HIDING
THE (

jo3m

FOR JACKIE.
WITH LOVE 'N' HUGS.
SIMPLY AMAZING GIRL
KEEP DOING IT..
YOUR FRIEND

jo3m

Published in 2018 by Stories from Silver Clouds

ISBN Paperback: 978-1-9998532-0-4
Ebook: 978-1-9998532-1-1

A CIP catalogue copy of this book
can be found in the British Library.

Proclaimers lyrics used by permission. Words and
Music by CRAIG MORRIS REID and CHARLES
STOBO REID ZOO MUSIC LTD. (PRS) All rights
administered by WARNER/CHAPPELL MUSIC LTD

Published with the help of Indie Authors World
indieauthorsworld.com

IndieAuthors
World

DEDICATION

This Book is dedicated with all my love and appreciation for Kirsty and all of our family who have made me feel so welcome and loved especially the superstars that are the weans, Isaac, Ethan, Sophie and wee Esme.

This debut novel is also dedicated with all my heart to the Memory of Sally Bell, Mary Meade, Taffy Meade, David Donald, Mamie Lang and Spoony. The world was a better place when you were all in it.

ACKNOWLEDGEMENTS

September 2018. Sinclair Macleod, Andy Melvin and I sat in All Bar One in Glasgow discussing the sins and successes of planet earth.

I said: "OK, I suppose we should talk about book stuff." I almost felt embarrassed to cut to business because my publisher and my editor had become my friends and I hoped that they felt the same.

Sinclair said: "We're nearly there, Joe, I just need a bit of blurb about the author, some acknowledgements, a dedication and we are good to go!"

I thought, no problem! I figured I could get my good lifelong pal Sue Ashcroft to do the 'about the author' bit and I could spend half an hour that night before Kirsty and I went to our local's pub quiz. Acknowledgements and a dedication. How tough could that be?

How far back should I go? Thanks to wee Mary and Taffy Meade, without whose love and support God only knows where I'd be. Who should I thank? Who do I leave out? Although I thought my English teacher in school was brilliant, I failed O Grade English twice. As I was consumed once again by reverie I looked back 16 years to 2002, standing on the 88th floor of our office block in Shanghai smoking a cigarette and wondering why I was so miserable. I had been described earlier that day as being at the top of my game. That was the moment when I decided I was going back to Scotland and I was going to write a book. I figured I could easily get a first draft sorted in six months, twelve months max. That was it decided. I was going home.

Shortly after returning to Glasgow I spoke with Castlemilk's Writer in Residence, Mamie Lang, on the phone. I told her I wanted to write a novel. She told me she didn't work with grown-ups. Just as six months turned into six years, my half-hour was up and the pub quiz was rapidly approaching.

There really are too many individuals to thank personally. So many family and friends that have supported me in this endeavour. As I thought about it all I became teary eyed and before I knew it my beautiful wife was giving me a hug and wiping my eyes. We went to the pub and I learned another lesson. Acknowledgements deserve some thought and the cold light of day.

There are those that I thank often in the privacy of my own mind for the motivation they gave me to be able to carry on despite their ignorance or best efforts to de-rail me. However, there are those that without their support this book would not have ended up in your hands.

So, a very special thank you to Kim and Sinclair Macleod (Indie Authors World) and the divine Andy Melvin. Mamie Lang said to me that to write is heavenly but to edit is divine. I have no memory of Mamie ever being wrong. Mamie then went on like Dumbledore and taught me more in one year about the craft of writing than most people learn in ten. Mamie deserves a special mention for breaking her own rule and taking the chance on a forty-year-old adolescent.

Writing, editing and publishing all requires proof reading. Thanks to all of my proof readers, but particularly Isabel Clough, who is the detail-meister. I have had much advice from several successful Scottish crime writers but a special thanks to Alex Gray, whose encouragement to embrace 'tartan noir' in the early days was fundamental. And to Netherton Writers Group, who all gave me so much brilliant feedback for my first chapters. Especially Karen Reynolds and my old pal Iain Johnstone who were the first to proof read the very first draft. Special thanks, too, to Jean Rafferty, her sister Mary and all the Scotia Writers who indulged my early scribblings.

By the end of 2002 I was writing my novel and bankrupt. There are several people who since 2002 and fairly recently who have helped me financially when the banks wouldn't; Donald, Gladys, Peter, Carroll, Nick and Marilyn, thank you. Most especially Jim Gisbey, who treated me like his wee brother when I was on the bones of my arse and still does. Last but by no means least Brian Woods, Dan McAlpine, his brother Billy, and Ronnie Alfield, who all invested their time in me and all the other lads at Gourock Youth Athletic Club. They taught us football, determination, discipline, integrity and a winning mentality. Thanks, too, to my professors at Glasgow Caledonian University, Alan Hutton and David Donald, for their continued interest after graduation in my sins and successes. Spoony (John Wotherspoon) also took the time to tell me how it was and then went on to put me right on several things, but that's another story.

PREFACE

"Stories are artefacts: not really made up things which we create (and take the credit for) but pre-existing objects which we dig up...."
Stephen King

Author's note

It is now my experience that original stories regarded as fairy tales, fables, legends and myths can be rejected, discarded, embellished or even blown up beyond all belief. And then, all of a sudden when they come back to life we find out that they are true after all.

When I first started to write the stories from Silver Clouds and embarked on this journey of discovery. Had I known in advance how challenging it would be, I fear I may have bottled it and chosen an easier task.

I'm happy to say that with hindsight I have no regrets. In fact I have gained so much from this adventure that I intend to continue it. I write because I now know I must.

The stories from Silver Clouds started with one question: Do we really have a choice or is life pre-ordained?

We all hope there is some sense and purpose to life and yet we also want to feel as if like King Canute we are in control and have choice. How can both exist? How can either exist? Is this an enigma or what?

When I first started this work of fiction I had no idea what the answers to these questions were. By the time I had finished book one, 'Hiding Under the Covers' I had at least an answer to my own questions. I feel privileged that I've had the opportunity to find this story and these truths.

It's amazing if you ask the right questions and look hard and long enough in the right places what you can find Hiding Under the Covers...

jo3m

omen n **1**. a happening that is regarded as a sign of how somebody or something will fare in thefuture **2**. to indicate the future course of events relating to something.

THE SICK ROSE

O Rose, thou art sick!
The invisible worm
That flies in the night
In the howling storm,

Has found out thy bed
Of crimson joy
And his dark secret love
Does thy life destroy.

William Blake

catch *v* 1 to capture somebody suspected of wrongdoing **2** to trap something or become trapped **3** to understand or manage to hear something that is being said **4** to trick or deceive somebody **5** to record something or somebody on tape or film…

January

Death has played in this room. Raymius can sense it. He moves his head a little. The outline of the vault door is around three feet by nine. The ceiling is around twenty, if his guess about the door is right. Each light overhead is protected by wire mesh. Apart from the trap door next to his face everything is covered with white tiles. There are little Perspex spheres in each corner of the ceiling. HTFO, hi-tech fibre optics – electronic eyes. On the plastic table there's a cup like the type you get from a water dispenser at the dentist. It has clear liquid inside. In between the tiles are intermittent dark stains that could've, once, been blood. He thinks about the 11th Commandment, *Thou shalt not get caught.*

Three people are seated in front of him. Raymius recognises the Honey Monster on the left but not the woman in the centre or the guy on the right with the white coat. On a trolley you'd see in any hospital operating theatre there is something hidden under a green cover. Behind the Three Amigos there's a console like any DJ would use. The room smells like a public toilet. His head is thumping. He recalls passing out earlier and collapsing over a beautifully varnished table like a bag of marbles. Now one side of his face feels nice and cool on the cold white tiles.

"Have a seat, Mr Raymius Scott," she says.

Well informed, he thinks as he opens his other eye and attempts to get on to one knee. The room feels like a little boat in the big blue. Her hair matches her outfit. Raymius wonders if she'd asked her stylist to fix it especially for the occasion.

"Does Madame have anything special in mind?"

"Yes Philippe, I have an execution on later and I'll be wearing my LBD, if you could do me something that looks demure and chic but frightening."

Apart from a subtle hint of lipstick, she's not wearing any make-up. Her eyeballs look like they come to a point. At the moment they're pointing at two chairs to his right. The black leather upholstery also matches the outfit. The furniture isn't typical DFS, more likely from eBay under the section, 'Second-hand recliners from Death Row'. They have all of those little extras that executioners must simply gush over – head, chin, arm, *and* ankle straps. Raymius thinks to himself about how the world has gone mad and what you can now purchase mail order. The chairs probably came with a free gift, an airport bestseller, 'How to get them to talk and still get home in time for tea', a wee gem for any self-respecting gangster. Raymius's head is swimming with all sorts of erratic shite, not because of the chairs but because of who is strapped into one of them. This isn't expected. It puts another perspective on the situation. It's un-fucking-fathomable. Raymius rapidly searches his brain for the logic in all of this. He thinks again about the 11th Commandment.

Raymius imagines the havoc that has been wreaked in order to create the mess in the leather seat. The face looks like it's been put through a blender and then stuck back together with dark red glue. The puddle beneath the chair solves the 'stench of pish' mystery. If he has to sum up this situation in two words it is simply, 'totally fucked'. If Raymius looks more

14

dazed and frightened than he really is then that's fine by him. He figures his chance of getting out of this one is a lottery win. There's no point in weakening the odds by looking more compos mentis than he has to.

The Honey Monster pulls a 9mm Beretta from inside his jacket and stands up. He points it at Raymius's right knee, a motivational gesture that really isn't needed. The Honey Monster makes it clear the woman's request is not optional.

"Take a seat, Raymius."

Raymius drags himself into the empty chair. He looks in the mirror attached to the armrest. His usually bright young eyes are bloodshot. The mess in the other chair is not unconscious. He thinks through this important implication and although it's not great news, at least it simplifies the situation. Now it's not even business, it's just arithmetic. However, although this is important, it's not urgent. What is urgent and important is the accessory situation. If the straps and clamps are administered then his odds are just about to go from winning a tenner to needing all five numbers and the bonus ball. Once again he thinks about the 11th Commandment.

The Honey Monster walks over and places the Beretta's barrel between Raymius's eyebrows. He pushes until Raymius's head falls back into the headrest. He grabs his right wrist and slams it into the groove on the arm restraint. Raymius notices the Woman as she turns to her left. She uses her finger and thumb to massage her earlobe with a slow pulling motion. Her long, perfectly manicured fingernails match her little black dress. She whispers to the Lab Rat and then turns back to face the Honey Monster.

"Vincent, hang on a second."

That's not actually what she says. Raymius had tried pinning her eastern European accent earlier and now has a short list. His best guess at the moment is Czech. Her 's's and soft 'c's sound more like the 'z' in zebra or in zeek – as in 'ZEEK-heil'. The Honey Monster keeps the barrel on Raymius's forehead as he lets go and turns back towards Psychoburd. *If she didn't look so scary, this would be funny,* he thinks. Her lips curl, her eyes close for the briefest of moments as her head shakes ever so slightly. Her body language signalling a final no, like the way you would to an auctioneer. *Going once... going twice.*

"Vinzent, letz see if Mr Scott will cooperate with our little inveztigation." She takes another puff of her cigarette. "I don't think we will need the reztraintz right now. If our guezt can clear up a few simple matterz for uz then we can let him go."

Raymius pretends to look pleased by the announcement and smiles as the Beretta is lowered. The Honey Monster's eyebrows crease and his nostrils flare.

"Of course, *Mr* Scott, if you decide to be silly we may have to put a few holes in you."

The Lab Rat bursts out laughing, like what the Honey Monster has just said is actually fucking funny, and then stops as abruptly as he'd started. The Honey Monster produces Raymius's cigarette packet in his outstretched hand.

"Would you like one, *Mr* Scott?"

Raymius doesn't want or need a cigarette right now but reaching for the packet gives him an opportunity to show the audience his outstretched hand tremble.

It has the desired effect. They all make a terrible job of concealing their knowing smiles. His hand stops just short of the packet.

"Go on, have a cigarette, Raymiuz," Psychoburd echoes, this time louder.

"Not just now, thanks." Raymius withdraws his hand, coughs and continues with a croaky voice. "Maybe later, if that's OK. I'm afraid if I have one now I might..."

It doesn't matter to his audience, they just continue to smile understandingly. The Honey Monster returns to his seat like a good little gangster. Psychoburd leans over and whispers to him as he sits back down. As the Beretta returns to its holster the owner smiles. It's her job to be soothing and convince Raymius that it's all an unfortunate misunderstanding that can be straightened out, *if* he cooperates. Soon he'll be free to go. They are all *still* trying to deceive each other, even in this room of death.

"Are you prepared to help uz with our enquire-eeze, Mr Scott?"

"Do I have a choice?"

"We always have a choice, Mr Scott."

Raymius thinks about the 12th Commandment: *Guard against your desire to believe them. It is natural to want to and natural to want to tell the truth. What they say means nothing. Giving them what they want won't help you – that's the thing you hold on to. That's the only idea that matters in this situation.*

She opens a folder. Her cigarette is clamped in the middle of her mouth with the smoke streaming into her eyes. She is smiling with her lips shut so the fag doesn't fall out but still smiling just the same. It reminds Raymius of black and white photographs, the Barras, the Saltmarket, noisy women gutting fish.

"Whatz your relationship with Emma Burgezz?" She asks.

"Who?" Raymius replies as he studies mixed reactions. Their heads move together to whisper.

"Emma Burgezz," she repeats, holding up a glossy photograph.

"I've never seen her before," Raymius insists.

Psychoburd shakes the photo in the air like she's on a protest march.

"You see? You see what happenz when..." she shrugs and the ash falls off her cigarette onto her lap. She brushes it off with her hand onto the white tiled floor. Raymius knows at once the photograph had been taken when Burgess was dead. The mark on her left temple could be mistaken for a bullet entry wound but Raymius knows it isn't. He watches and waits once again while they exchange their secret whispers. He knows the Honey Monster is now telling Psychoburd that their guest is telling lies. She takes out another photograph and holds it aloft.

"How do you know Helen Carter, Mr Scott?"

"I've never seen her before either."

"You want that cigarette now, I think," she says, nodding suggestively. Raymius shakes his head as she sighs and lights another for herself. Her eyes roll up to the left and then to the right. She seems to meditate, for a while.

"Put on the strapz," she says.

"Wait," Raymius pleads.

"What iz it now?"

"Where am I?" He asks.

She fills her lungs and blows out a huge ring of smoke before she responds. "That doesn't matter any more, Mr Scott." She looks at the Lab Rat. The Lab Rat looks at the Honey Monster and then gestures towards the console behind the chairs. The Honey Monster looks back at Psychoburd for the OK. She nods.

"OK, Vinzent, start the tape," she says. The Honey Monster once again pulls out the Beretta and moves towards the console. The Lab Rat gets up and starts moving towards the trolley. They both reach their destinations and look at her once more.

"Do it," she says.

The Lab Rat can't help showing his excitement and anticipation. The Honey Monster breathes a heavy sigh and shakes his head at Raymius. Psychoburd maintains her poker face. Raymius's heart starts to pound he looks down at his chest and can imagine it actually bursting out through his shirt. He closes his eyes, takes a deep, diaphragmatic breath to manage his state. She takes another lungful of smoke before throwing the butt on the white tiles.

"Damn it, do it now," she says again.

Raymius stands up. They all pause and look at him. What did they do to create the mess in the other chair? Who's the Lab Rat in the white coat? Why hasn't he spoken yet? Is he fucking mute? What's on the trolley hiding under the cover? Raymius takes a half step forward.

"Who-the-fuck's-in-charge?"

prologue *n* **1** preliminary discourse, introducing act or event, serving as an introduction

December... the previous year

It's dark, total blackness. Her eyes are wide open so she knows it's not a dream. The only sounds are her irregular breaths and the beat, beat, beat of her heart. Fear holds her chest the way the angler holds the fish. A vice-like grip moments before the metal hammer stuns the brain and ends life.

Helen Carter doesn't know where she is or how long she's been there. She knows what way is up and what way is down. She's curled on her left side. Her right side feels tender. She is free to move around but there is nowhere to go. The room is eight steps by six steps. The ceiling is out of reach. She is also free to cry out, but no one is listening. She can feel the needle holes in her arms and legs. He's done that, this much she's sure of. She wouldn't volunteer to be within a mile of a needle without good reason. She was squeamish at first, but not any more. Spiders and beetles are her friends now. Her hands are her eyes now. *This must be what it's like to be blind,* she'd thought, as she had examined each wall. No doors, no sockets, no beams, no holes, no vents, no drains, nothing, except cobwebs. She can hear the scraping sound of little claws and tiny teeth but that's OK because *they* must be trapped here too. But *they* are different from Helen. She'd been taken. She'd been put there. *Why? Why? Why?*

She wears what feels like a boiler suit. Her mind drifts back to when she'd still been with Raymius. They were painting his flat. She remembers how the material had chafed her nipples then too. Raymius had said it would be dead sexy if she had no bra and panties on. She puts her hand in between the buttons and rubs herself. Tears roll slowly down her cheeks. Her skin is smooth and smells of… peach? But that is not what's causing the tears. The baldness between her legs reminds her of when she had first come to and discovered the bump on her skull. Her head and eyebrows had also been shaved. There is not one single solitary hair on her body. She holds her head in her hands and wanders back in her mind to what happened.

How could she have been so stupid? She thinks. How many times throughout her life had she been told, 'DON'T TALK TO STRANGERS?' But it was 6am in the morning. She thinks. Still, it *was* dark. He looked so frail; a walking stick and two bags with messages.

It's an odd time to see someone with shopping bags, but we do have 24/7 now. Anyway, you always want to get an early start on a special day like that. You always want to get everything finished and get home early on Christmas Eve.

Helen's Gran used to get up at 5am every day and do all sorts, watching the TV or preparing the homemade soup for lunch. As soon as it was light she'd be off into the garden or out to the shops. "You need less sleep when you get older, darling," she used to say. But she also told her, all the time: "Remember, Helen darling, never, never, talk to strangers!"

He walked so slowly as he approached. Helen wasn't even a minute out of the flat. She still had the keys jangling in her hand and was putting them into her bag when she first noticed him. It's like he appeared from nowhere. Helen was startled and then he beamed a smile. Such a warm face, she'd thought, as she smiled back, unable to help herself. Then the most curious thing happened: he seemed to blush. He looked away. Helen felt sorry for him. She wanted to stop him, but didn't. She walked on. And that's when Helen heard it. It sounded like a yelp. She turned round. He'd fallen and was trying to use the metal railings to pull himself back up. Helen rushed over.

"I'm OK, honestly," he said, looking embarrassed. "Please don't bother, I'll manage," he pleaded. "You have a kind face," he conceded as he beamed his hypnotic smile again. Again Helen couldn't help herself and tried to reassure him.

"Kind face, warm heart," she said.

"My car is just over there," he said.

"My name is Helen," she said.

"I don't like leaving my wee Volkswagen in the car park, Helen. I get confused. I forget sometimes. When I forget, I get all excited. The doctor says I shouldn't get excited, Helen." His voice was so soft, so slow, so hypnotic. Before she knew it, they were both standing at his little red three-door hatchback. "Would you mind putting my shopping into the back seat, Helen?" He asked, so graciously. "The boot is full. I've been to the garden centre. I love gardening, watching things grow," he added, chatty now. " Oh listen to me. I'm such an old duffer. I'm sorry to trouble you, Helen. I'm so sorry for being such a bother."

"It's no bother," she said, folding the seat forward and stretching over to the far side of the back seat. She had to do that to avoid the plant pots that were nearest to her.

"Oh, silly me, I should really put those on the floor, shouldn't I?" he said.

"No, it's OK. I'll do it," she said.

Helen has seen wildlife programmes on the Discovery Channel. She and Marc have been chatting about going on a safari. He's been hinting how it would make a brilliant honey-moon. She's witnessed huge beasts brought to their knees with tiny tranquillizer darts. It takes seconds.

She felt the point of the needle in her neck. It wasn't sore. It wasn't even as bad as the prick they give you on your finger when you give blood. They reckon it's worse when you're expecting it. She wasn't expecting it. Maybe that's why it wasn't sore, just a scratch, really. The waves in her head were immediate. She'd fainted once before and that's what it felt like, waves. She heard his voice in the background, soothing, instructing.

"No it's OK. I'll do it... You feel dizzy now, don't you? You need to sit for a while now, don't you? You do have a kind face, Helen. You do have a warm heart, Helen. You'll be fine, isn't that how you feel, now? You'll be OK in a minute, won't you?"

She couldn't move. She just felt floppy, like a drugged dog on the vet's red leather table. Her heart raced and pumped.

"Your heart is racing now, isn't it?" he said. "You need a rest, don't you?" he said. "You're feeling flushed, your skin is so hot," he said.

She was panting when she felt his hand against her face. It felt soft on her skin. His hands were gentle. And then she saw his eyes, bright, young and piercing. Then came the darkness, and still it's dark.

Helen's eyes are stinging. Her head is drooping with dejection. On her knees now with clenched fists, she cries and sobs. She starts to choke. Warm, sticky liquid gargles in her throat and then dribbles from her mouth. She is beginning to realise the awful truth. A noise makes her stop. She holds her breath. It was from the ceiling. She definitely heard something. She didn't imagine it. Then it comes again. Click. If she's right, it's about twenty or maybe even thirty feet above. Her momentary exhilaration turns to dread. She figures out what is now obvious. She's in an oubliette.

oubliette n **1** a dungeon designed with only one method of entry or exit **2** an underground cell where the only way in or out is through a trap door at the top. **3** a dungeon with only one way out.

One week later...

It's dark, total blackness, until she lights the last one and collapses on the sofa, mashed with heroin. Four black candles blink in each corner of the room. Yvonne Morrison smiles across at Emma Burgess and then dares to deviate from the instructions. Yvonne doesn't normally walk around without anything on. She'll always don a pair of pants or even the littlest of towels to hide her modesty. She's not a prude, though. They've said many times.

"You really are quite liberated, Yve, aren't you?" She hates the way these posh bastards speak to her. Somehow, Yvonne feels more comfortable when she wears something, anything. A tiny thong, high heels, even a trick's tie removes that uneasy feeling of nakedness. If she stands in front of her full-length mirror wearing only a baseball cap, no problem. When she runs about wearing only striped socks that stop before her ankles, no problem. But remove that last item and it's like being bare arsed in the middle of a field trapped by a massive searchlight. Without one piece of clothing she feels that vulnerable, even when she's alone.

She stands up from the sofa, completely naked, not a stitch. Yvonne is far from alone. She blindfolds herself and swaps her feeling of nudity for a different uneasiness. She's conscious of her ears. They feel pricked and ready, like a keen fox before the hunt. Sensing terror, hoping for escape. She worries for Ryan. He hasn't spent one night without her since he was born four years ago. She'd left him with Aunt May and made the excuse she'd a job interview and had to stay in London for a few days. Every bit of evidence suggesting she has a son is hidden. *He'll be sleeping now. At least he's safe, whatever happens,* she thinks, she hopes.

She remembers the phone call. She'd panicked but had to act quickly. He never says exactly when he's going to appear but she knew it would be within a day or two. It had taken him just eighteen hours to land and she'd only just got back. She'd almost done a runner but there was no point. He's too clever. It may have taken a while, even years, but eventually he would have found her. Anyway, she owes him. It was a rotten deal at the time but Yvonne is the type of girl who keeps her word, pays her debts.

"Time to pay the piper," he'd said on the phone. *Full of fucking clichés,* she'd thought. Emma Burgess nibbles Yvonne's ear and whispers softly. "Stay focused, Yve, it'll soon be over."

Yvonne lies on the floor and closes her eyes. The room spins round and round and round. She starts to pass out. Ice cubes skid across the laminate floor. Cold water runs over her face, trickles down her back and wets inside her legs. She opens her mouth and gasps. A voice haunts her head. *God looks after good little Catholic girls.* Her chest heaves in and out like a paper bag. No, imagine a shell-suit sniffing glue. She is the paper bag. Emma ties thin red ribbons round Yvonne's wrists, ankles and neck. She'd seen them earlier and thought they looked Christmassy. Yvonne knows the instructions. It's been a long time since she's entertained him. Given him his special performance. But things like this you never forget, no matter how much you try. Emma's hands push at the inside of Yvonne's thighs. As her legs spread open, waves of drugs mixed with paranoia pan through her mind. She tries to focus and thinks of summertime, the beach, hot sand, warm sea air and Italian ice cream. Her stomach rolls as she holds her throat shut. The apartment upstairs is starting its Hogmanay celebrations early. They are playing their music too loud. She can make out every word of the world's latest pop diva.

"You are beautiful."

Yvonne squeezes her eyes but can't stop the tears. Her audience sit in their chairs and don't say a word.

> **Currency** *n* **1** The system of money in general use in a particular country **2** The fact or quality of being generally accepted or in use **3** From Medieval Latin currentia, literally: a flowing **4** From Latin currere, to run

The next day...

Emma's voice pierces the air like a spear. It comes from the corner of the room, defiant.

"You're fucking insane," she says.

His mobile phone rings. He answers her first. "Let me get rid of this call, then you'll have my undivided attention, darling."

He turns his back on her and puts his free hand into his pocket. "Yes, twenty-four red roses. Yes, the biggest you've got. No, no message. No, no card. Yes, just put it on my account. No, not at all, thank you. Yes, you too." Click. He ends the call, snaps the mobile shut, slips it into his shirt pocket. He's not big on conversation but when he speaks, you listen. "So you think *I'm* insane?" He laughs mockingly, shaking his head as he turns to face her. "*I'm* a celebrity get me out of here, Big Brother, Corrie, Easties, Emmerdale fucking farm. Pleeese! What's your definition of insanity? Go on, you tell me. Try this: Working forty years for an employer for a wage that keeps you three paycheques away from the building society repossessing your home. No, not *your house may be at risk if you don't maintain the payments of your mortgage.* Home as in homeless, as in shop doorways, as in the Big fucking Issue. Get it? Insanity, what do you know?

"Living with your 'significant other' in self-induced solitary confinement, unaware of the resentment that spreads like a vicious virus until your initial infatuation moves straight past that illusion called love and arrives at its destination. Loathing each other to the point you lie in bed facing opposite directions, unable to bear the touch of your partner's skin. There's loneliness and then there's the empty void of being in a relationship you hate, but don't have the courage to leave. Sorry, is this too honest? There's a sham. We all have our own definition of honesty. Ever met anyone who admitted to being dishonest, no? Ever met a dishonest man? *I did not have sexual intercourse with that woman... I'm not a crook...'* But let's not beat up the Americans and their presidents, they're only trying to do their job. What's important is *your* definition of honesty, *amigo.*

"But life's not all work, work, is it? Howz you? How's your social life? How often do you scoff with your peers, numb your little brain and rot your liver? What's your tipple? What's your latest liquid heroin, cunningly disguised by the psycho-mind-fuck marketing department and heavily taxed by faceless cunts you didn't vote for. Packaged in pretty Breezer bottles, frosted Aftershock glasses and dinky designer beers. You peer over the top of your Armani specs and run your manicured fingers through your highlights that have been kept exactly in place with fudge that smells funky, like coconut. It reminds you of the sun, the sand, Montego Bay or, more likely, Ibiza. There, once, you had a glimmer of happiness.

"You think that you think but the reality is, almost every moment of every fucking day, you are thought. Chasing a non-existent pot of gold at the end of a red and yellow and pink and blue that never has existed and never can. The multicoloured arc painted across a light blue sky is your subconscious fucking with you. You are in denial. Anyway, you didn't think of the rainbow. I gave you that.

"People like you never take the time to work out what it is you really want. Those who do are deluded by materialism and brainwashed by the media. What you've got now in your life is exactly what you deserve. Your life is down to one person only – you. No cunt else. When you stick in the DVD of your favourite movie, do you really think the end will be different from all those other times you watched? Of course you don't. If you continue down the same path, do the same things, make the same errors in judgement, day after day after day. If you continue to say you'll change but always put *it* off until tomorrow or next week or after winter or when the kids leave or whatever excuse you choose, guess what's going to happen? Guess what's going to change? Guess what life will look like tomorrow? Next week? Next fucking year? Guess? In the not too distant future you'll be sitting in your basket chair smelling of pish wondering why your life is the same as it's always been. Then the horrible truth will kick in. Doing the same thing and expecting a different result is insane."

He picks up a book from the table and thumbs through it. "**Insane**. *Adjective, lacking reasonable thought.*" He throws a copy of the Oxford Dictionary on the floor next to where Emma now lies silent. Her face is battered, her tears dribble over her swollen lips. She tastes the salt on her tongue. Sweat stabs at her open flesh and keeps her mind in the moment of now. He points at the book and continues. "Why should I pay attention to any of you, to what you think, to your rules, to your ideas of what's right and wrong, of what's fair and just? Day after pathetic day you continue to do the same fucking things and for some deluded reason expects a different result."

Emma screws her eyes into a scowl and once more attempts a defiant stare.

"I'm sorry, you're right, I'm repeating myself, excuse me." His eyes roll upwards as he presses his index finger onto pursed lips.

"**Insanity.** *Noun, extreme foolishness or an act that demonstrates it.*" He closes his eyes for a moment as he turns his palms upward. "Look at yourself," he says. "I'm successful in every way you morons would try to measure it. I'm healthier and fitter than most people half my age. I have wonderful relationships with family and friends and sex, oh yes, and definitely sex. I've lived out all of your fantasies and some you couldn't even begin to imagine. I do what I want, when I want. Am I happy? Good question. Well, what do you think? What do you think you think? What do you know?

"I've got cash, in fuck-you quantities. Isn't that how you measure happiness? With your brand new Range Rover or your Saab Convertible. Your regular visits to your therapist and weekend breaks to Paris, Brussels or Amster-damn! Sitting on the Champs-Élysées, chomping on your bagel and cream cheese, reading the Sonntag Times. How's the diet goin'? Drinking Coca-Cola and thinking you look kool. Hey, maybe you'll be the next Britney. Just ignore the sixteen heaped spoonfuls of poisonous, degenerative, man-made sugar in every single overpriced tin. Apologies if you only do *diet* drinks, we all know they're totally healthy. Aren't they? Deluded fuck-nugget springs to mind. Ever heard of ASPARTAME? Go on, pick the can up, it's there, right after sweeteners. Then go and get a medical journal or look it up on the internet. Or is that also too much like hard work? Here's a tip. If you own a racehorse that's worth a lot of money, make sure your trainer isn't feeding it diet fucking Pepsi.

"Telly-tubby or pencil thin, I'll bet you're still an Evian drinking, Nutra-sweet sweetening, caffeine counting, sodium sparing slave. You think being multicultural is having a pizza on a Monday, Chinese on a Wednesday, something from the chippy on Friday and a curry on Sunday. Choke to death on your Danish pastry. Drown in a lake of herbal fucking tea. If you're a privileged mother-fuqua you probably still think it's fashionable to have an alternative point of view. While you mingle with yo politically correct pals and listen to your latest CD of Pava-fucking-rotti, dwell on this: Money talks and whether you like it, or not. I've got cash in FUCK-YOU quantities. Is that a whimper I hear? Oh, I see, it's a why?"

He moves toward her. Emma's eyes widen. He grips a fistful of her hair and squashes her face into the pages of the dictionary. The black and white type changes to red and wet. "Go on, look it up," he says, shouting now. "**Why.** Interrogative adverb, meaning for what cause, purpose or reason. There are no causes. There is no purpose. There are no reasons, for any of it."

He studies the circular kitchen timer that's stuck onto a beer keg with its magnetic strip. He watches for a few moments as the digital display counts down. He opens up her mobile phone so that she can see it. His fingers find their way to her address book. He scrolls down to the letter 'R'. He smiles, his voice softer again. "Who is Raymius? Emma, you've got ten minutes."

introduction. *n*. **1**. explanatory section at the beginning of a book or a another piece of writing, e.g. one that summarizes what it is about or sets the scene.

January…

Another Monday morning, beneath a bright blue Scottish sky. Outside feels like being inside a deep freeze. They sit in their unmarked car with the windows down and the engine off. They look like two lumps of ice sitting in a frosted glass. DCI Ribbon's face is grey, but his ears, nose and cheeks are pink and sting like a well-skelped arse. He watches DS MacMillan use a half-eaten pencil to do battle with the daily crossword.

"What you stuck on, Mac?"

"Who says I'm stuck?"

Ribbon doesn't have to say anything. His look says it all. Mac scratches his head and continues.

"Indo-European languages in North Eastern Europe. Closely related to the Slavonic group, six letters, begins with a 'B'?"

Ribbon looks at the condensation in the inside of the windscreen and then down the street. Everybody has a scarf and hat on; well, almost. It seems everyone is smoking too, but of course they're not. Hot breath swirling in the morning air makes it look this way. That's Ribbon's job – to find out the way things really are, not the way they seem.

"So you're a detective then, Mac?"

"What's that supposed to mean?"

"BALTIC, Mac, you need me to spell it?"

Detective Chief Inspector John Ribbon loves his title. He's worked hard for it. His career is everything. He had almost married once. Ribbon's fiancée went missing one month before the wedding. That was twenty-seven years ago. There have been relationships since but they never last.

There's a noise at the bins along the lane they've sealed off. A cat lands inside the chalk mark and gives him that 'what-the-fuck-you-lookin-at?' stare. He catches himself smirking. It reminds him of a scene straight from an old Hitchcock movie. Only a few hours ago Emma Burgess lay there inside that white outline. A cold corpse on cobbled stones. His mind reels back as he feels the smirk vanish. He's seen lots of dead bodies but Emma's mutilations make him realise that now, finally, he's seen it all. Her wounds can mean only one thing. He has pictures in his head he doesn't want there. With eyes closed, his fingers attempt to massage away the frowns on his forehead.

Distinct bruises, handprints. How long had she been kept alive, how long had she been terrified? She has thin red lines on each wrist and around her neck. The peculiar red blotches on her heels are like the marks you get when breaking in new shoes. The round mark on her temple resembles a powder burn. Her skin has a faint smell of peach. Emma is black and blue around each orifice and has been penetrated, repeatedly. However, there is no trace of semen or any other bodily fluids, no DNA. Both CCTV cameras are broken, so there's no video evidence. Ribbon reads the report that indicates they'd been vandalised. He shakes his head and tosses the paper on the back seat to join the discarded crisp and sweetie wrappers. "Hooligans my hole. They've been disabled." Mac doesn't say a word. Ribbon knows the difference.

Glasgow is no longer the infamous gangland zone of the past. But crimes of this nature make Ribbon feel justified calling his home by the old tag, 'No Mean City'. They have four units looking out for Raymius Aaron Scott. The radio has been switched to a secure frequency, so when it crackles, John knows it's for him.

"Alpha One this is Delta Six, over." He holds the handset up to his face but not too close, he doesn't want to weld his lips to it.

"Go ahead Delta Six. This is Alpha One."

"Our man is approaching your location, over."

"Ok Delta Six, roger that. Out."

omen *n* **1** a happening that is regarded
as a sign of how something or somebody
will fare in the future…

The same day…

Raymius walks towards Glasgow Central railway station. He notices the morning buzz isn't there. It seems quieter. There's ice between the cobbles on the road and no wind. Damp skin clings onto his bones like wet clothes hanging on cold steel rods. He's not slept again and can't stop shivering. Last night it was raining cats and dogs.

Odd expression. It has been suggested that cats and dogs used to be washed from thatched roofs during heavy weather. Thick straw, piled high, with no wood underneath – these roofs were the perfect place for the little animals to get warm. Dogs, cats, mice, rats, bugs, all frequented the roof. When it rained it became slippery, so sometimes the animals would slip and fall off the roof. As an explanation it strikes Raymius as a bit thin. Still, odd expression.

No one knows the precise source of this medieval term but we can be sure that it didn't originate because animals fell from the sky. Small creatures can from time to time get carried skywards in freak weather but there is no record of dogs or cats being scooped up in that way and no need to study any meteorological charts for that. The most probable source is the fact that dead animals and other debris were sometimes washed up in the streets after heavy rain. There are of course mythological origins which are derived from the dogs who were attendants to Odin, the God of storms. And also witches, who often took the form of their familiars, cats, and are supposed to have ridden the wind.

Raymius looks across at Bothwell lane. He sees it's sealed off with blue and white tape. 'Police line, do not cross'. He looks down at the side of the kerb. There is a dead dog lying in the gutter. Nothing from Crufts, just another mongrel. Old Billy Smith stands at the west entrance to the station. He gives Raymius a newspaper and winks. No money changes hands. It never does. A sign of times to come.

"Mornin' Ray," he says.

"Hi Billy," Raymius replies.

"Daily Reck-ord, get yir Daily Reck-ord."

Raymius stops momentarily and stares at the headline. Billy gives him an odd look and asks how he is.

"Awe-right son?" Raymius is far from OK but says yes anyway. Well, you do, don't you? Let's face it, when someone asks if you're all right they don't really mean it, do they? For fuck's sake, where would you start? Raymius stares at the headline again.

GLASGOW WOMAN FOUND DEAD

Just outside the city's busiest railway station, a prostitute was found dead... In the early hours of this morning... The police are looking for anyone who can help with their enquiries...

"Whit's up, son?"

"Bad news, Billy."

"Whit some peepil dae furra livin', eh son?"

"Aye, Billy, ugly way to live, ugly way to die."

"Still, son, ye need tae earn a crust, eh?"

"Money, Billy, bits of paper, wee metal discs."

"Ahh, it's no everythin' son, member that Beatles song, canni buy me luv? Well yi can! But ah know what they wur tryin to say. Just wee boys wi' big ideas."

"Aye, that's right, Billy. There are treasures money can't buy, but that's bollocks when you're skint, eh? Being on the streets, that can happen to anyone, eh?"

"Aye son, that's fur sure, you tell it the way it is."

"Well it's a bit like the allegory of Animal Farm, Billy."

"The whit?"

"Animal Farm, the book, the film…"

"Is it like an omen son?"

Raymius asks, "Is what like an omen Billy?"

"Allegory, son, is that like an omen?"

"What?"

"The Omen, that wiz a film tae son."

"Not quite, Billy, but I suppose they are both metaphorical, in a way."

Raymius realises the insignificance of what he's just said and watches Billy, who now looks like he has a heavy breeze and a load of tumbleweeds blowing through his brain.

"Y'know, all animals are equal but in reality the **Pigs** were in charge. But if you've not read the book or seen the film that might not make much sense, Billy."

"Oh aye, son, ah get yi now." Billy looks around to make sure no one is listening and then whispers. "The fuckin' Polis. Bastards! But, whit can yi dae, eh?"

Raymius smiles right into Billy's eyes. "Aye Billy, that's right, Sir. You know it."

Raymius is playing Mr Down and Out and has time on his hands, to reflect. He walks around gazing into shop windows at luxuries that are no longer his. He wanders into the station on days like today and sits for a while, sometimes only for a heat. He knows aimlessness tells its story, just like the droop of your shoulders. He's discovering how the homeless are seen like casualties and are helped out for a while. He knows only too well that too few realise how borrowed money lacks the power of earned income. When you borrow merely to live, that on its own is depressing. If you need to borrow, borrow big. In the financial world that's called leverage.

If he was next to you it's unlikely you'd notice him. He's learning how to be anonymous. He's watching you all; butchers, bakers, burger bar attendants, lawyers, candlestick makers, all busy at work. Hour after hour, he argues with himself and his mind always arrives at the same verdict. Money equals freedom. Money makes a difference. Cash is King. The world, however, is changing and now you don't just need cash. You also need currency.

Inside the entrance, under the archway, he sits down, opens his bag, and takes out a bookmark. He'd found it at a second-hand shop, three years ago. Reading it, sometimes editing it, trying to make sense of it all every morning is a ritual, like daily prayers.

Do you think life is beautiful
Enough to try and figure it out
Do you still think about
Peeking into the wardrobe
Checking beneath the bed
Hiding under the covers
Have you ever been caught
Day-dreaming
Or
Lying under the stars
Do you believe in
People watching
Living under the rule of fools
Favourite colours

Dandelions

Tomorrow

Sleeping after the Tsars

Do you have courage

To dive into your mind

And go swimming?

If you are thinking of

Rising after the dead

True Love

Running under the radar

And...

Silver Clouds

Remember that when you are

Walking over the planet

Words can do more than plant miracle seeds

You can change

The world.

Raymius starts talking to himself.

"Beautiful words, mighty poet..." he stops, holds his hand over his mouth, closes his eyes and examines the ticker tape of his mind; *but what are we really suggesting? The pen is mightier than the sword? Over 2,000 years before Edward Bulwer-Lytton's fucking play, Socrates' star student was suggesting something quite different.*

His tongue and lips can't help themselves as angry words spit out. "We can do so much damage..." he stops himself again but hears his thoughts whisper, *with a knife or even our bare hands! Careful old boy, getting excited and talking out loud, not a good sign.*

He'd owned all the right toys. Had every *thing* he ever wanted. Deep down, he'd hated it. Sometimes he'd felt like someone else had the remote control and was pressing still frame advance. He'd been achieving other people's goals and living their dreams. On the surface everything had looked like ice cream and custard. Underneath, it was toxic waste on toast. He used to plan ahead, a year at a time. Mr Organised. Recently he'd read about a young woman who got cancer and never planned beyond the sell-by date on the milk and thought to himself, *When I get a fridge I'll do the same.*

Big Ben hangs in the middle of Glasgow Central, a giant egg timer, 8am. The clock's hands click away the day and the way we spend our days is the way we live our life. Isn't it? What would you rather be doing to occupy yourself on a Monday morning in January? He opens his notebook and clicks the top of his red pen.

"If you do not take an interest in the affairs of your Government, then you are doomed to live under the rule of fools…"

…Plato

To-Do's today

Tony says I should write to mum

Eat

Decide where to stay tonight

Tony says what goes around comes around

Tony says be happy

Raymius mumbles.

"Be Happy! Ha fucking ha. OK. Let's get started before the masses appear. At least I've broken free from the coma."

Raymius is referring to what the masses call 'nine till five'. He stops himself once more but this time has a look around before he thinks to himself, *careful, Ray, talking out loud again. Someone might be watching.*

His pocket radio is small enough to fit into a packet of ciga-rettes. **HS-USD: High Sensitivity – Ultra Slim Design**. He's always loved gadgets. He puts a tiny earpiece into his left lug and pushes 'on'. The volume is preset along with the station.

Classic FM. Raymius has always worked better with Baroque music, something to do with brain waves, alpha theta, the subconscious mind and all that shit. *Aye, whatever*!

He breathes in the aroma of freshly ground beans from Costa Coffee. The noise from the uneven symphony of Glasgow Central Railway Station fades into the background and is replaced by romance. 'Adagio ma un poco andante' spills from the receiver into his head. His brain becomes a sponge and soaks in the soothing sounds of the bassoon, the oboe and the clarinet. He smiles. Raymius likes Mozart. He lets go of a sigh and starts writing.

Dear Mum

This feels strange. I've never written to you before. Well, a good place to start, I guess, is to say thanks, for looking after me while you still could and for making sure I was safe before you left. I'll never understand how you must have felt. I'm sorry you had to deal with all that stuff. I felt responsible for you leaving. But now I know it must have been something else that drove you away.

Your grandson is doing great, he's almost four. His mother and I will sort everything out, eventually. She loves him very much. Hey! Look what you started.

I'm having a few challenges, but nothing I can't handle. Like Nan used to say, 'people are like teabags, you only know how strong they are when you drop them in hot water'.

Your loving son, Always

Raymius.

This is total bollocks, he thinks as he puts a line through the first entry on his to-do list. The numbers walking past are multiplying. The morning rush is on. A loudspeaker from high above echoes out.

"The next train to depart Platform One will be the 0900hrs Express to London Euston." A gaggle of girls walk out of Starbucks. One of them has her hands full. Café Latte, fudge

41

doughnut, banana, spring onion crisps, two Mars bars, and a large bottle of Diet Pepsi. Raymius almost understands the whole ensemble, even the two chocolate bars; morning and afternoon breaks. But he's stuck on one item only. He asks himself... *Why the banana*? They pass by.

"Aye Sheena, am the same. All a huv ti dae is look at a piece o choclate an ma arse gets wider. Am on-nat new Jennifer Annistun die-ut, it's pure magic, yi can eat as much as yi want." And so she goes on. A pound coin drops into his cup. Raymius looks up.

"Morning, Ray."

He pulls out his left earpiece and replies with no enthusiasm.

"Hi, Arthur."

"Get yourself a coffee, Ray. I hate to see a guy like you on the street. My offer is always open."

"Sorry, Arthur, fully booked this evening, but I'm tempted."

Arthur bends down before walking off. Raymius's face catches a whiff of his hot breath.

"See you tomorrow, Ray, you know I've got a wee soft spot for your hard... luck story." He winks before walking off.

"Yeah, I know, Arthur, you have a nice day." *Boxers or jockeys,* Raymius wonders. *Definitely underpants, probably Y-fronts, maybe even knickers?*

Raymius gets irritated when people stereotype the homeless. Assuming they're popping acid, dropping E's, shooting heroin and or want it up the bum. Arthur seems harmless enough, though. Clever-looking man and always smartly dressed, a big gentleman really. Shame he doesn't have someone special in his life. He's probably just lonely.

"Hello, Mister, lookin' for business?"

Raymius's face beams as he takes out the remaining earpiece, presses 'off' and throws his hands up.

"Clare!"

Clare's face beams as she throws her hands up, mimicking Raymius.

"Ray!"

His eyes narrow as he bites his bottom lip but he is genuinely delighted to see her. Clare has cropped black hair and a face that wouldn't look out of place on an elfin princess. Her long legs are complemented by a little red skirt and you sometimes miss her big brown eyes because of the glare from her lip-gloss.

"You're fucking hilarious. What you after, Clare?"

"I'm gagging for a coffee, and a ciggie. Let's go, my treat, drag yourself away from... what you doin' anyway?"

"Writing."

Clare opens her eyes even wider, tilts her head to one side and waves her hand, beckoning for more information. "A letter." Raymius thinks for a second and then adds, "To my mum."

"Are you on the scrounge for cash? You know, if you need a loan, I can always..."

Raymius interrupts. "No! You're all right, Clare. Thanks. So, what you after?"

Clare has a quick look around and then puts her mouth next to his ear. She always smells nice but the peppermint from her chewing gum kills the moment. She whispers.

"Look! I don't want to get into it here. Let's go, I'm much less wabbit after my caffeine fix."

"Later, Clare, I want to finish something first."

Clare stands back and searches her bag. "Later, LATER! Look, Ray, I've got to go down and see the cops at twelve o'clock. So if you can't help me I need to know now. I need to fuck off home and that's going to be a mare. I can't be arsed explaining to that old cow why I need to see the Plod. Listen to the, 'You should spend more time with your daughter' pish. I want a seat, I'm tired and my feet are killing me and I'm about to have my..."

Raymius interrupts for the second time and beams another smile. His eyelashes almost flutter. "Clare... Chill. Too much information, you're not making sense. Whatever the favour is, I'll do it, calm down. Give me half an hour, I just want to finish something first."

She finds her Zippo, takes out a cigarette, lights it and returns his smile. She adjusts her blouse the way women in her profession do.

"Who said anything about a favour? Are you still doing the song thing, then? When are you going to write a number for little old me? Café Alberta. Twenty minutes, MAX! Je ne peux pas attendre. Je dois partir maintenant. Ne sont pas en retard." Clare giggles.

"D'accord. Je comprends. Mon petite a tout á l'heure! I won't be late," Raymius replies, smiling smugly.

She snorts and giggles again at their pidgin French and at how sharp Ray can sometimes be.

"I see what you did there," Clare retorts as she wags her finger, smokes her cigarette and trots off, turning the heads of this morning's population. She most often does in her evening attire. And she knows it.

Raymius gets back to the task in hand. He studies the letter and seals the envelope. He stops for a minute, not sure where this temporary item should live. He puts it into his back pocket. His other bits return home into Deefor. That's what he calls his little grey day-sack: D for day-sack. He walks back along the archway, returns the Daily Record to Billy and winks.

"Thanks, mate," he says.

"Cheers Ray, not yersel today, son?" Billy enquires again, still looking concerned.

"Aye Billy, hungover, you know how it is." Raymius hasn't

had a drink for fifteen days. As he walks past Bothwell Lane one flatfoot remains alone, still guarding the entrance to the alleyway.

The River Clyde runs though the centre of Glasgow about five minutes from the station. Raymius pops an Embassy Regal in his mouth and sucks hard as he heads for the bridge. The trains clatter on the tracks overhead, the cars honk with rage. The traffic lights seem to pause, for only him. Nothing gets in his way. He walks slowly but deliberately. By the time he gets there his cigarette is all but finished. He holds it between the nail of his middle finger and thumb. He flicks it over the wall into the water. Just like the movies. He watches it float away and pass a rock that peaks out from the depths. On it an odd-looking bird stands tall and motionless on one leg. A heron. The Clyde is calm and perfectly clear. Perhaps his feathered friend also wonders about the reflection that looks back at him every day, from the mirror. Raymius takes the envelope out of his back pocket, crushes it in his fist and drops it over the barrier. He waits until he sees it make contact and watches it drift off with the current, or the tide. Whichever, it didn't matter; it was done.

serial *a. & n.* **1.** *a.* of, in, forming a series.
n.;(of story etc) issued ininstalments.

D etective Sergeant Macmillan chucks his crossword on the back seat.

"Finished?" Ribbon asks.

"Of course," Mac replies smugly.

The detective chief inspector gives his sergeant a look. He doesn't say anything. He doesn't have to. Mac knows what he's thinking.

"Oh! Eh, aye. So, boss. Will we bring him in?"

"No, Mac. Tell our units to keep an eye on him for another hour and then, stand them down."

"Are you sure, boss?"

"Yes Mac, I'm sure. Aren't you late? Shouldn't you be on the motorway by now?"

"I've warned them off, boss. They know I've been held up, it's being dealt with."

"What time has Buxton arranged to meet with you?"

"10am, boss."

"You better show her this," he hands Mac a letter addressed to: *John Ribbon.*

"Nice handwriting," Mac replies.

"Aye, that's what I thought. Here, you better read it."

Mac strokes his jaw until four fingers eventually end up covering his mouth. Shaking his head, he lifts his eyes from the page and looks at Ribbon.

"Jesus Christ, boss."

"It was in my pigeonhole when I got to the office last night. I opened it first because it had no postmark and like you said Mac, nice handwriting."

"But that means we'll have it on video."

"Only whoever delivered it. I requested the camera footage about a minute after I'd read it. It took me that long to decide it wasn't some sick joke. You know how the guys are sometimes, no sense of reality."

"So what made your mind up, boss?"

"Mac, you've just read it, eh?" Mac looks puzzled. Ribbon's finger pokes at the letter in Mac's hand.

"Do you think this could be a joke?"

Mac puts the letter carefully into his jacket pocket. His head drops slightly.

"Point taken, boss."

"We need to talk about this when you're finished with Buxton. You'll get me at home. I need to take a shower, I feel dirty."

"Ok boss. Does anyone else know about this?"

"Nobody apart from me, you and whoever wrote it. So tell Buxton this is off the record until I've had a chance to think. You reckon you can manage that, Mac?"

Mac replies with a look, like he's been wounded. Ribbon gets out of the car and begins to walk west, away from the station. He enjoys walking through the city. He believes it helps to clear his mind.

"Later boss," Mac shouts. Ribbon turns and acknowledges him with eye contact and then a nod.

Mac leaves Glasgow on the M8 and takes the M80 heading north-east. He chooses the Kincardine Bridge to cross the River Forth. A one-hundred-and-eighty-year-old cocktail of Gothic and Italian architecture rests in the centre of ninety acres of woodland. This is the home of Scotland's Police College. Tulliallan Castle is unique among all other UK law enforcement establishments. It provides senior, junior, traffic and detective training all on one campus. DS Macmillan is supposed to be taking a class at 9am. He's late. Mac is covering for an old neighbour who is off on a Mediterranean Cruise with a new wife. The newlywed and Mac have never lived next door to each other. That's cop jargon. When you see two cops walking the beat they're referred to as 'neighbours'. It's like time in the trenches. You get to know who individuals really are and develop unbreakable bonds. Another class of fresh-faced recruits will soon be pushed out of the factory to start their two years' probation pounding the beat on the Scottish streets. Mac will give them an introduction to Crime Scene Management.

"You're taking the piss," he'd said.

"You've got the syllabus and the books, how hard can it be Mac?" he'd been told.

Mac walks into the reception area of the Police College at 9.30am and holds back a grin. Standing under the coat of arms is his class, getting a history lesson from an instructor. The Drill Sergeant resembles a toffee apple. Orange cheeks and totally erect, like he's got a wooden rod up his arse. He's barking with the same authority as the Speaker from the House of Commons.

"The Lord Lyon assigned this coat of arms to the college in 1957. As you can see it incorporates a thistle surmounted by a crown on a diced Saltire cross. Pay particular attention to each side where two open books on a black background are supported by two oystercatchers."

A fresh-face asks a question without putting up his hand first.

"What's the significance of the birds, Sir?"

"Wind your neck in and get your hand up."

The red-headed freckled youth turns pink and complies.

"Sorry Sir, eh, what's the significance of the birds, Sir?"

The Drill Sergeant spots Mac. Remarkably, he manages to brace up even further. Mac takes a deep breath in through his nose and addresses the group of information-starved puppies.

"Good afternoon gentlemen and ladies, my name is Detective Sergeant Macmillan."

They all turn their head at the same time like they're at Wimbledon. Mac, having their complete attention, continues. "Your impromptu history lesson is down to me, apologies." He gestures to the Drill Sergeant. "According to legend, St Bride, while fleeing during a period of Christian persecution, fell exhausted on the seashore. The oystercatchers, seeing her predicament, covered her with seaweed so that her pursuers passed by without finding her. When our patron saint blessed the birds because they had saved her life, a cross appeared on each of their backs. Thereafter the oystercatchers became known as 'The Birds of St Bride'.

"Beneath our coat of arms is our motto, 'bi glic-bi glic'. This term represents the call of the oystercatcher and is also Gaelic for 'be wise, be circumspect'. This is something each of you should consider and aspire to."

"What about the college name, Sir? Is that Gaelic too?" asks the same fresh face, again without putting his hand up.

"What's your name?" barks the Drill Sergeant once again.

"Baxter Sir, sorry Sir."

Mac interrupts. "You always ask so many questions, Baxter?"

"Aye Sir, 'fraid I do."

"Good. I like that. Provided they're intelligent questions, though." Mac lowers his head in Baxter's direction and raises both eyebrows until the youth responds.

"Aye Sir! Fair enough, Sir."

Mac continues. "Tulliallan is not Gaelic but it does come from the Gaelic 'tulach-aluin', which means beautiful knoll." Mac's pleased with himself and smiles nostalgically. They all stare with their mouths wide open like little chicks waiting to be fed. Mac turns to reception.

"What room have we got today, Ruth?"

"101, Sir."

"Hmm. OK folks, follow me."

The Drill Sergeant with his shiny boots and shiny buttons lifts his hand and gives Mac a cracking salute.

"Thank you Sergeant Macmillan, I'll see you later."

Mac responds, unable once again to hold back his grin. "No, Tom, thank you."

They all arrive at the classroom and Mac watches them take their seats one by one. A silence follows. The fresh eager faces start to fidget. They still haven't gelled as a group yet. The bonding will start today, after lunch, when their Drill Sergeant administers an introduction to physical education. Soon every single one of them will be hacking up their rhubarb crumble and lumpy custard. They'll blow chunks like sick dogs. Mac remembers how it was for him, twenty years ago. He realises they're still, metaphorically speaking, shitting themselves. Mac sits on the desk at the front of the class and takes off his jacket. He looks round the room at every pair of eyes and smiles. His large dimples make him look jolly. He picks up a red marker and writes on the whiteboard. The felt tip makes that familiar squeak...

Managing the scene of a crime.

Preserve the integrity of the locus until the investigating officer arrives.

2. Only...

Their open mouths close as the silence is broken by a knock on the classroom door. Mac shouts. "Yes?"

The door opens a little and a half a body squeezes through the gap. Mac's face beams.

"Ah! Sheena, give me a second." Mac turns back to the rest of the class. "I want you to write down a list of what you must never do at a crime scene. I'll be back in a few moments."

A whisper travels from the back of the room, barely audible. "Now that's what I call a pair of tits."

Mac's head spins round and fixes on the perpetrator of the remark.

"You're now becoming well known for entirely the wrong reasons, Baxter!"

The police cadet feels his cheeks go to gas mark seven as the rest of the class witnesses his whole head turning bright pink. Mac leaves the classroom and closes the door carefully behind him.

"Good stuff Mac, very assertive, well done, good exercise. I'm impressed." Sheena Buxton laughs and shakes Mac's hand. She holds on much longer than she needs to. They study each other. Mac's eyes are sad but his face is content. He sighs.

"It's great to see you, Sheena."

"I got the message you were held up. Do you want me to hang about or come back later?"

"Speak to Ruth at reception. I've got us a room for as long as we need it. I'll be along in about an hour. Here's the folder with all my research on 'HOLMES'."

Mac hands her a folder and reaches into his inside pocket for the letter. He hesitates and then changes his mind.

"What's up Mac?" Buxton enquires.

"Nothing, Sheena, it can wait. I'll see you in an hour, eh?" Mac lets go her hand but Buxton is still holding on to his little finger. She gives it a squeeze before finally letting it slip away from her grip. Her head drops slightly as she looks up at him through her eyelashes.

"Don't keep your old neighbour waiting too long, Mac. We've got more than just work to talk about today, bi-glic bi-glic."

> **Allegory** *n* **1** symbolic work, **2** a work
> in which the characters and events are
> to be understood as representing other
> things and symbolically expressing a
> deeper, often spiritual, moral or political
> meaning **3** the symbolic expression of a
> deeper meaning through a story or scene
> acted out by mythical characters…

Raymius loves railway stations. He's drawn to them. Not a train spotter, though. Exit that thought. It's not necessarily only railway stations, though, it's Scottish architecture in general. Raymius does like to go unicorn spotting. A unicorn may seem an odd choice for a country's national animal, but perhaps not for a Scotland famed for its love of myth and legend. The unicorn has been in Scottish heraldry since the 1300s. Its symbols of innocence, purity, masculinity, healing powers, joy and even life itself are enough to make Raymius giggle, but he can become more serious when economics and politics are involved. He also appreciates a sense of irony. The British Royal Coat of Arms has the English lion on the left and the Scottish unicorn on the right. The Royal Coat of Arms for Scotland, however, has the lion and the unicorn the other way around. As early as 3500BC the unicorn was thought to be the natural enemy of the lion. No unicorns in Glasgow Central Station itself, though; you have about a four-minute walk to Jamaica Street for the nearest. But the station has its own appeal. This place is a good anchor for Raymius. It reminds him of day-trips, Nan's Cadbury's Roses, Pops' Liquorice Allsorts, Macaroon bars, the Beano Summer Special, Deputy Dawg and, for some reason, unicorns.

It's quicker to head back through the station to meet Clare.

He strolls through the south entrance and takes the escalator to the upper level. On his right is platform four and his favourite fast food stall. He breathes in the aroma created by the West Cornwall Pasty Company. *Hmmm. Home cookin'*. He passes under Big Ben and by the Belgian florist. He leaves the fun fair surroundings of the station and wades through the sea of black hacks in the taxi rank. Café Alberta is a honey-trap for tourists, TV celebs, the upwardly mobile and occasionally a certain prostitute who has just finished her shift. Clare has a table beside the window. She'd watched him dodge the traffic and skip up onto the pavement. He pushes open the glass doors and winds his way through the red and white checked covered tables. She greets him with: "Hell-loh!"

Raymius's mind is still on other things. His expression is businesslike. "So Clare, what's up?"

She glances up at the big round clock on the wall. "That's what I love about you, Ray."

"What?"

"I've already ordered for you." Raymius screws his face up.

"What?" he says again.

"Tea and toast."

"What?"

Clare grins, with a big cheeser.

"You're just so fuckin' reliable, Ray."

His features soften and a smile warms his eyes. He reaches for a newspaper off the rack.

Clare comments, "Yesterday's news?"

Raymius screws up his face again. "What?"

Her next comment is like Morse code. "You... are... readin'... yesterday's... news!"

Raymius doesn't bother to explain he enjoys studying the chess problem in the Evening Times. He used to play chess at school. Undefeated champion under-sixteen. He got bored with playing soon after that; lack of competition.

"Tonight's isn't out yet, Clare."

"Still… yesterday's… news!"

"Whatever."

Clare senses something's up and decides to give him a few minutes to chill. Ray doesn't normally get stressed. She lights up another fag. He studies the front page as his creamy coffee and hot buttered scone arrive at the table. He nods in appreciation to the waiter and then to Clare as he reads another ugly headline.

MOTHER COMMITS SUICIDE

Yvonne Morrison, a single mum, was found dead in her home in the Southside of Glasgow… The mother of four-year old Ryan had taken a lethal dose of heroin… The police are not treating the incident as suspicious but are looking for anyone who can help with their enquiries…

"What's up with your face now?" Clare snaps.

"Why would anyone give up the chance to see their son grow up? What could be so terrible to make you take your own life and leave a son without his mum?" Raymius sugars his coffee. Clare picks up the Times and studies the photograph on the front page. *Typical*, Raymius thinks.

"Eh, yesterday's news, Clare." He's about to ask for his paper back, when she goes off on one.

"No way! No fuckin' way!"

"What's up?"

"I know…" Clare pauses and sighs.

Raymius realises immediately her state has changed. Something is very, very wrong. He stays silent and lets her continue.

"…Knew Yvonne, for a long time. We were pals, best pals. We went to school together, went clubbing together. We even made the decision to go on the game together. Yvonne met some guy. They fell in love. Well, she did, anyway. Then she got pregnant. She said it was fate. She never asked him many questions; maybe she was afraid he might start quizzin' her. He got called away on business. Plan was to get married when he got back. I met her in Asda 'bout then. She was lookin' great."

Clare's big brown eyes fill with painful pictures. In her mind she hears Yvonne's voice."

"He says he loves me, Clare. The past doesn't equal the future, hen. What's the point in spoiling the party? Nobody wants to hear your sad stories. Life's too short, babe."

Clare grabs a napkin off the table next to them, which has been set for dinner. She blows her nose and carries on with her explanation to Raymius.

"Fuck, right enough, that must be about four years ago. I met her once again just after that. She'd had the baby and cleaned up her act. Yvonne always kept her word. He didn't. Cunt. She'd never heard from him again. Well, as far as I know. She always had a feelin' he was married. Bastard. Last I heard she was cleanin' school canteens. She loved wee Ryan, do anythin' for him."

Clare stubs her cigarette out like she's trying to squash an insect, lights another and carries on. "There's no fuckin' way she'd kill herself. And, there's no fuckin' way she'd leave her son on his own."

"Well that's what it says here in the Times, Clare."

"Fuck the Times, Ray."

"What makes you so sure she wouldn't kill herself?"

"If Yvonne was gonnae top herself she might slit her wrists, she might even blow her fuckin' head off. But, she didn't do drugs. And, she wouldn't take fuckin' heroin."

"Like I said, Clare, what makes you so sure?"

"Her big sister was a junkie."

"So what are you suggesting?"

"I'm suggestin' fuck all. I am stating fucking categorically Yvonne Morrison did not OD on smack."

His voice is sympathetic. "People change, Clare."

"Some people change, Ray."

He's not about to get into a discussion about someone he didn't know and feels a change of subject will make her feel better. He mimics her morse-code-like tone. "Fair... enough... Clare... So...anyway... What's the favour?"

Clare blows her nose again and looks into her empty coffee cup. She points at Ray's. He catches the waiter's attention. No words are required, just two fingers in the air. The waiter nods as Raymius gives him the thumbs-up. The waiter scurries off to fetch the refills. Clare grins at how easily he gets things done and starts her pitch.

"Some psycho is gettin' heavy on some of the girls, the new ones that don't know any better. The cops have got a description of him." Clare stops. She notices he has leaned back and is rolling his eyes up to the ceiling. She takes exception. "What the fuck is up with your face now?"

Raymius leans one elbow on the table and opens his hand like he's asking for something. "Clare, there's a point to your story some time this week?"

"You can be a real cheeky cunt at times, Ray. Last night DS Slater told me I needed to be in the plod office today at twelve to look at a photo-fit and answer some questions. I really don't mind. If there's a whacko out there I'd like to see him locked up just as much as the 'Filth'. But you know how I feel about spendin' time with cops down at Keystone fuckin' Central."

Raymius thinks for a moment before he asks. "So the dead girl in Bothwell Lane all over the news today. Did you know her?"

"Yeah, her name was Emma, gorgeous girl, from Newcastle. She used to lap dance, at Truffles. She was found with enough heroin in her arm to kill two rhinos. From what I hear she hooked up with a punter who was into fantasy games, rituals, domination, all that weird shit." Clare tilts her head to one side and looks up as if she can actually see a movie with Emma in it. She carries on. "Funny, she never struck me as the type to shoot up, either."

Raymius studies his thoughts carefully but doesn't say anything.

"I always thought she was a cokehead," Clare goes on. "She really did take a pride in how she looked; being full of holes from needles just doesn't seem like her bag. Snortin' spoonfuls of snow up her nose is more how I'd pictured her. She saw herself as being one of the 'beautiful people'. Always readin' Hello magazine and talking about 'one day you wait and see'. I guess she thought she was somethin' special. Poor cow."

Clare checks her cigarette packet. It's empty. She digs another packet out from her bag and tears off the cellophane. She offers him one.

"No thanks, I'm all right for now, Clare."

"So when you saw the headlines this mornin' were you worried about little old Mwah? C'mon, Raymondo, did you think wee Clare had met with an 'orrible end?" She teases Raymius and blows him another kiss. "Mwah!" He doesn't appreciate her attempt at humour but hides it well.

"It did cross my mind, for a nanosecond. But if there's one person I know who can look after themselves, you're it. So, Clare, there's a point to your story at some time this week?"

"Eh?"

"Clare, what's the favour?"

"Oh right, anyway. I met Lloyd last night, he gave me a lump of hash and there's no fuckin' way I'm going to march into the cop shop with it on my person. I'd melt with fuckin' paranoia."

"So you have drugs that need looking after till you get back."

"Aye."

Raymius sighs, shakes his head, smiles and holds out his hand. "Come on then. Give us it."

"Duh-uh! Don't be so fuckin' nice but dim, Ray. Don't you ever watch the telly? There's a way these things are done. Let's finish our coffee and zip up to Kelvingrove in a cab; we can sort my life out there." She looks around and leans over. Under her breath she says softly. "You never know who's watchin'."

Raymius beams the biggest of smiles. He hasn't figured out why he likes Clare yet or why he humours her. Her vocabulary is littered with lashings of 'fuck' but when she swears it doesn't sound offensive. Not to Raymius, anyway. He knows it's not a limited education that causes her overuse of the profane. Clare can be very articulate when she wants to be. He finds her voice pleasant and there's a congruence that exists in the content. Raymius likes to listen to Clare. Clare likes Ray because Ray listens. He thinks carefully before changing the subject back and asking his next question.

"So do you think Emma killed herself then?"

"Nah, wasn't the type."

"D'you think she was murdered by this whacko the cops are looking for?"

"I'm not sure."

"Maybe she'd had enough; saw it as a way out?"

"Nah, don't think so."

"An accident?"

"Well that's more likely than side-y-ways." Clare puts out her cigarette and starts to look for the waiter.

"So, Clare, how come you're the Detective Morse of suicide all of a sudden?"

Raymius isn't expecting what comes next.

"I tried to kill myself once."

Raymius isn't shocked easily but he didn't figure Clare was the type to opt out of anything. Again he hides his emotions well. There's a long pause as he looks at her and imagines all the maybes. He eventually asks., "Why?"

"I was terrified." Clare looks for the waiter again.

"Of what?" Raymius asks.

"You mean of whom," Clare replies.

His voice is soft and deliberate. "Who were you frightened of, Clare?"

Clare spots the waiter and snaps her fingers.

"I don't talk about it, Ray."

"Well, you just have."

She stands up and frantically waves both hands.

"Fuck off Ray, some other time eh? Christ! Have I all of a sudden become fuckin' invisible?"

The waiter finally acknowledges her. She holds the cash up. The waiter gives her the thumbs up. She throws it on the table.

"When you're ready, Ray. I'll get us a cab." She leaves. Raymius knows when the interview is over. He decides not to press it. He knows Clare is about to take a few days off, probably that time of the month, he figures. She isn't ever usually this touchy, though. He realises this subject matter is definitely off limits, for now.

They don't say much in the taxi. Clare is happy to just stare out the window. January is a great month to be in Scotland. It rains less then than any other month if you don't count snow. You actually get to see bright blue skies. They say it's the best time of year to climb Ben Nevis. On such a day you can see the peaks of Goat Fell on the island of Arran over eighty miles away. However, when you're in the park at this time in the morning it's hazy. Scotch mist. You get that eeriness associated with Sherlock Holmes and the Hound of the Baskervilles.

As the taxi zooms towards the West End Clare gets busy texting on her mobile phone and Raymius takes on the role of gazing out the window. They get off at the main entrance to

Kelvingrove Park and walk up the winding path. Clare takes his arm. Raymius knows where he's heading. They sit at his favourite spot, which is well chosen for its seclusion, quietness and the fact you can see who is coming before they see you. She gives him her mobile.

"I'll phone you when I'm done. I shouldn't be too long." She digs down deep into her shoulder bag and hands him the drugs. He looks at her in amazement, searching for the right words.

"What?" she says.

An explosion goes off in his brain but again he manages to hold it together. He hides it well.

"That isn't a lump of hash Clare. That looks like a Kilo of Moroccan."

Clare giggles. "Keep your voice down son. That's because that's exactly what that is. Look Ray, break a bit off, have a wee smoke, chill out, write some of your fuckin' songs. In fact write me a shaggin' song, before you know it I'll be on the phone and on my way back to collect it. I'll only be a couple of hours… max… I promise."

After Clare slips off he just sits there for a while holding the bar of hash, thinking. *Where the hell d'you keep a kilogram of drugs? Your inside jacket pocket?* He laughs at the ridiculousness of the situation. The lads would pee themselves to be sitting up the park on a Monday morning with so much Ganja. He pulls a piece of paper out of his bag and reads.

AIM FOR BLISS

If you can find

He crosses it out and starts again… and again… and again and again…

BLISS (for Clare)

If you're getting fat or simply growing older

Sometimes it's nice to hear

Beauty is in the eye of the beholder
If you're not being heard or simply getting bolder
"Fuck You!" will get your point across
If you crave excitement, embrace uncertainty.
But most of all
Follow the 'rolling stone' who gathers no moss
And, when you know
There is no better sight to see
Than someone with their love
Whatever or Whoever that may be?
Open your soul for them to visit
Enjoy life's gift called 'Bliss'
And be thankful that you didn't miss it.

He sits back and rolls himself a joint.

"Not bad son, even if you do say so yersel." Raymius has a lot on today and isn't sure if it's such a great idea to get stoned this early. But it's a lovely day and it's an awful lot of drugs. He talks it over with himself. He's been doing a lot of that lately.

"Go on son."

"Better not."

"One wee joint can't do any harm."

"Guess so."

"What's the worst thing that can happen?"

He lies back; the morning sun shines from behind a little collection of white puffy candyfloss clouds. It warms his face. His eyes shut.

"Monday morning, where else would I rather be?"

His smile widens in anticipation of that first long inhalation. His serenity is interrupted…

"Dah - Di Di Di - Dah Dah…"

Vivaldi. La primavera spurts out of Clare's mobile phone. He presses the little green picture of a telephone and a voice shouts: "Hi Ray! I'm done! I'll be about half an hour. Have you finished my song yet?"

He is about to respond with a resounding, 'Well actually yes!' when a voice from about six inches behind his ear says: "Hello son any chance of a smoke?"

Raymius spins round to face two of 'Strathclyde's Finest'. The chorus of, "Ray, Ray, Ray!" is getting louder from the mobile. He answers the phone first.

"Listen, Clare, something's come up, there's no point in popping round just now. Phone me in about half an hour. I should be finished then, bye."

He presses the red button before a confused Clare has the chance to respond or complicate the situation further. He smiles at the cops. The skinny one crosses his arms and smiles like Stan Laurel. The one that looks like Ollie speaks. "I suppose you're going to tell us the illegal substance held in your grubby little hand was given to you by a passing well wisher and you had no idea that it was cannabis?"

"We both know that wouldn't be true, don't we... Officer?"

Ollie's cheeks begin to flush. "What's your name, son?"

Raymius knows the next question will be for an address to check his identity on the voter's roll.

"Well?" the cop says, pressing for a response.

"Raymond Taylor."

"Address?"

"No fixed abode."

"Aye right. Well Mr Taylor, no fixed abode, this is not your day. Officer Currie and myself are in fact on our way back to the station, for a cuppa. So! Why don't you tell us the whole story down there? You're nicked."

Ollie picks up Deefor. "Is this yours, son?"

Raymius concentrates on the dull thud at the pit of his stomach. He breathes deeply as he forces a smile. "Aye."

Ollie and Stan escort Raymius to their car. They've been listening to Radio Clyde. Raymius's head is pressed down for him as he gets placed into the back seat. A Travis number sings out of the speakers. *Why does it always rain on me?* Raymius grins and then bites his lip to stop himself from laughing. He's always liked that song.

psychopath (sik-) *n.* person suffering from chronic mental disorder esp. with abnormal social behaviour; mentally or emotionally unstable person.

Sheena Buxton looks at her standard-issue wristwatch and decides not to take advantage of the large leather chesterfield; instead she sits by the dark wood writing bureau at the window. She enjoys the aroma of her fully leaded coffee even though it's cold. The room looks like a set from Petrocelli except the walls are stacked with volumes of *Scottish* case law. The log-effect gas fire reminds her of Colorado and a cabin at midnight in the middle of nowhere. She sucks hard on her Regal Kingsize and turns her head towards the corner of the room. The Grandfather clock strikes 11am.

Mac had said an hour. He's never on time. Sheena's known him for over twenty years. They met at basic training. He was her first and only neighbour. She'd left the force to do a degree in forensic psychology and has since worked with various 'high profile teams' all over the world. She'd become the first British woman ever to graduate from the FBI's Behavioural Science Unit at Quantico. In her travels she's worked with the South African Police's psychology service, the Dutch National Criminal Intelligence Service, the Austrian federal Criminal Psychology Service, the National Research Institute of Police Science in Tokyo and even the Royal Canadian Mounted Police. She currently splits her time between teaching at the department of Forensic Pathology at Dundee University and advising the Offender Profiling Unit at New Scotland Yard. Mac has said many times, "How can a woman with that body know so much stuff?"

Mac had been working on HOLMES when he noticed a correlation in specific murders spanning the entire country over a period of twenty-seven years. The 'Home Office Large Major Enquiry System' is a specialist filing facility developed as a result of the 'Ripper' investigations. It was those specific crimes that highlighted the limitations of card indexing and exposed how crucial information got lost. HOLMES remedies these problems, providing more effective cross-reference and retrievability. He had emailed Sheena:

hi sheena…

i've stumbled across something I need you to look at. you know I'm not an anorak but even the Boss thinks i'm paranoid. i hope so. i want to be wrong on this one. sorry if I sound like a drama queen. mac

He kicks the bottom of the door with one of his size tens and shouts, "It's me. My hands are full."

She turns the handle to find him with a fresh pot of coffee, forty fags and a plate of doughnuts.

"An hour, you said?"

Mac shrugs his shoulders as best he can and tries his charming look.

"Sorry Sheena."

"You planning on us bein' here a while then?" Sheena beckons him in like you do when you've ordered room service.

"As long as it takes, Sheena, as long as it takes." Mac puts the tray on the coffee table and tries hard not to look at the outline of her nipples. Her breasts are not making a good job of hiding beneath her white cotton blouse. Sheena sits down back at the window and has already read Mac's mind.

"This place is a bit swish, how'd you manage to swing this, Mac?" Sheena undoes the second-top button on her blouse to reveal a hint of cleavage and lights another Regal Kingsize. She holds the pack open and offers them to Mac.

"No thanks, not just now Sheena. Eh... the room is used for high-profile visitors, Sheena. Who, believe it or not, now happens to be you." Mac looks like an estate agent selling a house with dry rot, who's trying really hard not to think of the dry rot.

"That's not what I asked, Mac."

He scratches his head and tries to be more specific.

"Eh... Ruth sorts this stuff out, she looks after me, Sheena."

"Oh yeah, and what the *fuck* does that mean?"

"It means she gets me what I need, tells me what's going on and has a fetish for fresh doughnuts."

"Oh yeah, and what the *fuck* does that mean?"

"It means, Sheena, she's good at her job."

"Yeah, I bet she fucking is... Blow, job?"

"I'm not the one who jets all over the bloody world, Sheena."

"So what *do* you need these days, Mac? So what the fuck *is* going on these days, Mac? How's the wife and fucking kids, Mac?"

Mac sighs. "Ruth knows everything that goes on here, Sheena. She's well worth a few doughnuts."

"What else you giving her besides doughnuts?"

"Bloody hell, Sheena, let's not do this again."

"Don't treat me like an idiot, Mac. Are you really expecting me to believe the currency is *only* doughnuts?"

"I'm not even going to dignify that accusation with an answer." Mac changes the conversation back to the business in hand. "Let's get work out the way first. Eh?" Then attempts to lighten the moment by using an American accent. "So whadda ya think, Sheena? Am I losin' it or is it a case of *'Houston we have a problem'*?"

"Don't fucking patronise me, Mac. I'll tell you what I think in a minute. Yes, you are losing it and yes, you do have a fucking problem. But enough about you, let's get work out the way first. Eh?"

Mac crosses his arms and tries hard not to make a face but says nothing. Sheena turns her head again to the corner of the room. She pauses for a moment, takes a deep breath and flares her nostrils.

"Your clock's five minutes slow, Mac."

Mac still doesn't say anything. She opens one of the folders and her face manages to become even more serious.

"Your theory *is* probable."

Mac's eyes close and his cheeks puff up like he's blowing a trumpet. A load of air whistles out his mouth as he shakes his head.

"I was hoping you were gonnae tell me I was talking shite, Sheena."

She goes to respond but holds herself back as Mac shuts his eyes again and raises both hands like he's under arrest.

"Don't answer that, Sheena. Please, let me start again?"

It's Sheena's turn to cross her arms and say nothing. Mac starts again.

"How is it possible, Sheena? How can someone kill for nearly three decades and we don't know about him?"

"You want an example, Mac?"

"Aye!"

"Harold Shipman."

"But, he's surely a one off, isn't he? I mean all his victims essentially went to him."

"Yeah granted, I suppose he was more like a Venus Fly Trap. Your guy is more of a predator."

"If I'm right on this one, Sheena, this guy has struck all over Britain."

"It may be worse than you think, Mac."

"Worse? How the hell can it be worse? I can see the headlines already: Serial Killer! Murders on mainland Britain for 27 years…"

"He may be international, Mac."

Mac looks like he's just been told he has three months to live. Horrified would be an understatement. Sheena pauses for a moment to gather her thoughts. "Mac, how much do you actually know about my work? I mean, do you have any first-hand experience of this type of case?"

"Not much. I read all the general stuff but this is specialised, c'mon, you know that."

"No need to be so defensive, Mac, I'm just asking. If I start to tell you stuff you already know, stop me."

He pops a doughnut in his face and refills her coffee. Sheena lights another fag, takes a puff and carries on. "OK, Mac here goes. When I was Stateside I worked with FBI agent Robert Ressler. He's the one who first coined the phrase 'Serial Killer' in the early 80s. His term describes someone who kills repeatedly and obsessively. As you've quite correctly pointed out, unlike Shipman the modern serial killer tends to choose his victims at random, and the motive is usually sexual. Roger so far?"

Mac nods. "Aye, Sheena, roger so far."

"The perpetrator of this type of crime becomes an addict. Murder is his drug. Now, he's exactly like 'The Good Doctor'. These 'monsters' are terribly sophisticated and contrary to popular belief have massive IQs. Dr Hannibal Lecter…" Sheena stops mid sentence as Mac's hand automatically shoots in the air like he's back in the classroom at primary school.

"*Sir*, Anthony Hopkins, Silence of the Lambs!"

"Well done, Mac. Unfortunately, not total fiction. He is stereotypical of these individuals who are well read on criminology and psychology and, more often than not, socially articulate. They have the ability to argue lucidly in favour of their life and chosen profession."

Mac scratches his head. "Example?"

"Ian Brady, the 'Moors murderer', was most definitely of this mould."

"That was the early 60s, Sheena?"

"Well done again, 1963 to be precise, Mac. And your point, caller?"

"Surely things have changed since then?"

Sheena throws an empty notepad at Mac. "Take notes! You need a wee history lesson." Mac clicks his pen and Sheena smiles. "In 1970 an American publisher brought out a volume called *'Killer, a Journal of Murder'*. The world *I* live in trembled. We became aware of one of the most dangerous serial killers of the first half of the twentieth century. However, the autobiography of Carl Panzram was written more than forty years earlier. He was born June 1891 and was hanged September 1930 but it was regarded too horrifying to publish at that time."

Mac feels like he should say something but can't think what. Sheena carries on. "His last words to the hangman were: 'Hurry up you bastard, I could do a dozen men while you're foolin' around.'"

"Nice guy!" Mac comments.

"Yeah, a real charmer. When the book finally appeared it was hailed as a revelation of the inner workings of a serial killer's mind."

"Sounds like a right crackin' read."

She ignores his sarcasm and continues. "The 'travelling' serial killer moves relentlessly from place to place and is particularly hard to catch…" Mac interrupts.

"Why's that, Sheena?"

"Communications between law enforcement agencies were less efficient during the Cold War when..." Sheena stops mid sentence as, Mac interrupts again.

"The Cold *fucking* War?"

"I said history lesson Mac, didn't I?"

He holds his pen on the page at the ready but says nothing, Sheena continues.

"...Criminologists worldwide were trying to collaborate. But, one of the most frustrating things about the Iron Curtain was the difficulty in establishing if our Soviet counterparts were experiencing the same types of crime as us, in the west. The late 1960s accounts of Lucian Staniak made it clear the communist regimes spawned the same serial killers. In 1964, communist Poland was getting prepared to celebrate the twentieth anniversary of Warsaw's liberation by Russian troops. On the 4th of July, the editor of ..." She scribbles on a piece of paper and hands it to Mac.

PRZEGLAD POLITYCZNY

"I'm not even going to attempt to pronounce this one. It's the Polish equivalent of Pravda. You're familiar with the Soviet broadsheet, Mac?"

"Yeah, Sheena, I've heard of Pravda."

"Anyways, they receive an anonymous letter in spidery red handwriting."

Sheena pulls the top off a *red* biro and writes on a blank piece of A4.

There's no happiness without tears, no life without death.

Beware! I am going to make you cry.

Mac strokes his jaw and bites his lower lip.

"How d'you do that, Sheena?"

"Do what?"

"Remember all those bloody quotes?"

"Stop blowing smoke up my arse, Mac, and just listen."

Mac feels suitably scolded but remains impressed. Sheena continues. "The next day…" Sheena scribbles again:

DANKA MACIEJOWITZ

"…is discovered by a gardener at Olsztyn Memorial, a park for Polish war heroes. The blonde seventeen-year-old has been raped. Her naked body bears Jack-the-Ripper-type mutilations. The following day another letter appears: *'I picked a juicy flower in Olsztyn and I shall do the same again somewhere else, for there is no holiday without a funeral.'*

"The Red Spider's victims were hundreds of miles apart. He would never stick to the same area unlike the historical 'Ripper'. Also, he concentrated on the lower half of his victims. One case had a spike protruding from her sexual organ. An echo from the Boston Strangler, who like the Red Spider *also* had a strong sense of drama. Choosing national holidays for his crimes and using red handwriting for his philosophies, about death. Roger so far, Mac?" Mac nods and sighs with resignation.

"Aye, Sheena, roger so far."

"The Soviet Union had historically played down its crime figures. This changed in the mid 1980's. The Tass news agency admitted a man would go on trial for the murder of thirty-three women. In April 1992 a literature teacher…"

ANDREI CHIKATILO

"… was charged for the murder of over fifty children. During a twelve-year period, Chikatilo admits to luring eleven boys and forty-two girls into the woods. He ties them to trees, stabs them between the eyes, slices up the bodies and eats their flesh."

"Bloody hell, Sheena."

"Yeah, Mac, I know." She continues like she's reading straight from a script. "It became clear to law enforcement agencies that they were facing an increasing problem." Sheena pauses for a moment. She offers Mac another cigarette. He shakes his head. She lights up, breathes in deeply and wags her finger emphatically. "You have to understand, Mac. Killers who murder repeatedly and compulsively are a worldwide epidemic. Not just six times like the Ripper or a dozen like the Boston Strangler but twenty, forty or even a hundred times. In 1983 Henry Lee Lucas confessed to over three hundred and sixty murders. But, as I've already mentioned, until the 1980s cooperation between the various police forces was, to say the least, loose. In 1983 The National Centre for the Analysis of Violent Crime (NCAVC) was formed at the FBI Academy at Quantico, Virginia. It was obvious a single force was required and more importantly they needed to be linked, by a single computer."

"Wow, you're essentially talking about a worldwide version of HOLMES."

"Well done again, Mac. Yeah, absolutely, the centre is referred to as the Psychological Profiling Unit or PPU."

"Fuck sake, Sheena, I don't know any of this."

"Well, you do now. Anyway don't beat yourself up, Mac, like you said this is specialist stuff. And as you can imagine this is not the type of information we like to publicise. Also, compared to the rest of the world, Great Britain has had few cases of serial murder. The UK's murder rate is absurdly low. In the 60s it was around a hundred and fifty a year compared to over ten thousand per annum in the US. Los Angeles alone has more murders annually than the whole of Great Britain. But, and this is a big but, it's significant that in spite of this low rate, we have produced some of the most horrific cases of serial murder in the twentieth century."

"Example?" Mac asks with renewed enthusiasm.

"In the 60s the Moors Murderers…"

"Ah! I know this… Ian Brady and Myra Hindley."

"Top marks, Mac. In the 80s the Yorkshire Ripper, Peter Sutcliffe, caused the same fear among prostitutes as his namesake did in Whitechapel a hundred years earlier. And then in the 90s we learned of No 25 Cromwell Street."

Mac nods his head. "Fred and Rosemary West."

"Precisely!"

"I've got a really bad feeling about this, Sheena." Mac winces as he hears himself repeat the movie cliché. Sheena's nostrils twitch.

"Stay focused just a bit longer, Mac."

"Yeah, sure."

"You said earlier you wanted to know how someone like this could go un-detected by us for such a long period of time."

"Yes I did, I mean I do, or I mean… Well, you know what I mean."

Sheena peers into her mug, presses her hand on the plate and licks her fingers, finishing the last few sugary remains.

"Chill, Honey, I know what you mean."

"What are you giggling for, Sheena?"

"You're beginning to look like you've been caught having your first wank, Mac."

"Sheena!"

"We've run out of caffeine. You sort out another fresh pot and I'll dig out my notes and a transcript from the West case."

"You were involved in the Cromwell Street case, Sheena?"

"No, I wasn't, but one of my colleagues worked closely with the investigating officer."

"Who?"

"Detective Superintendent John Bennett."

"Aye Sheena, I've heard of Bennett, who's the colleague?"

Sheena frowns and wags her finger once again. "Arguably the greatest criminal psychologist we have."

"Should I know this guy?"

"What makes you automatically think it's a guy, Honey?"

"Sorry." Mac looks suitably scolded.

"Yes, Mac, you should be. You know the television series Cracker?"

"What, with Robbie Coltrane?"

"Yep, that's the one. Paul Britton is the real-life character Cracker is based on. I suggest you read Paul's book."

"Homework?"

"Yeah, something like that."

"What's it called?"

"It's called The Jigsaw Man."

omission *n.* **1**. the act or instance of omitting or being omitted. **2**. something that has been or is being overlooked.

MISSING

Helen Carter, a twenty-four-year-old art student, was last seen leaving an apartment in 413 Sunnyside Avenue in Kelvindale on Christmas Eve.

The Police are looking for anyone who can help with their enquiries.

If you have any information regarding the whereabouts of Helen call your local Police station

or

The National Missing Persons Help Line

0500 700 700

"Raymond Taylor?"

"Yeah, that's me." Raymius has been reading a poster on the wall of the entrance to Pitt Street Police Station. The third ugly headline that day. There are several other usual suspects waiting and now he's next. One of the civilian staff escorts him to Interview Room No 4. *Odd lot?* he thinks. Being on your own in a room with no windows and nothing in it apart from a table and a chair has a strange effect on your perception of time. Raymius had decided long ago to stop wearing a watch. He felt as a race we pay too much attention to the unforgiving minute. Anyway, there's always a clock somewhere or someone with a watch you can ask. Here there is no clock and nobody to ask. He isn't sure how long he's been waiting. A social worker appears with a chair in her hand. It's standard operating procedure when the Police apprehend a homeless person for such an individual to assist. She introduces herself as Ms Langan. Raymius notices she isn't wearing a watch either.

"Hello, Raymond. Do you mind if I call you Ray? Ray, we don't seem to have any record of you. Tell me, how long have you been homeless? Raymond, are you listening?"

Raymius doesn't care for his name. He cares even less for bullies. Here's a snippet of how he responded once, while he was training with the Parachute Regiment.

"**RAY**, as in drop of golden sun. **MEE**, as in you and me. **UHSS**, as in just the two of. It's not difficult: **Ray-mee-uhss!** Not my choice but who gets to choose what they're born with? Hey, call me what you like, Sir. I wouldn't want you to confuse me with someone who actually gives a fuck. What did they christen you, Sir stupid cunt?" Raymius didn't like that word most people don't. He figured the Sergeant Major wouldn't either. As usual he was right. Two words joined together to elicit a desired response. The Non-Commissioned Officer had been giving Second Lieutenant Scott a hard time, at a hard time. Only a few minutes earlier Sergeant Major Skilton had driven his left leg into the ground, snapped his arms to their sides and adopted the position of attention.

"My name is Sarrnt-May-jor…(pause for effect)… Skil-tin! For the purpose of protocol and this exercise I will call you sir and yooo! Will call me sir, the only difference being yooo! Will mean it." The rest of the story is irrelevant, what's important is that Raymius had decided the bullying had gone far enough. He got his desired response. The NCO grabbed him by the throat. That was all the excuse Raymius wanted to hug his assailant close. He then turned his head to the side and smashed it into the face of the Sergeant Major. There was a crunch like when you break eggshells. It was satisfying for Raymius to see a man twice his size buckle at the knees and crumple to the floor in a heap. The Sergeant Major was tenderly holding the piece of his face that had just been broken. His eyes were wide open and looking up tentatively, hoping there were no more lessons on the way. Raymius had always thought a more suitable career for the Sergeant Major would be the circus. He'd have fitted in perfectly with his big feet and big red nose.

He stood over the bleeding hulk and spat some more verbal venom. "You probably feel stupid now, don't you, **Sir**? Well don't, you're having delusions of grandeur. You feeling stupid is insulting to stupid people."

Raymius prefers to be called Ray.

At twenty-four, Raymius was on a roll. He bought his beautiful pregnant wife a Mercedes Sport, top of the range, **her** pride and joy. It came complete with purring roof, CD surround and matching Oakley sunglasses. Now, the marriage is over. Two weeks ago his son was five. Raymius wasn't there.

Susan Langan asks several more questions. No response. Her attempt to make sense of the situation amuses him. He's thinking, *She looks about forty but I bet she's older. Warm smile, she's definitely got that favourite aunt look. She seriously needs to rethink her hair, though. What really interesting eyes. They actually twinkle. Nice face too.*

"Raymond!" She has his attention. "Raymond, just answer me one question, OK?" He looks at her raised eyebrows and forces a grin.

"OK."

"Do you want to stay in a cell this evening? Or, would you prefer to leave this Police Station sometime today?" He understands the question. The cops can't let him leave the station with no fixed abode without her approval. If she has a plan to get him out of there today, it's worth listening to. Smoking a joint in Glasgow is no longer a serious criminal offence. It's tolerated so long as the perpetrator does not have a substantial quantity of weed on their person, which would suggest intent to supply. Supplying is an offence that still renders you very 'nick-able'. The cops are on a witch-hunt for drug dealers in any shape or form in the city. The two officers had thought he was a student. And, since many Glasgow undergraduates are upwardly mobile, there was a better than average possibility of finding the dealer. Someone with a future can be persuaded to offer better information. However, the homeless are viewed differently. Like smack-heads and shell-suits they are treated with the Gospel according to Bob Dylan; 'if you ain't got nothing you got nothing to lose'.

He'd been found smoking a joint nothing else, lucky boy. He'd placed the drugs under the large roots of the tree he'd been sitting at. If you looked closely you'd have seen there was something there but it was undetectable from more than a couple of feet away. PC Currie had only picked up the little day-sack. He hadn't bothered to look beyond it. So now the cops had someone with no fixed abode and no police record. For them, a lot of paperwork and no joy. They were glad to dump him on a social worker and are equally keen for Ms Langan to have him released. Raymius knows this but real- ises at the moment she holds the key.

"What have you got in mind?" he says.

"Just answer my questions and you can be out of here in less than an hour, Raymond." *More bullshit*, he thinks. He closes his eyes, takes a deep breath and nods. Ms Langan pulls out a Report Sheet and begins:

Interview Room No 4, Monday 9th January

Full name:	*Raymond Taylor*
Address:	*no fixed abode*
Date of Birth:	*09/01/77*

"How long have you been homeless, Raymond?"

"Call me Ray. A year."

"Exactly a year, Ray?"

"Exactly one year tomorrow."

"You became homeless on your birthday?"

"Brilliant! **You** should apply for Detective School. They've got a big recruitment drive on y'know!" He bites his tongue and removes the smirk from his face. *Couldn't resist it could you?* he thinks.

"I'm sorry, Ray. I can see you're uncomfortable. I'm only trying to help. What was your last address?"

"333 Woodlands Road, Glasgow."

"How long were you there for Ray?"

"Twelve months."

"What happened? "

"I got kicked out."

"By whom?"

"The building society."

"Didn't you pay the mortgage?"

"I was renting the flat. Benefits. The rent was paid direct to the landlord."

Susan smiles, looks straight into his eyes and tilts her head to one side.

"Yeah... go on."

"The landlord pissed off to Jakarta or somewhere, the property was repossessed. I got kicked out. I tried to get another flat but I had no job, no income and no deposit. So, no address, no benefits. No money no fucking home. I'm sure you've heard the story a hundred times."

"Mind your language, Ray. It doesn't cost anything for good manners."

"Whatever."

"OK, Ray, I get the drift. Would you consider taking work?" Raymius screws his face up and throws her a quizzical look. She tries to explain. "If it gives you the chance to get your life back."

"Thanks, but I'm more interested in finding somewhere to stay tonight. No address, remember."

"We have an arrangement with a respectable local property developer who has accommodation for rent." *There's a contradiction if ever I heard one.* Raymius thinks. Ms Langan continues. "I can only offer it to individuals who I believe really want to help themselves. It's a studio apartment, very comfortable, very clean, not a shelter. He does have a few deal breakers, though."

Raymius leans forward and strokes his jaw. "Go on.""If you're found with drugs on the premises **or** if you miss your rent the deal's off and you're out. We pay your deposit, you pay rent monthly in arrears and you must be recommended by us. Very few people qualify. It's only for those who we genuinely believe have a chance at getting back to grips with reality and fitting back in with society. If someone has been homeless for more than a year they don't qualify."

Raymius smiles. "So I have until tomorrow to decide?"

"No, Ray! You have until the end of this interview to tell me what I want to hear. Then **I'll** decide. So what do you think? Want to get your life back?"

"Sounds too good to be true – what's the catch? And, why are you doing this?"

"You look as if you could do with a bit of luck. Tell me a little more about your situation, I want to help you. Let's make it easy. When did you leave school and what's happened since then?"

"Please! No psychoanalysis."

"You want out of this Police Station today? You want somewhere to stay? You don't belong on the street, Ray. Let me help
you here. The catch is you convince me you're worth it."

Cognitive interviewing. He'd done the course. Got the
T-shirt. He'd sat across from more therapists than he cares to
remember. Raymius knows the script. However, he also now
understands what Ms Langan wants to hear. So he begins.
Making sure she hears everything she needs to. Paying
particular attention to all omissions...

omnivore *n* **1.** an animal that will feed on any kind or many different kinds of food including both plants and animals **2.** wide ranging and often undiscriminating in interests and tastes

Sheena Buxton changes her mind. She decides to take a shot on the leather Chesterfield and be mum. She pours the coffee. DS Macmillan is at the window closing the curtains. It's blowing a gale and torrential rain lashes the other side of the double-glazed unit. Outside, the new recruits are getting their introduction to physical education. The drill sergeant's smile is visible from over two hundred metres away. Mac stops shaking his head when he notices the internal latch is off. He takes a mental note to tell security as he locks it shut. His hand brushes against the windowpane; it's freezing. He increases the gas for the fire and lights up another fag. Sheena opens a brown case file. It has a whitish, worn-out adhesive label on the front:

West, 25 Cromwell Street.

She starts to read out loud.

"Thursday, 24th February 1994. 0900hrs

Investigating officer : Detective Superintendent John Bennett

Assisting : Paul Britton

We have a most unusual situation. Mr West comes across as cheerful, charming and straightforward. A workingman most people have a friendly word for. He and Mrs West have lived at the address for more than 22 years. By most accounts they are outwardly friendly and good neighbours.

*We have 3 bodies, none of which have been positively iden-
tified. The bodies were not left in a way we'd normally
expect..."*

Sheena pauses for a moment before she lights up. She points
the butt of the cigarette at Mac and asks: "Do you know how
the bodies were found, Mac?"

He recalls the feeling he'd had reading the original reports.
Once again the same alarm bells start sounding off in his
head as he answers her question. "They were dismembered
and decapitated."

She sucks on her Regal, takes a gulp of coffee and continues.
"It was immediately evident to Paul that they'd discovered a
sadistic predator with one particular dreadful feature."

Mac's eyes squint as he shakes his head. "I don't understand, Sheena,"

"Fred and Rosemary West didn't just wake up one morning
and discover they were sexual psychopaths, Mac. This behaviour starts early in life and doesn't end until they get caught."

"So what exactly are you saying?" Mac asks, still shaking
his head.

"Britton realised straightaway they were dealing with
prolific murderers, what people now call serial killers."

"I'm sorry, Sheena, I get that, but what's your point? I'm
afraid you're going to have to spell it out for me."

"How many bodies had they found, Mac?"

The extent of the nightmare is slowly sinking into Mac's
mind. "Only three."

Sheena gives Mac one of her a-ha looks. "That's right, only
three. Even though they'd only discovered three bodies
Britton knew even then there would be other..." Sheena's
eyebrows rise like the way a teacher does when she's expecting the pupil to find the missing word. Mac complies.

"Victims, Sheena."

"That's right, Mac, many, other victims. There could not have been a silence in between. That's not the way these things work. Everywhere he'd lived and everywhere he'd worked. Sexual psychopaths get comfortable with the particular way they dispose of bodies. Some are left in open ditches or beside rivers, some are buried. Fred West liked to keep his close."

"So that's why he used the back garden?" Mac asks, expecting another 'well done' and a gold star.

"No, not exactly, Detective Sergeant MacMillan." Sheena replies sarcastically. Mac's face tells Sheena he is now receiving her loud and clear. She continues in her primary school teacher tone, her head is nodding and her eyes are once again giving Mac an a-ha look. "He used the back garden Mac bee-cauwse…"

"Because he liked to keep his victims close?"

"No, Mac! He used the back garden because… the house…"

Mac finally gets it, although he feels suitably inadequate filling in the blanks. "Because, Sheena, the house…was full."

Sheena is tempted to applaud but decides not to. Mac puts out his cigarette and empties the ashtray. There is an old discarded milky teabag with blue mould at the bottom of the bin. He gets a waft full in the face and winces.

"Oh fuck, I need some air, Sheena. Let's take a break, eh?"

"A couple of minutes, just let me finish. Mac, you appeared surprised at the possibility of a sexual psychopath at large for over a quarter of a century. You shouldn't be. We live in a culture where people come and go all the time. Wives walk out on husbands, teenagers run away from home, hitchhikers fail to arrive. Their fate is unknown to their friends and families." Sheena holds up Mac's file with his findings on HOLMES and continues. "The data you provided me with suggests that the majority of victims you've highlighted were at some point possibly involved in prostitution, right?"

"Yeah, that's right, Sheena."

"Prostitutes suit the purpose for the sexual psychopath. They are easier to acquire and tend to be more anonymous. Their disappearance doesn't create the same headlines as a schoolgirl who is expected home. Hundreds of women who work as prostitutes disappear for days, even weeks. They leave some habitual red light area only to turn up in another; they're driven by trade, whimsy and fear. Far too many never turn up again. If they do they're entered into that ever-increasing file marked…" she gives Mac her teacher look again to make sure he's still paying attention. Mac plays along and finishes her sentence again.

"Unsolved Prostitute Murders."

"It's practically impossible to determine how many individuals are victims of violent crimes. Your theory is not only probable, it's our worst nightmare. Whether a person has been raped or butchered, without bloodstains, a body or the proverbial smoking gun we have little to go on. These individuals, as you have quite rightly suggested, end up in an even bigger ever-increasing file. These poor souls are simply… Missing!"

"Bloody hell, Sheena, this is all pretty bleak."

"Every day Mac as you well know girls and boys disappear all over the country. There are families who haven't seen their loved ones in years. When this type of news breaks people everywhere wonder, oh my God what if? And the media helps like paraffin on an open fire."

"So how bad can this be then, Sheena?"

"Good question. At best we only ever scratch the surface. As I said earlier and I'm sure you can appreciate, this is not something we like to publicise."

"OK, so what's next?"

"Let me talk to some people, I'll see what I can come up with. Anyways…"

Her head tilts to the side and her eyes fill with curiosity. "Mac? You were going to tell me something at the classroom earlier but changed your mind, what's up?"

Mac shuffles his feet, rolls his eyes to the left and gathers his thoughts. Sheena presses him again.

"C'mon what were all those cloak-and-dagger antics earlier? I'm a fucking psychologist, Mac."

He hands Buxton the envelope.

"You didn't say anything about a letter in your email, Mac."

"Hold on Sheena, fuck sake! My boss picked it out his pigeonhole last night. I got it early this morning. And the cloak-and-dagger antics are nobody knows about this yet. OK?"

Sheena makes a face and smiles in a way that has Mac wishing he hadn't stated the obvious. She opens the envelope and starts reading. When she's finished her face says all there is to say but just in case Mac isn't getting it she barks at him. "You should have given me this straight away, Mac."

omnibus *adj.* **1**. comprising several items.
2. serving several purposes at once.

Raymius's eyes scan round interview room No 4. Apart from the table and both their chairs, nothing, no posters no notices, nothing. It smells exactly like a cell. Raymius produces a smile for *Ms* Langan.

"Any chance of a cuppa?"

"Why not, Ray, give me a few moments."

"Is it OK if I smoke?"

"Sure Ray, just wait until they bring an ashtray, OK?"

Raymius nods in approval. She pops her head outside the door and speaks to the cop standing guard. *Marvellous,* Raymius thinks, *room service.* He carries on like Hans Christian Anderson.

"I left school at sixteen and went to the local polytechnic to study accounts. I wanted to do computing but I didn't have O'Grade Maths."

Ms Langan pipes in. "I'm not very good with numbers either."

Raymius ignores the remark. "I'd got thrown out of Maths when the Department Head decided he didn't like me. Accounts had plenty places to spare. Nobody wanted to do Accounts…"

She interrupts. "How do you know he didn't like you?"

"He told me."

"What did he say?"

Raymius leans forward over clenched fists with his elbows still on the table. "He said. 'I am going to have you thrown out of the Mathematics Department, I don't like you'."

Susan Langan is unaware of his body language as she continues to scribble away on her notepad. "Why do you think he didn't like you?" she says, still not looking up from her pad.

"His wife didn't like me first, so I guess he didn't like me either."

"Why didn't his wife like you, Ray?"

Raymius sighs. "I got picked on at school by neds who had something to prove and by teachers who wanted to make an impression. I got used to looking after myself. His wife, Mrs Barber, was my Modern Studies teacher and she'd told me several times my attitude was far too 'cavalier'."

Ms Langan looks up from her notes and peers over the top of her glasses like she is, ironically, a schoolteacher. "That was all?"

"No, there was an incident."

Ms Langan doesn't say anything and doesn't look like she is going to, so Raymius carries on. "Someone farted while her back was turned. It was wee Willie Young directly behind me. He was the proverbial little shite who made a career out of winding everyone up. Not just the teachers, he was forever getting smacked, by everyone. Anyway, she threatened to 'take me down a peg or two' and give me six of the best if I didn't own up or tell her who had been responsible. Well, no-win situation for me. So, I found myself on the floor in front of the classroom waiting for corporal punishment. Leather strap half an inch thick with a split at the end the teachers called the tongue. Not many of the teachers used the belt any more, just the sadists. It was more commonly used as a last resort. She made me take off my school blazer and jumper.

I then had to roll up my sleeves. The idea was to expose my wrists. You were expected to swap one hand under the other and get three on each during six of the best. She stacked a pile of reference books on her desk to about three inches below my fingers so I would have to keep my arms parallel with the ground. She then proceeded to give me six of the best on each hand.

"When she'd finished she was sweating and little droplets of blood had appeared on both my wrists amidst the bruising. She almost spat her next sentence at me. I think she expected me to show more emotion. 'So tough gu,y are you going to tell me who was responsible or would you like more of the same?' I actually felt like laughing. I'd guessed she'd been watching to many American movies. Whenever I think of this it reminds me of Billy Connolly. *'I suppose a kick in the testicles would be out of the question? Bike! I'll give you bike.'* Y'know, all that fucked-up adult-language that's designed to make you think they actually know shit. Around the same time in life you're beginning to realise that most adults don't have a fucking clue.

"I was in a lot of pain. I wanted to cry or even grass the wee shite up but that just wasn't done. When I stared into her eyes, all I could think about was how I'd been assaulted for nothing and how feeble she looked. She'd already lost. So, I put on my bravest face and gave her my reply. I don't know why I said it, the words just came out. My legs and arms felt like jelly but I just smiled…

"'Sorry miss it wisnae me, if you're no happy wi that, you'd better gimme mair o' the same. Mibbey yi should huv a wee rest first but, eh?'

"And that's really the way we spoke. I could speak properly. I knew how to act at home when my parents had their friends round. Nan used to call it minding your P's and

Q's. But I'd also learned how to speak at school in the playground. Now there's an interesting name for somewhere that regularly hosted extortion, sexual abuse and the occasional stabbing. Anyway, bilingual or not, I was of course bluffing. There wasn't a murmur in the classroom. Everyone eagerly awaited the next move. If wee Willie had chosen that moment to squeeze out the most silent of farts, you would've heard it.

"Then the entire classroom erupted in laughter and she lost the plot. She turned bright red and declared war. Another twelve of the best came thundering down on my hands and wrists, which were by this time in bits. I just felt numb. Most of the class were still laughing at the state she was getting herself into. But it wasn't funny. I had what alcoholics call a moment of clarity. I saw a chink in her armour; somebody had to lose and it was going to be her. By the time she had delivered another twelve thrashes at me with all of her might, she was panting like a rapist. I suspected this was the most physical exercise she'd taken in quite some time. Looking like a panic-stricken telly-tubby, she blasted at me: 'Right! Have you had enough?'

I considered saying yes but was afraid it might meet with a repeat of the same retort, 'Who was responsible?' and we would be right back at the start again. Anyway I was on a roll. Tourette's Syndrome, loss of inner monologue, I'm not sure. So, in my bestest poshest voice I said:

"'At fifteen seconds a go, Miss, it'll take three minutes for two 'sixes-of-the-best'. There's half an hour left of class, Miss. Do you really think you'll manage another hundred and twenty of those?'

"To this day I don't honestly know what she said, there were lots of stories and versions. All I remember was her shrieking and babbling as she burst into tears and ran out of the classroom. Mr Barber, the Head of Mathematics, told the class they should take an early lunch. I was told never to set foot in the Modern Studies or the Maths department ever again. I can remember it like it was yesterday."

"'I am going to have you thrown out of the Mathematics Department, I don't like you'."

The door opens, the coffee and ashtray finally arrives. When the door closes Raymius leans back and lights up a cigarette. Ms Langan is scribbling furiously. Once again she looks up over the top of her glasses.

"Tell me what happened after you left school, Ray."

Raymius sucks hard on his Embassy Regal and lets out another sigh.

"I went to the local polytechnic and left after two years with straight A's. I got accepted into Edinburgh's Heriot-Watt University. Four years later I graduated with a degree in Marketing."

"Your parents must have been really proud, Raymond."

"Eh… Yeah. Course they were. Please, call me Ray."

"They must have been chuffed to bits at your graduation, Ray?"

"They didn't attend."

"Why not?" she asks curiously.

Raymius decides Langan is going to keep him there at the Police Station until she feels she knows the whole three volumes of War and Peace. He thinks for a moment and pauses for effect.

"They died."

Ms Langan checks herself and begins to suspect that maybe she is being insensitive.

"Oh! I'm so sorry Ray, both of them died? Together? Was it an accident?"

"No! Just old age. Nan was seventy-four and Pops was seventy-nine, they both died within a year of each other."

She looks puzzled.

"They were my foster parents. Sally's aunt and uncle fostered me."

"Who was Sally?"

"Sally was my mother."

"So what happened to Sally?"

"She died too."

desire *v* **1.** wish for, to want somethingvery strongly **2.** find sexually attractive, to want to have sexual relations with somebody **3.**craving a wish or longing for something

Mac pushes his index finger between the curtains. He moves the dark blue velour back just enough to see the rain is still dropping out of the sky in lumps. The new recruits have disappeared from the playing fields. In the penalty box of the football park, a small lochan is emerging where earlier there was only a puddle. He looks at Sheena engrossed in the letter and thinks about his actions this very day. Why he has so much on his mind right now. *Why do we do the things we do?* A book on the shelf catches his eye, 'How to think like a millionaire'. He has a cynical snort to himself. *Bloody self-help books, if only it were that easy.* He thumbs through the small paperback and stops at the chapter entitled 'The Richest Man in Babylon'. He starts to read...

340 BC

Augustus sat sipping his tea in the Great Hall. A student approached and graciously asked for counsel. Augustus enquired as to what particular problem was troubling the boy. The youth's question was this.

"Master, how does one attain great wealth and possessions?"

Augustus replied, "The key to these treasures is desire. Do you desire such things?"

"Yes! Of course Master. Doesn't everyone?"

"How much do you desire these things?" Augustus further enquired.

The young student's face became bewildered. He was confused and unsure how to answer.

"Walk with me," said Augustus.

After some time they found themselves at the shore of the river. Augustus waded in until the water was above his waist. He beckoned the youth to follow.

"Do you trust me?"

"Of course, Master."

Augustus held the boy's head gently but firmly.

"Do not be afraid. Relax, close your eyes and take a deep breath."

And, like John the Baptist, Augustus proceeded to immerse the boy under water. It was not long before the youth began to flail his arms in panic. Augustus strengthened his grip and continued to hold the boy's head beneath the mighty river. Eventually he allowed the boy to surface. He waited until the boy stopped coughing and spluttering and asked: "What were you thinking?"

"I thought… I was… going to die."

"Yes, yes, but what were you thinking?"

"I couldn't breathe… I was thinking… I need air."

"And at that point you started to fight for your life?"

"Yes, that's right. At that point all I could think of was getting my head above the water to breathe."

"And, at that point did you crave for anything other than air?"

"No Master, nothing else."

"When you learn to express that very same emotion and passion at will, you can walk across the bridge between desire and attainment."

They strolled back to the steps leading to the Great Hall.

Before they parted Augustus turned to the youth and said this: "If the end of this day's business were known, there it comes. But suffice the day will end and then the end be known. Be mindful of what you wish for, young Alexander. Give great thought to your intentions for they are stronger than your desires. You are one of our brightest stars. But remember also the fire that roars twice as brightly burns half as long. If we meet again we will smile. If not, at least we'll know this parting was made well."

Augustus was a student of Plato and the great friend of Aristotle. He died in 340 BC. That same year a sixteen-year-old crushed a rebellion in Thrace. After seizing the principal city he re-named it Alexandropolis after himself. Alexander the Great was born in 356 BC and died in Babylon 33 years later.

The grandfather clock once again breaks Mac's concentration. His stomach groans as he turns his head towards the corner of the room. It's 2pm. They are both hungry but him especially. Sheena is more conscientious than Mac. She adopted the 'my body is a temple' attitude when she first visited California. Mac would be content to eat doughnuts and slurp coffee until it spilled out his ears. He could also gobble down a beef curry or a Big Mac and chips at any time of the day or night. Sheena used to tease him, hamburger by name hamburger by nature.

But it wasn't food that was on her mind. It was sex. Apparently you can survive without food for weeks and without water for days. It's argued that men think about sex every fifteen minutes. Sheena normally has lots to occupy her busy mind. It's like they say, though, about sex and cash. Whenever you're not getting any it dominates your thoughts. Well, from Sheena's point of view, food and drink is over-rated. Also, being together in an environment where you can actually take the chance and get right down to it isn't helping. Sex sometimes clouds everything else. *Doesn't it fucking ever!* Sheena thinks. She believes when it does you should satisfy your primal needs and get it out the way. Then life can get back to normal. Well, that's what she believes at the moment. Sheena is in touch with her needs and feelings. She considers how she could best describe her current state of mind. Her eyes roll up to the ceiling as she licks her lips and has a giggle. *Absolutely gagging for it. Big Mac. Hmmm, yummy!* So although Mac is thinking about food and Sheena is thinking about sex, they are both professionals. First they have work to attend to. Sheena holds up the letter and waves it at Mac.

"When exactly did Ribbon get this, Mac?"

"I'm not sure of the exact time. I only know it was in his mail when he got to the station last night."

"Delivered by hand?"

"Yeah."

"What time?"

"Jesus, Sheena."

"Mac, just give me your best guess."

"I think it was around ten o'clock."

"Why didn't you warn me off about this earlier?"

"I already told you. The boss only showed me it just before I left Glasgow this morning. Is there a problem?"

"I don't know, Mac, you tell me. You could have shown me this hours ago, why didn't you? Y'know, like outside the classroom earlier?"

Mac shrugs, his head falls to one side and he sticks his palms up with resignation. Sheena acknowledges Mac's inability to respond by pushing her hand into the air like she's halting traffic.

"It's all right Mac, forget it. Can you get me the use of a secure fax?"

Mac nods, still feeling a little wounded.

Sheena mumbles to herself as she powers up her laptop. "Nice handwriting."

"Yeah, that's what the boss said too."

Sheena scans in the letter and saves it onto her desktop. She hands the original back to Mac along with one of her business cards.

"Get Ruth to fax this straight away, make it for my attention. Also get her to send the original to the same address registered special delivery."

Once Mac closes the door she sends a quick text to her assistant at Dundee University. She then pulls the document back up on her laptop and reads the letter again.

Dear John,

We all make mistakes, but I am surprised none of your chaps have ever tracked me down. Maybe I shouldn't be. Your incompetence is totally congruent with the rest of the pathetic human race. Anyway, enough of my personal grievances, I digress. I know all about you. I've taken a great interest in your career, John. We are similar in so many ways, it's ironic. Example? I hear you say. Well for a start I know for an absolute fact we have the same tastes in women. Hmm, now I bet that's got your cerebral cortex vibrating at speed, eh?

Your seduction by the system is so very, very sad. You can be irritatingly average, John. You allow yourself to be deluded by an inaccurate belief system. It's your model of the world that makes you weak. That is why you avoid dealing with your demons and find sanctuary in a bottle of Glen-fucking-Ord. Malt whisky, John, is not the answer. Do you smile when you read above the Oracle's chair, John? Do you know yourself? Are you happy with whom you've become?

'...If any man is a habitual criminal, it is I. In my lifetime I have broken every law that has ever been made by God

or man. If either make any more, I will very cheerfully break them also. The mere fact I have done these things is quite sufficient for the average person. Very few people ever consider it worthwhile to wonder why I am what I am and do what I do. All they think that's necessary is to catch me, try me, convict me and lock me up. Life in prison is not necessarily miserable when there is a hope you'll be turned loose again... if someone has a young tiger cub in a cage and then mistreats it until it gets savage and bloodthirsty, when they turn it loose to prey on the rest of the world... there is a hell of a roar... But when people do the same thing to people, then the world is surprised, shocked and offended because they get robbed, raped and killed. They've done it to me and they don't like it when I do it to them."

Some things are inevitable, John.

Yours sincerely

αΩ

The door opens and Mac walks back in.

"Done."

"Thanks, Mac." Buxton scrambles through her notes and pulls out an old tattered, wine-coloured leather folder. She scratches through its contents. She hands Mac a single sheet of A4. He reads the first few lines and stops.

If any man was a habitual criminal, it was me. In my lifetime I have broken every law that was ever made by God or man...

"Jesus, Sheena, where did this come from?"

She hands him the file and he reads the front cover.

Carl Panzram. Killer. A Journal of Murder.

Macmillan, 1970.

She closes her eyes, raises her head and searches the hardware of her mind.

"He's copied Carl Panzram's quote and..."

"What is it, Sheena, what's up?"

"I'm not sure. I still can't figure it out, why he'd do that. Vanity perhaps? Arrogance?"

"Sorry Sheena but you've lost me again, what's going on?"

"He's quoted Carl Panzram, Mac, but he's fucking edited it."

"So what does that mean?"

"I'm not sure, Mac. I'm really not sure but this could be your guy."

"Bollocks! This is all too much, Sheena. C'mon, it's not fucking possible. I can't believe it."

"Can't or won't?" Sheena asks emphatically. With her hands planted firmly now on her thighs and her head cocked to the side, she waits for Mac's response.

"We don't get a whiff of some whacko for nearly thirty years and the night before I arrange to meet you and discuss the possibility, he decides to write us a bloody letter and have it hand fucking delivered? This is ridiculous. It's too contrived. It's not possible."

"OK Mac, consider this. If there is a sexual predator out there who has been collecting for three decades he'd need to have acquired some skills. We are not talking about Mr Average here. We are not talking about Mr Above Average. We are looking for Mr Top Two Per Cent." Sheena waves at Mac. "Hello! Are you OK with that?"

Mac nods.

"My profile for the author of this letter is something like this: Superiority complex…"

Mac screws up his face.

"Jesus, Mac, he's criticising a Detective Chief Inspector for fuck sake. He has demonstrated knowledge of psychology, philosophy, history and medicine. He's well read, especially in the field of psychological profiling, he sees himself as judge and jury. Do you know what this means, Mac?"

Mac looks confused, again. Sheena points at the signature at the bottom of the letter. Mac feels inadequate, once again. "No, Sheena, I don't, what does it mean?"

"α is the sign for infinity or Alpha, the first letter of the Greek alphabet in its lower case. Ω is Omega, the last letter of the Greek alphabet in its upper case. When both of these letters are placed together in this way it signifies the start and the end of all things. It is used to symbolise Jesus or in some cases... God!"

Mac looks and feels bewildered. Sheena hands him an old diary, her old diary. His eyes narrow and old memories flood his head.

"This is the year we graduated from..."

Sheena interrupts. "First year Police College, twenty-one years ago this month. Way to go, Detective Sergeant Macmillan. Read the first page."

Mac for the second time wishes he hadn't stated the obvious and reads the quote that has been hand written in the centre of the inside cover. It's Mac's handwriting.

"...When you have eliminated the impossible, whatever remains, however improbable, must be the truth..."

Sherlock Holmes

Mac feels nervous about stating the obvious for a third time. "Sheena! *That* was meant tongue in cheek a long time ago by a naïve young cop. Sherlock Holmes is a fictitious character from a book."

"Yeah, Mac. But Sir Arthur Conan Doyle was a real clever guy and so is your killer."

"It's all too much of a coincidence." Mac protests.

"Coincidence or providence, Mac?" Sheena replies.

legend *n* **1.** an explanation of the symbols used on a map.**2.** a caption for an illustration **3.** an inscription, especially a title or a motto, on an object. **4.** Somebody famous admired for a particular skill or talent. **5.** a popular myth that has arisen in modern times. **6.** an old story that has been passed down for generations, especially one that has been presented as history but is unlikely to be true. **7.** a story presented as history but unlikely to be true.

Raymius has been talking in interview room No 4 for what seems like hours. The ashtray is beginning to look like the morning after the night before. Susan Langan is engrossed in scribbling her notes furiously. Raymius tilts his cup and looks inside.

"Any chance of a refill?" He lights another cigarette as *Ms* Langan gets up from her plastic chair, pops her head out of the door and summons a uniform for more caffeine.

Sally had committed suicide on the 15th of January, one week after Raymius's 4th birthday. It had been a complete shock to everyone. No note, no rhyme or reason. Everybody was stunned. It was a real mystery. Sally was ambitious, outgoing and for a single mum very successful. She was the PA to a top CEO in the city's financial district. Well paid and seemed happy. The day before her death she'd travelled from the chaos of London to the little village of Doon on the West Coast of Scotland to leave Raymius with her favourite aunt and uncle. She flew back to London that night and was found the next day in bed with the contents of a full bottle of pills in her stomach.

Jim and Jean Scott brought Raymius up as their own. Raymius had reached the grand old age of twenty when James Christopher Scott retired from the police force. Three months later Jean died. She'd been ill for some time but everybody thought, or rather hoped, she'd be around for ever, especially her husband. Jim had never been ill in his life, not so much as a headache. Four weeks before the anniversary of Jean's death the widower passed away in his sleep. Many people find it difficult adjusting to retirement, especially after an active career. Jim, however, died from a broken heart. He'd been found sat up in bed with a book in his hands. He hadn't turned up for his lunchtime dominos match and the lads down at the Ex-Servicemen's club had become concerned. You could set your watch to Jim Scott. His false teeth were in a mug at the side of the bed and his bookmark was at the start of the last chapter. This was the main topic of conversation at the funeral, as if finishing the paperback was in someway significant.

"Imagine, auld Jimmy no gettin' tae finish his book…"

"A'know, bloody shame int-it…"

"He was a good man, it's jist no right!"

Raymius had listened to Pops' old cronies bleating all day and kept his smirk hidden. Pops was a wise old bird, a joker and a philosopher, he'd have been well proud. He never got stressed. He thought things through and he loved to keep people guessing. He'd said to Raymius many times, "All my westerns have the same ending, son…"

Raymius married Helen Carter in the March following his twenty-fourth birthday. She was only nineteen. December the same year his son Aaron was born. Sex between the newlyweds vanished shortly after the honeymoon. She'd stopped being a wife and embraced the prospect of motherhood. Like most young couples they didn't have a 'How to be a Parent Handbook'. The arguments followed rapidly by resentment booked in to the marital home. Like hordes of others who get married for the wrong reasons they went from 'you can't keep them apart' to 'nights out with lads' and 'nights out for the girls'.

Then came Hogmanay at Castle Carter, a New Year party for the movers and shakers. The Carters were popular because they were prosperous, not because they were lovely people to be around. Anybody who knew anybody in the West of Scotland business community would be there. It was a three-line whip for all of the Carter Clan. Helen and hubby were no exception. Raymius had passed out in one of the lounges in the wee small hours and usually that would have been him until the birds started to sing. Unfortunately, or fortunately, depending on how you look at things, a drunken blonde spilled her Bacardi Breezer all over him. She'd stumbled trying to squeeze by. He went upstairs to clean up. The loo he chose was occupied. He was about to go in search of another when he recognised a sneeze. It was unmistakably Helen's. There is not another sound like it in the world. Nan used to always say.

"There's a reason for everything, son!"

When he'd first met Helen he used to tease her about it. He'd thought often, *what in the world, Nan, could the reason be for that ridiculous bloody sneeze?* He considered an interesting theory that morning after he'd smashed the bathroom door in. Helen was on her hands and knees. On Daddy's instructions she had been working at Carter Cameron Fyfe since being kicked out of school. On Helen's instructions Thomas Andrews, a junior partner at Daddy's law firm, was also on his knees. He had her long blonde hair wound round his left hand and was spanking her with his right. Raymius found out later the term for this is 'riding rodeo'. It took four of the local rugby team to peel Raymius from Helen's cowboy companion. Thomas

Andrews realised fairly soon that he was lucky to leave the party on a stretcher headed for an ambulance instead of a box headed for a hole in the ground.

The fresh supply of caffeine arrives. Ms Langan looks up from her notes.

"So how did Sally, eh that is…your mother die, Ray?"

Raymius lowers his gaze and pushes out his bottom lip.

"Car crash."

"Oh, I'm so sorry, Ray."

"Its OK, I was very young. It was nobody's fault, just one of those things, but if it's all right I'd rather not talk about it."

"I understand, Ray. Let's move on then. Are you married, divorced, separated?"

"Single."

"Any dependants?"

Raymius tries not to think about Aaron's first day back at school today and the conversation on the telephone where he'd recently been told that he still had no access. In terms of life he'd always thought of his son as being his first teacher. But that's another story.

"No, none."

"Can we go back to just after you graduated, Ray? Tell me about your working life."

Raymius lights up another cigarette.

"Within three months of graduation I'd started work with Orbital PLC in the marketing department. Later that year I moved into management and was shooting up the career ladder. When I was made redundant it felt like being sent to the gallows. I'd never ever considered the possibility of not being employed. I'd become very attached to my lifestyle.

"My depression got steadily worse. I stopped talking, stopped washing and then stopped eating. After my house was repossessed I moved to Glasgow with only enough deposit for a small flat. I signed the lease and got the keys for a bed-sit at 333 Woodlands Road. As I said to you earlier, one year later my flat was repossessed when the landlord, Martin Singh, did a bunk to Jakarta or somewhere. I was homeless. I wandered around the streets of Glasgow wondering what had gone wrong. I'd said to myself many times, 'Things can't get any worse'. I know now no matter how bad things are, they can always get worse. I wasn't sure where I was going. I kept heading towards Glasgow Central Station as if I were going to get the last train down to the West Coast and go back home.

"Lloyds TSB is on Bothwell Street, diagonally across from the Central Station. I was sitting on the stairs of where I used to bank. It was a cold night but dry. My bones felt brittle. I'd been crying, not sobbing, just lots of tears. A young couple walked up the stairs and passed me to use the cash machine. I held my breath and tried to be invisible. I hated the way they looked at me. I felt like a stray dog lying dead in the gutter. On the way back down the stairs the guy threw a pound coin at my feet. I heard him whisper to his girlfriend, 'See, Honey? I don't mind helping them. I just hate the ones that hassle you and ask…'"

Raymius lowers his head and covers his eyes.

"I went below street level under the stairs where I was out of sight and stayed there until morning. Everything I owned was in a leather holdall. I put it into a black bin bag because it had started to rain. The following morning was torrential. I wandered around pretending I had somewhere to go."

Raymius looks up and stares at Susan Langan. "The only trouble I've ever had was stealing apples from a back garden when I was seven years old. I'm going to be thirty years old tomorrow. I'm in a Police Station blabbing with a social worker I've never met before, dredging up stuff I'd rather leave buried. I'm not a bad person. I don't deserve this!" Big round tears fill his green eyes and roll down his cheeks. "So, how do I get out of this Police Station today, Ms Langan?"

Susan Langan sits upright, smiles sympathetically and offers him a paper handkerchief.

"Right, Ray, this is what I need you to do. Do you know Govanhill?"

Raymius wipes his eyes and lights another cigarette. "Yeah."

"Be at 104 Albert Road today at 5pm on the dot. I'll meet you there and we'll organise you keys for your studio apartment." She hands him a card. "Phone Martin Williams tomorrow on this number."

Raymius screws up his face. "A shrink?"

"Martin is a therapist. He'll help you address those demons that you've been dealing with yourself. Don't fall into the trap of thinking you have to face all this stuff on your own, Ray. Your life is fixable and... it's part of the deal."

Susan Langan hands him another card with her own details on it. "I'll organise an appointment for 9.30am next Monday at my office to get an update on how you're doing. In the meantime if you need to talk to someone phone me. Oh and Ray..."

"Yeah?"

"Call me Susan."

"So, Susan, why are you doing this? Are you not taking a big chance on me? When do I get the, 'You'd better not let me down' speech?"

"I'm not the one with something to lose, Ray. You're clever enough to work that out."

"You don't have to do this, though. Why are you helping me?"

"No, you're right, I don't." She looks at him once again with her sympathetic social worker smile. "My brother had eyes that sparkled when he was trying to be brave."

"So that's it?"

"He had an honest face too."

Susan completes all the necessary paperwork and escorts him past the front desk. As Raymius walks down the steps of Pitt Street Station she shouts after him...

"What about your father, Ray? You haven't mentioned him once."

Raymius turns round. "What about him?"

"Well clearly he must exist. Do you know anything about him?"

"No, nothing."

His face is expressionless as he shrugs. Susan Langan tilts her head to the side and smiles. Her eyes are filled with admiration and pity. He looks at her standing in the doorway and continues down the stairs with his head hung low. He holds back a grin as he thinks to himself, *Good job, Raymius, a masterstroke adding the whole tears thing...*

> **loyalty** *n* **1.** the quality or state of being
> loyal,a feeling of devotion **2.** duty or
> attachment to somebody or something

Sheena excuses herself, goes to powder her nose. That's always been her preferred expression. She can be really crude sometimes and yet at others she's sweet as honey, or at least that's what Mac thinks. He stares out the window and wonders where the years have gone. The rain has stopped. The countryside is like a wet facecloth hanging over the shower rail. Mac looks past the rugby field he'd played on as a young cop and down the hill to local civilisation. In the nearby village of Kincardine the chimney pots puff pollution into the sky. The smoke swirls up through the candyfloss clouds heading for the ozone. Mac sighs.

Today is a special day and he must tell Sheena. He looks into the corner of the room. Sheena has been away for fifteen minutes. He checks his watch to make sure. Correction, twenty minutes. He remembers the grandfather clock is slow. Mac's watch keeps perfect time. It's not exactly a Rolex but it was a 40th birthday present from Michael and Maureen, his dutiful son and daughter. They're good kids and Mac has always tried to teach them to 'do the right thing cause it's the right thing to do'. He's worked hard at being the dutiful father and of course, husband.

Michael wasn't planned, and the reason they married. Mac doesn't believe he's ever been the type of person to shirk his responsibilities. Opinions vary. Maureen arrived a few years later. A naïve plan by a couple attempting to improve their marriage who were resigned to a sentence of 'till-death-us-do-part'.

Mac fell in love with Sheena Buxton the first time he laid eyes on her and still feels the same way. She left him for her career. He was young, angry and desperately lonely. The next time he saw her he was married with a child on the way. At least once a year since he's been married, Sheena visits Glasgow. They always hook up. They always sleep together.

The door opens and in she comes.

"Ah! That's better. I feel almost human again."

"I thought you'd fallen down the pan, Sheena."

"Aye, Mac, very good, very original. My grandmother used to say that y'know?"

Mac ignores her comment looking at his watch again. "Did you get confirmation that the fax has been received?"

"Yeah I did, thanks, and you're right, what's-her-face at reception is very helpful."

"Her name is Ruth, Sheena. Do you want to order something in?"

Sheena turns on her mobile and is checking her messages so Mac continues. "Or, we can go out? There's a wee hotel not too far from here that does magic food but they stopped serving at three o'clock."

"Yeah, I know. I remember." Sheena laughs through the next sentence. "Sweet and sour King Prawn and a squeaky four-poster."

"Sheena… I've been meaning to tell you." Mac's face flushes pink. Sheena switches off her mobile, crosses her arms and sits down on the Chesterfield. But Mac waits for a response.

"Yeah, go on," is all he gets.

"I miss you, Sheena. I miss you a lot and always look forward to seeing you. I want to be with you. But today of all days, it's just not possible."

Sheena smiles openly and has that 'Aye right' look on her face. Mac continues. "No, honestly, Sheena at close of play Ribbon is expecting me back at Pitt Street. And, as soon as I've finished at the office..." he hesitates.

"Well?" She says.

"I've..." He hesitates again.

"C'mon, Mac, do I need to beat it out of you?"

"I've... a table booked at Di Maggios."

"Oooo! Mrs Mac's favourite Italian restaurant. What's the special occasion Mac, is she going to be a grandmother?"

"Fuck no. Christ, God forbid. However, the amount of shagging young Michael's doing it's not totally unimaginable."

"Like father like son, eh?"

Mac says nothing.

"So what's the gig then, are you two trying to get things sorted out, new start, new beginning all that shite?" Sheena giggles again. This time she resembles a mischievous elf. Mac stays silent and gives Sheena one of his stares.

"Well, Mac, the begging is about to stop and the beating is coming next. Fuck sake Mac, it's not like I don't know the score. What's the big secret?"

"It's our anniversary."

"Ahh!" she says.

On their anniversary Mr and Mrs Macmillan normally go for something to eat and have some wine. Well, actually lots of wine. That's normally what's needed for them both to get in the mood and do what they feel is required, the obligatory annual shag. Christmas is easy to avoid since the kids are always around. On his birthday he's allowed to get so pissed that it's unlikely he'd manage sex even if he wanted it. Her birthday usually involves having a weekend away with the girls under the guise of shopping. London, New York, Paris, Brussels and even Brighton, anywhere really so long as it's not Glasgow. It's her treat for all those years at home looking after the children. That just leaves two dates for keeping up appearances. The Wedding Anniversary and the 14th of February.

If Valentine's Day falls on a school night they can normally get away with the 'have to be up early for work in the morning' excuse. Today was that occasion when they'd each make an effort to forget the big mistake they made and tonight, they would both fulfil their obligations.

"How many years now?" Sheena asks, making conversation.

"Twenty."

"Jeeze-us doesn't time fly?" Sheena giggles again. Mac looks out the window again.

"Yeah, I know, Sheena. I was just thinking that myself."

"Sorry, Mac. If I'd remembered. I'd have got you a card."

"You're fucking hilarious, Sheena."

"Awe! Calm down, Mac. It's not a day I care to remember. While you were up to your ears in confetti I was sat at home all day crying my eyes out."

"Yeah and how was I supposed to know that? You were the one that left, remember."

"Well, if you play your cards right I'll give you an extra special anniversary present."

Mac shakes his head in disbelief and turns his palms skyward hoping to catch a little sympathy. "Sheena…" He is halted mid sentence as Sheena interrupts him with the 'old finger over the lips' thing. Her eyes close as she starts to get her head round the reality of the day. They have other things to talk about and there's much Mac still doesn't know.

"Let's get out of here for a while."

Mac looks at the clock and checks his watch, shaking his head he says, "We might get a sandwich at the hotel."

Sheena switches her mobile back on and rummages through her purse. She pulls out a business card and dials in a number.

"Hello, yeah, the restaurant please... Is that you Carlo? ... Yes, it is Sheena, clever you... Yeah, thanks. A colleague and I want to have lunch but obviously haven't made the three o'clock curfew, is that a problem? ... Eh, yeah sure, have you got sweet and sour King Prawn on the board today? ... Brilliant, I'll have that then, just a second..." Sheena cups her hand over the bottom of her mobile looks at Mac and beams a big grin.

"What you want for lunch, Mac?"

"Cheeseburger and chips." He replies, Sheena snorts, shakes her head and puts her mobile back up to her ear.

"Burger and fries please Carlo... yeah bacon, cheese and all the trimmings too. Thanks Carlo we should be there in about half an hour, you're a star. Oh Carlo just one more thing... No, cheeky, not that! Can you just charge lunch to my room? Thanks again, you're a dear. See'ya." Sheena can't wipe the grin from her face as she presses the picture of a red telephone on the keypad. She flips her mobile closed and pops it back into her handbag.

"Right, let's get some food and finish off what we've started, DS Macmillan."

Mac gives her a curious and cynical look.

"Don't worry, Mac, I won't rape you. Unless you beg me to."

"Thanks Sheena, I knew you'd understand."

Sheena had flown up last night and booked into the Kincardine Hotel, she couldn't resist it. Flights north are always quieter on a Sunday evening and cheaper. So what she saved on the travel she is happy to splash out on a bit of comfort. Anyway, most of it will be claimed back on expenses. She has to be in Dundee on Wednesday and back in London at the Yard on Friday. She was looking forward to catching up with Mac tonight and having a lazy day tomorrow. C'est la vie.

Sheena isn't sure if she'd want to marry now, too used to doing her own thing. She likes her independence and is never short of offers. She's already convinced that Carlo will literally jump at the chance. Her marketability in the dating scene is top quartile and unlikely to change in the foreseeable future. Who would want kids at her age? Fuck sake, she has a life. Why spoil that with nappies and school fees? Sheena doesn't want the burden of having anyone dependent on her. Who in their right mind would? Sheena has four older sisters therefore she has a plethora of nieces and nephews. She is a full-time favourite Aunt. She works hard at it; Christmas, Easter, birthdays, the shows, the theatre, boat trips and of course the footie. However, at the end of any day she can leave the little people in question with their parents and go to the pub. If you count up the days that Auntie Sheena spends with the kids it amounts to treble the 'quality time' spent by most doting parents. It's easy, when it's not a chore.

Mac always did know how to press those buttons, though. The way nobody else could. He always used to make her laugh and still has his moments. She really had sat at home all day and cried twenty years ago. And yet, in a way she's pleased the way her life has turned out. She has always felt she's had her cake and is always able to have another slice whenever it takes her fancy. There are a few men in her life that are only a phone call and a flight away. And she knows she can have Mac, any time.

They both button up their coats as they slip out the back entrance of the Police College. They head for the path that winds down the hill through the forest to the local hotel. As they continue walking Sheena grabs his arm and pulls herself close. Mac feels uncomfortable and gives her a look.

"Chill out Mac, we're just walking. So tell me about your boss. Who is John Ribbon? What's he all about?"

"What do you want to know?"

"Why didn't he go upstairs with this letter right away?"

"I'm not sure, Sheena, why?"

"What's he got to hide, Mac?"

Mac considers the question but doesn't respond. Sheena continues to fire questions into his ear.

"What skeletons does he have in the cupboard, Mac? Will he confide in you? Will he speak to me? Do you trust him?"

Mac stops and turns to Sheena he pulls away with his arm and she lets go.

"Hang on a minute, Sheena, this is my boss we're talking about here. You're bang out of order."

"Really! If he's dirty and it comes out later that you helped keep this under wraps, how does that look for you? Has anything like this ever happened before?"

"That's enough, Sheena. Yes, I do trust him and no, nothing like this has ever happened before. Well not to my knowledge, anyway."

"Aye Mac, indeed. How's he been acting recently?"

"Pretty much the same as always, Sheena."

"OK, so he's still drinking heavily, still chain smoking and still in therapy?"

"Yes, no and yes."

"Is he in a relationship, Mac?"

"What the fuck has that to do with anything, Sheena? Where are you going with all this?"

"What taste does he have in women? Do you know where he goes when he's off duty?"

"Make your point, Sheena. I'm losing my patience."

"Did you know he has an apartment in Amsterdam and visits it regularly, Mac?"

"No, I didn't."

"Did you know he's being investigated by Special Branch, Mac?"

"No, I didn't."

"The author of the letter believes they have the same taste in women. Chances are Ribbon has seen him, spoken to him and might even know him. Find out if Ribbon has any idea who this guy might be."

"And what if he doesn't want to go there, Sheena?"

"Then you have a choice to make, Mac. You need to convince your boss to do the right thing here."

"And if he doesn't see it the way you do, what am I supposed to do then?"

Mac feels droplets of water on his face. The rain starts. Not full on, not yet. But the sky is definitely about to open up. Mac pushes open his red and white golfing umbrella. Sheena moves under and close. She takes his arm once again and looks up at his face. She feels as if this time she's been too hard on him. She lets out a sigh as she smiles.

"Don't be so defensive. You're the detective, Mac. Be professional about it. You'll figure it out."

Mac looks at his watch and winces. Sheena arches her eyebrows and asks like a primary school teacher.

"So, Mac, you got any other prior engagements that I should know about?" Sheena checks the time on her mobile phone as they walk off down the hill. It's ten minutes past four.

omerta. *n* the code requirement alleged to apply to members of the Mafia, requiring that they remain silent about any crimes of which they have knowledge.

Have you ever been to the movies in the middle of the afternoon? When you come out you expect it to be dark but it's still broad daylight. You feel disorientated. That's how Raymius feels when he walks out of Pitt Street Police Station. He heads for the Inner Circle. Not an elaborate labyrinth like the London Underground but Glasgow's system is cheap and efficient. St George's Cross and then Kelvinbridge, only two stops between his current location and the abandoned hash. Raymius turns on Clare's mobile. Within seconds Vivaldi once more is spewing out of her phone. He presses the button with the little green phone and speaks.

"Hello?"

He holds the earpiece at arm's length.

"WHERE the FUCK are you? I've been goin' out my fuckin' mind."

"Relax, Clare."

"Relax! What do you mean RELAX? Where the fuck are you? I need to see you right away."

Raymius responds calmly. "Sorry Clare, no can do."

"Eh? What d'yi mean? Fuckin' talkin' no can fuckin' do? You and I need to meet right away."

His voice is soft but assertive. "Clare."

There's a momentary silence at the other end of the phone. He takes advantage of it. "Have I ever let you down, Clare?"

Clare closes her eyes and takes two deep breaths. Once she feels she's back below fifty thousand feet she responds.

"I've been worried sick, are you OK Ray?"

"I'll be at the Scotia around seven tonight, meet me then. I'll bring you up to speed with my interesting morning and give you your mobile back."

"What about the 'gear' Ray?"

"Sorry 'C', I had to stash it but I can get my hands on it tomorrow."

"That's goin' to be a problem, Ray. Fuck! Tell me again there's no way I can get the gear back tonight?"

"There's no way you can get the gear back tonight, Clare."

"Cunt. Fuck! See you at seven then. Don't be late."

Raymius hears her giggle before the phone clicks. At times Clare amazes him. He walks along the pedestrian precinct. A grin appears on his face as he remembers an old Glasgow gag. What does a cop do if he arrests you on Sauchiehall Street? Drags you round the corner on to Hope Street 'cause it's easier to spell.

Raymius takes note of the triangular contrast before him. On his left the dark smoked glass windows of the Scottish Television Studios. On his right Glasgow Caledonian University campus sprouting bright gleaming silver build-ings from out of lush landscaped gardens. Straight ahead is the grubby graffiti-ridden underpass at Cowcaddens under-ground station. It's like a deserted bombsite from the holo-caust. The platform smells of pish and if you had an inkling to clean up the litter it would only make the dog shit more obvi-ous as you navigate carefully along the chewing-gum-ridden walkway. In a few hours this little hamlet will be a hive of activity with jakeys and junkies.

It is literally a breath of fresh air when Raymius gets off at Kelvinbridge in Glasgow's West End. He enjoys his short walk through the cosmopolitan part of the city. He's whistling and almost skipping en route to rescue the abandoned hash. Most people would have been apprehensive returning to the scene of the crime. Most people would have been anxious, wondering whether or not it was still there. Most people would be nervous carrying about that amount of drugs on their person. Raymius isn't most people.

Normally Raymius will take advantage of the fresh weather and do his travelling by foot, but his to-do list is getting stretched and time is zooming past. *Busy, busy, you get days like this, don't you?* Raymius thinks as he jumps on the No 44, with his booty safely tucked away in his day sack. In less than twenty minutes he'll be back in the sunny Southside. Raymius sits downstairs at the back of the bus and practises being anonymous. He gathers his tasks and thoughts for the rest of the day, a mental to-do list. Some things are best not committed to paper. He needs somewhere safe to hide the drugs. He doesn't want to push his luck at the new apartment and he is actually excited about the possibility of clean sheets.

So much has happened over the last twelve months. Raymius can't help chuckling out loud to himself. A wee wifey sitting opposite looks over, Raymius smiles sheepishly and pretends to be embarrassed. He lets his mind wander back. Three hundred and sixty four days ago he'd joined the ranks of the homeless. The rain had poured out the sky like a burst tap. He'd headed for the oldest and most famous of Glasgow bars. Raymius remembers how he sat dripping in the corner of the pub with his black bag under the table. He remembers how he'd enjoyed the live music, sipped his pint and contemplated his story, no fixed abode. He remembers the old guy warming a barstool. A woolly hat, National Health specs, a brown cardigan, the bottom half of a shell suit, no socks, tartan slippers and a big heavy jacket; a peculiar but familiar jacket.

When Raymius was very small the coal lorry used to come on Saturday mornings. Big dirty men with big dirty hands carrying massive sacks of coal and wearing black jackets with shiny leather patches on the shoulders and elbows, *'Donkey Jackets'*. *Yeah, that's what Pops called them, 'Donkey Jackets'!*

The old guy on the stool could have been a coalman. Round reddish cheeks and big dirty hands. He seemed content. He might have actually been happy. *Ignorance is bliss,* Raymius had thought.

Glasgow is a city where you can't be alone for very long. Within ten minutes of his arrival in the pub that day two men are interrogating him.

"Rela-ax, wee ma-an. We're no the fuckin' Krays y'know. Although we are actually twins. Ah-know... Ah-know, yi widnae think so tae look at us. We look as much alike as big Arnie an wee Danny De-fuckin Vito. But nevertheless we urr whit we urr and we urr indeed twins just the same. Ma name's 'H' an this is ma bro. He calls himsel 'The Man'."

Raymius had been trying to get his head round how he was going to handle his first day. He wasn't prepared for company this early on. He also knew that bursting into laughter wouldn't go down very well. H had offered him a drink several times now and it was becoming clear that Raymius would have to accept soon or leave. Those phrases with warning bells attached had already been said.

"Oor company no good enough fur yi, ma ma-an?"

"You got a problem wi the colour of ma money, wee ma-an?"

"Urr we fuckin' botherin' yoo?"

His options were clear: have a drink and join their company, or fuck off. H didn't actually say that but fucking off had started to rapidly disappear as an option. To stay and ignore them would result in only one possible outcome. A thick glass-bottomed ashtray across the face. He had seen it too many times now.

The Man, AKA Michael Anthony Noonan, and his twin H, AKA Howard Eric Noonan, were nothing alike. Michael hates being called Mick or even worse Mickey. In school he tolerated Manza but would go into a blind rage if he was referred to as Mani; he thought it sounded Jewish and was proud of his Irish heredity. Like most nicknames you get in school it gets twisted and inevitably shortened. An unfortunate tried to shorten it to M but when Michael realised that was 'an old burd fae the Bond films' the individual concerned ended up in intensive care. Sticks and stones? Bollocks! Some words can get you killed.

Just the same way as one spends time perfecting one's autograph in the childlike hope of one day being famous, so too Michael toyed endlessly with his name. He himself came up with The Man. He claims to be the most sensible of the twins. What he means by this is that he's been arrested least and has never been convicted. The thirty-one-year-old has attended college since leaving the Royal Marines. He regards himself the big brother and looks out for H.

H is addicted to drugs. Not a heroin addict or a cokehead or even an acidhead; a proper drug addict. He's tried everything. He'll snort anything up his nose, swallow anything down his neck and stick anything up his arse in an attempt to get a buzz. He is simultaneously on several other planets and very rarely visits this one. He has fits of violence and is a compulsive liar. He is, however, also loaded with cash. When it comes to funding his addictions he is motivated and focused. The Man calls him the family accountant.

They have a two-bedroomed flat in deepest darkest Govanhill. It's a real tip. The Man had given Raymius a key and an open invite to doss. The twins' flat was always busy. There were always drifters, neds and slappers hanging around sponging for drugs. It was more like a bus station than a home. Raymius never slept there, he just dozed, too wary of being robbed, shagged or stabbed with a dodgy needle. One night six heavies kicked the door in and gave H a tanking which put him in hospital for four weeks. Everybody else had been thrown down the stairs except Raymius. He'd been made to stay and watch. Normally Raymius is happy to wade in and is very comfortable getting in amongst it, always has been. But it's difficult to object with the barrel of a shotgun between your teeth. He was told to tell The Man: "Putting H in the hospital is just a warning."

The next day Raymius sourced an allotment at the top of Queen's Park. There are a few huts that don't have a lock on the door. He uses the one that doesn't leak. It isn't as warm as the twins' squat but it's quiet, just him and the local residents. Raymius doesn't mind vermin that goes about its own business. He's been managing to sleep there, from time to time. Well, at least until today.

The bus stops at the traffic lights at the entrance to Queen's Park. His reminiscing stops. *So much can happen in one year.* He picks up his little day-sack and makes sure everything is secure. Another poster of Helen's face is pasted behind the driver's cabin, MISSING! He stares at it for a few seconds before moving off. He holds the back of his hand up to the bus driver and points to where he'd wear a watch if he had one. The driver obliges. Raymius glances at the time before stepping off the bus.

"Thanks mate," he says. The driver nods. It's ten minutes past four.

> **vice, n 1**. a tool with two jaws that close
> by a lever or screw that is used to hold an
> object immobile so that it can be worked
> on. **2**. an immoral or wicked habit **3**.
> depravity or immoral conduct, especially
> prostitution **4**. a mild failing or defect in
> somebody's behaviour or character **5**.
> in place of or instead of somebody or
> something (*eg: Vice President*)

John Ribbon creaks open one eye and glances at the carriage clock on the mantelpiece. *Fuck*! he thinks. He's fallen asleep on the sofa, again. He squints at his pale white hairy legs protruding from his bathrobe. Both eyes barely open but still surveying. He's got that horrible feeling and doesn't want to look. But he's going to anyway. His two mini searchlights creep reluctantly from his size twelve feet in a line past shins and nobbled knees. Finally, they reach the source of the uncomfortable warmth. He stares at his manhood. One meat and two veg lie lazily basking in a ray of sunlight from the patio-doors. Ribbon covers himself and utters another expletive, this time under his breath.

"Fuck!" It's easily done. He'd only fallen asleep after he'd come out of the bath. John Ribbon has nothing to be ashamed of even if there are prowling voyeurs. In the old days during basic training the lads used to tease him constantly.

"Hey, Johnno! If you don't make Sergeant you can always go into zee movies vit zee pretty girlz und zee dizco dawnce-zing."

But what if the milk boy or a nosey neighbour had peeked in? There was never any chance of that. It's a fair hike up the garden to the house and no one ever stops by. Anyway, he doesn't have his milk delivered. John enjoys his own company.

His neighbours know who he is and of course what he does. But none of them really know him, except Heather. She lives two houses along the street at number twelve.

John joined a creative writing group just over a year ago and attends religiously. He gets excited about going and gets grumpy if he misses it. This is where he met his neighbour Heather. They have never met outside the group, not even for a coffee. He's never been to visit her and she has never called on him.

John has been writing poetry since he was a boy but it's not something he talks about, until recently. Before, when the poem was finished he'd throw it in the bin. To him it was just like doodling. Didn't mean anything. It was simply a way of passing the time, like a puzzle or a crossword. He'd had an inclination to write something bigger, a crime novel. Well, he has seen enough of it and he's always liked the idea of writing a book. He's always been an avid reader but has yet to find a story where he can't guess the outcome well before the end. So he thought, *Why the fuck not? Can't be that difficult.* And that was the reasoning behind the writing group. The group consists mainly of budding novelists but there are a few unlikely suspects who contribute poetry and the odd Haiku. Not quite sure where he was going with the novel, he would scribble a few verses together a half an hour before. The group loves John's poetry. He can make them laugh and he can make them cry.

"What a gift, what a talent," Heather had said. John Ribbon is not often surprised. Heather surprises him. They're not friends, they are writing enthusiasts, fellow artists, kindred spirits. He hasn't felt this comfortable with anyone since Diane. Every room in John's house has memories of Diane; there are photographs, jewellery, ornaments and fragrances. He can't accept she no longer exists.

John was studying law at Glasgow University and had fallen in love with the most adorable medical student in first year, Diane Fisher. They wanted to get married straight away. They thought it through and planned to make it legal in twelve months. John calculated how much it would cost to pay for the wedding and put a deposit down on a small flat. Both families were against the idea. They believed the couple were being rash and making a mistake, they were too young. The families withdrew all financial support in order to discourage them. Unfazed and even more determined, Diane and John carried on with their plans. He left at the end of his second year with straight A's and joined the Glasgow Police. It was 1974 and he was twenty years of age. He'd decided to support Diane until she graduated and became a GP. Diane made a big deal about him giving up uni for her but he was never really interested in becoming a lawyer. He just thought it sounded cool. He jumped at the chance of leaving University and becoming a cop. Two months before the wedding both families accepted the inevitable. The in-laws actually began to admire the couple's devotion and commitment to each other. One month before the wedding, Diane disappeared. Her body has never been found.

He attempts to get up from the sofa but has been sleeping in that stupid-fucking-awkward position. He has an almighty fuck-you Jedi-master crick in his neck, a-fucking-gain. He feels like someone has broken it, sawn it off and super-glued it back on in the wrong fucking position. He makes a mental note. If it's still the same at 4.55, call the chiropractor. John sighs to himself. *Another fifty pounds an hour to be snapped and re-fucking-set.* John rarely swears out loud. When he does it's deliberate and usually for effect. He doesn't lose his temper at work, it's unprofessional. His inner monologue is quite differ-ent. *That's normal though!* he thinks. *Isn't it?*

John is very confident and can at times even appear arrogant. *If only they knew what is really going on in my head.* John Ribbon can win the Olympic gold for beating himself up. *Aye, go on mate, buy yourself a fucking sickle and do the job right.*

One of those pictures of Jesus Christ whose eyes follow you round the room gives John a Mona Lisa grin. *Smug bastard!* John strokes his jaw as a sinister smile appears on his face. *You could live in the drawer y'know. Mother won't care. I'll just take you out once a year before she visits. She'll be none the wiser.* He stands up and walks over till he's nose to nose with the Nazarene. He lifts Jesus off the wall, looks around and giggles to himself before incarcerating the holy photo in the sideboard drawer. *Thought I was fucking bluffing, didn't you? Only way to bluff is not to bluff.* Feeling pleased with himself, John heads for the study.

He sits on his favourite chair. He leans over and presses 'on'. VH1 Classics. *Hmmn?* He presses the CD function. Mr Reed blares out. *Oh fuck! Way too early. Sorry, Lou.* He presses the CD changer. *Ah that's better… Vivaldi. Four seasons. Concerto No 1. La primavera. Spring!* John picks up the photograph of Diane he keeps on his desk. It's that clichéd pose of them both on the promenade with embarrassed smiles. A passing stranger had captured that special moment for them. A seaside town, endless blissful days of laughter, ice cream, fish-suppers, sex, complete intimacy, falling in lust and growing in love.

He holds his memories of Brighton beach in its wooden frame and glances at his graduation photograph on the wall. What a contrast; no hugs, no kisses, no party there. He looks around his study at all his achievements and compares them with the picture of two young lovers smothering each other in an embrace. The room is beginning to resemble a shrine, but to what? His degree certificate mounted and framed. Law, First class honours, First division. He'd completed it on a part-time basis, at home. For what? For whom? He lays down the photo-graph in its place of rest and reaches for the drinks cabinet.

He selects a wooden box and slides off the carefully engraved cover. His finger traces the serial number. His mind flits back to the Jameson distillery in Dublin. He lifts from the tiny bed of straw a twenty-five-year-old bottle of Midleton Rare. He licks his lips. His mouth salivates. He picks up a heavy crystal tumbler that's also engraved, from the lads. "Thanks for everything John, all the best for the future." He opens a little mini fridge, grabs a handful of ice from a bag that's half full. He makes another mental note. *Wow, I just opened that yesterday, better order another.* His ears enjoy the clink, clink, clink in the glass. A tidal wave of the very best Irish whiskey covers the cubes; they crackle. He smells first, gargles and then swallows. With gums and tongue still tingling, he closes both eyes. After a few moments he opens them. His eyes are more focused and his face feels content. Now he is ready to tackle the day. His left hand gently strokes his forehead. His middle finger and thumb ease their way to the bridge of his nose. They pinch it gently. *Ahhh… That's better. Vivaldi. Concerto No 2. L'estate. Summer!*

He mentally reviews what he must do today. He clicks the left button on the mouse. He checks his diary first and then his email. *How the fuck did we manage before Mr Gates?* Meticulous and diligent would be an understatement. He considers each task and then actions it before moving on to the next. *Measure twice, cut once. Ahh… Vivaldi. Concerto No 3. L'autunno. Autumn!*

He moves onto his snail-mail, his answer machine and finally his texts, all with the exact same attention to detail. He presses the button on the circular kitchen timer that is attached to the filing cabinet with its magnetic strip. It makes a satisfying bleep. It has taken thirty-two minutes to complete his admin. He has a clear desk once again. *Vivaldi. Concerto No 4. L'inverno. Winter! 8 minutes 43 seconds.*

He fills his mouth with another helping of best Irish. He taps his finger on the desk as his daydreams drip back to the past.

Di Di Di,

Di Di Dahh,

Di Di Dahh!

He looks at a plaque on the wall, two Griffin's wings and a sabre. He rubs his left shoulder and remembers. Three short sharp taps in his mind. *Dot-Dot-Dot.* His fingers continue to tap but now a different tune another three taps with his finger but this time longer, slower, more deliberate.

Dash… Dash… Dash… The last three taps the same as the first. Dot-Dot-Dot.

He repeats the whole process again, the muscle memory of his finger in complete harmony. Dot-Dot-Dot. Dash… Dash… Dash…. Dot-Dot-Dot. The international signal for distress. S.O.S.

He repeats the process once more but this time a small change that makes a world of difference. Dot-Dot-Dot. Dash… Dash… Dash…. Dot-Dash… Dash… Dash… Dash…. Not S.O.S this time. S.O.1.

John stops himself. No one is listening but it isn't the message in Morse that concerns him. He had started to do it unconsciously. *Have I done that before? Is my mind slipping? Maybe it is time to retire?*

There's a knock at the front door. Seconds later the doorbell rings. *Fuck*! Nobody ever sees it first. The knocker is obvious, the bell is almost covert. He keeps meaning to move it or change it but there are a thousand other things to do. Anyway, nobody ever calls. He listens: silence. Maybe they've got fed up and gone away. He checks himself and takes a deep breath. Walking to the front door, he glances at the carriage clock. It's ten minutes past four.

omnipresent *adj* **1.** present everywhere at the same time. **2.** widely or constantly encountered

Helen's eyes are still stinging. Her head feels like it's packed with lead. She gets off her knees and unclenches her fists ready for her daily routine. The warm and sticky liquid is no longer dribbling from her mouth since she has stopped choking. The tears always ceased long before the sobs. All is quiet now because she is listening. It's the noise from above that makes her stop. She holds her breath again. It's definitely from the ceiling. She's definitely heard something again. It doesn't matter if it's twenty, thirty or even fifty feet above. She isn't imagining it. After the click she knows what's next. A soft humming like a computer rebooting, then whirring, mechanical unnatural. Then another three sharp movements like before, only louder, echoed in the blackness. Click. Click. Click. Then bolts, yes, definitely bolts. Metal against metal. Thump. Thump. Like deadlocks on a safe door. But this was on the ceiling. Her ears are her eyes, calculating, recalibrating. And finally, that familiar noise, so familiar that she doesn't want to let her mind go there but she can't help it. Helen squeezes her eyes and tries hard to erase the memories in her head. Trying to stop the search-party programme in the dusty caves of her mind, searching the vaults of childhood, teenage and then adult thoughts. She bangs her smooth shaven skull.

"Stop, stop, stop!" And then she gives up. Another small moment of exhilaration as she remembers the similar sound of an electric sunroof in a car, stop. She waits to see what the cardboard box will contain today. Something is coming in but it looks different. Different shape. She is standing directly under it, looking up. How can she be so stupid, standing there transfixed? She leaps for the corner as it comes crashing in. She cowers in the corner trying to make herself small. Trembling like a mouse would before a huge tom, like prey before predator. It was a wooden sound that crashed against the floor followed by a few moments of silence. She hears footsteps far above and a door closing, in the space above the ceiling. It sounds like a big door, a big heavy door. Like the door you'd have for a vault. A light flickers above and then a brightness shines through the square in the ceiling. A roped ladder hangs all the way to the concrete floor on which she sits. She stares at it and then looks up. The light makes her eyes blink and then water. She rubs them. Breathing heavy again. But this time like when you've been under water too long and have to come up for air. Need more air, greedy for oxygen, now. *Get out*, she thinks. *Get up*. Instinctual, natural, rapid response. *Head for the light*. Halfway up the ladder she misses a step and stops. She grips on with everything that is left in her. Controlled breathing, focused now. She closes her eyes. *Slower*, She says in her head, like a mantra. *Be careful, don't fall. Be deliberate, get up, get through the gap, go into the light*. How many days has she been there? What is happening? Where is she going? *Doesn't matter, focus, focus. Get into the light*. She hears a tune in her head. Massenet the French composer, meditation and the theme to an advert: St Ivel Gold.

She pulls herself into a white room. Her first thought is the smell – it's clean – and then the touch of the tiles – cold and smooth but also clean. She can see but only barely; her eyes are sore because it's too bright. She crawls on hands and knees to what appears to be the nearest wall, trying to gain a sense of perspective. She fingers the tiles, big squares, twelve, maybe fourteen inches each way. She looks over at the black gap in the middle of the floor, from where she's just emerged. And then that sound again. She looks over and down. A soft humming as the computer reboots again. Whirring now. The steel sunroof in the middle of the floor begins to shut. Like an elevator door but smaller and slower, an electronic guillotine. Two sharp movements. Thump, thump... Metal against metal. The deadlocks marry back into position. She knows what to expect next. Click. Click. Click. The door of the oubliette is now locked. And she is now in a bright white room.

She surveys her new home. The outline of the vault door is around three feet by nine feet. The ceiling probably eighteen feet if her guess about the door is right. The lights are cupped in wire cages. Apart from the vault door and the entrance to the oubliette everything else is tiled with bright white tiles. In each corner of the ceiling tiny little Perspex spheres. No bigger than small marbles. Electronic eyes, HTFO, hi-tech fibre optics. Helen had read about them in her dad's magazine. He was into all those James Bond gadgets and things. On the cheap white plastic table, two feet by three feet, three items. A little cup like the type you get at the dentist. It has clear liquid inside that has no smell. An envelope with her name on it. A small plastic clock. She opens the envelope and takes out the letter. Before she starts to read she thinks, *nice handwriting.*

Dear Helen,

Welcome to the entertainment industry. You have been chosen for your beauty.

You are in the Deconsecration chamber. You will have other questions and in time they may be answered. You are being held against your will now, but this may change.

I have been studying you for some time and it seems you are not happy. If you work hard and choose well, I can show you happiness. If you do not I will show you suffering. This choice is yours to make.

Everybody has a purpose and everybody works for somebody, Helen. Now you belong to me…

αΩ

She hears another click but this time it's from the table. The noise has come from the clock. It's ten minutes past four.

justice. *n* 1. fairness reward of virtue
punishment of vice

They both sit in the Italian bistro at the Kincardine Bridge Hotel while the last of the other diners pay their bill and leave. Outside lumps of rain bounce off the concrete patio. The gusts of wind lash wave after wave of weather against the glass panels of the conservatory. In the north of Scotland rain can be relentless. Mac doesn't relish the idea of eating lunch in a greenhouse, especially when it's beginning to feel like a submarine. He doesn't say a word while he's gobbling down his burger and fries.

Sheena feels relaxed in her surroundings. She is glad to get away from the hospital-type smell of the Police College and breathes in deeply the hot wafts of garlic and basil from the kitchen. For her the piped classical music is aptly accompanied by the sound of the torrents outside. Like a monotonous drum roll without crescendo, a mantra. Mac seemed jealous of how happy the restaurant manager had been to see Sheena. Especially when she'd giggled as Carlo had kissed her hand.

A young waitress with the traditional black dress and white frilly bits places a double espresso in front of Mac and a cappuccino in front of Sheena. An Irish accent asks if they want to have a look at the dessert menu. They both decline; too many doughnuts earlier. Sheena smiles in appreciation at the young girl but waits until the nubile leaves the conservatory before she leans over and puts a spoonful of brown sugar into her espresso. She then takes a folder from her briefcase and puts it in front of Mac. She drops it on the white linen tablecloth where his cutlery had been but now only a dried-in tomato ketchup stain remains.

"Don't say anything until you've read all of it, Mac."

He goes to speak. Once again, Sheena gives him the one finger over the lips – international shoosh sign. Mac complies. Sheena sips her espresso and continues, "I have plenty to do so please, Mac, don't speak, read." Sheena opens her mail. Mac opens the file.

Confidential Report:

DCI John Bernard Ribbon

Supervising Officer:	*Eamond McLeod*
Rank:	*Detective Chief Superintendent*
Recommended	
for promotion:	*NO*
Born:	*17 January 1954*
Height:	*6ft 3ins*
Weight:	*18st 7lbs*
Complexion:	*swarthy*
Colour of hair:	*black*
Eyes:	*blue*
Heredity:	*Mother, Elizabeth (Brown) born 1923 in Glasgow's West End...*

Mac continues to read the hard facts about his boss and takes a pride in not being surprised at any of it. They'd spent many hours in their unmarked car and got to know each other pretty well, or at least that's what Mac believed. He knows Ribbon's mother keeps fairly good health and lives with his older brother Bernard. His father, also Bernard, was born in Oxford, 1921. The family moved to Glasgow when Ribbon's dad was thirteen years old. Bernie met Liz at school and they became sweethearts. They were married as soon as Bernie passed basic training. He became an RAF pilot. It was his ambition since he could point at the sky and say 'plane'. He fought in the Battle of Britain and survived the war but died driving his sports car in the countryside a few weeks before John's birth. He was only thirty-one years of age. It's believed he hit oil on a notoriously bad bend. However, he liked to drive fast and was fond of a drink. Bernie was the only fatality in the crash.

Ribbon's brother was born in 1943, so there's an eleven-year gap between them. They've never really been close although they do keep birthdays, the anniversary of their dad's death and of course Christmas. Bernie followed his dad into the RAF, did his twenty-two years and then joined the board of an American oil company, where he worked until he was given a very large golden goodbye last year. Bernie is married with three sons and two daughters. They've all had a university education and are all now married, with children. Bernie is a very proud grandfather and has always been teetotal. They live in Oklahoma, USA.

Ribbon had studied Law at Glasgow University but left at the end of his second year. He was top of his class with straight A's. He swapped his remaining years of student life for two years' probation pounding the beat as a cop. He joined the Glasgow Police in 1974, which became Strathclyde Police the following year. He was twenty years of age.

Ribbon spent four years in uniform at the blue end of the city. Impressing all the right people, he became the youngest ever Detective Sergeant in the history of Govan CID. He enjoyed increased pay and better conditions during the 'Thatcher Glory Years'. He evolved in a period when criminal justice became increasingly hard-line but he'd always felt uneasy with the Thatcher 'poodle' tag. In 1982 he was promoted to inspector and joined the Serious Crime Squad. He was exposed for the first time to solving 'high-profile media interest cases'. His success under the spotlight earned rapid promotion again within three years. Detective Chief Inspector; Serious Crime Squad, Force HQ, Pitt Street. He had joined the 'A list' of Strathclyde's finest.

From 1985 to 1987 he was responsible for solving several high-profile murders. His reputation as a man who can get things done *and* being in the right place at the right time put him in prime position for his next promotion up the greasy pole to Detective Superintendent. He was only thirty-two and on track to go all the way. During probation, he'd known a high-ranking officer who had been tipped to be the next Chief Constable but then subsequently arrested and sentenced to eighteen months in prison. Ribbon's Sergeant at the time asked him how far he thought he'd go up the ladder. He responded with the diplomatic. "I'll be happy to make Sergeant, boss." In reality he believed, *if that daft crook was en route to becoming Chief Constable it couldn't be that difficult.*

Ribbon knew that one of the necessary factors in making it to Chief Constable is for your presence to be made known to the powers that determine the career paths of senior officers. He had been the youngest… and the first to… many times in his career but his notoriety took a different tack when he attended his senior command course at Bramshill Police Staff College.

Sheena notices the folder is closed and breaks Mac's daydreams.

"He'll be fifty-two this year, Mac. He's been a DCI for twenty years. He was a rising star and on the way to becoming the youngest Chief Constable ever. He's been passed over for promotion a dozen and a half times now… Why? He's a clever man. He was on track. What do you really know about your boss, Mac?"

Mac shuffles in his seat, loosens his tie and lights a ciga-rette. He barks back at Sheena, defensively: "I know he's made enemies and doesn't do politics..."

The official report of the Bramshill Senior Command Course 'incident' doesn't differ much from many of the stories that have followed Ribbon over the last eighteen years. Albeit, there have been the odd exaggerations. On the last evening of the course a senior officer made reference to privilege, marbles in one's mouth, rods up one's arse and the RAF. Ribbon was furious. Having a short fuse and too many whiskies in him, he did what he basically always does – the sensible thing. He got up to walk away. The other officer in question took exception to this and grabbed Ribbon's wrist in an attempt to yank him back. What followed took seconds, a rush of blood and an instinctive response for someone who teaches Aikido. However, it was still an out-of-the-ordinary reaction for John. He swung his assailant's arm in a wide circle and slammed it on an adjacent table. He was now eyeball to eyeball with the overweight and overbearing loudmouth, Hugh Halford-MacDonald. John watched as big Shuggie's eyes watered and then went out. John had broken his arm in three places. It wasn't just what he'd done. It was also who had been there and whom he'd done it to. The Halford-MacDonalds were steeped in police lore and well connected. Ribbon had started to slide down the greasy pole. It was a tough way to learn his next lesson. He was now out of the meritocracy and up to his waist in the political arena. He had dipped his toe in the big pond and he was a very green, doe-eyed, small fish. For the first time in his life Ribbon realised he was out of his depth.

"Aye, Mac, Ribbon does have enemies, but you don't get passed over for promotion for twenty years for making one mistake. Here's our Special Investigation file on your boss. It's my duty to remind you, DS Macmillan, this is classified and not to be discussed with anyone, especially not Ribbon. You hear me?" Sheena offers Mac an A4 brown Manila envelope with nothing on it. Mac holds it in both hands and although its contents feel light, it weighs heavy on his mind.

"You're putting me in an awkward position, Sheena."

"Hey, you can walk away now. I know you have a dinner engagement that's pressing. Don't let me keep you. You don't have to open it. You don't have to read it. But, how well do you really know your boss, Mac?"

Mac reads the file. He knew about the apartment in Amsterdam and the extensive property portfolio and even that Internal Affairs were sniffing around. John Ribbon had never been Mr Conventional and his holidays and investments may have not been approved officially but they weren't crimes. He knew about the whisky and the gambling but John was a cop not a saint and he could afford it.

Sheena started again. "He could have taken voluntary redundancy aeons ago. He has already put in for another extension. He's got expensive tastes. Why's he hanging on? Is it money? What's keeping him in? Who's he connected to, Mac?"

"Are you asking me to help you find some filth on my boss, Sheena?"

"No, I'm asking you to dig deep, be a detective and do the right thing. If your boss is clean then you both have nothing to worry about."

"And if he's not?"

"Well, that's his problem and not yours, so long as you cooperate."

"Is that a threat?"

"That's advice, Mac. Why are you being so god-damn defensive? Are you telling me everything there is to know here?"

"I don't like what you're trying to do, Sheena."

"I'm doing my job and you would do well to take my advice and do yours. Remember, Mac, Bi glic-bi glic…"

Secret. *n, adj* **1.** not widely known and intentionally withheld from general knowledge. **2**. undercover working or operating without the knowledge of the general public. **3**. acting or feeling a particular way without admitting it. **4** known to very few people and consequently quiet and secluded. **5**. mysterious and often beyond common understanding. **6**. a piece of information known to only a few people and intentionally withheld from public knowledge. **7**. a little-known technique, approach or piece of information that is the key to success in a particular endeavour...

Sheena is sitting on the bed in her hotel room. Mac is looking out of the window thinking about his wife and contemplating the worst possible thing that could happen if he cancelled their table reservation on their anniversary. His wife will be getting ready for their yearly visit to Di Maggios. She could go out with a pal; hell, she'd probably have a better time without him. Maybe this was the push she needed to finally kick him out and save him the agg' of leaving her. Maybe she'd get pissed, go out to a club and meet someone. He looks across at Sheena. She smiles as if she's reading his mind. Sheena is thinking about fucking Mac in the shower.

"So! How long have you got, Mac?

"Good question, I'll phone the boss." Mac reaches into his pocket and pulls out his mobile. He presses last number dialled. He hears the tone purring. Four double rings now and Ribbon still hasn't answered. *Not like him,* Mac thinks. He checks his wristwatch.

Back in the West End John Ribbon answers the phone and opens the door at the same time. He's not expecting anyone but especially not her. He has a mental double take.

"Give me a couple of minutes, Mac, I'm busy. I'll call you back." Click!

John ends the call without waiting for a reply and feels like stepping back in amazement. He thinks for a moment and gathers himself before addressing his caller.

"Heather! Hello ehmm…" John isn't usually stuck for words but he's realising what an idiot he must look and sound standing there in a bright orange bathrobe. Heather blushes and makes a stab at some humour.

"Hi John, I'm so glad you're not bald or I may have thought this was the Buddhist centre." Matters go from bad to worse. Ribbon doesn't hear her right. He gets the wrong end of the stick and checks to make sure his appendages aren't parading themselves again. Unfortunately, he isn't subtle enough with his checking procedure. When you're a small woman standing in front of a big guy and you're two steps down it's advisable to keep eye contact. However, you'll tend to look at what he's looking at. Heather can't believe she's staring at his… well, you know. Her slightly pink cheeks go from gas mark six to flaming red.

"Oh!… I'm sorry John… Eh, look I've caught you at a bad time, I should've rung but I couldn't find… Oh fuck, maybe I should've… Christ, never mind."

John holds his hand up and interrupts. "Heather, please… come in." He shows her through to the kitchen and continues with attempts to remedy the situation. "Make yourself at home, Heather." He introduces the tea-making facilities with a wave of his hand and then holds his mobile phone in the air like a magician who's going to make a card disappear. "Sorry, but I need to take this. I'll try not to be too long." He walks off and takes refuge in his bedroom, feeling awkward for the first time ever in his own home. *What's she doing here?* he thinks as he stands in front of the mirror, inspecting himself. *Could probably exercise a bit more. Why do you always looks so bloody serious John? Lighten up.* He examines the small chip on one of his front teeth. It's hardly noticeable unless he gives you a big cheesy smile and that doesn't happen very often. He thinks back to when he chipped it. He was ten years old and the aggressor was the crossbar of his bike.

Ribbon selects last call redial. He hears the click and the phone being answered but no words are forthcoming. He barks down the phone: "Hello!" He hears a faint flustered response.

"Hello, eh sorry, hello…"

He barks again, still irritated. "Hello!"

"It's me, Boss, Mac."

"Well that's grand, Mac. Now I can sleep easy knowing both of us have got that. Is that all you called to tell me?"

"You called me, Boss…"

"Way to go, Detective Sergeant, you'll be looking for promotion to the Intelligence Corps soon."

"You sound pissed off, Boss."

"Another pearl of information which gives me an enormous feeling of enlightenment. So is that all you have to say, or is there more?"

"OK, OK, Boss, I get the drift. I forgot to tell you that I have to be away sharp after our meeting this evening."

"What's the drama?"

"No drama boss, it's my anniversary and I've…"

Ribbon interrupts. "Ahhh! I see. Where are you now?"

"Still up here in sunny Stirlingshire, Boss. I'll be leaving shortly though."

"How did things go with Buxton?"

"Interesting, Boss, interesting."

"Ah, so she's still there then?"

"Aye, Boss."

"What time's your dinner with the Mrs?"

"Eight."

"OK, Mac, I'll tell you what, when we get together I need you to actually be there. Forget our six o'clock meeting and I'll see you in the morning at..." Ribbon pauses for a minute to stroke his chin, before he continues.

"...7.30am, in the office. Don't be late."

"Are you sure, Boss?"

Ribbon raises his voice again. "Have a good evening, Mac." He doesn't wait for his sergeant to respond and presses the little red picture of a phone. Click. He studies the screen. There are only two bars indicating battery strength. He goes to join his guest.

Heather has made herself a cup of tea and has wandered through to the study. She's already had a nosey around John's memorabilia and is now at the reading rack. Under a complete row of books on Scottish history there are a number of classics; Oscar Wilde, The Importance of being Earnest; Pride and Prejudice... The Times crossword, completed... Online Dating Monthly... an Aikido instructor's manual and, on what appears to be an altar, a Samurai sword. She starts to work her way through the photographs on the wall.

Ribbon goes to the kitchen and discovers she's not there. He hears his own words in his head. *Make yourself at home, Heather.* He heads for the study. He stands behind her and watches for a moment as she tries to pick him out of a sea of faces and uniforms. Her finger traces the words Scottish Police College. He speaks matter-of-factly. "Front row centre..."

"You look good in a uniform, John."

"Thanks."

"I guess there are lots of things I don't know about you?"

"Aye, lots."

"We all have secrets, John. Maybe I should tell you mine?"

"Aye, Heather, maybe you should."

Heather hasn't come round to talk about herself. She did originally have another agenda but now he looks so appealing in his semi-attire. Why is she having these feelings, why is she seeing these pictures in her head and why does he smell so damn good? What she would give to have someone who could understand her needs, who could love her for who she wants to be. Dressing up is just fun and games. The double life she's invented is exciting but she now wants more, she wants to feel alive, she wants to be herself, she wants John Ribbon.

She notices him turn his head slightly to the side as if he suspects what she's been thinking, as if he's reading her thoughts. Her heart starts to pump faster, she tingles all over and her face flushes once again. Heather stares hard at John. She searches deeply but still nothing is said, nothing is hinted but she knows they are going to be fine, she just knows. The silence is not uncomfortable, it's exhilarating. The expectation is crushing. She holds her breath for a moment, feeling like a party balloon that's about to burst. Heather knows John Ribbon is a gentleman and she'll wait a hundred years for him to do what she wants, so she will have to take control. She will have to make the first move. The muscles on the insides of her legs twitch at the thought.

Don't let him speak, she thinks, as she moves towards him, strong eye contact now burning her wishes through his retina and onto his mind. His mobile phone is still in his hand and the cord for the battery charger is still attached. It hangs down below his knees. His robe is securely fastened but she is sure she can detect the outline of a bulge. Maybe it's only wishful thinking. She's close now and his breathing is calm. This is not a man who gets easily flustered. Faint subtle smells, after-shave from his neck and mint from his breath. She takes his phone and places it on the desk. He reaches for her shoulders with his large hands. Heather takes both of his wrists in front of her as if to say no. He hesitates as she guides his arms and places them back at his side. For a moment he looks confused, disappointed, almost embarrassed. Her smile reassures him. He motions to speak but she raises her hand this time. In front of his face she presses her fingers gently on his lips and speaks with the firmness of someone who is in control.

"You have something I need." Her words hold menace and excitement. John closes his eyes as her hand slips into his bathrobe. There's a knock at the front door.

"Shite!" he says as the doorbell rings for the second time that day. "Fuck! Shite," he says again.

"Fuck-shite?" she says inquisitively. They both let go a nervous laugh.

"I'd better go and see who it is. My house is like Sauchie-bloody-hall Street today.

"I'll go," she says, raising her eyebrows. "You're not really in a position to." She looks down below his waist with her eyebrows still raised and a satisfied grin beginning to appear. Ribbon's eyes follow hers. His face feels warm as he gets the point. His mobile phone starts to vibrate on the desk.

"Fuck!" he says. She laughs and heads to the front door.

Ribbon reads the text message. His face changes from surprise to thoughtfulness.

Heather comes back into the room with her grin fully developed.

"Who is it?" he asks.

"It's the Boy Scouts."

"What do they want?"

146

"In my day they called it Bob-a-Job," Heather replies, still laughing.

"Tell them…"

She holds her right hand up like she's stopping traffic and continues, "I've sent them away, John. Is your call very important?"

"It's a text."

She notices he's now changed back to Mr Serious. She sighs with the realisation the moment has gone. "So, I guess I should go?"

It's John's turn to sigh. He sucks in his lips and thinks for a moment.

"I'll have to attend to this text, Heather, I have to get ready now and go. How about we do dinner tonight though, my treat?" He isn't pleading but she can tell he is anxious for a yes. She puts him out of his misery by beaming a smile.

"I'd love that." Her head cocks to one side as she notices the little chip on his front tooth.

"I'll pick you up at eight and take you to my favourite eatery," he says, bursting with boyish enthusiasm. She scribbles down her mobile number on a Post-it and sticks it onto the screen of his PC.

"Just in case you get held up, John. I'll let myself out," she says as she pecks him on the cheek and pats his bum. As he hears the front door close he daydreams for a moment before looking at the clock on his desk. It must have stopped. It still says ten minutes past four.

sentinel *n, v* **1.** sentry or guard **2.** to stand guard over something or a group of people **3.** to provide a guard for something or for a group of people.

Raymius is heading for his new apartment but first he'll stop by a regular haunt which is only a few minutes away, Govanhill Public Baths. Every day he goes for a swim, shower and shave. Pops always used to say, "Clean hands, clean face and neatly combed hair are better than all the fine clothes you can wear." *It's amazing the shit you keep stored away in your head,* Raymius thinks.

He pushes the old school-like wooden swing doors at the entrance to the reception. It was like the Mary Celeste. On the notice board among the mass of how to leaflets, how to read Spanish, how to learn Aikido and what's on in the Southside, there was another 'MISSING' poster. In his stomach it feels like a guitar string has just snapped. Her face is stalking his mind now. He thinks hard, forgetting, focusing on the task at hand. A big toothless grin pokes its head round the corner. Raymius smiles.

"Hi Joe."

"Hi Ray."

"Quiet today, Joe, anybody in I might know?"

"Just the regulars son, the old and bold, naebody interesting."

"You mean the auld dears and the auld queers?"

Old Joe puts his finger up to his lips and checks round about to make sure no one's watching before he rocks into a kink of laughter, blowing air out of his mouth like a whistling kettle and shuddering like an old washing machine. Pulling himself together and wiping the tears from his eyes, he asks Raymius: "You in for a swim then?"

Raymius squeezes his eyebrows together and can't take the smirk off his face. "So where's your teeth, Joe?"

Old Joe rolls his eyes and goes slightly pink. "Oh Jesus, this must be what they call a senior moment. Hope it's not early Alzheimer's, son. I didn't even notice." He tries hard to hold back the chuckles but can't. Off he goes again in a fit of laughter. Raymius waits for him to calm down and produces another grin.

"Bit of a rush today, Joe, I've got to meet a social worker at 5pm."

"Oh aye," Joe replies with eyes wide open now.

"Looks like they've found me somewhere to stay."

"Awe, that's great news Ray, well done son. You'll be taking your stuff then?" Joe Bell, the pool's caretaker, had seen Raymius leave some of his possessions in a locker months ago. Raymius had given Joe the same story as the twins and explained how he didn't have anywhere to leave the few important things he had left for safekeeping.

"Not just yet Joe, we'll see how it goes. Flats get robbed too y'know. I'd feel safer with the lockers for now if that's OK?"

"As I said before Ray, long as I'm here, son, you'll always hae somewheres to keep yer stuff safe."

"Thanks Joe, I appreciate that."

"Big nae probs son, big nae probs. Anyway, fancy a cuppa?"

"Yeah, cheers Joe, that'd be great."

"I'll stick on a brew then, an' leave you to sort oot yer stuff. Milk an' two, Ray?"

"Aye Joe, thanks, milk and two."

Joe was really chirpy for an old guy with only one foot. During the war he'd come off worst after kicking a mine. He'd constantly say, "I only lost my foot! Bloody lucky, that's me." Joe had also lost his son, to heroin. He'd have been the same age as Raymius.

When Joe closes the door Raymius looks around to make sure there is no one else about. He reaches into his locker and pulls out a dark blue suit. He unzips the inside jacket pocket and takes out a mobile phone. He switches it on and presses the profiles function immediately to make sure its status is still on silent. There's an envelope on the screen. Select. Messages. Text. Inbox. He has three all from the same number. He looks around again before his fingers effortlessly work the keypad to create his response. He waits for a few seconds. Message sent flashes on the screen. He turns the mobile off and puts it back inside the jacket. He zips the pocket shut, looks at the clock on the wall and smiles. Just enough time for a brew and a quick blether with old Joe before he has to meet the social worker.

When Raymius arrives at 104 Albert Road he spots Susan Langan parked at the front gate in her Peugeot 206, furiously reading her mail. It's probably been a busy day for her too. The whole affair of getting the keys, getting a copy of the rules and being briefed on the regulations takes about an hour, just as Raymius expected. Raymius has to hold back his impulse to burst out laughing when he is first introduced to his new landlord, Mr O'Hare. It has been a long time since Raymius needed to pay attention to such an anally retentive individual. Although O'Hare is average build, his head looks too small for his body and his face is pointy. Raymius reckons he has a coupon perfect for throwing a dartboard at.

The three of them, led by O'Hare, complete the layout brief, shortly followed by the fire brief, the security brief and finally how everything works, which of course is the appliances brief.

Raymius guesses immediately that O'Hare is ex-military. He just can't imagine peaked cap and the pay stick though, albeit O'Hare would love you to think that. No, Raymius guesses that Simon O'Hare was either a paymaster or a quartermaster; a number cruncher or a blanket counter. His safety boots are still highly polished, like black PVC, so that definitely ruled out the Intelligence corps. At the end of the briefings Mr O'Hare checks his army issue watch with a contented grin. Raymius guesses that Adolf has just broken another personal best. He assures Ms Langan that her new recruit will be well looked after and almost bangs his heels together as he about-turns and leaves. The door clicks shut, leaving Susan Langan and Raymius alone in his new studio apartment.

"So! What do you think, Ray?" Susan asks.

"Well Ma'am, I think he should definitely see your pal the therapist." Raymius comes to attention and salutes. It seems it's his day for making people laugh. Langan can't help herself.

"No Ray, c'mon, you know what I mean," she says through girlish giggles.

"Brilliant, Susan, I can hardly believe it. Thanks, I owe you one." Raymius almost blushes.

"OK, Ray that's only one down, two more to go. I've already spoken to Martin, he's expecting your call tomorrow evening before 6pm. I'll look forward to hearing how your week goes at our meeting next Monday. Any questions before I go?"

"Nope."

She heads for the door. "Good luck, Ray, you have a good week." She pauses in the doorway, takes her hand off the handle and searches her bag. She peeks back into his room. "Since I don't expect to hear from you until next week, this is for you." She tosses an envelope onto the bed. With a big cheesy smile and a twinkle in her eyes she closes the door and skips along the landing. She loves her job.

Ray picks up the envelope and reads the front.

Ray Taylor

He takes the card out.

Good Luck

Ray

Happy Birthday

Raymius lies back on his bed and closes his eyes. He breathes in the whiteness of the hospital-like cotton sheets. He looks round the room and listens to the birds chirping outside the window. There's an opportunity clock beside the bed. An old memory makes him chuckle to himself. *I can remember a time when I used to think that was an alarm clock.* There's a knock at the door.

"Who is it?"

"Pizza for Taylor."

Raymius smiles to himself as he recognises the voice.

"I didn't order any pizza."

"I've got a pizza here for Raymond Taylor."

Raymius can't wipe the smile off his face at the ridiculousness of protocol.

"Two minutes, mate."

Allegory II *n* **1** symbolic work, **2** a work in which the characters and events are to be understood as representing other things and symbolically expressing a deeper, often spiritual, moral or political meaning **3** the symbolic expression of a deeper meaning through a story or scene acted out by mythical characters…

Year of the RAT. Last – 1996. Next – 2008

As his eyes track the second hand on the opportunity clock, his mind remembers basic training, another commandment and a whole load of random shit. Time to kill. Two minutes can be a very long time.

Rats, rodents with long tails, pointed noses, and wee whiskers. They are associated with filth and disease. If someone calls you a rat it's an insult. Like when Jimmy Cagney famously said the line, "You dirty rat." Except you remembered it wrong. Another famous misquote. You can't believe anything you hear any more.

Some people keep rats as pets. Scientists study rats because their psychological behaviour is similar to that of humans. We know that cocaine is pretty powerful stuff because of the way it seduces the pleasure centres of the brain. Rats will choose cocaine over food, over water, over sex, even over life itself. Although rats' and humans' psychological behaviour is similar, their brain function is obviously very different. Pablo Escobar created a drug empire on the basis that the brain function of rats and humans are very different, except when it comes to certain things like cocaine.

Rats are intelligent and adaptable but their negative traits have led to negative PR. Liar, double-crosser. You can also use

153

rat as a verb, meaning to betray or to snitch. A person who is deemed to be a RAT is despicable, contemptible. Someone who would reveal confidential information in return for money. Someone who would be an informer or a decoy for the police.

If you are in urbania, you are never more than six feet away from a rat. In reality, it is much more likely to be 164ft. Fifty metres if you've gone metric. 164ft just doesn't have the same sort of shock factor as 6ft. It also doesn't specify what type of rat. White rat, brown rat, non-educated delinquent rat, junkie, crook, drug- dealer or undercover fucking cop.

And, two minutes can seem like forever.

Although Raymius knows the voice of the pizza delivery guy, he doesn't yet know if the individual is alone or in some sort of fucked-up coercive situation. No point in looking through the peephole in a fucked-up situation that might be a hit either, because you're only making it easy for them. So, although protocol can be silly, it can also save your life. Raymius is more than happy to play along with protocol and respect the two minutes' silence. Not a second more, not a second less.

Two minutes can be painful in some situations, especially if you are holding a gun to someone's head and have no idea that there is a protocol under way. The second hand completes its second revolution. Raymius breaks the silence.

"What kind of pizza?"

"Domino's." Now Raymius knows the delivery guy is alone.

"What kind of Domino's pizza?"

"Pepperoni, chicken and green pepper."

"That's my favourite." Now the delivery guy knows that Raymius is alone too, and everything is cool. "Yeah, come on in, the door's open."

Raymius stands up as Detective Chief Inspector Ribbon walks towards him.

"How are you, fella?" Ribbon asks, as he reaches out for Raymius's hand.

"Nice outfit John, it's good to see you too," Raymius replies.

They both laugh as John Ribbon surveys his red, white and blue attire.

Raymius doesn't need to look out the window to know that outside there will be a Domino's Pizza van along with at least one unmarked car and, somewhere close, Support Group.

"How long have we got, John?"

"Not long. Are we going to eat this pizza or what, fella?"

"It is my favourite!"

John Ribbon takes out a brown file a book and a pizza box from the DP satchel. He opens the pizza box and offers Raymius the 16-incher.

"We've got a problem with our plumbing, Ray."

"Got any napkins, Sir?"

John hands him a bundle that he takes from his DP jacket pocket.

"How big a problem?"

"Not sure yet. I'll have a much better handle on everything within the next 24 hours, fella, but as you and I know by then you'll be in so deep, well, you know the script. I just thought I'd rather speak to you myself and give you what I can before you go in any further."

"Fair enough. So, what's the headlines? Hmm, good pizza!"

"It's Domino's!"

Raymius holds up his arms in the air in apology, wipes some pizza from his face and puts a hand to his lips. He burps.

"Sorry, John, probably just eating this too fast. I don't have anything in the fridge yet. Want some water?"

Ribbon now can't hide his pleasure and Raymius can see that wee chip on his tooth.

Ribbon opens his jacket to reveal two inside pockets. He produces two bottles of Stella and a can of Sprite. Raymius's head falls to one side and his face beams as he strokes his finger down the side of one of the bottles. The Stella is not quite frozen but almost.

"Top fucking drawer, Sir."

Ribbon covers his top lip with his bottom lip and raises his finger. He pauses for effect and then produces two miniatures of Uisge Beatha. Raymius can only say one word.

"Classic."

Ribbon enquires, "I don't suppose you've had a chance to fill up the ice tray?"

It's Raymius's turn to hold up a finger and he goes to check. Ribbon hears the fridge door being opened and Raymius shouts through.

"Bingo!"

He appears a few seconds later with two tea cups and ice. Ribbon laughs out loud and now he can only say one word.

"Brilliant!"

"Anyway, Boss, back to business. Do we know the source of the plumbing problem?"

"We know one of the sources."

"How many sources?"

"Not sure yet."

"Fuck! That's not good news."

"Look, Raymius. I hate to have to tell you this now but what you need to know is that other than yourself and Emma there were, or in fact are, another four SO1 operatives in deep cover in Glasgow."

Raymius looks like he's just swallowed a dodgy piece of pepperoni.

"Six of us altogether?"

"Yes?"

"For how long?"

"Can't tell you that."

"Who are my co-workers?"

"Can't tell you that either."

"Is it possible any of the others are responsible for the leak?"

"Well, I know that Emma wasn't."

"That's not really very helpful, John, what about me?"

"Well, I know it's not down to you, son."

"That's really not helpful either, Boss. What about the powers that be?"

"The powers that be, Raymius, don't know about two of you at all."

"Emma and I?"

"No, not you and Emma, Raymius. You and another. It's complicated."

"I don't understand, John."

"At this moment in time and under these circumstances you don't need to. I know when you get a chance to think about it you'll work it out eventually."

Raymius sighs. "Thanks for the vote of confidence, Sir."

"You're welcome. Going forward it's necessary for you and the four other operatives to use the following protocol."

Raymius nods. "Go for it."

"That sounds like something a cop would say."

"I am a cop, John."

Ribbon lowers his head and looks as if he is looking over the top of his glasses. Except he's not wearing any.

"Really!"

"Sorry, couldn't resist. Seriously, word for word, John?"

"No, Ray, anything that effectively accuses the individual of being a cop will work, but the operative word is 'sounds'. So with that in mind the first trigger is accusatory and auditory."

"Got it. What's the second trigger?"

"Defensive and visual."

"OK, so anything like; Do I 'look' like a fucking cop?"

"That's it. You've got it, fella."

"And the third trigger?"

"Kinesthetic."

"OK, so basically any kind of statement that describes how I or they are feeling like; I'm getting annoyed. I'm getting angry. That sort of shit?"

"Almost Ray but you must use the operative word 'feel'."

"Got it, sounds, looks, feels. What's the safe word?"

"Nexus."

"As in nexus 6."

"Aye."

"Cute. Fair enough, Boss." Raymius starts smiling.

"What's funny, fella?"

"You make this one up yourself, John?"

"Just the safe word."

"Who all knows about this protocol apart from you, me and the other four?"

"No one."

"Cool beans. Great pizza. What's the book?"

"Well, it is your favourite, Mr Taylor." Ribbon's chipped tooth is visible for the third time today. "How long do you have before you head out?"

"Not long."

John hands Raymius the brown file and the book.

"You'll figure it out."

Raymius starts flicking through the brown file.

"OK, Sir, give me the headlines."

"You remember all the psychological profiling in the initial brief for the professor. All of that stuff about the Messiah Complex and the Jerusalem Syndrome."

"Yes, of course."

"Well, it turns out that the family name Oldman has been connected with Glasgow Breweries for several hundred years, at least. I am 99% positive that the Professor is already in Glasgow. I also know that he wants us to think he's in London. I am assuming that something is wrong and he's going to oversee the cleaning before he disappears again. We know there are many entry points to our catacombs in the Merchant City. We need to start figuring out WTF is going on down there.

"We know that Lloyd Oakley was recruited or at least interviewed by the professor in Paris. We also know that Interpol want to talk to Lloyd about a number of bodies that were discovered in their Ossuary."

Okay John, roger all of that."

"You do the maths on this, Ray, and Grahamston becomes an important part of the puzzle. For obvious reasons, we can't cordon off the city centre and send in a regiment of law enforcement to check out what is going on under our feet."

Ray throws the brown file onto a chair and retorts.

"Until we know what the fuck is going on under our feet."

"Exactly."

Raymius necks his whisky and Sprite.

"Fucking hell, John, this is all getting a wee bit too much like the Da Vinci Code for me. You're not going to tell me that one of my SO1 co-workers is Tom Hanks, are you?"

John laughs.

"That's too cute, Raymius, very good. Actually, for me it's all a bit too much like Lethal Weapon One."

"What do you mean John, thin?"

"Yes Raymius, absolutely fucking anorexic."

The both laugh. It's now Raymius's turn to offer Ribbon the open pizza box.

"Last bit of pizza, Boss?"

"All yours, fella."

Ribbon holds out his hand. Raymius puts the box down and shakes Ribbon's hand.

"Later, Sir."

Ribbon's eyes narrow and his voice has an air of determination.

"Later."

Ribbon sees himself out. Raymius sits and demolishes the last bit of pizza listening to the different car engines outside starting up and moving off. He necks the last of the Stella and chases it with the last of the Laphroaig and Sprite as the last support vehicle drives off. He picks up the book and flicks through all the sections with Post-its first, then has a look at the contents page at the front before studying the title.

Glasgow Myths, Legends and the lost village of Grahamston.

providence. n. **1** God's guidance, the wisdom, care and guidance believed to be provided by God **2** God perceived as a caring force guiding humankind **3** Good judgement and management **4** foresight in management of affairs or resources **5** Capital of Rhode Island. **6** where imbecilic best friends Lloyd And Harry are from...

Raymius examines the book Ribbon has given him, *Glasgow Myths, Legends and the lost village of Grahamston*. He thumbs through to the section where Ribbon has stuck the first yellow Post-it and starts reading.

Grahamston vanished beneath the foundations of Glasgow Central Station more than 100 years ago but its memory lives on in buildings, in street patterns and not least in the urban legend of an abandoned village beneath the platforms of Scotland's busiest railway station.

Most books on Glasgow only mention Grahamston in passing, at most a paragraph or just a few lines if at all. This seems odd, given that Grahamston was not some obscure, far-flung part of the city. It occupied a very important location and was to play a significant role in the development of the city. From its earliest years, it stood en route between the city and the main towns of central Scotland.

Grahamston was first noted on maps of Glasgow around 1680, and grew over the next two hundred years from a row of thatched cottages to an important commercial and industrial centre at the heart of Glasgow, before it was demolished in the late 1800s and early 1900s to make way for the Caledonian Railway Central Station.

Going west from Glasgow along Anderston Walk (now Argyle Street) one would have passed the village of Grahamston, which possessed only one main street, running north and south, known as Alston Street. This is where the first permanent theatre in Glasgow was built in 1764. Ransacked on its first night by a mob claiming it was the work of the Devil and eventually razed by a fire sixteen years later.

Grahamston is now covered by the Central Station, but it is thought by many people that Alston Street still exists intact beneath the foundations of the station. It is also reputed that quantities of silver were left abandoned in the shops of this street and never claimed!

The crossroads – Union Street and Jamaica Street with Argyle Street – became one of the busiest in Europe, perhaps in the world. It was best known to Glaswegians as the location of Boots Corner. All over Glasgow, and indeed the world, you can find people who declare with pride that their ancestors hailed from the Calton, Bridgeton, Anderston, Springburn, or the Gorbals. But you have probably never met anyone whose family came from Grahamston. Odd, when you consider that the village only disappeared just over 100 years ago.

Millions of people pass through or by the Central Station each year, and never give a moment's thought to the fact that they are virtually on Grahamston. They are essentially walking above Alston Street and the site of Glasgow's first theatre.

Of all the illustrations and sketches of this part of Glasgow, there are very few that actually show the village. It is usually just out of sight, just over the hill, just behind the trees. There is very little pictorial evidence of Grahamston, apart from the odd photograph of the demolition work and the building of the station. Grahamston is always, at best, just edging in to the left or right of the lens; like the ghost in the camera.

The only remnant that marks Grahamston's existence above ground is a small aluminium plaque mounted at the top of the escalator at the Hope Street entrance to the station. This village that stood in what is now the heart of Glasgow for 250 years, through the whole of the industrial revolution and the Scottish Enlightenment, this village that served the city so well during the most important period of its growth, has been allowed to slip from the consciousness of citizens and visitors alike.

The only two Grahamston buildings that have survived are Duncan's Hotel (currently the Rennie Mackintosh Hotel) in Union Street and the Grant Arms in Argyle Street.

Many cities owe their existence to a river that runs through it. But Glasgow, like St Andrews, also owes its existence to a Saint and a Cathedral. Glas-cu means 'dear green place' and on its coat of arms St Mungo stands over a fish, a bird, a tree and a bell. The inscription or riddle has remained unsolved for over a millennium.

"The tree that never grew, the bird that never flew, the fish that never swam and the bell that never rang, let Glas-cu flourish."

Raymius lights another cigarette and flicks to the next Post-it.

The Scotia Bar is Glasgow's oldest public house and is situated on 110-114 Stockwell Street, the western point of what is known as the Stockwell Triangle. Between this handsome building and the River Clyde was once a stretch of grass that provided grazing for sheep and entry to the shore at low tide for watering the horses. This stretch of grass on the Broomielaw was called Horse Brae and is part of what is still referred to as the Merchant City.

The Merchant City emerged above Glasgow's Catacombs. These underground cemeteries do not measure up to those in Rome. However, they still extend to over one square kilometre and are at least equal to the Catacombs of Paris. There you can find the remains of up to seven million Parisians who still lie neatly stacked. There are more than two dozen big bones in the human body, not counting the little ones like toes and fingers. For perspective, layer upon layer of neatly stacked skeletons.

The Ossuary in Paris is now a major tourist attraction. They call this labyrinth of caverns the Empire of the Dead. It has several entry points and the most well-known is across from the Metro Station at Denfert–Rochereau. After descending two thirds of a mile below street level, you reach the entrance altar. Its inscription, translated from the Latin, says:

"Man, like a flower of the field, flourishes while the breath is in him and does not remain, nor know longer his own place, in peaceful sleep rest."

Contrary to the myths that have been created by Hollywood, catacombs are simply ancient underground cemeteries. In the beginning, they were only intended for burial and only much later did they become shrines to martyrs and centres of pilgrimage.

Christians have historically rejected the Pagan custom of cremation and believe you should respect the bodies that will one day rise from the dead. They have a strong sense of community and wish to be together even in the *"Sleep of Death"*.

Economics also always has its part to play. It was cheaper to dig underground corridors than to buy land. Early Christians who lived in Pagan societies were subject to varying degrees of hostility. Their religion was considered a strange and illegal superstition. They were mistrusted, accused of crimes, persecuted, imprisoned, sentenced to exile and even condemned to death.

Unable to practise their faith openly, early Christians began to use catacombs for secret meetings and communicate with cryptic symbols. Similar to the style of the Old Testament, these cryptic messages are written for only those who know the code. Many were trained in the use of this allegorical cryptography and examples can be found in numerous gospel texts. Normally these cryptic messages are heralded by the words;

"For those with the ears to hear or the eyes to see."

The Tree and the Bird are symbols of peace. More specifically a dove holding an olive branch symbolises a soul that has reached divine peace. The Fish or 'ictus' is a widespread symbol of Christ. Placed vertically, the letters of this word form an acrostic. The first letters of every line or paragraph spell a word.

I
Ch
Th
Y
S
Iesous Christos Theou Yios Soter
Jesus
Christ
God's
Son
Saviour

The Anchor and the Bell are symbols of salvation. More specifically the dropping of an anchor or the ringing of a bell symbolises a soul has peacefully reached the port of eternity. In 1992 Glasgow became the European City of Culture and well and truly landed on the tourist map. There are many fascinating tourist attractions in Glasgow, but the Catacombs still do not feature. There are many reasons for this. Every city, like every person, has a skeleton of some description in the closet. Glasgow is no exception.

One of the entry points to the city's underground cemetery is situated in the Merchant City at 110 to 114 Stockwell Street. After descending two-thirds of a mile below street level, you reach the entrance altar. On it is a coat of arms, St Mungo standing over a fish, a bird, a tree and a bell. The inscription, of course, is in Latin. Translated it reads:

"The tree that never grew, the bird that never flew, the fish that never swam and the bell that never rang, let Glas-cu flourish..."

Although to flourish means to be healthy or to grow well, it is also an ornamental trumpet call, a fanfare that heralds the arrival of an important person, or their return. There are many versions of Glasgow's riddle. Here is the one that's inscribed on the wall in the cellar of the Scotia Bar:

His soul will remain here.
Our saviour will take his rightful place
And reach divine peace
Destined for eternity.
He waits and we wait.
Let this dear green place
Herald his return.

Under the inscription is a picture. Some argue that it is a flaming dragon, others say that it is a phoenix. According to the ancient seers, the phoenix, after a thousand years, arises from its ashes.

Raymius checks to see how many cigarettes he has left. He lights another and flicks to the next Post-it.

The Bloodlines of the Dragon and the Dragon Court.
The Imperial and Royal Dragon Court recognised as the Sovereign Court of the Sovereign Dragon Nation is a closed fraternity of individuals, representing those who would trace

their ancestry and affiliations back to the ancient Grail and Dragon families.

The Imperial and Royal Dragon Court was reconstituted by King Sigismund in 1408. It was based upon an ancient bloodline which Sigismund assumed he had inherited from his Egyptian and Scythian ancestors through the Pictish Dragon Princess Maelasanu of Northumbria and the Imperial Duke of Angiers of the Angevin Royal House, Vere d'Anjou. This line had descended through the Dragon Kings of Anu on one side and the Egyptian Dragon Dynasty of Sobek on the other. The latter included the bloodline of the Davidic House of Judah who married into the descent of the Merovingian Kings of the Franks.

Raymius closes his eyes finishes his cigarette looks at the clock and then flicks to the next Post-it.

The Priory of Sion and the Knights Templar

The secret society known as Priory of Sion has a long and illustrious history dating back to the First Crusade starting with the creation of the Knights Templar as its military and financial front. The Priory is devoted to returning the Merovingian dynasty, which ruled the Frankish kingdom from 447 to 751 to the thrones of Europe and Jerusalem.

The main elements of the theory are that Jesus had a child with Mary Magdalene.

The descendants of this child became the Merovingian Kings of France. A secret order protects these royal claimants because they believe that they are the literal descendants of Jesus and his wife, Mary Magdalene, or, at the very least, of King David.

The following claims have been made about the Roman Catholic Church. The Church has suppressed the truth about Mary Magdalene and the Jesus bloodline for more than 2000 years. The Church attempted to kill off all remnants of the

Merovingian dynasty and their guardians, the Templars, during the Inquisition. The Church did all of this in order to maintain power through the Apostolic succession of Peter instead of the hereditary succession of Jesus and Mary Magdalene.

Raymius scratches his head and lights another Embassy Regal. He looks again at the time on the clock and moves to the next Post-it.

The 6th Century

The period from 501 to 600 in the West marks the end of Classical Antiquity and the beginning of the Middle Ages. Following the collapse of the Western Roman Empire late in the previous 5th century Europe fractured into several small Germanic Kingdoms which competed fiercely for land and wealth.

From this upheaval, the Franks rose to prominence, and carved out a sizeable domain encompassing much of modern France and Germany. Meanwhile, the surviving Eastern Roman Empire began to expand under the emperor Justinian, who recaptured North Africa from the Vandals and then attempted to fully recover Italy with the aim of re-establishing control over all the lands once ruled by the Western Roman Empire.

St Mungo, also known as St Kentigern, established a Monastery on the banks of the Molendinar Burn, a tributary of the river Clyde, in the 6th Century. St Mungo is celebrated in Scotland on 13th January, the date of his death. He died in 614.

Yvain ou le Chevalier au Lion or Yvain the Knight of the Lion is an Arthurian romance by French poet Chrétien de Troyes. It is a story of knight-errantry, in which the protagonist Yvain is first rejected by his lady for breaking a promise, and subsequently performs a number of heroic deeds in order to regain her favour.

Yvain's story bears a number of similarities to the hagiographical Life of Saint Mungo.

One version depicted in a carving has a Knight slaying a Dragon which is threatening a Lion. The lion is subsequently shown wearing a rich collar and following the knight. Finally, the lion appears to be lying on the grave of the knight.

In Wales, Myrddin or Merlin appears in the 6th Century as a forlorn old man blessed with the gift of prophecy. According to medieval sources, Merlin's mystical powers come to the attention of St Kentigern AKA St Mungo. The two men are supposed to have met several times with Merlin detailing various prophecies for the Saint.

Merlin is alleged to have been buried by the Powsail Burn near the town

of Drumelzier on the banks of the Tweed. A strange prophecy existed that if the Powsail and the Tweed ever met at Merlin's grave, England and Scotland would have the same monarch. The Tweed burst its banks and flooded the Powsail on the 24th March 1603, the exact day that James VI of Scotland was crowned James I of England. Stranger still, at his birth James was hailed as "little Arthur" since he had a direct claim to the thrones of both Scotland and England.

Raymius looks again at the clock and takes a deep breath as he flicks to the second last Post-it.

In July 1614, Pierre de Bourdeille, the third son of the Baron de Bourdeille, died. His mother and maternal grandmother were both attached to the court of Marguerite of Navarre. He had many important benefices, the most notable the Abbey of Brantome in Southern France. With no interest in an ecclesiastical career after concluding his education in Paris he became an officer and met with many of the great leaders of the continental wars. He travelled extensively to Italy,

England, Morocco, Spain, Portugal, Malta and Scotland. In Scotland he accompanied Mary, Queen of Scots, who at that time was the widow of Francis II of France.

A fall from his horse compelled him to retire into private life, where he spent his last years writing his memoirs of the illustrious men and women whom he had known. He spoke of an illegitimate child whom he knew of but never got the chance to see. The child was born in Edinburgh on the 13th January 1614. This child was to become the maternal grandparent of John Law, who was born on the 21st April 1671.

Raymius flicks to the last Post-it.

An infamous Glaswegian born at the beginning of the twentieth century, the eccentric Robert Dreghorn was better known as Bob the Dragon. He was said to have been the ugliest man in Glasgow. His body was of a tall, gaunt, and lean nature. He had an inward bend in the small of the back of his head, which was of enormous dimensions. His nose was aquiline and skewed considerably to one side. He was blind in one eye and squinted with the other. His cheeks had been dreadfully furrowed by the small-pox. He dressed generally in a single-breasted coat which reached below his knees. His hair was powdered, and his queue, or pig-tail, was ornamented with a bow of black ribbon. He always walked the street with a cane in his hand. He lived his final years at 110 to 114 Stockwell Street.

Raymius looks at the clock, puts the book on his bedside table and lights up the last Embassy Regal. He crushes the box in his left hand and tosses it into the empty pizza box. He closes his eyes and breathes deeply. He can sense that it's going to be an interesting evening...

pantomime *n* **1** a style of theatre, or a play in this style, traditionally performed at Christmas, in which a folk tale or children's story is told with jokes, songs and dancing **2** a ridiculous and farcical situation that results from confusion and misunderstanding **3** a performance in ancient Rome by one masked actor who plays all the characters using only dance, gesture, expression and no words **4** an actor in Roman pantomimes. *Greek, pantomomos, 'complete imitator'*

It is a typical Scottish winter evening. No night sky, no stars or moon. Just grey clouds. The air is cold, dark and wet. If there's a werewolf howling you can't hear it for the noise of the wind lashing the trees.

Raymius has his collar up and his hands deep in his pockets. As he strides through the streets of Glasgow his feet disturb the tops of the puddles of slush. Raymius left his new apartment with a contented smile on his face and a good feeling in his heart, even though he suspects shit is about to happen. He feels good. He always does. He sees the lights of his local and hears Bono from U2 blaring out of the Jukebox and into the night air.

Sunday bloody Sunday!

Raymius smells the homemade steak pie and can almost taste the mashed spuds. He pushes the doors and feels like the sheriff walking into a saloon in an old western.

A cheer explodes from the lads sitting in their corner. The two Donnies, wee Dylan and of course The Man. The Merchant City's Usual Suspects. The Man pushes his chair back with the heel of his right foot and steps round from the table. He stands with both arms outstretched, his grin becoming a smile.

"Ray-Mondo!"

Raymius narrows his eyes and then allows them to sparkle as he delivers his own retort.

"Bonjour, Kemosabe!"

The lads look confused. They generally do. If you know anything about Michael Anthony Noonan, you don't call him anything other than The Man, or just simply Man. They also know that Ray doesn't appreciate being called anything other than Ray.

However, both men have a special dispensation for such things and ignore this etiquette as they hug each other like two line-backers celebrating a touchdown.

Every Monday in the Scotia bar is Lyrics in the Lounge. It's a bit like an open mic jam session for writers and poets. The lads like to sit in and do some serious heckling. Well, that's the official party line. The unofficial is that big Donny Malone fancies himself as a bit of a singer-songwriter. Although he doesn't admit that openly, it's common knowledge.

Why Big Donny is reluctant to 'come out' is a bit of a mystery. Donny is pretty talented, the size of a baby hippo and a self-confessed totally mad Irish cunt.

To say he is fast with his fists for such a big lad would be an understatement in the same league as saying Tiger Woods is 'not bad at putting'. Donny Malone, 18 stone, 6ft 4in tall, 32 years of age, die-hard Celtic fan, Dublin born and bred. He was once asked if he was vegetarian. His reply was, "Naw, Sagittarian". He's been in Glasgow now for over a decade and has managed to maintain his Irish lilt. He sounds a little like Dougal from Father Ted but again no one has been brave enough to tell him that.

Big Donny interrupts the hugging by tapping Raymius on the shoulder. Raymius turns around and opens his arms, also inviting big Donny for a hug. Malone backs off with his hands in the air.

"Away-yi-go Ray, ya fockin' eejit!"

"So, what's been happening tonight then, big guy?" Raymius asks, unable to remove the smirk from his face.

Big Donny scratches his blond crew-cut scalp with the digits of his massive right hand, takes a huge deep breath and responds.

"The fockin' theme tonight is 'Bank Holiday Monday'. Since when does Glasgow have a bank holiday in fockin' January? I ask yi? And then, am writin' a poem four the day y'know, while the lads are deliberatin'."

He takes another gulp of air.

"Every Monday is a Bank Holiday Monday four me but they don't come too often four ma likin'. Am tryin' ti tink of an end four ma poem when some fockin' eeejit wants me ti buy the Da Vinci code forra fiver. I can get it four less at Bargain-fockin'-Books. Then, this joker's pal wants ti sell us a leather jaykit. Forra tenner, then a fiver, then two pound-fockin' fifty. I contemplate a poem about the black economy, leather apparel and Dan Brown."

All the lads are giggling like wee boys as big Donny goes for another intake of air.

"Then, we all click like we're all tinkin' the same ting, at the same fockin' time. We all shout like we are synchronized fockin' swimmers all doin' the booin' and the hissin' and shoutin' that HE'S BEHIND YOU SHITE at a fockin' Panto, it wiz tree-mendous, am telling yi, we all sayze it at the same time... FOCK OFF YI CUNT! See how they all come to it? Brilliant! And that's before they started all that shite about fockin' TV licences."

Raymius looks at Noonan. Noonan shrugs his shoulders and holds his hands palms up like Jesus at the last supper. Neither of them says anything; there's no need. Big Donny adds: "David Bowie knows what am talkin' aboot."

Everybody exchanges bewildered expressions as Donald McGee, not to be confused with Big Donny Malone, returns from the bar and hands Raymius his usual.

"Thanks, D."

"Nae problem, Ray."

It would be difficult to confuse Donald McGee with big Donny Malone. McGee is younger, slimmer and has ginger hair down to his shoulders. It covers most of his face and hides most of his freckles. Although McGee is also Irish, he was born and bred in Belfast. McGee is in Glasgow because he isn't welcome anywhere on the Emerald Isle. He came to Glasgow a year ago to watch the 'Old Firm' and decided just to stay. Behind their backs they're fondly referred to as the two Donnies.

A woman's voice shatters the air like a banshee in a chapel. They all shoosht and peek around their corner like they're sneaking a peek at a lassie having a pish up a close.

"Wan singer wan song."

She shrieks again, waving her arms and stomping her feet like Bonnie Langford. Her hubby pulls her hands down and presses her shoulders together like he's playing the accordion. He then throws the audience an apologetic grin while he ushers her out the swing doors heid first. The doors creak back into place and there's quiet for just a moment. It's as if the whole pub's waiting for some tumbleweed to roll by. Big Donny breaks the silence.

"Happy days."

Wee Dylan decides it's his turn to add in his penny's worth.

"I was happy once, until I found out my mother was my father, but now my skin is Teflon coated."

Nobody laughs.

"That'll explain yer shiny heid then, wee yin," Big Donny says.

Wee Dylan aka Brian Brown is the youngest of a family of twelve. He hails from the Highland town of Oban. He came to Glasgow to study Social Science and is currently repeating first year. Everybody knows wee Dylan is gay but for some unknown reason he has not yet got around to admitting it. If you asked him why he's called Dylan he'd tell you it's because he is a mad fucking Bob Dylan fanatic. Which is somewhat true. If you asked any of the usual suspects they'd tell you that it is on account that he is going bald and looks like Dylan from the Magic Roundabout. A hippy-like, droopy-eared rather dopey guitar-playing rabbit.

He pipes up again with another worn-out gag reminding all the lads that Mr Billy Connolly would like to thank the rhythm method for us all being here. Still nobody laughs. It is painful to watch the wee atmosphere hoover try so hard.

"Can't take yoo boyz nowhere except the Scotia bar," he says. Still nobody laughs. "Hey, Donny see that sci-fi story you read oot earlier?" Dylan now has everyone's attention.

"Aye, whit aboot it, wee yin?" Donny asks.

The Man interrupts before Dylan has the chance to respond.

"Be careful, Dylan, you know how big Donny is about his writing. Tread carefully wee yin. Is it going to offend anyone?"

Wee Dylan thinks and shakes his head.

"Is this going to be funny?"

Wee Dylan thinks and then nods slowly.

"Are you sure?"

Again, he thinks and then nods more confidently.

"On yi go then, Dylan, go for it."

"Getting sucked tae death by aliens sounds better than being hit by a bus."

Still nobody makes a sound because everybody's looking at Big Donny.

Big Donny bursts out laughing, rolls his eyes up to the wooden timbers and then hits the lads with another one of his trance-inducing contributions.

"Nice one Dylan. I'll try and avoid all those swallows but what about the Amazons?"

Everybody's looking up to the heavens and pushing hard to get their eyebrows to touch together like they've got some kind of chance of getting a fucking clue what Big Donny is talking about.

"David Bowie knows what I'm talkin' about."

Donald McGee has got his glower-thing happening. Big Donny notices and questions him.

"Yoor awfy quiet McGee, everythin' all right?"

McGee speaks. While he's still got his glower-thing going on.

"I've been thinking, big guy. You lads are all flying too close to the edge of the doughnut. I often wonder why we awe suffer each other's company. Anyway, Donny, here's an end to yer shagging poem, sonny bhoy.

"Every Monday is a Bank Holiday Monday for me, but they don't come too often

for my liking. Some Bank Holiday Monday..."

All the usual suspects including those at tables nearby who are earie-wigging look in and hold their breath, so as not to miss a word. Big Donny's getting impatient. "C'mon McGee, four fock sake, spit it oot, MAN." Big Donny turns to The Man and holds his hands up. "Sorry, Man, no offence meant."

Noonan shrugs. "None taken."

McGee takes a drink of his pint and waits until he's got their attention before he starts again.

"Right. I'll start again. Every Monday is a Bank holiday Monday for me, but they don't come too often for my liking.

I'll try and avoid all those swallows but the Amazons can fuck right off. Some Bank Holiday Monday, I'm gonni buy me a gun.

Bee-cause….

Getting sucked tae death by aliens sounds better than being hit by a bus."

McGee winks at wee Dylan and smiles at big Donny.

Donny starts shouting and applauding like a big kid.

"I like it McGee, naw, I fockin love it, tree-mendous."

Raymius moves closely to the side of Noonan's head.

"Where's your brother, Man?"

"H is yappin' at the bar, dude."

"Let's give him a hand, hombre."

"OK, Raymondo, let's leave the proletariat to it."

They both head for one of the booths at the other end of the pub. It's nowhere near Noonan's brother.

murder *n* **1** unlawful killing of human being with malice aforethought **2** highly dangerous or troublesome state of affairs **3** *v* kill (human being) unlawfully with malice aforethought **4** *v* kill wickedly or inhumanely **5** *v* utterly defeat **6** *v* spoil by bad performance, mispronunciation, etc.

Michael Anthony Noonan aka The Man, had spent time with the Royal Marines. On his favourite T-shirt is a picture of Che Guevara with a green beret. On his arm there's a tattoo of a dagger and beneath it says… "God is Airborne because he failed Commando Course!"

Raymius points to another booth at the back of the bar where the artists tend to hang out.

"Who's the Red Head?"

"Amigo, you brought me here to ask me that?"

"No."

"Not sure. She's got great tits though. Thinkin' aboot shaggin' it?"

Raymius and Noonan have two types of dialogue. Normal-speak and, when they mimic the lads, shellsuit-speak.

"C'mon Michael, you know everybody."

"Yeah, I know, muchacho. So what's the fascination with this colita?"

"She hasn't taken her eyes off me since I walked into Dodge."

The Man bursts out laughing but Raymius's face remains expressionless.

"Are you laughing at me, Noonan?"

Michael Noonan raises both his hands like he's under arrest and tilts his head to one side. His mouth is the shape of an inverted U, like Brando in the Godfather.

"No way, dude. Well I suppose yeah, I am. But amigo, honestly, I mean you no disrespect. Fuck me, I expect the chemical heads to be paranoid but not you, buddy. Is your head so far up your arse at the moment you don't know when a woman wants into your pants?" This time they both laugh.

"Can you tell me anything about her? Apart from the obvious fact she's got great tits?"

"Maybe."

"Maybe? What the fuck d'you mean maybe? Maybe you want to keep her for yourself? Maybe you want to just answer the fucking question?"

The Man starts laughing again and takes a few moments to compose himself. "Ah Raymondo, that's one of the things I love about you, dude. I really am that transparent to you. True?"

"True!"

"Be warned, though, she's got her relationship beacon on! I'm not sure if you've got enough experience to shag her and bail out unharmed."

Raymius scratches his scalp and screws up his face like he's just sucked on a lemon. "I know I'm going to regret asking this but what-the-fuck is a relationship beacon?"

"Picture the lads out on the pull at the end of the night around kebab o'clock. They've decided they'd better get a 'burd' while they can still actually speak."

Raymius folds his arms and leans back. "Aye. Go on."

"That look they have as they scope for prey is as subtle as a Corporation 'Road Sweeper' with the yellow flashing lights. Steamin' and dreamin' about stickin' their cock in anything warm and moist."

Raymius leans forward. "So, what the fuck has that to do with the redhead?"

"Patience Raymondo, patience. If you were close enough to the lads at that particular moment you would see their pupils were dilated."

Raymius starts looking round for a waiter. "Stunning, Sherlock, have you considered that this earth-shattering observation might have something to do with the amount of alcohol and drugs they've thrown down their necks? Fuck sake, has the entire pub went on their break?"

Noonan tosses Raymius a Juicy Fruit.

"Chill Whin-stan, chew on this a while, pay attention amigo, maybe you'll learn something. Yes, of course, mind-altering chemicals affect the involuntary dilation of the pupil. However, the facial muscles react differently when emotional excitement is experienced. This look I am referring to is different than that of someone who is merely nuggets. It gives the impression of someone who has been transfixed, momentarily frozen in time."

Raymius folds the wrapper into the silver paper and drops it in the ashtray. "Ahh, Juicy Fruit. Yeah Man, this chewing gum is as fascinating as your conversation. How about explaining in layman's terms what the fuck you're talking about?"

"Women who are looking for sex, amigo, give themselves away with their eyes. Women who are thinking about love have the same look in their eyes but are also trapped in the moment. Usually with that goofy-fucking-looking smile." Noonan gestures over to the Red Head, whose grin is painted from one side of her face to the other and still locked on Raymius from across the room.

Raymius nods, breaks eye contact with psycho-chick and grudgingly concedes Noonan's point with a small flare of his nostrils. "You really believe all of that shit, don't you Michael?"

"Yep, and you should too. Amigo, trust me, that Red Head with those beads, those boots and that whole fucking Kate

Bush thing happening has got her relationship beacon on. At the moment the red dot is on you. Be warned, Ray. She's in loa-ve, dude!"

"Well, thanks for sharing that with me, Michael, but is there any chance you can tell me anything other than her subconscious fucking emotions? Like her address, age, occupation, any maniac brothers or, more important, is her old man quoted in Gangsters'R'Us? And if I shag her am I likely to wake up with Shergar smiling at me from the top of my duvet?"

"Very cute amigo, very cute. I'm happy to oblige with the bint's bio but it looks as if that'll have to wait." Noonan's eyes shift upwards, his forehead creases and he nods to indicate behind Raymius. The Red Head has already decided to make the first move. Before Raymius has the chance to turn round his nose fills with the aroma of expensive perfume and he feels a finger tap his shoulder. His ears tune in to her voice and he figures it wouldn't sound out of place in any popular porn movie. The only thing missing is the elevator music.

"Hi gorgeous. God! Have I just died and went to Heaven? I suppose you get compliments about your green eyes all the time? What do I call you, then?"

Amanda Blair is a size fourteen body trapped in a size twelve's mind. She has a degree in Literature from Glasgow University and lives alone in a three-bedroomed West End apartment which Daddy funds. Amanda comes from the socio-economic group that believes in order to really find oneself one simply must get down to grass roots and keep one's life in perspective by getting to grips with not 'losing the common touch' and then make sure they know one is quoting Kipling. Amanda hangs around the Merchant City bars in the hope that soon she will find her true self. Amanda plays the guitar, the piano and the violin. She is in musical terms incredibly talented. She's only recently found out about the Scotia's 'Lyrics in the Lounge' and so far the night is just simply fabulous. Amanda thinks Billy Joel's Uptown Girl really is a song that's about her.

Despite Noonan's warning, Raymius decides to play along. But before he responds he takes a moment to survey the goods from up close. Amanda has red hair, not strawberry blonde, not auburn, not mousey with a reddish tinge, but flaming red. In fact Raymius has always wondered why they call it red hair because to all intents and purposes this Ghinger's hair is actually closer to orange.

"You can call me whatever you want provided you're going to buy me drink," Raymius replies.

"Well, well! Whatever you want, what would you like to drink?

"I would like a pint of St Andrews and a Black Bush."

Amanda gives Raymius a curious look and isn't quite sure what to say, which in itself is off-putting for her since she normally never shuts up for a minute.

"It's beer and Irish whiskey," Raymius explains.

"What, in the same glass…or…?"

Raymius interrupts her mid sentence. "No, it's two different drinks in separate glasses. Look, never mind, just tell the barman it's for Ray, he'll know what to do, thanks."

"Do I look as if I'm loaded? You said a drink, not the whole fucking bar!"

"Yes, actually, you do. You also look too intelligent to be littering your vocabulary with expletives that imply procreation so early in our relationship. If you are trying to impress me you'll do well to do what you say. You said 'whatever you want'. You shouldn't make offers to strangers, especially if you don't mean them. But hey, if you haven't cashed your giro yet, don't bother."

Amanda loves assertive men. "Oooh! Touchy, humorous and gorgeous. How fucking shaggable are you? Yum yum. Don't you dare go away, drinks are coming." Amanda skips off to the bar. Raymius turns to Noonan and mimics the Ghinger.

"I fucking love the way posh people swear, especially posh fucking women. They pronounce each fucking syllable so crisply and they deliver their profanity with such confidence and such fucking assertiveness. To quote the Merovingian, it's like wiping your arse with silk." Raymius has a giggle to himself.

The Man appears to be getting bored with it all. The whole time she was talking to Ray, Noonan felt as if he was invisible.

"So, gorgeous, before psycho-burd gets back maybe you can enlighten me as to why you lured me into the booths in the depths of the Scotia Bar?"

"I need your help, Michael."

"Sorry Duderino, I'm not in the 'help' business any more and I'm a wee bit busy right now."

"Busy doin' what?"

"Stuff."

"Stuff! Don't give us it Michael, you don't do stuff, you don't DO fuckin' anythin' you're the laziest fucker I know."

"Well if I'm so lazy, dude, how is it you're coming to me looking for help? And may I compliment your sales approach, a nice touch brandishing all these wonderful endorsements and compliments."

"It's because you're so fucking lazy I want your help, Michael."

Noonan doesn't often look confused but his eyebrows push together for the second time tonight. Raymius smiles as Michael Noonan pulls out a liquorice cigarette paper and expertly rolls in some Old Hoborn.

"Don't allow my look of intrigue to get mixed up with that of confusion, Raymondo. So what's with your recruitment drive for hombres with a lazy disposition?"

Raymius eventually spies a waiter and summons him.

"You guys eating tonight?" asks the waiter.

"Naw, just drinks."

The waiter lifts the menus off the table.

"Beers or shorts?" Raymius looks at Noonan they exchange knowing nods and speak in tandem.

"Both."

The waiter grins. "Your usual, guys?"

Once again they both respond like a well-rehearsed duet.

"Aye."

The waiter heads for the bar and Noonan raises an eyebrow. "So I guess you're getting these in just in case the Ghinger goes missing?"

Raymius shrugs his shoulders and this time it's his turn to make his mouth into the shape of an inverted U. "Always have a plan B, Man, always have a plan B."

As if by magic the music stops at exactly the same time the saloon doors swing open. Clare walks in. She spots Ray and Noonan in their booth. She goes straight over and sits down beside them. The waiter looks across and shouts, "What can I get you Clare?"

"Tequila, Babes, thanks."

"In a hurry tonight?"

"Aye, somethin' like that." She kisses Raymius full on the mouth. Noonan puckers his lips. "Me next, Colita."

"In your fuckin' dreams, Man."

They all laugh. Noonan stands up and reaches for her hand. He gently kisses her fingertips.

"I'll leave you two alone. Later, Princess, later, Kemosabe. To be continued." He nods his head at Raymius and then gestures to Amanda, who is returning from the bar. Raymius raises his shoulders and grins. The Man goes to head psycho-chick off at the pass.

Clare lights up a cigarette. "Mobile phone, darling? Any messages?" she asks.

Raymius places the mobile in Clare's outstretched hand. "No messages, Clare."

"Enough chitchat, to more important matters. We, as in you and I, need to go to Janus."

"Why?"

"To meet Lloyd."

"Who the fuck is Lloyd?"

"Lloyd owns the 'K' you've assured me is safe."

"When?"

"Now."

"Why?"

"Because he was expectin' a package from me tonight and since I can't deliver, he wants to see the person who will. Provided you've not been bullshittin' and the goods are safe, then we have nothin' to worry about. Lloyd just likes to be thorough. If there's a problem, now is the time to talk so I can explain how fucked we both are."

"The goods are safe, Clare, and accessible first thing tomorrow, is that cool?"

"Yep, great. Let's go then." Clare turns her head to face the Red Head. Amanda brushes past Noonan and arrives back at the booth armed with drinks.

"Here you are, Gorgeous, one Pint of St Andrews and one Black Bush with lots of ..." She stops mid sentence like she's just realised she's forgotten to put any knickers on. Her mouth falls open as she gawks at Clare. Raymius shrugs with resignation at Amanda as Clare takes his arm, stands him up and pulls him out of the booth. Raymius opens his mouth to speak as he's walking away backwards. Clare is amused at both of them standing silently with mouths open, ready to speak but saying nothing. She beats them both to a response.

"Nice dental work, Ginge. Don't worry about this guy, I'll take good care of him. I shouldn't need him for too long. C'mon Ray, chop chop!"

Noonan, who has clocked everything, takes his opportunity willingly and moves in on Amanda, lifting the glasses from her, placing them on the table and helping her sit down as the booth becomes vacant again. He shouts at Raymius: "Hey, Kemosabe, I'll look after these until you get back. Cops and buses amigo, cops and buses!" This is one of the Noonan's well-used expressions. It suggests that women, like buses and cops, are never there when you need one. Then all of a sudden a bunch of them appear at the same time.

Still being dragged backwards Raymius smiles with arms out and palms upturned. Noonan watches Amanda's gaze as Clare disappears out of the Scotia with Raymius in tow just as her tequila arrives. His eyes move to study the other side of the table. *Great tits*, he thinks to himself again.

"So, Colita, what do we call you, then? Tequila?"

"Eh… Amanda."

He takes a mouthful of Irish. "Hmm, haven't seen you here before, you must be new." He holds out his hand. She takes it. He gently kisses her fingertips.

"Hi, Amanda, my friends call me The Man. How would you like me to tell you the history of the Scotia Bar?"

tolerance *n* **1** the acceptance of different views of other people, fairness towards people who have differing views. **2** the act of putting up with something or somebody irritating or otherwise unpleasant **3** ability to endure hardship, to put up with harsh or difficult conditions **4** allowance made for something to deviate in size from a standard or the limit within which it is allowed to deviate **5** ability to remain unaffected, the loss of or reduction in the normal response to a drug, or other agent, following use or exposure over a prolonged period. **6** ability to survive extreme conditions

Janus is only fifteen minutes' walk from the Scotia Bar. Clare hails a cab within seconds and responds to his quizzical look. "High heels aren't designed for walkin' and trainin' shoes don't work with this outfit. Anyway, this is Glasgow and it's January, are you fuckin' mad?"

"I was actually thinking about your entrance and our exit from the Scotia."

"What?"

"I just think it was a bit melodramatic, are you OK?"

"I guess I'm a bit tense, premenstrual. How, you worried about your Red Head? She'll keep, y'know? She knows a good catch when she sees it."

"So I'm a good catch, then?"

"Like you don't fuckin' know that? You expectin' me to blow smoke up your arse all night, Raymondo?"

"You know I don't like being called that, Clare."

"So how come your pal The Man gets away with it?"

"It's just a joke, a long story. I'll tell you about it some time."

Clare lights a cigarette and notices the driver's eyes in his rear view mirror.

"If you want to smoke, hen, roll doon yur windy?"

Clare opens her legs to reveal the tops of her stockings and a black G-string. She winks slowly at the two eyes peering back at her.

"Awe, don't want me to catch a chill, do you Daddio?"

The driver doesn't respond.

Janus is an upmarket venue. Very swish, very posh, very expensive. There was a time when Raymius would have been at home there but it's not the type of place he's been frequenting recently. As they leave their taxi and walk up to the door, a steward makes towards Raymius. He is about to deliver one of the many lies bouncers use to refuse someone they either don't recognise or simply don't like the look of. Clare speaks first.

"He's with me, JJ, we've got an appointment to see your boss."

"Sorry, Babes, didn't recognise you there. This meeting, with or without drinks?"

"Cocktails."

"Lucky girl. You stay safe now." JJ turns to his colleague beside the door: "Two guests to see the boss, Frank, take them upstairs and bypass the cash desk mate, they're on the guest list."

Frank studies the clipboard he's holding. "What's their names, JJ?"

"Donald and fucking Minnie, don't keep the boss's guests hanging about the door, Frank."

"But I can't see their names on the list, JJ, and at the briefing Cha said…"

JJ interrupts. "Fuck the list, fuck what Cha said, take them upstairs and when you get back we'll discuss the fucking briefing."

"Nae bother, JJ."

Clare and Raymius do their best not to laugh. JJ apologises. "Sorry, Babes, he's from a big family and they're on a share plan. It's not his turn for the brain cell tonight."

Clare kisses JJ on the cheek. "Thanks, Babes."

Frank escorts them upstairs. Raymius whispers to Clare, "Cocktails then?"

"Fuckin' hope so," she snaps.

Lloyd. S. D. Oakley AKA Lloyd Shar Mercano was born in the Port of Spain on the Caribbean island of Trinidad fifty-one years ago. His family moved to Europe when he was five years of age. Not many know the reason why. Without a grey hair on his head, he regularly boasts he's fitter than most men half his age. At only twenty he left the back streets of Paris for an apprenticeship in the London underworld. Lloyd has long black wavy hair gathered in a ponytail with a black silk ribbon. His eyes are deep, dark brown, almost black. He's always clean-shaven and his skin looks like satin. His smile makes you feel warm. He is articulate, charming and carries every inch of his 6ft 4 frame around like an American General. Lloyd knew poverty. It was his job to put food on the table for his baby bother and sister from the age of six. By the age of ten he was dealing drugs and by eighteen he was managing drug dealers. If you were smoking, snorting, injecting or in any way partaking in any illegal substance and you were in Paris then the chances are you were buying from Lloyd.

Lloyd's mother, a devout Christian, helped the authorities get evidence for the arrest. Three days after he'd been dragged from his home it was razed along with everybody in it. Lloyd's orders were specific. His sister and mother were to be sacrificed in the fire. He made bail, attended the funeral and left France.

Clare and Raymius are escorted to an alcove where a log fire gives the impression of being in someone's front room.

There are three gorillas in suits sitting across from Lloyd. They stop speaking and stand up. Lloyd remains seated.

"Sit down, gentlemen, we haven't finished by a long way." He turns and faces Clare. "Sorry, darling, this won't take long." He pats the cushion for her to join him and then points at Raymius's chest. Raymius follows Lloyd's finger as it moves to indicate an empty chair left of the gorillas and at the end of a beautifully varnished table. Lloyd's intention is clear. Raymius sits down and says nothing. His mind reels back to Ribbon's files. He recognises some of the players in this act and the name tags fill in the blanks. He draws a seating plan of the alcove in his head, imagining how it would look to a fly on the ceiling:

Darren   Ronnie   Liam

JJ   Ray   BEAUTIFULLY VARNISHED TABLE

Clare   Lloyd

FIREPLACE

Lloyd turns his attention back to the suits.

"Gentlemen, the two roads that lead to success and failure travel in opposite directions, yes?"

"Yes Boss."

"Yes Boss."

"Yes Boss."

"Therefore if you wish to succeed then you must avoid failure at all costs, yes?"

"Yes Boss."

"Yes Boss."

"Yes Boss."

"In my last estimation there were at least two dozen ways to fail. May I elaborate?" He smiles at the suits and waits for their eenie meanie and miney combined responses.

They all repeat once again, "Yes Boss."

Lloyd puts his left hand on the table and makes a fist. He sticks out his thumb.

"One... insufficient education." He takes the time to look at everyone before he sticks out his forefinger and continues to count. "Two... lack of control of sexual urge." Lloyd sits back, his left hand now in the shape of a gun aiming at Darren. Darren has been sneaking glimpses of Clare's cleavage. Not a crime given she's in the advertising game. Lloyd has made his point, though, at least to Darren, whose neck is now beginning to blush. Lloyd sits forward, produces his middle finger and continues to count. "Three... wrong selection of a mate in marriage." Lloyd's attention switches to Raymius. Neither man so much as blinks. "Four... a negative personality and five... wrong selection of associates in business. Gentlemen, are we there yet?"

They all respond like a musical trio. "Yes Boss."

Clare and Raymius look at each other but say nothing. The fingers of Lloyd's left hand are now spread out wide. He turns his palm towards the table and bangs it down like when you're playing snap. The suits and Clare jump. Lloyd tilts his head slightly to one side and studies Raymius. Lloyd's left hand remains on the table. He places his other hand next to it and once again makes a fist. He sticks out his right thumb and continues counting. His eyes are fixed once more on the suits.

"Six... inability to cooperate with others. Seven... wrong selection of a vocation. Are you gentlemen sure you're in the right job?"

The gorillas look at each other and then sing out again, "Yes Boss."

Lloyd continues. "Eight... lack of enthusiasm. Nine... lack of ambition to aim above mediocrity and ten... intentional dishonesty!" Lloyd bangs his right palm on the table. This time nobody moves. "Gentlemen, I seem to have run out of fingers, would one of you be good enough to lend me a hand?"

The gorilla in the middle places his right hand on the table and makes a fist. "No problem, Boss."

"Thank you Ronnie, but I was hoping Liam might help me out."

As Liam puts his fist on the table he looks at Raymius. Raymius notices an involuntary twitch at the side of Liam's face before he stutters, "N-not a problem Boss." It's clear to everyone that it is.

Lloyd raises his eyebrows and nods his head towards Liam's fist. Liam sticks out his thumb and Lloyd shakes his head while continuing to count.

"Eleven... lack of self-discipline."

When Liam sticks out his forefinger his hand starts to tremble.

"Twelve... lack of persistence. Thirteen... lack of ability to make decisions. Fourteen... lack of a well-defined purpose. Gentlemen, were my instructions nebulous?"

Liam stutters. "S-sorry Boss?"

"Were my instructions ambiguous; were they cloudy, confusing, muddy?"

The suits glance at each other. Liam stutters again. "S-sorry Boss?"

"Did you understand my instructions? Were my instructions CLEAR?" He stares at them individually.

"Yes Boss."

"Yes Boss."

"Y-yes Boss."

Lloyd gestures to Liam's right hand. Liam sticks out the remaining pinkie.

"Fifteen... egotism or vanity."

Liam puts out his right hand.

"That's not how I showed you earlier, Liam. Pay attention, son."

Liam spreads the fingers of his hand and places his palm face down. He looks at his boss for approval.

"Come on, Liam, you can do better than that! Slap it down. What are you afraid of, boy?" Liam feebly slaps his palm on the table. Lloyd rubs his eyes and shakes his head. "This is your last chance, son."

Liam bangs his palm on the table as hard as he can.

"THAT'S BETTER! God that feels good, doesn't it?"

"Y-yes Boss." Liam places his other hand on the table and makes a fist. He sticks out his thumb and Lloyd continues to count. "Sixteen, procrastination, seventeen, ill health. Gentlemen, are you all well?" Once again he stares at each of them individually.

"Yes Boss."

"Yes Boss."

"Y-yes Boss."

"Eighteen, superstition or prejudice, nineteen, the habit of indiscriminate spending. Are you enjoying your new car, son?"

"Y-yes B-boss,"

"Twenty, an uncontrolled desire for SOMETHING for NOTHING. Gentlemen, are we getting there yet?"

They all nod before responding, "Yes Boss."

Liam raises his hand to slap it on the table as before. Lloyd turns and points at Liam's raised hand.

"Hold it right there, son, be still."

Liam's arm freezes in mid air. He looks like he's asking permission to go toilet. Lloyd keeps his finger pointing at Liam's raised hand and turns to Ronnie.

"Ronnie?"

"Yes Boss?"

"Do you still drive that dinky little Volkswagen?"

"Yes Boss."

"Do you still have that dinky little key you showed me a few weeks ago?"

"Yes Boss."

"Can we see it?"

Ronnie produces a remote control fob from his trouser pocket. The ragged part of the key is not present. It's black with a metal rim and has a little silver button on the top right hand side that bears the popular logo VW.

"Now, the more intelligent of you might be thinking, where is the bit you put into the ignition? Show us the key, Ronnie." Ronnie presses the little silver button and the key flips out from the side like a switchblade. After the click Lloyd smiles like a kid on Christmas day who has just opened the present he'd asked Santa for. "How cool is that?" Nobody moves.

Clare looks at Lloyd, nodding her head like one of those little dogs at the rear of a car. She says, "Yeah, I must admit, that's pretty fuckin' cool."

Lloyd slaps his thighs and goes into a fit of laughter. Clare joins him. The gorillas chuckle nervously. Raymius stays silent but glances at Liam's arm, which is still hanging in the air and is now shaking. Lloyd produces a similar gadget from his pocket. It has a circular logo sliced into four wedges. Two light blue triangles, two white triangles and the letters BMW. He taps it on the desk for what seems to everyone like an eternity. Raymius has been counting in his head; he reaches sixty-two. Liam's doe eyes are expanding like a hedgehog's on the highway. He knows something the others don't. Lloyd presses the little silver button and the key flips out. Raymius notices the key comes to a point and resembles a little sgian-dubh that would stick in the top of your sock when you're wearing a kilt.

Lloyd continues., "Ah... German engineering. You can't beat it. Efficiency at its best. Vorsprung durch technik. Continuing and never-ending improvement. Eh, Liam?"

He glares into Liam's eyes and gestures to the raised arm. Liam slaps his hand on the table as hard as he can. He feels the relief of the blood rushing back into his hand after having had it aloft for so long. As he makes contact with the table Lloyd stands up and throws down his own hand on Liam's wrist, pinning it to the wood. With the speed of an accomplished magician pulling a rabbit out of a top hat, Lloyd drives the metal key through Liam's hand, nailing it to the beautifully varnished surface. Liam lets out a scream like a cat being strangled. Lloyd grips Liam by the throat. His thumb wraps itself round Liam's windpipe and squeezes, gently. "Twenty-one, the inability to realise the necessity for concentration of effort. There are people trying to enjoy themselves this evening, Liam. You're embarrassing me. Stop crying like a little girl. Take the pain."

Liam closes his eyes, sucks in both lips and bites hard. With a firm hold of Liam's throat Lloyd continues, "Twenty-two... over-caution. Twenty-three... guessing instead of thinking, and last but by no means least... intolerance."

snuff *n* **1** tobacco in the form of powder taken by sniffing it up the nostrils **2** *v* to inhale something through the nose **3** *v* to extinguish a flame to **4** *v* to put an end to something or someone **5** *v* to destroy…

"Well, Amanda, in order to help you understand the significance of the history of the Scotia Bar let me put it all into context by first telling you a little about this wee place called Glasgow."

Noonan looks around the bar and motions towards several dark timber beams. He puffs out his chest.

"This fine establishment is part of a construct that dates back to 1515 originally built by a Dreghorn and his roots have a direct lineage to one of Glasgow's Tobacco Lords.

Alan Dreghorn. Let me explain. This area, which of course you know as the Merchant City, was developing around the mid-18th century in terms of residences and warehouses for the Tobacco Lords. The Merchant City was competing in real estate terms with what is now sadly the lost village of Grahamston, but that's another story."

Amanda looks confused and transfixed. She is thinking that this is becoming one-fucking-hell of a chat up line. She really likes the attention.

"English literature and music?"

"Yes, that's right. I'm impressed."

Noonan starts rolling himself a smoke.

"OK, so here is Economic History 101. Feel free to take notes, Amanda. When you look at the history of Europe, the

Medieval period or the Middle Ages lasted from the 5th to the 15th century.

"It started with the fall of the Western Roman Empire and then merged into the Renaissance and the Age of Discovery. The Medieval period is therefore the middle period of these three divisions in Western history.

"It all kicked off in the 6th century with St Mungo at the Molendinar burn and it all sort of gathers momentum in the final period during the age of discovery. Bearing in mind, Pumpkin, that at that time Glasgow was the second city of the British Empire.

"In 1707 the Treaty of Union between Scotland and England gave Scottish merchants access to the English overseas territories, especially in North America.

"Glasgow's position and the River Clyde gave merchants a two- to three-week advantage over all the other ports in Britain and Europe. This position was enhanced by the French monarchy granting it a monopoly for the importation of tobacco into French territories."

Noonan smiles. Amanda smiles back.

"Go on."

"The tobacco trade was part of the trade linking exports of consumer goods from Britain to North America and…"

He takes a beer mat and tears it in half to create a triangle. His finger traces the edge of the new visual aid.

"OK, so this is the Stockwell Triangle."

He points down at the floor.

"This is the Scotia Bar."

He points over to the north exit to the pub.

"Out that door and across the road is the Victoria Bar."

He then points over to the door at the south exit and says,

"…and over there, as you know, is the Clutha Vaults."

Once again his finger traces along the edge of the beer mat, touching each of the three corners.

"Scotia, Victoria, Clutha. Got it?"

Amanda nods.

"Got it."

"Imagine that across the road the Victoria Bar is Britain, or more specifically Glasgow."

He points to the floor again, then the north exit and then to the south exit.

"Here in the Scotia bar is North America and the Caribbean. So Glasgow exports goods to the Yanks and then collects tropical goods like tobacco, sugar and rum from the Caribbean. Got it?"

"Got it."

"Later, a third leg was added by English merchants carrying slaves from West Africa, thus establishing the so-called triangular trade."

He points over to the south exit towards the Clutha Vaults.

"So, the Clutha Vaults is West Africa Amanda, got it?"

"Surprisingly I do. You do have a very brilliant way of explaining things simply you cheeky Man."

"Just Man. You ever been to Havana?"

Amanda smiles and flutters her eyelashes.

"Havana?"

"Aye, Cuba, Havana?"

"I know where Havana is."

"Cool, ever been?"

"No."

"Wanni-go?"

Noonan pauses for effect, rolls another rollie and continues.

"Glasgow became the focus of an economic boom which lasted nearly five decades. This was the age of the Tobacco Lords, the nouveau riche of the mid-18th century. Arguably the greatest of these merchants was John Glassford, who gives his name to the street that connects with Stockwell Street heading north past St Enoch's towards the Italian Centre and George Square."

"John Street?"

"No. Glassford Street."

"Oops, sorry, silly me."

Noonan continues.

"Glassford was the most extensive ship owner of his generation in Scotland. Glasgow merchants made fortunes and adopted the style of aristocrats – though their Calvinist background was displayed in their sober choice of materials. Black silk clothes, startlingly set off by scarlet cloaks. Black three-cornered hats, silver or even gold-tipped ebony canes, mahogany furniture and classical architecture.

"Their mansions were laid out on the western boundaries of the city where they latterly gave their names to streets. Andrew Buchanan, James Dunlop, Archibald Ingram, James Wilson, Alexander Oswald, Andrew Cochrane, Alexander Speirs and John Glassford. Other streets refer to the Triangular Trade more directly, Virginia Street and Jamaica Street especially.

"St Andrew's Parish Church in St Andrew's Square was built by Alan Dreghorn as a demonstration of his wealth and power.

"In the Merchant City it was usual for individuals to be involved in several businesses. The Dreghorns were no exception and had interests in property, plumbing, engineering, lead, timber, tobacco, banking and the retailing of snuff.

"Robert Dreghorn l died in 1742, leaving two sons, Arthur and Robert II. Robert II built a four-storey tenement block on Stockwell Street for the purpose of office houses."

Noonan once again looks around and points to the Scotia's timbers and ancient structures.

"Robert II died, leaving his widow, Isabella, with four daughters and a son. Robert III the youngest of five, inherited the Dreghorn fortune. As a child he contracted smallpox and was later also plagued by infamy; he became known as the city's ugliest man. The deadly disease spared his life but disfigured him. It deprived little Robert of an eye and half a nose and left his face with bits missing. He was nicknamed Bob the Dragon."

Noonan takes a long drink of his pint. Amanda is enjoying the history lesson and is not making a good job of pretending not to.

"If you're trying to get into my knickers you're going to have try much fucking harder than that."

Noonan puts his pint down and blows out a huge smoke ring. He has no intention of hiding the delight on his face.

"Bob the Dragon could be seen daily, walking down Argyle Street past the Trongate, dressed in a single-breasted coat that reached below his knees. His hair was pigtailed, powdered and boasted a black silk ribbon. In his hand he carried an ivory wooden cane with a solid gold handle and tip. Bob never married but was rumoured to have an illegitimate son. He disappeared January in 1806, the day after his 40th birthday. The body of Bob the Dragon has never been found."

Noonan takes another drink of his pint and starts to roll another cigarette. Amanda is actually amazed at his skilful articulation and storytelling ability. She starts to look a bit doe-eyed. Noonan lights his little dark brown masterpiece and blows another ring of delight. He looks around with upturned hands like he's a guide showing tourists round a gallery.

"The Scotia claims to be the oldest pub in Glasgow. Once you've passed the rather dreich exterior and settled in beneath these low ceilings and dark-stained beams you may be excused for feeling that you've passed through a portal and went back in time. This is not just a bar, this is a Glasgow institution."

Noonan points at the many pictures and photographs that paper the walls of the Scotia.

"Billy Connolly, Gerry Rafferty, the Humblebums, the Sensational Alex Harvey Band. These guys used to play here for the price of a pint."

Noonan looks at Amanda the way you do when you're peering over the top of specs. Amanda plays along.

"Oooh! Well, there you are!"

"Cute, Amanda, very cute."

They both laugh.

"You're making this all up, aren't you?"

Noonan puts his finger up to his lips and then points above her head. There is a large parchment framed in glass. Its title is **'The History of the Scotia Bar'**. Amanda starts to get up. He stops her.

"Be patient, Colita, you can check it in a minute."

He crouches a little and starts to speak softer like he's telling a tale round a campfire.

"The licence was granted to 51-year-old Mary Oldman on April 1st 1792. A spinster of considerable wealth for a woman of that time. Before moving into the licensed trade, Mary Oldman was in the world's oldest profession and had the most intimate of information on some of Glasgow's most prominent men. Although she never married, she devoted her life looking after whom she referred to as her nephew. Her nephew's heirs were to look after this establishment for the next 137 years until his remaining descendants sold up and moved to America in October 1929."

Amanda is quiet although Noonan can imagine the noise in her head since her eyebrows are propping each other up and she looks like she's trying to see out of the centre of her forehead. Noonan is still sipping his beer and puffing away in between paragraphs.

"This is totally bollocks, Mr Man, you're making this all up."

Once again Noonan puts his finger up to his lips and stops her from getting up. She's beginning to enjoy his big hands on her bare arms.

"Be patient for just another few minutes. I promise you won't be disappointed, you can check it all in a minute. And it's just Man."

He crouches again and is now almost whispering. Amanda is warming to his voice and his big smug grins.

"Not many people are aware of this but I'm the type of guy who likes to know what's going on, especially on my turf, y'know what I mean?"

He nods at Amanda. Unconsciously she nods back.

"In 1929, John Jones, a well-known publican, was eventually granted a licence for the Scotia. He ran it until the '60s when the licence holder changed to Mr James Sherry. He ran the hostelry throughout '60s and '70s. This was when the notorious Glasgow bikers the Blue Angels frequented the 'howff', believing it to have some significance in Devil worship. That era ended with the 'Winter of Discontent' – unemployment, violence and lack of clientele. The doors closed again for almost a decade."

Amanda is starting to get bored and is also now out of alcohol.

"So is that it then? Can I check the parchment now? Is there no big Scooby Doo punchline?"

Noonan puts his finger up to his lips for the third time. He points again to above her head.

"You can check that any time. There is just one more thing. So shoosht and listen. When I'm done I'll get the drinks in since you've been a good wee lass."

Amanda is enjoying being told what to do by 'The Man'.

"In 1987 the restoration battle began and this handsome building was refurbished. Mr Brendan McLaughlin and his wife Maureen became known as the team who blew life back into our historic hostelry. Today the Scotia is famous for folk music, rock music, bootleg music malt whisky, hospitality, beer and Glasgow banter. The bar stools are now frequented by, as you know, the Glasgow University creative writing fraternity, poets, painters, poofs, musicians, tourists and of course, the occasional shell-suit. You can buy anything in here from a bacon joint to the latest movie in the cinema. However, when Brendan and his wife retired from the licensed trade last year they allowed it back into the hands of the breweries. Above the door currently reads..."

Noonan grabs her wrist and drags her up and out of the booth. He catches the eye of one of the bar staff and shouts, "Same again, Daz, we'll be back in two."

What seems like only seconds later Amanda is outside in the freezing cold looking above the main door. There are menu boards and coming attractions;

Mon... Skinny dippers
Tues... Bottleneckers
Wed... Big George and the Business
and right above the door...

It's great, isn't it?
The way words fall
Fae mouths and minds and pint glasses
Pure class
Poets'n'dreamers
Creepin' roond corners

Waitin' fur buses
Pens at the ready
Watchin'
Listnin'
Weighin' things up…

The Man waves a hand in front of her after he's spotted the confusion on her face. "Not the plaque above the door… the engraving on the wooden panel, below the doorframe."

She starts reading again…

Custodians: United Breweries PLC
General Manager:
Mr Robert Oldman (IV)

Below the plaque there is a picture of what looks like a dragon on fire.

Amanda's mouth is wide open. Her face has an expression like a rubber doll.

"WOW! Is that a dragon?" is all she can muster.

Noonan is rolling another cigarillo.

"Some people argue that it is a phoenix."

"If this is a total noise-up you are so dead," she says, almost running back into the pub towards the booth to check the parchment. "I'll admit I'm intrigued but this doesn't mean you're getting a shag. You're still cocking your leg up the wrong lamppost, Mr Man."

"It's not Mr Man, it's just Man, Amanda."

They arrive at the booth the same time as their drinks. Noonan takes the framed parchment from its home on the wall and hands it like a priceless antique to Amanda, who is now sitting down and gulping her Black Russian. He pays the waiter, who's giving Noonan a knowing grin.

"Keep the change, dude."

The waiter's grin becomes a smile before he walks off. "Thanks, Man."

"You do realise it's your pal I fancy and not you?" Amanda says, getting the impression that Noonan now thinks he's in with a chance. But at the same time she is furiously reading the History of the Scotia Bar. She is more than impressed. One of the hardest things for her in acting class is remembering her lines.

The Man must have a photographic memory, she thinks.

Apart from his own obvious little additions it was practically word for word, almost as if he'd written it himself. Amanda has another go.

"You do realise I'm going to blow any chances I've got of shagging Mr Green Eyes if I jump into bed with his best pal."

"Trust me, sweetie, Ray is nobody's best pal. And if you want to stay in his favour I wouldn't call him anything other than Ray. That also includes all your wee adjectives like Gorgeous. Anyway, you don't know him and I can't figure how you can compare me to Ray because you don't know me either. You in the habit of buying the first thing you see? Downside of a middle-class upbringing, I guess."

Noonan is busy lining up the side of the frame to coincide with the nicotine marks on the wall when he plays his trump card and asks Amanda: "So, have you ever passed out after you've come?"

"Excuse me?" Amanda asks, figuring she hasn't heard him right.

"Just after the point of climax, when you've come, y'know, had an orgasm... have you ever passed out? And I don't mean because of the amount of chemicals or booze you've consumed, I mean..."

Amanda interrupts. "I know what the fuck you mean."

"Well?"

"Nope," she says quizzically, still scratching her orange locks.

Noonan gives her another one of his big smug grins.

"Wanti-try-it?"

"OK, Man, I'm interested."

"Good girl."

"Bye the way, Man."

"What?"

"You had me at Havana."

"Cute. When we're alone, you can call me Michael."

"OK Man, deal. What kind of music do you like?"

"You heard any Biffy?"

"What's Biffy?"

"Not what, Pumpkin, who."

"Who's Biffy?"

"Kilmarnock band, pals of mine. Literature and music, right?"

Amanda's cheeks go a little pink.

"Should I have heard of them?"

"Abso-fucking-lutely!"

Amanda giggles.

Noonan looks towards the bar and shouts: "Daz!"

No response. Louder.

"Daz!"

Still no response.

"**Darren!**"

Daz looks round and shouts back.

"Sorry Man. What's up?"

"Stick on Biffy."

"What one?"

"You know what one."

Daz smiles.

"Sound."

The Jukebox gets paused and the in-house system kicks in...

They both pause to listen to the lyrics. She looks deep into his eyes. She says: "I like that, that's good, that's really good. So, are you going to take me for a ride?"

"Absolutely! To the bottom of the ocean."

"I'm liking this. So, what's this called, Tiger?"

Noonan shakes his head, grins and stares deep into her eyes. "It's called Mountains, Amanda, and I told you already who I am. How's your Henry V?"

Amanda looks like she's just eaten some dodgy yoghurt.

"Y'know, *once more unto the breach, dear friends…*"

Amanda smiles, interrupts and carries on.

"*…once more; Or close the wall up with our English dead.*"

"Is that all you know?"

Amanda nods her head. Noonan smiles but this time you can see all of his teeth.

"*In peace there's nothing so becomes a man as modest stillness and humility: But when the blast of war blows in our ears, then imitate the action of the tiger.*"

"As I said earlier, you had me at Havana, Michael."

tip *v* **1** to cause something to slant or become slanted **2** to turn something on its side or upside down **3** to dispose of refuse **4** a rubbish dump **6** an extremely untidy or dirty place **7** *v* to touch or lift a hat as a greeting **8** *n* the pointed end of an object, or form the end of something **9** *n* a light glancing blow **10** *n* a helpful hint. **11** an item of advance, inside or confidential information given, e.g. to warn of something about to occur or to help in solving a crime **12** *n* gratuity a gift of money for a service especially as an amount above what is owed...

Lloyd sits back down when JJ returns to the alcove. Liam's left hand is still pinned to the beautifully varnished table. His skin is grey and although the whimpers have stopped he's still shaking like a blender. JJ fingers the diamond stud in his left ear and studies the situation before he speaks.

"Everything OK, Boss?"

"Yes, JJ, thanks for asking. Can we help you?"

"Eh, no, I mean aye, eh – fuck. Boss, we have a situation."

"Enlighten me."

"We've got two uniforms on their way up the stairs as we speak. I figure they just want a nosey."

"Are they on the payroll?"

"No Boss."

"OK, JJ, get one of the girls to take them up to the VIP area and get them on the payroll. But first, show Darren and Ronnie where to deposit this shit once they've scraped it off my car key."

"Sorted Boss."

"School's out gentlemen, we can continue this later. If you'll forgive me I have another small matter that needs my attention."

JJ retrieves the car key and wipes the table with a white handkerchief. The four men leave without speaking.

"Clare! You're looking delicious, as always. Thank you so much for delivering my little caretaker. Be a darling, Clare, and order me a bottle of wine from the bar, anything un-oaked and over twenty pounds, tell them it's for me. Please, leave us for a while."

Clare gets up and turns to leave.

Lloyd adds. "Oh, darling?"

Clare stops and looks back.

"Take your time."

As Clare leaves, the watch on Lloyd's arm beeps. It catches Raymius's attention. Lloyd smiles at Raymius and then explains. "It's a heart rate monitor. At my age you can't be too careful, Ray."

"Yeah, you shouldn't exert yourself so much."

"Are you disturbed by my approach to management, Ray?"

"It's not my preferred style but I'm sure you won't be surprised if I tell you that's not the first time I've seen someone stapled to a piece of wood. I also noticed you didn't mention the most common reason for failure."

Lloyd chuckles. "Ah yes, **Fear!** An educated man and you're right, I'm not surprised." Raymius doesn't respond. Lloyd continues. "How does someone like you end up, well let us say, between projects, Ray?"

"Just lucky, I guess."

"Hah and humour, be careful Ray. I could end up liking you."

Raymius still doesn't respond.

"So Ray, which one of the ghosts of fear cast you into the abyss?"

Raymius shrugs but still says nothing.

"Let me guess. Fear of death? No. Old age? No. Ill health? No. Criticism? Of course not. The most common fear, poverty? Hmm, unlikely. Ahh! Of course, of course, lost love?"

"Sorry, Mr Oakley, you're guessing and you're wrong."

"So then, young Ray, what was it that cast you into your current situation? I'm intrigued. Do you know?"

"Yes I do. I'm surprised you haven't mentioned it yet."

Lloyd looks like a kid who's just been told he's going to Disneyland. He beams eagerly. "Ah yes… Intemperance. But, in what, sex? No. Definitely not food. Drugs…? Ah… of course. Relax, Ray, I'm getting some wine but if you'd prefer something else I'll be happy to oblige."

"Whisky will be good. Malt whisky will be better."

"Malt whisky it is then."

"Lloyd hands Raymius the drinks menu, hails a nearby steward and carries on talking. He seems comfortable doing lots of things at once. Raymius watches him produce two little porcelain Chinese balls. He rolls them in his left hand.

"Do you believe in **tips**, Ray?"

"Yes, I guess I do."

"And when would you say was the best time to tip, Ray?"

"After you've had good service. I guess."

"When did Noah build the Ark, Ray?"

This time Raymius's eyebrows crease before he shrugs. Lloyd leans back and holds his chin; he taps at his lips with his forefinger.

"Do you believe in **insurance**, Ray?"

"Yes."

"And when would you say was the best time to have insurance, Ray?"

A lightbulb switches on in his brain.

"Before the rain. I guess."

"EXCELLENT! You guess right Ray! BEFORE! BEFORE! Before the rain. Do you know what tip stands for, Ray?"

Raymius shakes his head. The steward arrives and is standing patiently waiting for Lloyd to stop speaking. Lloyd smiles. "To **insure** promptness, Ray, to insure promptness. Sophisticated people don't like to take risks, Ray. Example: When I go out for dinner I ask for the headwaiter. I tell him my guest and I want to be taken good care of. When you smile at someone, Ray, they'll smile back, they can't help it. When the waiter smiles back I'll hand him a £50 note. Before I hand over money, Ray, I feel it's polite to smile. I'm never disappointed with my service, Ray, never disappointed."

Lloyd's eyes are fixed on Raymius.

"So, I believe you have something that belongs to me?"

Raymius orders his whisky.

"Eh, The Macallan please, and twenty Embassy, mate. No ice, thanks."

The steward shakes his head.

"We don't do Regal, is Marlboro all right?"

"Marlboro Lights?"

"Coming right up, sir."

"Excellent choice of whisky, Ray. There's a twenty-year old, bring the bottle."

The steward nods.

"Right away, Boss."

Raymius watches him head off. Lloyd seems happy to discuss his merchandise in front of the staff. Raymius isn't. Once again Lloyd's eyes lock onto Raymius.

"Now, Ray, quote me happy."

"Mr Oakley..."

As Lloyd interrupts his tone becomes even more stern and direct. "Please, call me Lloyd, but let's dispense with the pleasantries and get down to business. Now! Tell me that my goods are in safekeeping."

The steward returns with a bottle of the Macallan, a packet of Marlboro Lights and two crystal glasses on a round silver tray. Raymius gets out his wallet. Lloyd raises his right hand.

"Not necessary, Ray, on me."

The steward nods and walks away. Raymius puts his wallet back.

"Much appreciated, Lloyd. Your goods are in safekeeping."

Lloyd remains silent so Raymius continues. "I just can't get my hands on them until tomorrow morning, sorry." Lloyd snaps, "Why not?"

"I'd rather not say. But I promise they'll be OK." Raymius definitely wishes he hadn't said 'sorry' or 'promise'. It sounds weak.

"I don't care much for what you'd rather, Ray, I'm looking for some reassurance. NOW! PLEASE! Humour me."

"Your goods are safe. I can't say where they are but I can have them for you tomorrow any time after 7am. I assure you, I give you my word."

"Can't or won't?"

"Won't."

Lloyd says nothing. He looks like he's attempting to read Raymius's mind. Raymius starts counting in his head again; this time he gets to 121. Eventually Lloyd leans back in his chair and smiles. "Well well, a man of his word, a rarity these days. OK, young Ray, if that's the way it is, then that's the way it is." Lloyd stands up, his face unable to conceal the expression of boredom.

"The Club opens at 11am for breakfast. I like to have my meeting with the staff and conclude all my business before the first punter walks through our doors. Be here at 7am tomorrow with my goods and I will be assured. I don't think we have to discuss what will happen if you let me down." Lloyd picks up on Raymius's slight hesitation. "Too early for you, Ray?"

"Eh, no that's fine," Raymius responds unconvincingly.

"You got another engagement tomorrow, Ray? Somewhere else more pressing that you need to be?"

"No, it's fine, I have a few bits and pieces but I can do them later. You can be assured, I'll be here at seven."

Lloyd turns his back on Raymius and walks towards Clare, who is still chatting patiently to the barman. He has a few words, pecks her once again on the cheek and then leaves. Raymius gulps his Macallan and pours another. Clare arrives back at the alcove.

"Well, that seemed to go well, I think he likes me."

She squashes her cigarette into the ashtray, hands Raymius an envelope and then lights up another. He notices her hand tremble.

"Well done, Ray, you're on the payroll now," she says as her eyes well.

"What's this for?" Raymius asks.

"Lloyd told me to tell you it's a tip."

Raymius puts the envelope into his jacket pocket. "Are you all right?"

"Just feeling a bit emotional. Don't ask."

"I'm feeling that I am over-staying my welcome. Are you coming?"

"Not right now, you crack on, Ray. I'll get a cab and join you in the Scotia shortly." She pecks him on the cheek, looks him in the eyes and nods.

Raymius smiles back and goes to find his way out.

fear *n* **1.** feeling of anxiety **2.** an unpleasant feeling of apprehension or distress caused by the presence, anticipation or perception of danger...

Clare and JJ head downstairs to the cellars. She feels like she's on her way to the gas chamber. Clare has only heard rumours but JJ knows firsthand what it might mean to take a trip to where the beer kegs live. She's witnessed this scene in a thousand movies. A single light bulb, a man battered, bruised and tied to an inanimate object. There's no one behind the damp walls to care and the civilised world is too far above to hear. The whimpers inside his hood are shared with only three sets of ears. Clare doesn't know him, JJ has never liked him and soon Lloyd will be the only one who knows the whole truth behind how badly Liam fucked up. Liam, who has developed too much of a fondness for food, wine and women, is well aware of how he's upset the boss, but now none of that matters.

Liam is squashed into a wooden basket chair. Although he's a big guy his feet are not touching the ground; this is because the legs of the chair are also not touching the ground. The chair is curiously resting on top of an aluminium beer keg.

Liam's left shoe is missing and his bare foot is experiencing more than the odd involuntary twitch. There's the smell of something that has been burnt. Beside the waste paper basket there's a large pair of industrial wire cutters, and the little stump where his big toe used to be is charcoal black. Clare feels the food slide back down her throat as she swallows and then takes a deep breath. Lloyd pours himself a glass of wine. He swirls the contents of the glass and sniffs at the aroma before taking a gulp.

"You see, Clare, it's not so much the pain as the anticipation of the pain that helps us find out all we need to know. Liam has tried to convince us that he is telling the truth. But of course we already knew what lie he was going to tell. So now he doesn't know what we know and what we don't know, so the only thing he can do is to tell us the truth, the whole truth, and nothing but... Because now, if he even forgets to tell us the slightest of details that we already know, we will have to assume that he's lying. And he also knows this will result in no mercy. Liam knows exactly what we must do to liars. He also knows that we must show mercy to those that tell the truth. Our whole system stands and falls on these two principles."

Lloyd continues as if he's still reading from the training manual for Investors in People. "You see, Clare, liars have to be made an example of. They have to die so horribly that nobody would even contemplate the possibility of lying to us. At some point real soon, Liam will be begging us to put a bullet in his brain and he'll be praying that we comply. However, at this moment in time he is in a phase we call denial. It's the ego, a self-preservation system, it's that little bit of you that still thinks there is a way out of this, it's the little voice that tries to pretend this really isn't happening. It's how a psychologist would explain how a person with throat cancer believes having just one more fag won't do them any harm. Its technical term is cognitive dissonance."

Clare looks confused. Lloyd just smiles and continues talking. "Anyway, that's why Liam finds himself in this position. It's so that we know when he gets the chance to talk for the last time, he'll use his opportunity wisely. We are helping Liam think things through."

Liam has an old coal sack over his head with a rope tied round his neck to keep it secure. He can hear everything, including the scraping noise that's coming from the beer keg. His senses are taut like a guitar string just before it breaks. But he doesn't need to guess what the scraping is because he already knows. He's played this game many times before but not from this perspective. That's why he is so keen not to topple. If he rolls forward, backward or to either side he'll crash to the floor and that's bad. Because he knows exactly what will happen next.

"You see, Clare, there are six rats in the aluminium beer keg that Liam's chair has been secured to and they are currently just as confused and frightened as Liam. If the keg crashes on its side they will move into a blind panic and start biting at everything, including each other, and although they will have no joy with the aluminium, once they discover the little round hole at the top of the keg they will eventually gnaw through the base of the wooden basket chair. Shortly after that they will discover Liam's anus and once they have squeezed through that they will eventually eat their way to freedom through Liam's stomach.

"Liam knows this is not a good way to go. It's terrifying, it's agonising and it takes a long time. While this is going on we will administer morphine to help with the pain and to stop him dying from shock. Also, a little heroin will help with the hell of hallucination."

Clare has seen and heard enough. "Why are you telling me all of this, Lloyd? Why am I being privy to your little torture scene?"

"Well, Clare, it really is very simple: I want you to understand that it's not good to lie to me."

"But I haven't lied to you, Lloyd."

"Oh, I know that. If you'd lied to me, darling, you'd be currently sitting in a basket chair balancing on top of an aluminium beer keg, with a hood over your head. I just want to make sure you're not tempted to, once I've asked you the questions that I need to. It's called a pre-frame."

Clare tries to hold back a gulp but can't. Her paranoia magnifies the sound in her ears. She's petrified but manages to hide it well. She does her best to look defiant before she responds. Lloyd likes strength, hates weakness; she at least knows that.

"Look, Lloyd, I respect you and all that but I don't need all this Dungeon-Master shite in order to tell the truth. I've got fuck-all to hide so whatever you want to ask, ask away and then I can get on with what's been a total cunt of a day and **you** can get back to playing with your chums." She lights a cigarette but can't keep her hands from shaking. Lloyd smiles like a proud father would if he were watching his daughter stick up for herself for the first time.

He sighs deeply before saying, "So, how well did you know the dead girl they found in Bothwell Lane that's been all over the news today?"

"Not very well. I met her a few times, we called her Emms. She was gorgeous without the make-up and came... originally from Newcastle, I think."

"Anything else?"

"What you want to know?"

"Everything."

Clare lights another cigarette. "She used to lap dance, at Peaches. She was found with enough heroin in her arm to kill a couple of phants."

JJ screws up his face. Lloyd smiles and says, "Elephants, JJ." JJ's face says, oh!

Clare continues. "From what I hear she hooked up with a punter who was into fantasy games, rituals, domination, all that weird shit." Clare tilts her head to one side and looks up as if she can actually see a movie with Emma in it. She carries on. "I thought she was a cokehead. Didn't realise she was into smack. I reckon she saw herself as being one of the 'beautiful people'. Always had a copy of Hello magazine in her bag and talkin' about 'one day you wait and see'. I guess she thought she was somethin'. I guess deep down we all delude ourselves wi' that. Poor cow."

Clare checks her cigarette packet. It's empty. She digs another packet out from her bag and tears off the cellophane. She offers JJ one.

"No thanks, Babes, I'm all right the now."

"Is that it?"

"That's it."

"Are you sure?"

"Positive."

Lloyd meditates for a while before asking his second question. "How does your friend Ray know Emma Burgess?"

Clare doesn't even think before she screws up her face and says, "He doesn't."

"What makes you so sure?"

"Cause only today I was talkin' about her and he was asking me if I knew her."

"Oh?"

"Well, if he did know her he certainly didn't let on. But he didn't behave like he knew her."

"And?"

"And fuck-all, that's it."

"So basically, Clare, he could've known Emma but you just don't know about it?"

"Yeah, Lloyd, I suppose so, but he didn't appear to know her and he's got no reason to pretend not to. But hey, for all I know you, Ray and JJ could all have been bangin' her."

Lloyd looks at JJ. JJ shrugs, seeming to be convinced that Clare is telling the truth. Clare has a wee think and becomes curious. "What makes you think that they knew each other?"

Lloyd nods to JJ and JJ responds. "We found his name on her mobile telephone."

Clare looks amazed. "What, Raymond Taylor?"

"Naw, just Ray," JJ replies.

Clare raises her hands, almost pleading. "For fuck sake, JJ, did it ever occur to you that there might be more than one fucking Ray on the planet?"

Lloyd interrupts, "Yes Clare, thanks, that did occur to us, but I don't trust fucking serendipity and so I just thought I'd practise a bit of diligence and ask you. You don't mind me doing that, do you, Clare?" Lloyd's tone is calm but peppered with menace. Clare decides it's time to wind her neck back in.

"Can I go Lloyd? I'm tired; I really have had a bastard of a day." Her eyelashes almost flutter.

"Show her upstairs, JJ, and bring me down an ice bucket, this is getting warm and it might be a long night."

JJ looks over at Liam. "You want a drink, Liam?" They all look at Liam, who is silent and isn't moving apart from his foot that's still experiencing the occasional twitch.

"Ah well, at least you tried, JJ. I think he might be in a huff."

JJ replies, with a big pleased smile, "Or... maybe the rats got his tongue." JJ and Lloyd giggle like two little boys who are about to pull the legs off a spider but want to finish their sweets first.

Just before Clare goes to climb the stairs with JJ she turns to Lloyd. "Was it a mobile number or a landline?"

Lloyd looks at JJ and nods. JJ responds, "Mobile."

"Naw, that definitely rules out Ray then."

"How's that, then?" Lloyd asks sarcastically.

"He's the only person I know who doesn't have a mobile, he's always needing to borrow mine and he's a fucking nightmare to get hold of sometimes."

Lloyd has that bored look on his face again. "Aye, OK Clare, thanks, darling. You try and have a better evening, OK?" He has another gulp of his wine and closes the door. JJ and Clare climb the stairs.

"So, Babes, are you staying for a while or will I get you a cab?"

"Thanks, JJ, but I think I'll walk for a bit, I can feel a bit of a head coming on, wrong time of the month and all that."

JJ holds up his hands. "Nae probs princess, already too much info. You stay safe, eh?"

Clare kisses him on the cheek. "Thanks JJ."

She leaves Janus and heads for the taxi rank at Asda. It's about five minutes' walk, but she's hoping she can flag one down before she gets there. She's not dressed for shopping. She takes a side street as a short cut to a main road where the Hackneys usually hunt for fares. She stays in the middle of the dark road to avoid the shadows and the puddles of slush on the pavement. It is still a typical Scottish winter evening. This means the possibility of at least three seasons in the same hour. There are no stars visible but a little bit of black sky and the moon pops its head occasionally from behind thick grey clouds. It makes their edges appear silver. The air is freezing and Clare's feet are already wet. The wind howls behind her. She looks back along the street as she nears the main road. On her right there are a few parked cars. They all have melted snow on their windscreens apart from one, a little red hatchback. As she turns the corner onto the main street she can see Asda in the distance like a mother ship in a sci-fi movie. An old man is on the same pavement walking towards her with a couple of shopping bags in one hand, a walking stick in the other. There is nothing else around other than the noise of the odd random car passing by. Monday night is obviously not a big hit for shoppers around here.

Some people are hard to faze. Some people aren't afraid of the dark. Some people don't do 'things that go bump in the night'. It's Clare's job to talk to strangers. His walk is slow but purposeful. Clare smiles back when he beams at her. He has such a warm face that she can't help herself. She's tempted to ask if he's lookin' for business but doesn't want to give him a heart attack **or** take his Building Society savings. Clare sees his red cheeks before he looks away. She walks on only a few steps when she hears what sounds like a yelp. She turns round. He's fallen and is trying to use the metal railings to pull himself back up. She rushes over.

"I'm OK, honestly," he says, looking embarrassed again. "Please don't bother, I'll manage," he assures her. "You have a kind face," he concedes, beaming another smile. *An old charmer*, Clare thinks.

"Let me help you with that," she says.

"It's no bother, honestly," he says.

"Kind face warm heart," she says.

"My car is just round the corner," he says.

"My name is Clare," she says.

"I don't like leaving my wee Volkswagen in the car park, Clare. I get confused. I forget sometimes. When I forget, I get all excited. The doctor says I shouldn't get excited, Clare." His voice is soft, slow, almost hypnotic. Clare hears the diesel engine of a Hack. She looks up and sees the bright yellow light engraved with the distinct black letters spelling TAXI but, more importantly, signifying it is for hire. She waves her hand instinctively. The cab's left indicator starts to flash, acknowledging contact and suggesting, 'wait there'. She turns to the old man, who is now on his feet and looking less feeble.

"Hang on till I speak to my cab and then I'll help you with your shopping."

"It's OK, Clare, I'll be fine now. Thanks anyway."

The cab screeches to the side of the pavement beside Clare. The cab driver's window is down.

"Where are yi goin', hen?"

"Scotia bar, Stockwell Street."

"Mon-well, time's money."

She turns to the old man. "Are you sure you'll be all right?" And then to the driver, "He fell a wee minute ago and his car is just roond the corner."

The driver asks, "Are yi wantin' a haun wi yer shoppin', auld yin?" They both look at the old man.

"No, honestly, I'll be fine. You are both very kind." He turns and walks up the side street. Clare jumps in the back of the cab and notices the driver is smoking. She pulls one out of her packet and holds it up for the driver to see.

"Mind if I...?"

"Nae probs, hen, you crack on."

joke n **1** something or somebody that is laughably inadequate or absurd, **2** cause of amusement anything said or done to make people laugh eg dressed up the dog in a hat and sunglasses as a joke **3** funny story, anecdote or piece of wordplay that gets passed round and repeated, **4** not to be serious, trying to be amusing rather than being earnest **5 beyond a joke**, having become a serious or difficult matter...

Raymius leaves Janus and happily takes the fifteen-minute walk back to the Scotia bar. He takes stock of the day so far. The early start, the news about Emma, getting arrested, getting released, recovering the merchandise, getting an early birthday card, clean sheets. He smiles as he fingers the envelope in his back pocket. Receiving his first tip. And, how could he forget, getting chatted up by the Red Head, Amanda. No one has shown that much interest in him in a long while. Some things can wait until tomorrow. Some things can't. Birthdays are here to remind us life should be celebrated. It was also good catching up with an old friend.

Raymius walks onto the suspension bridge still thinking back to earlier this morning where he'd seen his one-legged friend on the river. In his mind's eye he once again watches the letter he'd written to his mum float down the Clyde. He remembers the day she died. He won't cry, even though he wants to. There have been enough tears. He couldn't even make the funeral because of work. What employer justifies keeping a son from his mother's funeral? Tony, his therapist, had suggested he could exorcise a lot of demons by simply writing a letter and then posting it. Raymius doesn't have the address for the hereafter and reckons that's maybe why it isn't working. Tony didn't find that funny, he'd just smiled understandingly the way therapists do. It's a cunt when the only person you have to talk to has the power to say you're a danger to yourself and others. It's a cunt when the one person that is willing to listen has more important agendas than you. It's a cunt when the only fucker that's willing to listen properly works for the system. It's just a total cunt. It all seems such a long time ago but it was only first thing this morning. He looks up at the church clock. A new day and last orders in two hours. The usual suspects will be melted by now but hopefully Amanda is still warm – although Raymius is under no illusions and realises this might be because Noonan is currently attempting to fire into her pants.

Raymius looks in awe at how the lights from the Broomielaw illuminate the court house and then splash onto the river. He stops dead centre on the bridge and looks east towards Lanark. The song of the Clyde springs to mind. He then looks west to where the sun has set hours earlier and where a few years ago life was so different in sleepy hollow.

"Aahhh-naw!"

He hears what can only be a mad junkie. One of those 'awe-naws' that suggests it's run out of chocolate, dropped its ice cream or stood on a shite. These are big issues for lost souls that are strung-out. Raymius snaps his neck towards the offending commotion at the end of the bridge he'll shortly be heading for.

Fuck, this is all I need, he thinks. Raymius doesn't relish the idea of nursemaiding some smack head. Then it comes again.

"Aahhh… Naw! The scream sounds like Eliza Doolittle in My Fair Lady.

"How-naw? How-naw? I jitht waant a hole-iday, a wee hole-iday, at-th awe. Awe-ma-life uh've only ever wantid wan thing. A hole-iday. Tenner-eefe mibbey, a thwimmin' pool, an-a-bit-a thun. Awe-ma-life, it-th no much ith-it? How Naw? Eh? Fur fuck-thake ma-an, how-no?" And, then there is sobbing.

Raymius's immediate response is to pish himself laughing. The crowing of this bilious doo and its detestable boo-hooing is almost hilarious until Raymius realises the shell-suit is a man, a very big man. He's somewhere in between a docker and a heavyweight wrestler. In his left hand, hanging like a Colt 45 in an old western, is a bottle of Buckfast. The golden screw top is missing along with three quarters of the contents. Raymius reckons it could easily have swallowed the cap without noticing. He puts the humour on hold when he notices the XXXL red, white and blue shell-suit staring his way.

Raymius turns to face him and takes a moment to smirk to himself. He's seen this still in a thousand spaghetti westerns. But once again he puts the humour on hold as reality kicks in and reminds him he doesn't have a gun. Raymius focuses on the big guy's face. Showtime! Giant Haystacks' look of surprise changes from disorientation into embarrassment. His face is soaked with tears and he is unquestionably mingin' on both counts. Like a big kid he turns and runs away. His body language resembles someone who's been caught in the act but this guy has 'victim' beaming out from him, like a neon sign. Raymius feels guilty because the big drunk's misery helps Raymius feel better about Raymius. It's easy not to laugh, though, once you realise that this degenerate's lack of ability to articulate will keep him in the gutter. And his only parole will be when it's time to put him in a box and plant him in the ground. Raymius shakes his head in pity.

"If you're listening, God, give the cunt a break. Whatever it costs, send him on holiday and take it out of what's coming to me. Give him his wish and stop his bleating. It's not dignified, it's not right, is it?"

Oops! Talking out loud again, Ray. Tony won't be impressed. Raymius pauses for a while to enjoy the peace and quiet again. He gathers his thoughts and looks once more at the church clock. *Time, Tony, like a snowflake, disappears while you're wondering what to do with it.* Ah well, fuck it, at least the whisky's kickin' in. His mind wanders back to another conversation with Tony about why going to the pub is important for men.

"Have you ever thought about why pubs are so well frequented, Raymius? To have a beer, catch up with friends, escape from your other half? For most men the pub is more than that. Women like to chat about their problems. Men, on the other hand, need an activity. Ministers, Rabbis and the Catholic Church would do better if they frequented 'the local' to practise their priest-craft. All you have to do is look at men watching 'the footie' on Saturday. When their team scores, notice how many of them are in desperate need of a hug. So tell me, Raymius, why do you go?" Raymius has several reasons for spending so much time in the Scotia Bar. Some of them are obvious, but some are not.

It's still Scotland and still winter. The night sky is now littered with stars and the moon is occasionally poking its face from behind silver clouds. The air feels clean and crisp. Raymius stops for a moment to watch a fox crossing the road; it walks deliberately, like a Lord Provost who belongs there. There's no wind and the trees seem fast asleep. Raymius turns his collar down and lights a cigarette when he sees the lights of his local. Once again Bono blares out of the Jukebox and into the night.

Raymius pushes open the saloon doors. Another cheer explodes from the 'usual suspects' sat in their corner. Déjà vu. Michael Anthony Noonan for the second time that night pushes his chair back and stands up with both arms outstretched, his smile switching on like floodlights.

"Raymondo, you're back. You miss me?"

Raymius's eyes narrow predictably.

"Naturally." Both men laugh as they shake each other again. Raymius moves closely to the side of Noonan's head.

"Where's the Red Head?"

Noonan gestures towards the bar. "Gettin' served, dude. Let's have a word while she's busy, eh?"

Raymius's eyelids close momentarily while he thinks and then nods his head in agreement. Before they both venture back to the booths, Noonan hands Dillon a twenty and stares at the two Donnies.

"Look after Amanda till we get back. Yoo hear me?" They all agree with their heads bobbing like three little chicks in a nest. Donny Malone turns to Donald McGee and whispers in an exaggerated posh voice, "Oooh! Look after Amanda till we get back." They all wait till Ray and The Man are out of earshot before they start laughing.

As they're walking past the bar Noonan establishes eye contact with the barman, gives him the peace sign and then turns to Raymius.

"So, amigo, exactly why are you here tonight?"

"I like the taste of alcohol."

"No shit, is that a fact?"

"Aye Man, that's a fact. So who the fuck is Lloyd?" Raymius surveys the room while Noonan rolls himself a cigarette and thinks. Big Donny Malone is scratching his blond flat top as he starts one of his infamously long funny stories. He's telling the joke about when the Pope visits the little island of Corsica and tastes his first Phucka fish. Raymius can make out every single word Big Donny is saying from across the room. Not just because he's heard the joke a dozen times but for the same reason he knows that the black BMW outside the front door is owned by the guy opposite him and the guy's girlfriend is telling the guy to call a taxi because he's had too much to drink. It's the same reason he knows the registration of the black BMW and the two cars parked on either side. It's the same reason he also knows it's a minimum of thirty seconds to get from where he's sitting to the furthest exit. Noonan lights his roll up.

"The Jamaican who runs Janus?"

"Aye."

"Someone not to be fucked with, he's heavy duty, amigo."

"Is that a fact?"

"Aye amigo, that's a fact."

"So back to what we were talking about earlier before we were so beautifully interrupted. What's the chat on the Red Head, Michael?"

Noonan turns round and looks up above his own head. Raymius looks confused.

"What the fuck you looking for, Michael?"

"Sorry mate I was checking to see if there was a sign above my head saying Citizen's fucking Advice Bureau?"

"Aye awe right, Michael, calm down, very funny," this time it's Raymius's turn to flare his nostrils. After a brief pause they both burst out laughing, seeing the funny side. The laughter subsides. As their drinks arrive, they clink glasses.

"Slainte."

"I'll tell you what, amigo."

"What?"

"There's stuff you want to be knowing about Clare Stephens, Ray."

Raymius's nostrils start to twitch again. "What the fuck has Clare Stephens got to do with the fucking Red Head, Michael?"

"Calm down, amigo, trust me, this is stuff you want to know."

Raymius's nostrils are in full flare again. He puts down his glass, sits back and folds his arms. Noonan raises his arms in defence. "OK, Kemosabe. I'll tell you what. I'm going for a slash, when I get back you tell me if you want to hear what I've got to say. If you don't then I'll let it go, but trust me, Ray, you want to hear this. And I want you to hear it. Deal or no deal?" Raymius nods. Noonan wanders off to the toilet.

Ray's seat has an elevated position with a view of both exits, both toilets, the door to the office and the entrance to the cellar. Raymius knows about the difference between cover from view and cover from fire. He knows the partition his arm is resting on will stop a 9mm round from a handgun but not a 7.62 full metal jacket from a rifle. At this moment there is no threat from anything or anyone but something is going to kick off tonight, he can sense it, he can smell it, he can taste it. Raymius feels cold blood will be spilled this evening. Although he knows this might be paranoia and he may be wrong, so far he's fed up being right. Raymius surveys the room again, the booths, the snug bar itself, the lounge where the band usually play but where at the moment the artists and poets are doing their thing. Then there's the family area that is used for feeding time during the day and where at the moment is his elevated position, giving him the best view, with the best cover from fire. As Noonan sits back down they both watch Noonan's brother H returning from the bar laden with drinks and joining back in to big Donny's story about the Pope and the Phucka fish.

"What's up with your brother? He looks unusually quiet, Michael."

"He's waiting on a delivery tonight so he's a wee bit strung out. Although he's a head case, amigo, when it comes to work it's business first and party later so he'll have a few quiet pints and stay low profile until the deal is done. But H, amigo, is not the question, is it?"

"Look, Michael, don't treat me like a fucking halfwit. What is it that you want?"

Noonan strokes his chin and thinks for a minute. "I just think if you get hooked up with this Red Head it'll be a mistake. It appears to be something that you've obviously not thought through."

Raymius reaches over with his arm outstretched, offering Noonan his hand. Noonan's hand responds. Raymius's grip is like a vice. Noonan forces a smile.

"OK, Michael, answer me straight: Are you interested in the Red Head?"

Noonan looks Raymius straight in the eyes and grins. "Absolutely."

"Then let's not complicate the situation with bullshit and stories about Clare."

"But you're getting the wrong idea amigo, Clare..."

Raymius interrupts, letting go of Noonan's hand and raising his own up like he's about to give an oath.

"I get it Michael, I swear, I get it." Raymius looks across to where Amanda is still sitting engrossed in the Pope and the Phucka fish story, which is now in full swing. He lowers his hand and gestures like he's laying out his stall. "The Red Head, Kemosabe, is all yours. As of this moment, I'm not fucking interested, OK?"

"Fair enough, amigo, fair enough." Their glasses clink once more.

"Slainte." The moment is cut short as they both look to check out a Beckham clone walking past the family area with a bimbo on each arm. They sit down at the only table that's free. The table that's immediately adjacent to where Big Donny Malone is still pontificating with the Phucka fish tale. Wee Dillon can't help himself.

"Ho big man, you're a dead ringer fur that English cunt that does the footie. Y'knaw that wee fucker eh, Barry Lineker?

In sayin' that you're much better lookin' and aboot twice his fuckin' size. There canni be much porridge left when you're done big yin, eh?"

Big Donny stops the story for a moment to put Dillon right. "His name is Gary Lineker, ya daft wee prick, and he disnae look anythin' like him." He then whispers to Amanda. "Apart frae the sticky-oot ears." Amanda bursts out laughing. The big guy grins, underwhelmed. Amanda gives the bimbos her best dirty look as they give her that up their-own-arse look. Both the big guy's girlfriends force a polite smile and they all start to suspect they might be the wrong people in the wrong part of Dodge.

> **Allegory** *n* **1** symbolic work, **2** a work
> in which the characters and events are
> to be understood as representing other
> things and symbolically expressing a
> deeper, often spiritual, moral or political
> meaning **3** the symbolic expression of a
> deeper meaning through a story or scene
> acted out by mythical characters…

Most stories begin with the end in mind. Raymius always felt that if he were going to write a book he'd end it with the beginning in mind. Today started off with the usual shite and no doubt it will end with the usual shite. Michael Anthony Noonan had rattled his cage with regards to Clare. WTF was all that about? Maybe he is hanging on too tight. Maybe he is flying too close to the edge of the envelope. Maybe it's time to become an instructor at Top Gun. Maybe it's time to just call it all a day. Like Vinnie said at the end of his autobiography: It's been emotional. As he looks about and tries to take it all in he thinks about that cartoon he loved when he was that wee boy. Deputy Dawg. Once again, WTF was all that about?

Michael shakes his head. "What a fucking tool."

Raymius almost pleads with his hands. "Which one?"

Noonan can't help but agree. He uses his head to point in the direction of Beckham and his bimbos. "Captain Rugby, you know him?"

"Somewhat, Kemosabe, somewhat, but first things first. Are we clear the big orange bird is now all yours? Let's not complicate matters any further. You have my full attention, Man. What should I know about Clare?"

"She's one to be watching, Ray."

"Aye and, why is that then?"

"So, you basically want me to spit it out, Ray?"

Raymius looks at the outside of his left wrist and imagines a watch that is not there. He then gives Noonan his big doe eyes and still feels that he does not have any other appropriate response.

Noonan shrugs. "What do you want me to tell you?"

"Man, you said, and I quote: 'There's stuff you want to be knowing about Clare Stephens, Ray.' So if you and I are using the wrong crypto, get the right fucking crypto or get to the fucking point, mate."

"Crypto?"

"Aye, Crypto. Cryptography. Michael. You do know what cryptography is, Marine, don't you?"

"Yes, Ray, I know what cryptography is, but I don't know what you think is going on here."

"What I think is going on here, Michael, is that you are on a fishing trip."

"Fair enough."

"Cool beans, so cut the crap and tell me the stuff I need to be knowing."

Noonan leans back, palms facing towards Raymius. They exchange glances, sizing each other up, until Noonan decides that he needs to be the one to blink first. If for no other reason than there is enough shit going on tonight without them both falling out. There is drinking and shagging to be done.

"Look, Ray, there are things that you don't know about me. There are things I don't know about you. I've been wanting to chat to you for some time but it never felt like the right time."

"So does it feel like the right time now, Michael?"

"Well to be honest and fair, it doesn't, but let's jump in and see how warm the water is."

Raymius leans back, necks a suitable quantity of his amber ale and nods his head. "Over to you."

"Earlier on, Ray, I explained the whole road-sweeper scenario with Orange-burd. I really meant it, mate – she does have her love beacons targeted on your good self. But I really like her and in many ways she's kind of my type. When I say I like her I mean I aim to shag her and take it from there."

"Go on."

"It seemed like an appropriate moment to give you the heads-up on Stephens. I realise I've hit a raw nerve and I do apologise for that. I also didn't think you'd hang on to this like a mental dog with his favourite bone. But there you go."

"Fair enough."

"I know that you and Clare are pals but I realised a wee while ago that Clare Stephens actually cares for you, and I don't mean in a road sweeper sort of way. I mean in a way that a sister would look out for her brother. Stephens is street smart and she's mixed up with some really heavy fucking individuals. I'm guessing that you know what she does for work."

"Yes, Michael, I know Clare's a working girl."

"Again ,Ray, being totally up front. This is my neck of the woods. I take a keen interest in everyone and what the fuck is going on. I have no idea what you are all about. But I know when someone is a dick and I know that you are not. I'm guessing you've made a few mistakes and like most people have your story, but like I said you seem to me to be an all right guy."

"Awe shucks, thanks Man, I appreciate that, but with respect is there a fucking point to all of this?"

"OK, OK, OK… I can't figure her out, Ray. Something doesn't add up and when it comes to checking her out, it only goes so deep and then nothing. I think she might be a cop."

"Clare?"

"Aye, Clare. So if you are into any dodgy shit just be aware of any odd questions she asks you."

Raymius bursts out laughing. Noonan is not impressed.

"Is that it, Man?"

"That's it, Ray."

"Cool beans, Man. Noted."

Man offers his hand. "We cool?"

Raymius takes it. "We're cool, but before we crack on with the rest of the night, Man, let's just do the bunnit-bit. Dog or a cat?"

"Is this some clever psychometric shit?"

"Does it matter, Man? Y'know Top Cat, Deputy Dawg, Bewitched, Scooby fucking Doo? Dog or cat? Go with it Man, indulge me."

Noonan smiles. "CAT Man. That's definitely me, as in cool as a cat."

Raymius retorts, "How about as complicated as a cat, or even curious?"

"How about intelligent as a cat?"

"How about as cute as a cat as in computerized axial tomography?"

Noonan rubs the hair on his forearms.

"How about a domesticated carnivorous mammal with soft fur and a short snout?"

Raymius adds "…and retractile claws."

"You've got me all wrong, Ray. I was really heading more towards Cat as in the north American jazz enthusiast way of suggesting, well, you know what I mean."

"Aye, Michael, I know what you would like me to think but to be honest Man I don't really know what you mean. I never really thanked you for the key to your pad but then again we never got the chance to chat about your visitors after H spent all that time in intensive care."

"That all got sorted, Ray. No longer a problem."

"You never asked me why I handed you back your key."

"Figured you got somewhere better."

"Fair enough."

"Did you?"

"Aye."

"Nice pad?"

"Aye, bangin'."

"Well, let's face it, mines and H's wasn't exactly the Ritz, was it? If you were still dossin' there I wouldn't be thinking that you were one of the brightest bulbs on the tree, mate."

"Fair enough. You got yourself another place, Man?"

Noonan laughs. "What do you think?"

"Anyway, Man, you haven't told me what Cat you identify with. What's your cartoon world?"

"Ah, so that's where you're going with that?"

"Aye! What's it to be then? Bewitched? Top Cat?"

"Clarence from Daktari."

"Good choice Man. Big cat."

"Aye big cat." He rubs the hair on his arm again. "Soft fur. So, since it looks like none of us are going to ask the obvious question, do I get a go at cats and dogs?

"No problem Kemosabe, go for it."

"What's good for the goose, Raymondo. You choose. Cat or dog?"

Raymius looks like he's just pulled the fourth ace from the deck in stud poker.

"I'm a dog, Man, BIG DOG."

"What, as in domesticated carnivorous mammal that typically has a long snout, acute sense of smell and barks, howls or whines?"

Raymius smiles. "Cute, Man, are you saying that I have a big nose?"

"Well it's certainly longer than mine. So is it because you hang onto bones like a mental dog, or maybe you just like dogging?"

"Happy to hang onto the things that matter to me, Man, but I've never really got my head round the whole voyeuristic nature of outdoor shagging."

"Don't knock it till you've tried it, my friend."

"Fair enough, Man, so I'm sure you can understand what I mean when I say to you – if you can't run with the BIG DOGS then stay on the porch."

"Is that a threat, MATE?"

"Definitely not."

"OK, cool. I'm guessing Scooby Doo, then. Big Dog."

"Sorry Man, guessed wrong. DEPUTY DAWG.

"Noonan raises his hands in surrender. OK, you got me Sheriff." Raymius doesn't take the bait. "To be honest and fair, Ray, it's not a cartoon I ever really got into. So why don't you give me the headlines."

"Well other than the Deputy, Man, my favourite characters were two of the varmints, Muskie the Muskrat and Vincent Van Gopher."

"Like I said Ray, DD is not ever anything I got into. So what's your point?"

"Well, most of the storylines involved DD protecting his shit from Muskie and Vince, battling with some of the peculiar indigenous population and, of course, trying to please his boss. Pig Newton."

"That doesn't seem too tasking on the brain, Ray, not exactly my kind of literary masterpiece. You still watch a lot of DD?"

"Aye, very good, Man. Not lately but recently got a new TV and a wee bit more time on my hands so looking forward to finding out where I can get a hold of those re-runs. I love those re-runs."

"OK, fair enough, that's intriguing – maybe I'll give it a go. What's the hook?"

"Well, Man, most of the crimes committed by Muskie and Vince were never really treated seriously by DD. In fact, he was on friendly terms with both of them most of the time. Except of course when he had to perform his duties as a lawman and keep them from causing trouble."

"Cool beans, Sheriff, so basically DD is a big softie?"

Absolutely, Man, you got it, the biggest of softies. DD would pal around with Muskie and Vince just as often as he would lock them up in the jailhouse. When the varmints weren't locked up or involved in mischief the trio would engage themselves in their all-time favourite pastime."

"What was that then?"

"Fishing."

"Any particular type of fish?"

"Of course."

"What?"

"CAT."

"Fair enough then, Ray, we should definitely chat some more. Can I assume we are now using the same crypto?"

"Couldn't agree more, Marine. I have enjoyed our conversation."

"To be continued, then?"

"To be continued."

Cryptography n **1** the science or study of the techniques of secret writing, especially code and cipher systems. **2** the procedures, processes, methods, etc., of making and using secret writing, as codes or ciphers. **3** anything written in a secret code or cipher **4** from Greek kruptos; 'hidden. **5** Historically used in warfare, cryptography is now used routinely in computer networks. **6** This often pits the desire of individuals and businesses to keep Internet information private against the need of government to investigate crime and terrorism

Raymius lowers his head uses thumb and middle finger to massage his eyebrows. He manages to hold back his amusement but not his grin.

Noonan asks, "What is it now, Ray?"

"The Beckham tribute is Gavin Brookfield, Michael."

"And?"

Raymius looks up and over at the speakers.

"Sunshine on Leith, Man, the Proclaimers and a sense of irony."

They both listen to the lyrics.

> *'My heart was broken, my heart was broken*
> *Sorrow... Sorrow... Sorrow... Sorrow...'*

"Sounds interesting, Ray."

"Aye Man, long story for another time."

"To be continued then?"

"To be continued."

They both laugh. Raymius knows Brookfield from days of old. Mummy and daddy sell swimming pools and are part of the Greenock business elite, a group of individuals who wouldn't look out of place in Salem's Lot. Gavin was at the Hogmanay party the night Raymius broke Thomas Andrews' nose for shagging his ex-missus doggy-style on the bathroom floor.

> *'My heart was broken, my heart was broken*
> *Sorrow... Sorrow... Sorrow... Sorrow...'*

Although Brookfield was one of the four rugby players who eventually managed to pull Raymius off the bleeding mess, he probably won't recognise Raymius now. But Raymius angles himself just to make sure.

> *'My tears are drying, my tears are drying*
> *Thank you Thank you Thank you Thank you...'*

Raymius and Noonan watch Brookfield as he passes by on his way to the bar, give each other a knowing grin and continue to look discreetly with interest.

The barman barks at Brookfield. "What can a get yi, big guy?"

"A Pernod and orange. Hmm, and, a Gordon's with tonic please, make them both large ones if you would, my good man?"

"Yi want ice in them?"

"That would be lovely, thank-you."

"And what are yi-havin yersel' big fella?"

Gavin almost sneers at the comment as he produces a twenty from his money clip. "The P&O is for me, old boy."

The barman holds back his desire to laugh. "One of the ladies not having anything then, sir?"

"Do you do coffee?"

The barman gestures toward the coffee machine on the bar about a foot away from Brookfield. "Aye." The barman smiles understandingly. He's too much of a professional to let Gavin know what he thinks, and what he thinks is that he's in the company of an Olympic wank. Also, a fleecing opportunity is rapidly approaching.

Brookfield continues obliviously, "Can you do me a latte for Siobhan? The old girl's driving my rig home on account of us stuffing Pollok today on their own turf. She feels I should chill out, it all got a bit ugly today, tempers fraying and all that, but hey, that's rugger for you. If you can't stand the heat, get away from the Aga, eh?"

The barman scopes the bimbos again. They both look about nineteen.

"Aye sir, I guess so. So, you're a rugby man then?"

Brookfield flashes his ivories and says proudly, "Captain, Greenock Wanderers."

The barman put on his best 'wow' face. "Pollok at home, sir, impressive." Although Pollok is only a few miles away, the barman doesn't even know that Pollok has a rugby team. He hands the drinks across the bar and, smiles again.

"You've obviously had a big day, sir, you go and sit down and I'll bring the lady's latte over."

Gavin hands across the crisp twenty-pound note that looks as if it's been ironed. "Marvellous, have one for yourself my good man."

The barman beams a contented grin.

"Don't mind if I do, very kind of you, sir. I'll have a Peroni if that's OK."

It isn't a question. The barman already knows it's OK, that's why he picks the dearest designer beer they have.

"Ah, a man with taste, good choice. We're over ..." Gavin is attempting to point with both hands full as the barman interrupts.

"That's all right, sir, I know where you are."

'While I'm worth my room on this earth
I will be with you...'

241

As they both watch Brookfield return to his seat Raymius notices an old man appear at the far away exit. There's something about him that catches Raymius's attention.

He might be fooling the rest of the pub, but not me, Raymius thinks.

Noonan has just finished expertly rolling another cigarette. He lights up.

"Are you OK, amigo?"

Raymius doesn't respond because he's still studying the 'old guy'.

"Are you fucking OK, amigo?" The Man repeats, firmly this time.

"Aye, sorry Michael. The old geezer that's just walked, in do you know him?"

"Nope, never seen him before, probably a tourist."

"What, with Asda shopping bags?"

"Aye fair enough, good point, but nope, never seen him before. I'll ask the boys at the bar, they know every cunt and anyway the bar is now three-deep so, it's probably quicker if I go and get the drinks in. Check out the bar staff, they've got that stressed-oot-tae-fuck look."

Raymius goes into his pocket for cash.

"It's awe right, amigo, I'll stick it on your tab we can square later."

"Sound."

Noonan goes to the bar. Raymius adjusts himself again so that he can keep tabs on the mystery shopper. It's the little things that give you away; the way you hold your cigarette, the way you light it, the way you smoke it, the way you act casual and uninterested but are actually surveying the room systematically. The way you stay in focus a little longer on certain parts of the room, like the exits and the elevated positions. Raymius looks away just before the old guy looks his way. Raymius pauses long enough and then glances back to watch the old guy complete his survey. *This guy is well trained but what's he doing here?*

His attention switches back to Gavin Brookfield getting his apology from the barman as Siobhan's latte eventually turns up. The barman is explaining that the bar has become unexpectedly busy. Gavin sits back down, satisfactorily appeased.

Raymius's attention is now becoming unexpectedly busy; the old guy, both exits, the entrance to the office, the door to the cellar, the guy with the black BMW, his girlfriend's advice, which he's not taking, Brookfield, Big Donny telling the Phucka fish tales to the other Donny, Dillon, Amanda and Michael's brother H.

> *'While the Chief puts sunshine on Leith*
> *I'll thank Him for His work*
> *And your birth... and my birth*
> *Yeah, yeah, yeah, yeah, yeah, yeah'*

Although Raymius finds it exhilarating, he also finds it easy. Just like watching a bundle of CCTV monitors, you get used to what it all looks like and only have to focus in when an image on the screen changes. Or looks like it's about to change.

Raymius notices that Noonan is getting served and asking about the mystery shopper. He lights an Embassy Regal as he focuses back on the usual suspects. H is watching Gavin Brookfield return from the bar. Raymius could tell earlier that H doesn't like anything about him. His physique, his clothes, his manner, his education, his accent, his girlfriends, his drinks, his hairstyle, his smile and not least his place in life. Gavin Brookfield represents everything that H fucking detests about life and it reminds H of what he's never had and will never get. They are poles apart and it will always be that way, except for one thing. Gavin Brookfield is in H's house. The Scotia is somewhere Brookfield really must mind his Pints and Quarts.

Like a lot of big guys Brookfield can be really clumsy sometimes. People don't normally give them any bother though because, well, they're big guys. But big guys don't get to use the big-guy get-out-of-jail-free card in the Scotia Bar. As Brookfield makes his way back to his table with another tray of drinks and nibbles he smiles the way he normally does, assuming that everybody is noticing him. The punchline of the Phucka fish story is about to come to a head. Big Donny bawls out.

"… so he sits back and lights up a big Cuban and says, 'You cunts are awe-right'."

Brookfield has no idea of the joke that has just been delivered but the whole table is falling about laughing and the two bimbos who have been listening in can't hide their amusement either. Brookfield feels a wave of paranoia wash over him and as he moves towards his seat he forces another grin in the direction of the Two Donnies. By mistake he treads on H's foot.

"Ahh. Fuck!" H cries out.

Brookfield stumbles but manages to keep his balance. He puts the tray of drinks on the table and turns around.

"Jeeze-us. Fucking hell, my man, watch your big feet, will you?"

Everybody at H's table stops laughing.

H just giggles, hunches his shoulders up to his ears and shakes his head as if indicating to an auctioneer, 'no thanks'. The Two Donnies get the message that no action is required. H puts both hands up. He then produces a smirk before sniggering the next line.

"Sorry, mate."

Brookfield detects the sarcasm.

"I'm not your mate, fella, and you should take more care about where you put your feet, people have to pass y'know. If I'd have fallen someone might have got hurt and I don't think you realise that. Also, I find your attitude a tad cavalier."

Raymius is watching every word from across the pub. He sighs as he puts his hand over his eyes and thinks to himself, *just, shut up Brookfield, for fuck's sake, just shut up.*

H is thinking the same thing but his patience is starting to wane.

"I said, I was sorry big man, so don't push it, awe-right?"

Brookfield takes a step towards H. The Two Donnies look at each other in amazement. Dillon gets up and says, "Ma round lads," and fucks off quick style to the bar.

They all respond, "Aye, awe right, wee man," in unison but none of them look round because all their eyes are fixed on Gavin Brookfield. Raymius prays again in the confines of his mind, *just shut the fuck up, Brookfield, don't do it son, just walk away, just walk away.*

The Captain of Greenock Wanderers Rugby Club can't help himself.

"Look here my man, maybe that tone works with your chums..." he looks towards Amanda and pauses for effect, "...or your slapper there."

Everybody within earshot seems to cringe and then hold his or her breath as Brookfield continues. "I'll have you know, I, my man, am not intimidated that easily."

H lights a cigarette and offers Big Donny the packet. Malone takes three; one for himself, one for Amanda and one for the other Donny. H then offers Malone his Zippo. They all light up. While this is all happening at no point does any one of them take their eyes off the Captain of Greenock Wanderers. The scene is beginning to resemble Gunfight at the OK Corral.

H stands up and speaks in a slow, soft, deliberate tone.

"Right, ya big cunt, too far."

Brookfield is looking down at H, who even at 5ft 10in is about six inches shorter and considerably slimmer than himself. Brookfield moves his right foot back and adopts a karate stance.

"I have to inform you that I am trained in martial arts..."

H doesn't expect this, it totally takes him by surprise. He can't stop himself. He bursts into laughter. Even Amanda, who up until this point has been stunned into silence by the whole episode, has an uncontrollable fit of the giggles. Whoever the Proclaimers fan is has another of the choices start on the Juke Box. Irony. The Joyful Kilmarnock Blues.

> *'I'm not gonna talk about doubts and confusion*
> *On a night when I can see with my eyes shut'*

Raymius and Noonan look at each other and read each other's minds. Brookfield's ego is dented and he now has no doubt about what everyone is laughing at. They are both too far away to do anything.

Siobhan pipes up, "C'mon Gav, just leave it, let's go."

Brookfield looks round at both of his acquaintances and puts his hand up.

"In a minute, ladies." He turns to face H. He's about to say something he's rehearsed in the mirror a hundred times. "I'm warning you. If you continue with this aggressive tone I will have no option but to assume that you intend violence, and I will take the initiative. I will strike you first. Terminate your aggressive and insulting behaviour and sit back down."

Raymius arrives at the bar. "Call an ambulance."

The barman is in still pause. "What?"

"Call a fucking ambulance, now," Raymius blasts again.

The Two Donnies are studying the situation and contemplating what part of this big guy they're going to attack first. Brookfield is waiting for everyone to quieten down so that H can deliver his retort. The cabaret has the whole pub's attention and all the laughter has started to subside. Brookfield doesn't get to utter another word. As the barman picks up the phone and punches in the necessary numbers for the emergency services, the giggles also stop as if everyone apart from the Juke Box is now paying attention and waiting for the curtain to be raised for the last act of the Panto.

'But I'm not gonna talk about it
On a night when I can see with my eyes shut
No I'm not gonna talk about it
On a night when I can see with my eyes shut'

H drives a thick, glass-bottomed ashtray square into Brookfield's face. There's a crunch but the ashtray is unfortunately still in one piece. The second blow is to the top of Brookfield's head. His knees give way just before H is about to deliver the third lightning blow. He doesn't have to. Like a building that's just been demolished with explosives, Brookfield collapses into a crumpled mess. While the Pernod and orange crashes down and the latte soaks Siobhan, Brookfield's skull smashes on the wooden floor. His eyes roll back. For a moment everyone just looks, no one says anything. Brookfield stirs, groans and tries to get onto his knees. He's in an environment where he should just play possum. Even shell-suits know the script with wounded animals. Before H or the Two Donnies can react, the smallest most unlikely assailant, the one with the most to prove, enters stage left.

"Hawd that, ya big posh cunt."

Lots of people see what happens but now there is nobody who is going to say. It's like when you see a dog shite on the street, you don't want to get too close in case you can smell it and you certainly don't want to stand in it.

Dillon leans over and thrusts five inches of steel into Brookfield's back, completely missing the ribs but ripping straight into a lung. He then stabs him twice in the neck. As Brookfield becomes panic stricken his arms flail erratically and he starts to drown in his own blood. All the bimbos can do is scream and cry. Raymius, who is now standing over Brookfield, looks at H before he turns to face Noonan who is right behind him.

"Low fucking profile?"

Noonan shrugs as Raymius fixes his stare on Dillon.

"Give me the knife, ya wee prick."

"Wha-at?"

"You heard me, just give me the fucking knife."

Dillon hands over one of those wee commando knives with the serrated edge that are bought mail order. Brookfield has lapsed into unconsciousness. Raymius expertly cradles his head and makes to cut a surgical incision in his throat. Siobhan screams, "NO, STOP!"

"I'm going to puncture his windpipe, Siobhan. There's an ambulance on its way." He holds up the plastic shell of a Biro. "If I don't put this into his windpipe before they get here, he won't be able to breathe. If he can't breathe, he'll die. Do you understand, Siobhan?"

She nods her head, still sobbing. Raymius makes the cut and inserts the makeshift tracheotomy tube.

Raymius then grabs a bumper packet of crisps from the table and empties the contents. He puts the plastic crisp packet over the punctured lung. It immediately makes a sucking sound. He grabs Siobhan's hand and places it over the crisp packet.

He says. "Watch and listen, OK?"

She says, "OK."

"When he breathes in you'll feel it suck the plastic, that's good. When he breathes out relax your hand slightly so the air can get out but keep the plastic in place. Got it?"

He helps her with the first few breaths.

She says. "Got it," and nods her head.

Raymius smells Clare's perfume and looks up.

"Where did you learn that?" Clare asks.

"Vietnam."

"Cute."

Noonan can't help but comment either.

"Aye amigo, impressive."

Raymius gives Noonan a knowing nod and grabs the jumper round Brookfield's waist. He collapses the damaged lung and wraps the jumper around the tube like a big light blue doughnut, holding it in place and soaking up the excess blood. He summons the remaining bimbo.

"You, hold this here. Hold his head like this. Don't move him until the paramedics get here. He's going to be fine."

Noonan hands Raymius a bar towel and he wipes his hands clean. "Thanks, Man."

Noonan nods. Raymius grabs Clare's hand.

"OK hen, time for us to go too.

"I just got here."

"No shit, let's go."

Noonan is at the table issuing instructions to the Two Donnies.

"Get H up the road pronto." He grabs Amanda. "Show's over, sweetheart, let's get a cab."

In his peripheral vision Raymius sees the old guy look over just before he disappears out of the furthest away exit, slipping off into the night.

249

jo3m

"Shit," Raymius says.

"What the fuck's up now?" Clare asks in her to-the-fucking-point eloquent way.

Raymius leans his head to one side as he hears the sirens.

"I'll tell you later, let's GTF."

He starts laughing.

"What's funny?"

"You like the Proclaimers, Clare?"

"Definitely."

Raymius looks up at the speakers.

"Listen."

> *'It's over and done with, it's over and done with*
> *It's over and done with, it's over and done with'*

> **missing** *adj* **1** not present in an expected place, absent or lost **2** not yet traced and not known for certain to be alive but not confirmed as dead. **3 go missing** to disappear or become lost untraceable or unaccounted for...

Sheena stops and looks round her hotel room. For a moment there isn't a sound. She is mentally running through her checklist of things to remember and last of all is the final visual once-over. Sheena is what you call a frequent flyer and pretty much always on the go. She places her matching suit-case and flight bag down on the aluminium carpet runner that separates her room from the hallway and walks back across the room to open the white gauze curtains. Although it's a smoking room she still feels the need to let some air in. She opens the latch of the top window and feels the cold outside against her face. Walking back now to the centre of the room she stops when her shins touch the mattress. She gets down on one knee with her hand firmly grasping the duvet. A smirk appears on her face while she surveys under the bed and then reaches for what she's remembered. She walks back to the door, pops open her suitcase and drops in little red panties with tiny white letters on the waistband boasting the brand Calvin Klein. *Too expensive to lose and part of a set after all,* she thinks as the smirk turns into a giggle, playing once again the movie in her head of how they ended up there.

Sheena walks down the hallway and into the lift. At recep-tion she notices the exhaust fumes emitting from the tailpipe of her cab right outside the swing doors. The porter doesn't have to ask, he knows the drill. Sheena nods her head and smiles a thank-you. As she climbs into the back seat she presses the picture of a telephone on her mobile and notices the cabbie has a cigarette in his hand. She puts her phone on the cold leather seat beside her and pulls one of her Embassy Regal King Size out of its packet. She holds it in the air high enough for the driver to see it in his rear view mirror.

"Mind if I...?"

"Naw, hen, you go right ahead, fill yer boots."

"Thanks," she says.

"There's nae ashtrays in the back though, ye'll huffti use yer windae."

Sheena winds the window down just enough. As the mini-cab whisks her off to the airport she looks up the hill at the Police College and lets out a large sigh. She's been fortunate to get such an early flight to London at such short notice. She'd hoped to stay in Fife for a little longer. Traffic permitting she'll be at Scotland Yard before tea break. Because of several recent developments, her Friday meeting with Michael Shepherd now can't wait. Or at least that's what her boss had said in his message last night. She looks over the cabbie's shoulder and winces as butterflies start to flutter in her stomach.

"Excuse me, is your clock the right time?"

"Naw, hen, five minutes fast. How, ur you in a rush fur yer flight?"

"No," she replies with relief, "we're fine, I'm just expecting a phone call." Sheena's mobile starts to vibrate.

"There yi go hen, somebody's keen, eh?"

Sheena takes a larger than normal puff from her Embassy Regal, widens her eyes and nods with agreement at the eyes in the rear view mirror.

"No shit," she says pressing answer and then raising her tone to, "Morning, Mike."

"You on schedule?" the voice asks.

"Bang on," she replies.

"What's your ETA, Sheena?"

"Depending on traffic should easily make tea and buns."

"Listen, Sheena, I can understand why you might not be over the moon coming down at such short notice…"

Sheena interrupts. "I'm coming to see you on my day off, Mike, of course I'm over the fucking Moon.

"Well, you'd better wipe your diary till Friday, Sheena."

"I'm supposed to be in Dundee tomorrow, Mike. I faxed the letter yesterday to the University and need to get it authenticated but if I can…"

It's Shepherd's turn to interrupt. "Wipe your diary till Friday, Sheena," he says again, emphatic this time.

"OK, Mike, I get the point, what can you tell me?"

"It's shit, not love that's in the air."

Sheena switches to solution mode. "Do I need to prep anything for our meeting?"

He hesitates for the slightest of moments. "Eh, no Sheena, you just get here as speedily as possible."

"So who's on the guest list?"

"Sorry, you'll have to wait till you get here."

Sheena understands the veiled speech and can guess the rest but is determined for more information to confirm her anxiety. "Are any of the departments not going to make it, Mike?"

At the other side of the phone Mike smiles at her cleverness. "No, Sheena, they're all going to make it."

Sheena gulps before she responds. "OK, Mike, no probs. See you when I get there."

She'd given Mike the big, brave I'll-take-everything-in-my-stride response but now her stomach is doing the tango. Because they are speaking on an unsecure line, she knows not giving her a heads-up on the guest list can mean only one thing: VIPs. And, if all the departments are going to be represented, shit, the P-fucking-M could be there.

Mike Shepherd is the CCLO for the Government with every department that you can think of and some that you can't. The Chief Coordinating Liaison Officer has the ear of Whitehall, the Met, Special Branch, MI5, MI6, SO1, the military and any of the foreign agencies such as the FBI, the CIA and Interpol. He might not necessarily be the guy in charge but he is pretty close to being the guy who always knows what the fuck is going on.

Sheena's stomach eventually stops dancing and by the time she boards the aircraft she's ready to do her usual and doze off as soon as she gets in her favourite seat over the wing. She's snoring before they take off. But, for some reason, whether it's a domestic flight or long haul she always wakes up just before the Captain says, "Cabin crew prepare for landing." On the ground she whizzes through arrivals and her black Hack gets her to the Yard for 9.20am. It's a bright sunny morning in the nation's capital, a complete contrast from the recent torrents of rain and the green rolling hills of Fife. Mike Shepherd is, unusually, waiting at reception for her.

"C'mon, this is no longer research, have you got your ID?"

Sheena nods and has too many questions in her head to know which one to ask first. She manages to mumble out, "Where are we going, Mike?"

"The boardroom," he says, matter-of-factly. As they make their way through the Special Operations room amidst all the packets of cream doughnuts and iced buns, she reads a few of the slogans and messages on the various mugs left about on the desks of officers who essentially live in 'OPS'. I'M NOT FAT, I'M JUST NOT TALL! ; THE WORLD'S GREATEST DAD.; C'MON YEE REDS. And, one of her favourites of all time,

SEX is not the answer, sex is the question. On the other side, the mug reads, *YES is the answer.*

Sheena's doing all of this to take her mind off walking into the boardroom, that first few seconds where everyone becomes quiet and focuses their gaze on you, the proverbial spotlight. That's when you smile and pretend you're calm and in control but everybody already knows that you're absolutely fucking shitting yourself. The lift goes ding and the doors slide open, they get in and Mike pushes a six-figure code into the control panel before pressing for the 12th floor. Sheena takes a deep breath; she's never been above the 5th floor. Mike continues, "Anthony Brookes is the NSA to the PM. It seems our Prime Minister's National Security Advisor has taken up a new hobby of tearing people new arseholes and has asked for a briefing with all the heads of department. The ones that can't make it in person will be watching on the video conferencing facility."

Sheena asks the obvious question. "So what's all the excitement about, Mike?"

"You aware of the Helen Carter missing persons case?"

Sheena doesn't have to think about this. "Yeah, of course, she's our very latest might-be victim that fits the profile for an Alpha Omega abduction. She was last seen in Glasgow last year on Christmas Eve. So, how come this missing person has become a concern for the PM's National Security Advisor?"

Mike's eyes flick up to the left as he accesses the memory of how he'd been briefed. "OK, you've asked so here goes; the PM was chatting to the French Prime Minister, probably about Champions League football – apparently they're both big Arsenal fans." Mike turns his hands palms upwards and shrugs sympathetically as Sheena's screws her face up. She now gets that all he's doing is regurgitating what he's been told. Mike Shepherd continues with the brief.

"The conversation goes to American football and then supposedly to the OJ Simpson trial. They then have a heart-to-heart about secrets that are kept under wraps for years and years. Eventually the French Prime Minister starts talking about their Secret Service file on Alpha Omega. Our PM asks his National Security Advisor to brief him on the same. Unfortunately for all concerned he hasn't ever heard a peep about any such file or any such individual but tells his boss he'll find out ASAP. That was yesterday. Now, our PM's NSA has found himself a new hobby."

Sheena screws her face up once again in bewilderment. "Am I missing something here, Mike? What's the connection with Helen Carter?"

"It turns out Helen Carter is the PM's niece."

They get to the 12th floor and the doors ding open.

"But Mike, that would rule Helen Carter out of Omega's MO. If he really has nabbed the PM's niece then he's broken his own rules and made a mistake."

They stride along the passageway. "That may well be, Sheena, but right now we have a Prime Minister who wants to make himself an expert on how we deal with missing persons."

Sheena stops dead like a hedgehog on the highway. "Oh fuck," she says staring at the two uniforms guarding the door of the boardroom. One of them grins, the other one speaks. "You've to go right in, Ma'am, they're expecting you."

Sheena cocks her head to one side as she addresses her boss. "Mike, who's giving the briefing?"

"If you study a subject for over three years, Sheena, you are regarded as an authority. If you study something for over seven years you are regarded as an expert in that field. How long have you been working project Alpha Omega, Sheena?" Sheena pauses before she answers. "Over eleven."

"The PM's National Security Advisor doesn't do bullshit. Don't waffle, keep to the point and speak your mind. We don't have a profiler who knows project Alpha Omega as well as you do. You're the expert here Sheena – act like it. You come here today highly recommended."

"By who?" she says, almost hysterically. It's Mike Shepherd's turn to take a deep breath. "By me, Sheena, by me."

Sheena holds all the air in her lungs as she walks into the boardroom and surveys the sea of faces looking at her. They all finish their conversations. The room goes quiet. Mike Shepherd's voice is strong and authoritative, like the Speaker in the House of Commons.

"Gentlemen, Sheena Buxton."

As Sheena scans the suits and the visual buffet of uniforms it reminds her of many movies she's watched over the years. All the decision makers cluster in one room round an electronic image of the planet to discuss what move Doctor Evil will make next and what options they have to overthrow their adversary and save the day. Worldwide battleships and cruisers. She nods graciously while she examines the faces looking at her and wondering what on earth she has brought to the party. One face in particular sticks out, an anomaly. He is somehow out of sync with the rest of the hierarchy and looks like a prisoner of war, a refugee, a white-faced junkie who has been washed, shaved and prepared for court. He looks like he needs a good feed and a good sleep, and his appearance also suggests that he's borrowed his big brother's suit. Sheena realises that she's been staring at him for an inappropriate length of time. Her gracious grin turns to embarrassment when he smiles back like he's just read her mind. She takes her place next to the screen and gestures to the Yeoman who is working the PowerPoint equipment. She picks the file up from the table and thumbs through the summary of slides available. She pulls the whiteboard into the centre of the floor and, with a red felt-tip marker, begins to write.

αΩ
Alpha Omega

"Alpha is the sign for infinity and the first letter of the Greek alphabet in its lower case. Omega is the last letter of the Greek alphabet in its upper case. When both of these letters are placed together in this way it signifies the start and the end of all things. It has historically been used to symbolise Jesus or, in some cases, God. For the purpose of this brief I will refer to the subject by his Special Branch file name, Professor O.

"Gentlemen, we live in a world where individual parts can sometimes be worth more than the whole. The same way a car can be broken down in a scrap yard and sold in pieces for more than the cost of the vehicle, so too can a person. There are those in underground organisations who still trade in flesh for a number of reasons; prostitution, pornography, medical and chemical research, organ transplants. And, of course, the ever-increasing world of making snuff movies." Sheena pours herself some water. The weight of the glass jug wavers in her hand and for a moment; everyone in the room thinks she's going to drop it. She doesn't. She continues.

"We have identified data to conclude a correlation in several hundred missing persons over a thirty-year period. Even our most conservative estimates make Omega potentially the most prolific serial killer in history and, as I'm sure you've already been briefed, this highly sensitive information has the possibility of creating a national fucking nightmare." She thought that adding an expletive might help build some rapport with her male audience. No one flutters so much as an eyelash. She continues. "One specific and significant yet peculiar factor is that we have never, not once, ever managed to recover a body."

Sheena drinks the water from her glass and refills it, this time more comfortable with the weight of the jug. No questions are forthcoming; she suspects some of the audience have heard all of this before but there are some who seem a little awe-struck. She continues.

"It is pointless putting any of the professor's photographs on screen since there are so many conflicting descriptions for this individual. He's changed his appearance and has re-invented himself more times than Michael Jackson. For a period of over three decades he has apparently headed various underworld activities. But when we get close to any of his operations they get closed down and anybody who could have possibly identified him vanishes. There is a possibility that he has some sort of 'New Deal Strategy', an idea similar to that of our American colleagues' FBI Witness Protection Programme, except for villains. It's possible that he organises plastic surgery, new identities and a brand new life. However, even if this is true it's only for the minority since few ever get to see him and not many want to. Gangsters are not stupid. They all know that soon after you meet Omega, you vanish.

"But this too may be just a front. He may simply have them all cleaned. Because what we do know is that to date, not a single one of our villains has ever turned up, anywhere. And, although reduction of the criminal fraternity is a positive by-product, it still leaves us back at square one in regards to the identity of Omega. It would be easy to feel embarrassed about discussing this case because although we know what he's done and what he's capable of, he is essentially a ghost. I can at least give you a description of Santa Claus. I cannot give you a description of Omega. He's like a submarine that disappears over the horizon and leaves only an oil spillage in its wake. This guy is a broken window, graffiti on the wall, a tyre track in the mud."

Still no questions are forthcoming. Sheena is beginning to think that before she got there they were told to leave questions till the end. *Fuck it,* she thinks. "Any questions, gentlemen?"

A few unfazed glances are exchanged between various parties throughout the room. The NSA speaks. "You carry on, Ms Buxton." She looks at Mike Shepherd. He gives her one of his approving nods. She feels better.

"As I'm sure many of you gentlemen are aware, since the tearing down of the Berlin Wall and the disappearance of the Iron Curtain, certain facets of organised crime have flourished. The international criminal has developed much quicker than the international authorities, which are still hampered by politicians and civil servants and swayed by public opinion. Many of the international atrocities that are regularly committed are kept secret in order to maintain the average person's peace of mind. If the average Joe or Jean really knew the risks they were faced with each time they stepped out their front door, they would simply stay at home."

The NSA no longer seems happy with the way proceedings are going, and after massaging his forehead for the briefest of moments he asks, "Ms Buxton, do we have any hard evidence that can prove this person actually exists?"

"The short answer, sir, is," Sheena stops for a moment and gulps some water. "No, we don't."

"So he could be a group of people or an organisation who for multiple obvious reasons are invested in keeping this myth alive?"

"Yes sir, that's right. And although we know this myth has been alive for at least thirty years, our International Psychological Profiling Units have only been researching and working on it for just over a decade. But irrespective of whether it is an individual or indeed a group of individuals, it is evident we now have a different breed of monster, a predatory entrepreneur that has perfected a method of getting rid of the evidence. But with the greatest of respect sir, remember the best trick the Devil ever spun was to get some people to believe that he didn't exist. Do you believe in the Devil, sir?"

Sheena notices Mike Shepherd lowering his gaze and he too now feels the need to massage his forehead. She decides to carry on just the same. "The majority of communications with Omega are carried out via couriers, letters, emails and telephone conversations, which when traced always lead to the same place – nowhere. It's a bit like chasing rainbows in winter, sir; there are footprints until the sun also melts the snow."

The NSA speaks again. "Is there anything you can tell us, Ms Buxton, that can help us find him?"

"We know he pops his head above the covers for years at a time. We also know that he disappears for years at a time. And as I mentioned earlier we can only guess the reason he disappears is that he has either accomplished his aim or his operation has been compromised. He never takes chances and he never makes mistakes. We never know if he's around and we only know he's been here after he's left. Omega is so thorough there have been times we've wished he was on our side."

"I'm sorry, Ms Buxton, but I'm afraid that's all just a bit too vague for me. Could I ask you to be a little less dramatic and a little more specific?"

"Sir, he normally informs us he's around and then seventy-two hours later he tells us he's gone." Sheena takes another gulp of water.

"And, Ms Buxton, how exactly does he do this?"

"He writes and tells us, sir."

"And when, Ms Buxton, was the last time he wrote to us?"

"A senior police officer received a letter from Omega on Sunday evening." Sheena checks her watch. "That was around thirty hours ago. At this moment the letter is still to be authenticated, sir, but for what it's worth I believe it to be genuine." Sheena pours another glass of water from the jug. She is starting to crave a cigarette. "It's worth pointing out, sir, that all our handwriting experts agree that all the letters so far have been written by the same author."

"So then, Ms Buxton, your conclusions."

"My conclusion, sir, is that we've got forty hours to close the stable door."

"And what are your recommendations?"

Mike Shepherd interrupts immediately, before Sheena has the opportunity to respond. He raises his arm like all of a sudden he desperately needs to go to the loo. "Sir, if I may?" The NSA makes a gesture with his hand for Shepherd to continue. Mike Shepherd stands up and starts to resemble the ringmaster just before he announces the Big Top's main act. "Gentlemen, Daniel Harris."

Minus the threads and a few days without a shave or a wash he'd look like anyone you'd see sitting outside a bus or railway station begging for change. Sheena's jaw drops and a lightbulb goes off inside her head as the white-faced junkie look-a-like she'd noticed earlier gets to his feet. He has an air of confidence that reminds her of a Royal Signals Colonel she once knew and he too sounds like any Conservative MP you'd hear on the front benches of the House of Commons.

"We support Buxton's conclusions that Omega will generally operate until either his aim has been achieved or his operation is compromised. Nothing surprising about that really, bog standard SOPs for any covert op." He notices some of the suits squint as he pauses and pours a drink from his own glass jug. "Sorry gentlemen when I refer to SOPs I am of course referring to standard operating procedures. I'll do my best to refrain from any more usage of TLAs, ehm...

three-letter acronyms, ehm… jargon." He takes another drink and looks at Sheena as she smiles back, clearly indicating that she already knew exactly what he meant.

"We have identified several patterns over the last decade. The average time Omega operates for is two years and the average time of hibernation is eighteen months. This ties in with the standard amount of time for corrective plastic surgery to take place and heal. We believe he has been up and running now for less than twelve months. However, over the last two weeks in certain geographical locations the criminal fraternity has rapidly diminished and several villains who we believed maybe Omega's farmers are among those who have disappeared from our screens. We believe it is too short a duration for him to have concluded business and therefore believe that somehow his operation has been compromised and he is about to bolt. We did reckon we had around one week tops to find him before he once again vanishes but since we had authenticated the letter Buxton is referring to," his eyes narrow as he once again glances at Sheena apologetically, "on Sunday evening, we now also support Buxton's conclusion that the stable door needs to be shut within thirty-six-hours. The question is, which stable?"

The NSA takes off his specs and pinches the bridge of his nose with thumb and forefinger. "What are your recommendations, Harris?

"Well, sir, because of the time constraints this will require us to concentrate all our resources in the one area; we'll only get one shot at this. He may think he's a magician but we've seen his tricks before and it doesn't matter what smoke and mirrors he uses, this time if we move quickly enough we'll have him. The majority of activity has been around the London area so basically if we lock down everything around the M25 perimeter and then reduce the circle, he's ours."

Buxton can't hold her tongue any longer. She bangs the table with her hand as she stands up in protest. "Jesus, gentlemen, I know we're pushed for time but Christ, are we maybe being a little over impetuous and gung-ho? Can I suggest perhaps a more balanced approach than two up the middle, one back and bags of smoke?"

She looks at Mike Shepherd and realises that when he said speak your mind he didn't mean that. Shepherd's nostrils flare as he looks skywards, hoping that the Enterprise is watching and is going to beam him up. The NSA is halfway between amazement and bewilderment. He'd love to play with this woman for a while if only he had more time but he doesn't, so he switches to his political tone.

"Ms Buxton, we are not looking for problems now, we are looking for solutions. Do you have any?"

"Sir, may I address Mr Harris directly?"

"By all means."

"What makes you think he's in London, Mr Harris?"

"Four years ago, Buxton, we started hiding SO1 units under the covers as moles. It's a bit like the strategy counter-espionage agencies employed during the Cold War. Each unit has two members, one male and one female. These are operatives who are highly trained and specialise in long-term undercover operations. They are a bit like the classic sleepers you read about during the days of the good old KGB. They know about each other but work independently. Generally, all operatives on the ground know if there are any other units working on the same operation. This is the one crucial element where Operation Hide and Seek differs from anything we've ever done before. And, it is because of this, ehm, sir, that you were not informed of its existence. This way we can authenticate every bit of information we receive, just the same way as psychologists use double blind experiments to prove scientific theory. It's maybe now clichéd to the point of annoyance but it is on the highest level of ehm, need to know. And, well basically, ehm, if you don't ask then you don't need to know."

The NSA tries to hide his fury, without success. But he realises there is no point in venting his venom at the messenger. Harris pauses and waits for the NSA's wave of frustration to bear fruit or wane. "Go on, Harris, go on," urges the NSA, now totally aware that every single minute counts.

"The idea was to infiltrate underground criminal organisations from different angles at ground level and effectively get promoted through the ranks. It's the biggest undercover operation that we've ever embarked on and in order to maintain the integrity of the operation none of our operatives know the magnitude of the operation. So although we have SO1 units in the same city, on the same op, ehm, they don't actually know about each other. So far we have not suffered a blue on blue but it is in this instance a risk and a possibility. To get to the point, and I suppose to answer yours, Buxton, we therefore have operatives reporting on operatives who don't actually know about each other and this is of course the double blind authentication process that I mentioned a moment ago. So at the risk of becoming repetitive, we believe he has been up and running for around twelve months, in the London area." Harris takes a large gulp of water and refills his glass.

"So *at the risk at sounding repetitive*, Harris, what makes you so sure he's in London?" Sheena demands. "What makes you so sure he can't operate from outside London? I'm sure you're aware that he's done that before. What makes you so sure he's not somewhere else?"

"I'm sorry, Buxton, I can understand your frustrations but you are simply not authorised to get any more detail than this. We are confident we can pin the location of Omega if we have sufficient resources."

"Do you place any SO1 units in Glasgow?"

Harris looks at Mike Shepherd. Shepherd nods.

"Yes."

"How many?"

"Two."

"Two personnel or two units?"

"Two units."

"So that's four operatives altogether?"

"Correct."

"What's their reporting procedure?"

"I'm sorry, Buxton, but you're not authorised for that."

Sheena holds up her hands. "OK, OK." She pauses and thinks for a moment. "When was the last time you heard from them?" Once again Harris looks at Shepherd. Shepherd sighs before he nods with approval.

"We had two SO1 mole units working under the covers in Glasgow. We lost a female operative about a week ago and the same night your letter arrived she turned up dead in an alleyway. The male half of that team has failed to call in today."

"How long is he overdue?"

Harris looks at the round analogue clock on the wall. "Just over an hour now."

"How long has he been in active duty?"

"A considerable length of time, and yes, he is one of our most experienced operatives. And to answer your next question, no, he has never failed to report in on time before."

"And I suppose you think all of this is just fucking coincidence?"

"Sheena!" Shepherd has heard enough. The NSA is looking a little confused. Sheena sits back down. Harris finishes his water and pours another glass before he continues.

"Ms Buxton, as you know, if Omega was involved we would not have seen our SO1 operative again, she would not have turned up anywhere."

"What about the other unit?"

"We are considering pulling them in."

"Can I ask why?"

"Well frankly, some time ago we identified an individual in Glasgow who we believe has been involved in the snuff industry for a considerable time. We thought he was potentially one of Omega's farmers but as we have all already agreed it doesn't fit with the MO. People disappearing, yes; bodies turning up dead, no."

"So tell me, Harris, how the hell can you rule Glasgow out when the letter was delivered there?"

"Don't you think that's just a little thin, Buxton?"

"Don't you think he knows we'll think that's thin, Harris?"

"C'mon, Buxton, on the balance of probability..."

Sheena butts in again. "On the balance of probability, Harris, we didn't even know about Omega for two decades and for the last ten years you haven't even had a sniff of what he looks like. He's the one who has always been at least two or three moves ahead of us. So at the risk at sounding repetitive, again, what makes you so sure he's in London? What makes you so sure he can't operate from outside London? And, what makes you so sure that this potential farmer of Omega's hasn't gone renegade and disobeyed orders?"

"All this is still a bit thin just because of where the letter turned up."

"I think, Mr Harris, you're forgetting the main reason we're all here today." Harris smiles and folds his arms before sitting down. "And why's that, Ms Buxton?"

"Helen Carter went missing in Glasgow."

"As we've agreed, this is not the typical MO for Omega. His victims are usually selected very carefully and he's not stupid enough to target a celebrity's niece. If what you say is true and he has made an error, both Helen Carter and the farmer will be cleaned."

It's Sheena's turn to cross her arms and as she sits down she looks first at the NSA and then at Mike Shepherd, before returning her gaze to Harris and saying emphatically: "Exactly." Sheena's career-move performance is based on nothing more than a hunch. Although what Harris is proposing is logical and concentration of effort is a sensible priority, if the farmer in Glasgow has not been cleaned yet, he will be, which means Omega will visit Glasgow before he disappears under the covers. It's just a hunch and it's wafer thin. But when you have three things on a to-do list, what does anyone normally do first? That's right, the easy thing. Not Omega. He will always follows the path of most resistance. She's sure of it, at least enough to try to get them to commit some resources north of the border.

The NSA stands up to bring the meeting to a close. "Mr Shepherd, your conclusions."

"It depends, sir, on what the main objective is. Is it to locate and lock down Omega before he disappears again? Is it to save Helen Carter if she hasn't already been cleaned? Or is it to make sure that the lid remains tightly on this so that the public are kept in the dark but are able to go about their daily business without the extra stress of mass hysteria?"

"Well, Shepherd, as always the objective is win-win."

"I'm sorry, sir, at this time there are insufficient data to support any conclusions that might result in a win-win."

Just like in the Batman movies a red light starts to flash on a phone next to the NSA. He unconsciously looks up at the video conferencing camera before picking up the receiver. He listens for a few moments before he responds.

"Yes…of course… I will, sir… Yes, if you say so, Prime Minister." Click. He replaces the handset and addresses the audience who are waiting like information-starved puppies. "OK, gentlemen, that'll be all." The suits and uniforms start to filter out like disgruntled fans at a concert that's just been a flop. "Ms Buxton, if I could have a moment?" It isn't a request and Sheena knows that.

As Mike Shepherd files out with the rest of the supporting cast he walks past her and whispers into her ear. "Christ, Sheena, I know I said you were the expert here but fucking hell. Look, come straight to my office when you've got your new arsehole, there's more." He's grinning as he walks off, holding back his laughter.

The NSA waits until the last of the suits and uniforms leave the boardroom. The door closes behind the last one and all of a sudden it feels like talking to teacher after class. "Now we're on our own, Buxton, I can be frank and I'm now pretty aware that I don't need to ask you to be..."

Sheena interrupts, despite appreciating his mellower tone. "I'm sorry, sir, but..." It's the NSA's turn to interrupt. "Sheena." The NSA puts his finger to his lips like he's about to tell his daughter a secret. He sits on the desk, pulls out his cigarettes and offers her the packet. Sheena glances at the video conferencing camera and notices the little light at the side is still green.

"No thanks," she says.

The NSA flashes a broad Hollywood smile. "It's OK, Sheena, the boss knows that we both smoke."

"No thanks just the same."

"I understand you play pool and that you can be a bit of a hustler?"

"I'm not that good, sir, but then again neither is the competition."

"I'm a politician, Sheena, which means I like to keep all my pockets covered. The PM wants you to take your hunch to Glasgow. If we instruct the remaining SO1 unit to stay in play, will you go up there? This of course, as you can understand, will be unofficial." Her butterflies start to flutter once again. The NSA continues. "As you and Mike already know, if this story gets out and some career journalist suspects there is a Professor Moriarty that's been on the loose for over thirty years, the missing persons help-line will effectively melt. So the public and their peace of mind is always the official priority.

"However, the PM is a human being and any uncle will always look out for his niece. Helen does not fit the normal profile but if she hasn't been abducted by Omega then she's been kidnapped by someone else or is simply missing. As you know there is no ransom note and you can take it from me Helen is not the kind of girl to just run off. So, we are not interested in whether or not she has been abducted by Omega, whether or not he's made a mistake, whether she's been cleaned or has less than forty hours before she is. We deal in results, Sheena. So to hell with what you know, tell us what you think. If it were your niece, what would you do?"

Sheena's butterflies are now doing Olympic gymnastics. She gets the whole unofficial bit but also realises that this has just become much more than her biggest career move. This is no longer about being right, it is about, as the NSA has spelled out, getting a result. She takes a deep breath. "OK Sir, I'll have that cigarette now." As she lights up she nervously glances at the little light on the video conferencing camera. It's still green. She takes in a lungful of smoke before starting.

"I think we've got a farmer who's gone maverick on Omega. Omega will know this and take his time to have him cleaned along with any mess that's been made. But this means that he'll be around to make sure all the ends are tied up before he vanishes off the screen. Omega is always a few steps ahead of us, I don't know how but he always is. So if we're committing all our resources to London he'll probably know this. Christ, he probably thinks that he's engineered it that way. So while everybody's chasing ghosts in London everybody else connected with him in Glasgow will disappear, including the PM's niece. I say let Harris carry on with what he's got planned but keep an eye on the farmer in Glasgow and I'll bet that Omega turns up."

"So will you go, Sheena?"

"Aye sir, I will."

The NSA flips open his mobile phone. Sheena squints up at the camera in time to see the light change from green back to red.

"OK, Mike, I'm sending her up to yours. She's going north, tell her what she needs to know." The NSA flips his mobile shut and gives her a look that reminds Sheena of when she told her dad she was going to be a cop. "Good luck, Sheena," he says.

"Thank you, sir," she says instinctively. She walks out the boardroom almost in a trance. She pulls the door shut behind her. The click brings her back into the moment.

"Went OK then, Ma'am?" It's the uniform on guard who was grinning earlier. She replies with a nod and a resigned smile while thinking, *Fuck, if you only knew.* The uniform walks with her to the lift. He leans in and punches in the security code.

"It'll take you to any floor you want now, Ma'am."

"Thank you," she says to his back as he marches back to his post. When she gets out the lift the journey to Mike's office is a bit like that daily car journey you make unconsciously where you don't remember any of it. She knocks on the door and walks right in to find Mike sitting with a small round gentleman in a grey pin-striped suit. He stands up and offers Sheena his seat.

"You'd better sit down, Ms Buxton." He hands her a light brown Manila file. "I'm sorry this is all a bit James Bond,

Buxton, but I am duty bound to remind you that all the information in this file is protected by the Official Secrets Act. It is strictly and exclusively for your eyes only." Just in case she hadn't understood the instruction, the Ministry with its usual belt and braces approach had two words stamped in dark red on the front: TOP SECRET. She opens the file and reads his name. As she reads John Ribbon's Special Branch File, she's glad she's sitting down.

> **clean** *n* **1** unadulterated containing no foreign matter or pollutants **2** free of problems or difficulties **3** complete and unqualified **4** with no flaws **5** containing few mistakes or corrections **6** played, fought or won with strict compliance to the rules **7** *v* prepare a dead animal for cooking by removing its entrails **8** v to rid something of incriminating evidence…

Vincent leans forward and presses the aluminium buzzer. A voice blasts out of the intercom.

"Who is it?"

He leans forward again.

"I'm here to see your boss."

"Who is it?" the voice asks again.

"I have an appointment to see your boss."

There's a pause before the voice replies.

"Hang on a minute."

Vincent takes a step back and removes a bar of chocolate from his pocket. He tears at the wrapper, exposing the rich, milky interior. He breaks off a few chunks and pops them into his mouth. He enjoys the smooth, creamy texture of his favourite treat. He then presses the speed dial function on his mobile phone. He lets it ring three times before ending the call. Seconds later, his mobile vibrates. He answers it immediately with a jovial, "Good morning, Professor."

"I'm sorry, Vincent, I don't have any time for pleasantries this morning. Are you there?"

"Yes, Professor, I'm just about to go upstairs but I thought I'd check in just in case anything has changed."

"Thanks Vincent, I appreciate that. However, it is situation no change. Text me when the job's finished."

Vincent hears the click and smiles as he turns his phone off and stores it away.

The Professor checks the time and sets the alarm function on his mobile. The professor likes routine. He will do twenty-one minutes of yoga followed by sixty-three minutes of deep meditation. After that he'll read. He prefers to clear his mind before he puts intelligent thoughts in there and gets on with the task of meeting the day. He has only just settled down to read when he is disturbed by an unsolicited knock on his office door. He checks the time and calls, "Come."

She turns the handle and walks in. He peers at her for the briefest of moments from behind his reading glasses.

"Sit."

She sits in a standard-issue red leather Chesterfield. He continues to browse at his own pace through a French translation of Mein Kampf. He holds it cradled in his right arm and turns the pages with the fingers of his left hand. He ignores the pages for a moment to remove his glasses. He holds the frame delicately in his fingers and taps the stem against his short white teeth. He forces a grin but still says nothing.

Siobhan for a sharp second thinks she can hear the sound of his stare until she realises what she's hearing is her heart and veins working overtime. All of a sudden, maybe this isn't such a great idea. She's not usually lost for words but has a momentary feeling of being struck dumb. Siobhan Finch is the envy of her peers. She's top copy for the sycophant fraternity. The girls want to be her pal and the guys want to be in her pants. It's not just because she's great to look at, intelligent and has a celebrity dad. Or even that her family are minted. She has an air of superiority that gets things done. She's got charisma, charm and that whole attractive personality gene. She's the type of person you enjoy being around; she oozes natural magnetism. She doesn't even think twice about what she had planned to do this morning. She gets something in her head and that's pretty much it. In many respects she truly is daddy's little girl. Since she was a toddler he's drummed it into her head, the code.

"You see it, honey, you want it? You go for it."

She feels mesmerised, paralysed, excited. His small eyes must be dark brown but they look black. Every little hair on her body stands to attention and presses against her clothes. She can't bear it any longer.

"Sir, I know you don't…"

He raises his hand and again she has the feeling of being struck dumb. His voice is cultured but has a steely rasp, an edge to it that reminds her of a master butcher sharpening his knife. The professor considers her as he carefully places his spectacles on the desk, pouts his lips and presses his index finger against them.

"It's Miss Finch, is it not?"

She nods.

"Chanel eighteen."

"Pardon me?" she asks.

"Chanel number eighteen, Miss Finch, you are wearing Chanel number eighteen. The mingling of rose, ambrette and musk, intended to evoke sensual opulence. Isn't that how they market it, Miss Finch?"

Again all she can muster is a nod.

"Good grades, Miss Finch, in fact excellent, probably my top student. So let me see, what would motivate you to interrupt me, in my study, thirty minutes before our class?"

Siobhan inhales in readiness to respond but again he raises his hand. "Please, Miss Finch, relax, humour me." She slumps back into her chair. "I suspect, Miss Finch, that you want permission to miss one of my classes, probably next week. And, since I do not produce handouts for my lectures, I suppose you would like to get a heads-up on what you might miss. I am correct, am I not?" Every 't' at the end of a word sounded like a wooden cane striking the desk.

"Next Monday, sir." Siobhan feels relieved that she still has the capacity for speech. "I'd really appreciate it, sir. I'd like to top out on this subject, I really want that distinction."

"And, why is that, Miss Finch?"

"Strathclyde Police have a fast-track graduate programme but only have one place a year for Forensic Science. I figure if I can get distinctions straight through to honours they'll have to offer it to me."

"Yes, Miss Finch, you are probably right. How could they not?"

Even though Professor Oldman's diction is perfect and he shows little sign of emotion, Siobhan's razor-sharp ego can still detect the hint of insincerity.

"I always get what I put my mind to, sir. I believe success is a choice." She slumps back in the chair again, realising that she probably didn't need to share that.

"Don't be so defensive, Miss Finch. It's not attractive on you. And choice is not where it all starts."

She looks puzzled by her professor's response.

"Awareness, Miss Finch, awareness. Be careful what you put your mind to." He checks the time on his pocket watch. "Give me your email address and I'll send you what you need next Monday."

"But sir, don't you want to know why I can't make it?"

"I'm guessing that your other engagement is important or you wouldn't be here, so no, Miss Finch, I don't need to know." He makes a deliberate point of looking at the clock behind his head on the wall. "Now, if you'll excuse me, I would hate for any of us to be late for this morning's lecture."

She scribbles her email on a Post-it and leaves it on his desk. She gets up and heads for the door. "Thank you, sir. I appreciate it."

He replaces his glasses and continues reading his French translation of Mein Kampf. "Hmm!" he grunts as the door clicks shut. He then closes his eyes and breathes in deeply the aroma she has left in his study. *Les Exclusifs de Chanel dix-huit*. Dee-lightful.

At 8.55am the University's biggest lecture theatre has a full house. Having a class bursting to capacity first thing on a Tuesday morning is uncommon in itself. What is even more staggering is that it's part two of a weekly lecture that started yesterday morning at the same time. The question is, what spectacle motivates first-year undergraduates to pack themselves like tinned fish at two out of the three most unpopular slots in the entire student timetable? To give an idea of the magnitude of this anomaly, last Friday at 5pm the lecture had three attendees and one of them was the lecturer. In point of fact these days it is uncommon for any lecture to have a full house, at any time of the day. So, what is the attraction?

You might think that the reason for such a full attendance is that the lecturer is Miss Scotland or some other charismatic celebrity. Nothing could be further from the truth. Oldman could by no stretch of the imagination be mistaken for the most popular professor at Glasgow University. Perhaps, then, the subject matter is the reason for the full house. Once again it couldn't be further from the truth – first-year Applied Chemistry. Oldman does have that Howard Stern quality whereby even though students don't like him they are nevertheless intrigued by him. They want to know what he's going to do or say next. The large numbers are also partly due to the reality that all first-year science and engineering students are required to include Applied Chemistry in their timetable in accordance with the new broad based curriculum. But that doesn't explain why maximum numbers attend. Professor Oldman is the only lecturer in the University who produces

277

zero notes for his classes. If you don't attend his lectures, you can't pass his class. He doesn't even give you the new syllabus at the beginning of the semester. Like an episode of 24 he gives you the story in small weekly chunks, minus the cliff-hangers. By the end of the semester the numbers will dwindle as reality kicks in and people decide they want to switch to social science and other subjects that doesn't include Monday and Tuesday morning concentration camps.

He rolls the blackboard to the middle of the stage, revealing a trolley that might be seen in any hospital operating theatre. There is something hidden under a green cover. No one at the University other than himself tends to use blackboards any more. With a piece of white chalk in hand he scrapes 'Applied Chemistry' on the black surface at 9am precisely, accompanied by his normal introduction.

"Good morning, underlings, so what is our topic for today?" A sea of eager-to-please arms are quickly produced by the majority of the congregation. Everyone in the front row has their hand aloft except one half-asleep spotty youth whose face has already started to flush crimson.

"You! Yes... You! Could there possibly be another you?" The youth in question looks up reluctantly. "What's the point of coming if you're not going to pay attention, son? Would you like me to repeat the question?"

"No sir."

"What did you say?"

"I said no sir, I understand the question. I'm afraid, sir, I just don't know the answer.

"Are you, in the wrong class, son?"

"No sir."

"Is this an attempt at humour?"

"No sir."

Oldman studies the youth, who now looks in a state of panic.

"If you have not come prepared to my class then why on earth have you not hidden yourself away out of sight in the back of the lecture hall? Are you stupid?" Oldman looks around to see that there is not one empty seat left in the hall. He waves his hand in front of the youth and shakes his head, making it clear he doesn't need a reply. "What's your name, lad?"

"McGregor, sir."

"Get out, McGregor."

"But sir…"

"Don't 'but sir' me, son, GET OUT! And I suggest you prepare for next Monday's class or don't even bother to come back." Oldman steps back to address the mass of stunned students who are now thinking that their professor has completely lost the plot.

"This seat is now reserved for McGregor until further notice. Sit in it at your peril." As McGregor collects his chattels and shuffles out of the theatre, Oldman continues like the lad doesn't even exist.

"OK, underlings, let's get back to work. Hands please?" He points at another victim in the front row. "Miss Finch."

"Industrial Chemicals, sir."

"Correct." After scraping Industrial Chemicals on the blackboard he continues to write.

DOT Label: corrosive

CAS Registry number: 7664-93-9

STCC: 4930040

CHRIS: SFA

UN Number: 1830

Chemical name: ?

"OK, my little amoebas, you know the drill, fill in the blank. Hands please." Not a single hand goes up in the ocean of worried faces. Oldman smiles contentedly. "I suggest, ladies and gentlemen, that for the exam you start to recognise these chemicals without their formulae." He gives the bemused congregation the missing info and writes on the board:

Formula: H2SO4

Every hand once again is aloft. Everyone has either checked their textbook, asked their swotty pal or is simply bluffing and hoping they won't get asked.

He ignores the hands and continues lecturing.

"At the end of today's lecture I will furnish you with an example of how effective this industrial chemical can be. But first let me explain the pertinent facts about…"

He writes on the blackboard:

Sulphuric Acid

"Little Johnny took a drink but he shall drink no more,

"What he thought was H2O was H2SO4"

…and continues, "H2SO4 is a colourless liquid, with a specific gravity of 1.85 and is most commonly identified with battery acid." He looks up to witness the sea of activity. Laptops, palmtops, Dictaphones, notepads are being bashed or frantically scribbled upon. He continues.

"During the 19th century, the German chemist Baron Justus von Liebig discovered that sulphuric acid, when added to the soil, increased the amount of phosphorus available to plants. This discovery gave rise to an increase in the commercial production of sulphuric acid and subsequently to improved methods of manufacture. It has a variety of uses and plays some part in the production of nearly all manufactured goods. Although the major use of sulphuric acid is in the production of fertilisers it is also widely used in the manufacture of chemicals, the refining of petroleum, the processing of metals and…" he takes in a large breath, "…in pickling, which is, essentially, the cleaning of iron and steel before plating them with tin or zinc."

He stops to take a drink from a small bottle of Evian. "Questions, comments?" He scans the hall. "Although sulphuric acid is one of the most important industrial chemicals and more of it is made each year than any other, it has to be treated with the utmost respect. Breathing sulphuric acid mists can result in tooth erosion and decrease the efficiency of the respiratory tract. Even small droplets of sulphuric acid that may exist in polluted air make it more difficult to breathe. Basically, sulphuric acid is very corrosive and can cause adverse effects on the skin, eyes and gastrointestinal tracts. Prolonged exposure through inhalation, ingestion, or contact with the skin can cause pulmonary edema, bronchitis, emphysema, conjunctivitis, stomatisis, tracheobronchitis, and dermatitis. It can cause blindness if thrown on the eyes and if taken orally, sulphuric acid can burn the mouth and throat, erode a hole in the stomach, and cause death."

He takes another drink. "Are there any questions or comments so far?" He scans the hall once more as he picks up the remote for the big screen. "Put down your pens, turn off your machines and pay attention." Over the next few minutes, while the screen shows graphic images of people and inanimate objects burning, melting, exploding and in some cases spontaneously combusting, the professor continues to talk above the bangs and explosions. "Concentrated sulphuric acid can be extremely volatile. It can catch fire or explode when it comes into contact with certain chemicals, alcohols, and metals. When heated, it emits highly toxic fumes that include sulphur trioxide."

Oldman switches the screen off and a volley of hands shoot up. "Since we are running out of time I will now take questions at the end of class. If I could ask you to keep your pens and laptops off and once again pay attention." He picks up a cardboard box from the side of the hall and drops it in McGregor's empty seat. "Miss Finch."

"Yes sir."

"If you would be good enough to select a few volunteers from the front row and distribute these."

"Certainly, sir." While Siobhan and her usual sidekicks distribute the industrial disposable facemasks, Oldman asks one of the University staff who has arrived on cue to make the extractors ready. The buzz in the room starts to resemble the activity before lift-off at an Apollo mission.

"Quietly, please." On the trolley next to the lectern Oldman takes off the green cover to reveal what looks like a tropical fish tank. He rolls the trolley to centre stage. There is no water and instead of its usual inhabitants there is what appears to be a dead baby pig. Oldman puts on his protective clothing, which includes the regulation gloves and over boots. He looks like something from a 1970 science fiction movie. He asks his auxiliary to open the doors and switch the extractor fans to full. He then scans the entire house to make sure everyone has on his or her facemask and only then proceeds with his demonstration.

Before the subject is completely immersed in H_2SO_4 the congregation are already amazed at the speed of this chemical at work. The smell of melting flesh isn't quite at the point where anyone needs to vomit but it's strong enough for those who have been holding in one of those silent but deadly farts to let it go without fear of discovery. The bell marking the end of this morning's lecture rings. Nobody moves. All eyes are fixed on the rapidly disappearing flesh and the bones that are becoming increasingly visible.

"Next week I will explain the difficulty H_2SO_4 has with the chemical structure of bones."

As Siobhan's crew and the auxiliary help to collect the facemasks for appropriate disposal, the congregation make their way out of the great hall and on to their next class. Oldman flips open his mobile phone, which has started to vibrate in his trouser pocket. He has two text messages. One of them is expected, the other isn't.

destiny n the apparently predetermined inevitable series of events that happen to somebody or something. **2** the inner purpose of a life that can be discovered and realised **3** a force or agency that predetermines what will happen **4** a particular fate or destination...

Janus is the Roman god of beginnings, of the past, of the future, of gates, doorways, bridges and of peace. He, or she, is traditionally depicted as having two faces. Lloyd likes that. His nightclub finishes around 3am for everybody apart from those who get a lock-in with the staff, who generally party on until 6am. Lloyd very rarely stays till the end. He'll tend to retire to his magnificent penthouse apartment by the river with spectacular views over the city. Recently he's been reading the Sunday Times Rich List and one of the serious players had said, "Managers have meetings, successful people have parties." Lloyd likes that too.

Tony and Stefano run the kitchen. The 'Brothers Grim' very rarely do any cooking; they're there to make sure the food is impeccable. At Janus you don't get praise or a bonus for high standards, they are expected. If you get sloppy or fuck up, you pay. So you don't get sloppy or fuck up. Janus is not the type of organisation where you get a written warning or an interview with your line manager. It's also not the type of firm you leave. You work hard and please the boss or you are well and truly in the shit. At Janus not getting a good reference is the least of your worries. However, there's always a plus side. The wages are fantastic and you don't need a university degree to work there. And the personnel

department don't get all bent out of shape over little character flaws like having a tendency towards violent conduct. Or
blips on your employment history like having done a bit of
bird at Her Majesty's pleasure.

A nightclub is a strange place during daylight hours; everywhere you go has a feeling of returning to the scene of the
crime and everybody is on edge, hungover or both. After
dark, when the lights are on along with everybody's face
paint and makeup, is when she looks at her best, like any
other woman in the entertainment business. First thing in the
morning when she's just got up is the best time to see what
she's really like. Although Lloyd's not one for meetings there
are some matters that need to be attended to in the cold light
of day. Every morning at 6.15am sharp he has what he likes
to call 'Prayers'. If you're on that day or called for, you are
present, no excuses. You only miss prayers once, never twice.
Generally, prayers last for fifteen minutes. Any longer means
there's bad news. There is no bad news today.

Lloyd has breakfast immediately after prayers every morning. On Tuesday he has his favourite, steak brunch. Rump
steak, 8oz, medium rare, grilled so slowly it melts in the
mouth. Two fried eggs, sunny side up, chestnut mushrooms,
two crispy hash browns, sun-dried tomatoes. Rocket salad
dressed with roasted pine nuts, virgin olive oil and balsamic
vinegar. Two freshly baked hot buttered croissants, all washed
down with a pot of hot black Jamaican coffee. Arguably the
best breakfast brunch north of Texas; well, that's what it says
on the menu. But then again if you're expected to pay £55
for breakfast then you expect it to be out-fucking-standing.
Albeit the punters do get a flute of champagne with that.

Lloyd uses a napkin to wipe his mouth and leans over to
pour himself some coffee. While he's flicking through the
latest edition of FHM there's a knock on his large wooden

office door. It sounds like the police. He has only one ex-cop who's on the payroll. The door opens a little and a head pops through. Lloyd doesn't need to look up.

"Fuck off, JJ!"

"Sorry Boss, but there's some big cunt here to see you."

Lloyd screws his face up and thinks for a moment before he replies. It's because JJ himself is a big cunt and he's more accustomed to hearing him talk about hobbits.

"Tell the big cunt to fuck off. I seem to remember saying earlier I only wanted disturbed for one reason, until after 10am. So unless it's that one reason or you're here to tell me I've lost the ability to tell the time, fuck off."

"The gentleman says he's got an appointment, Boss. Says you're expecting him?"

Lloyd looks at his desk diary and frowns while scratching his ear.

"Who is it, JJ?"

"Dunno, Boss."

"What the fuck d'you mean you dunno? Since when did we start letting people into the club we don't know? Have you gone fucking insane?"

JJ's face starts to go red. "Look, Boss, I ask this big joker who he is and what he wants. He barks at me, he says, 'Fuck you, cunt, doesn't matter who I am, what matters is that my boss has a message for your boss and your boss is expecting me. So if you don't want to upset your boss, my boss and more importantly me, go tell your gaffer there's someone here to see him'. I think, cheeky bastard, but at the end of the day, Boss, he seems pretty sure about himself."

"He alone?"

"Aye Boss."

"He tooled up?"

"Dunno Boss, wouldn't be surprised but."

"Where is he?"

"Boss, despite what you think I haven't went insane. He's still standing outside at the front door. I've warned off four of the lads and they're now standing inside the front door waiting for the word. And yeah Boss, they are all tooled up."

"Marvellous, JJ." Lloyd rolls his eyes to the ceiling. "OK then, bring the big fucking joker up."

After JJ closes the door Lloyd reaches into his drawer and takes out a sawn-off shotgun. He clicks it open and checks there are rounds in both chambers. He clicks the safety catch off. A few minutes later, the same knock on the office door.

"OK, JJ, in you come."

JJ walks in first and is dwarfed by the Big Joker, who is over 7ft tall and at least twenty-two stone. The other four stewards file in behind him and stand in pairs either side of the door with their backs against the wall. The Big Joker smiles as Lloyd stands up and offers a seat to the big guy like he's a matador ushering a bull into the ring.

"Have a seat."

They both sit there for what's at least thirty seconds, just eyeballing one another. Lloyd is his usual calm-as-fuck self and the Big Joker is also displaying cucumber-like qualities. The four stewards and JJ are all looking at each other and trying to figure out what the fuck's going on. They're getting twitchy and now all looking at Lloyd for some kind of direction. Lloyd decides to break the ice before it all gets silly.

"We can all see you've got balls, big guy, but since I don't read fucking minds, perhaps you will be good enough to tell me, one: Why you lied to my steward about having an appointment. Two: Who the fuck you are. And three: What it is that you think you want."

The Big Joker smiles again, leans forward and gestures towards the piece of hardware on Lloyd's desk. "Expecting trouble?" No response, so the Big Joker continues. "It's a pleasure to finally meet with you, Mr Oakley. Before we get into the pleasantries may I be so bold as to bother you for a coffee? I've had a long journey this morning, I've just eaten a full bar of Dairy Milk and my throat's feeling a little dry."

One of the stewards at the back coughs and then splutters like his chewing gum has gone down the wrong way. JJ pins him back to the wall with a look.

"Sorry Boss," he mumbles.

The Big Joker rolls forward on the balls of his feet and cocks his head round to view the steward, who is wiping his mouth with a handkerchief. He then looks back at Lloyd before once again smiling.

"I'll say this, Mr Oakley: You have them well trained."

Lloyd knows exactly who is sitting in front of him and whom he works for. He'd figured that the moment he'd opened his mouth, but doesn't want to let on. They've spoken on the telephone three times now but it doesn't make sense for him to turn up unannounced unless…

"Look, you and I both know that you've come here without an appointment and I'm happy to organise you a coffee but you do have me at a disadvantage. Perhaps you'd be kind enough to tell me who the fuck you are?"

The Big Joker folds his arms. His face changes from quizzical to resigned. "You know me as Vincent, we've spoken on the phone three times and I work for the Professor."

Lloyd watches his men's response. As he expects, none of them are any the wiser. Lloyd is the type of individual who likes to make sure just the same. He turns to JJ. "Its OK, JJ, get the boys back to whatever they were doing. I'll handle this now. Oh, and can you sort us out with some fresh?" Lloyd holds up the pot as he checks the clock on his desk. "JJ?"

"Yes Boss?"

"I'm expecting that delivery any time now. Show him to the alcove and sort it like I told you earlier. I'll be there presently."

"Sure, no probs, Boss."

They all file out behind JJ just as puzzled as they were when they got up this morning. Once they are alone Lloyd offers his unexpected guest a cigarette.

"No thanks, I don't."

"So, Vincent, what's the problem?"

"May I be candid, Mr Oakley?"

"I'd appreciate that."

"The Professor has found out about Yvonne Morrison, Emma Burgess and Liam McKinnon."

"How the fuck…"

Vincent holds his hands up to interrupt. "The how at the moment is not important, Mr Oakley. Have you disposed of McKinnon's body yet?"

"No."

"Good."

"Why?" Lloyd asks, still trying to hide his concern.

"I'll arrange for his body to be cleaned immediately. The Professor, Mr Oakley, would like to know why both girls were cleaned but more importantly why they weren't cleaned in the appropriate manner?"

Lloyd starts quick thinking. "Morrison was a mistake, she simply OD'd. So there was no need to complicate the situation with another missing person. Burgess, however, is another story. She was working for someone else. At the time we thought it might have been the filth."

"And was it?"

"No, whoever she was working for, she was more scared of them than she was of us. She didn't tell us anything. As you well know, cops aren't that motivated. The methods we use are thorough; if there's anything to tell, we're told. So contrary to your boss's instructions, she was dumped, on my say-so, as a warning to her employer."

Vincent's nostrils flare. "The Professor has asked me to convey his disappointment. He's asked me to get your assurance that these mistakes will not be repeated and that any future disposals will be approved, by us, first."

Lloyd isn't used to being spoken to like this. "Vincent, this isn't a McDonald's fucking franchise. Are you threatening me?"

"Mr Oakley, I am making a request from my employer. I have no emotions attached to this work or any of its associates. I apologise if my manner is insensitive but like yourself I am busy and this is just business."

Lloyd for the first time hesitates. "Apology accepted."

"Mr Oakley, do I have your assurance?"

Lloyd's neck starts to become red hot. He forces a wide smile. "Certainly. Anything else?"

"We have a few challenges with your most recent abduction. Apparently a few basic procedures in the vetting process have been missed and as such we have a situation."

"Really? And what is that?"

"We are still checking but it appears you may have snatched the PM's niece."

Lloyd has to make a huge effort not to gasp. If this is true then heads will roll.

"We are not pleased with the way you've conducted your business, Mr Oakley. We know about the filming you've been doing on your own."

There's a knock at the office door. Vincent loses his calm demeanour for a split second as his hand instinctively reaches inside his jacket. It's Lloyd's turn to hold his palms up. "Stay cool, Vincent, it's only JJ." JJ opens the door and one of the lads from the kitchen walks in with fresh coffee. Vincent takes in a deep breath.

"Ahhh... smells good, Mr Oakley."

JJ gives Lloyd a look. Vincent notices. "Everything OK, Mr Oakley?"

Lloyd rolls his eyes to the ceiling once more. "Yeah, everything is fine, Vincent. What is it, JJ?"

The waiter is just about to leave the room. JJ waits until the door closes. "That's your delivery arrived, Boss. He's in the alcove getting his coffee as we speak."

Perfect timing, Lloyd thinks to himself. "Vincent, this is something I have to attend to personally. Will you excuse me?"

Lloyd stands up. Vincent stands up.

"Mind if I tag along?"

"What about your coffee, Vincent?"

"Coffee can wait."

Allegory **n 1** symbolic work, **2** a work in which the characters and events are to be understood as representing other things and symbolically expressing a deeper, often spiritual, moral or political meaning **3** the symbolic expression of a deeper meaning through a story or scene acted out by mythical characters…

Raymius enjoys the feeling of the clean cotton sheets as they envelope his nakedness. He hears the door click shut and as he becomes fully conscious he breathes in deeply the distant smell of her, on the now available pillow. He rolls into the emptiness next to him and finds its warmth comforting. He opens one eye and looks at the space between the curtains. It's still dark out there. He focuses on the clock next; it's around 5am. He smiles at the remains of last night's feast. Hawaiian pizza, mixed pakora and chips. Glaswegian cuisine at its best, all washed down with the customary bottle of Châteauneuf du Irn-Bru, Scotland's other national drink. Barr's Irn-Bru, any morning's magical hangover cure, made in Scotland from girders.

He presses the remote for the small television set and immediately turns on the mute button so that he can see but not hear Good Morning Britain. 5.15am. He turns the telly off and adjusts the clock from ten minutes slow to ten minutes fast.

Old habits die hard. Better get my arse into gear and my head out of clichés. Party's over, son, time to work.

He grabs his cigarettes out of his pocket, lights up a Marlboro and walks to the window. He pulls one curtain to the side so that he can look out into the blackness. One fox closely followed by another cross the road and into the bushes. *Wow!* In all his time in Glasgow he's seen many foxes but never two together. He then sees the cub. *Amazing.* A tear runs down his cheek. He takes in a lungful of smoke and smiles. *Fucking beautiful. Life can be so fucking beautiful. Do we really create our own reality? What about destiny?*

He turns around and walks towards the bathroom, still surveying his new surroundings. He throws the cigarette end down the toilet and thinks about how in a few months the entire nation will ban smokers from inside their establishments. *Maybe I should quit while it's still my choice?* He flushes and examines his new en suite. Nothing too complicated in here. He pushes the button for the shower and has a seat while the hot water turns the cold air to steam. He gets up off the big white mint and flushes the toilet again. After being on the streets for a year it'll take more than a shower to stop him feeling dirty. But Raymius knows the score, it's well documented now. If you roll about in a sty long enough you'll eventually end up smelling like the locals. However, it still feels good to scrub up.

Raymius could easily have spent longer under the hot spray but there'll be plenty of time to relax later. With wet hair and a damp towel draped over his shoulder he lights another cigarette and switches on the kettle in the little alcove that's supposed to be the kitchen area. It is still a massive improvement on last week's living arrangements. He laughs as he looks down at the miniature fridge. *Mon the Shire*, he thinks as he opens its little door to see nothing inside. *I'd better get myself some milk.* He stirs sugar into his cup of black coffee and flicks his ash onto a saucer that is now full of fag ends. With Deefor in one hand he glances at the clock and takes out his little notebook. He clicks the top of his pen. The clock reads 6.05am.

To-Do's Today

Govan hill Baths to Janus 20 mins

Leave 6.30.

Milk, decent coffee and brown sugar

Tony says what goes around comes around

Tony says be happy

Fuck Tony

Txt Clare???

Daily Prayers

Do you think life is

beautiful enough to try and

figure it out?

Do you still

peek into the wardrobe

check beneath the bed

hide under the covers...

Raymius is in that state of automatic pilot you get into some mornings when you feel you're watching a movie of somebody else. Time becomes illusory. The streetlamps switch themselves off, heralding another day. He leaves his new apartment with an even more contented smile on his face than usual. He breathes in the smell of cooked bacon wafting over from the corner shop. It's quiet, there's still ice between the cobbles on the road and not a drop of wind. His freshly showered body feels like toast under his dry clothes. He's not had much sleep but at least he feels rested. He'll have an early night tonight. He doesn't bother lighting up because Govanhill Public Baths is only a few minutes away. It's another typically dreich Scottish morning with no sky, no sun and just one big gloomy grey blanket of cloud.

As he reaches the top of the stairs at his first port of call he carefully opens the doors the way you do first thing in the morning, when there is no one around and every noise seems to be amplified. He lets the old wooden doors go and they swing back and forward as he makes progress on the short walk down the corridor to the reception. Although it defies logic, Raymius figures that it's not the dark wooden surroundings but the smell of chlorine that makes it feel like the Mary Celeste. A familiar grin sticks its head around the corner. Raymius smiles back.

"Hi Joe, I see you've got a full complement of teeth present today, then?"

Joe giggles like a child and titters his response.

"Aye Ray, very good son, very good." He looks up at the big round clock on the wall. "You're in a bit sharpish the day son, in for a swim, eh?"

"Naw Joe, 'fraid not. I've got a few errands to run. I just want to grab a few bits from my locker and I'll be on my way. Might pop in for a wee sauna later on though."

"Big nae probs son, big nae probs. You'll no hae time for a cuppa either, then?"

"Naw Joe, sorry, like I said, maybe later though, eh?"

"OK, Ray, I'll leave you to it son. You take care, eh?"

Joe sits back down continuing to read his paper and Raymius heads across to the locker room. Even though there are no punters in yet, he goes through the standard procedure to make sure there is no one else around. Satisfied he's alone, he turns the key, reaches into his locker and pulls out his dark blue suit. He unzips the inside jacket pocket and takes out his mobile phone. After switching it on he checks the profiles function immediately to make sure its status is still on silent. There's an envelope on the screen. He has four messages from the same number. They are always from the same number. He looks around again before his fingers effortlessly work the keypad to create his response to John Ribbon.

'Managed to get on the payroll, running an errand for new employer at 7am this morning, may be a little late for breakfast regards, R.'

He waits for a few seconds. After 'Message sent' flashes on the screen he deletes all his inbox and outbox messages. He turns the mobile off, puts it in his back pocket, looks up at the clock on the wall and smiles. He places Lloyd's merchandise at the bottom of Deefor and then locks up.

Since he's ahead of schedule he decides to go back past the corner shop and get in on the bacon roll deal. Less than ten minutes later he's on his way to the heart of the Merchant City. As he negotiates the morning traffic with bacon butty in hand and laden with a kilo of top quality Ganja, he thinks deeply about the recent choices he's been making.

Raymius walks past the glass architecture of St Enoch's Square. If the giant from Jack and the Beanstalk had a greenhouse then this would have been it. *People who live in glasshouses shouldn't throw stones.*

His mind is all over the place but that's normal first thing in the morning. That's what he believes. He walks through Trongate and past the Tollbooth tower. One of Glasgow's oldest streets and the location of the city's last hanging, or at least that's what the locals would have you believe. Raymius remembers his brief on the Dark Side of Glasgow 101. Peter Manuel, hanged in Barlinnie July 11th, 1958. Manuel was suspected to be responsible for the deaths of more than fifteen women. Bible John, preyed on women who frequented the Glasgow Barrowlands in the 1960s but was never found. The story of Bible John inspired Scottish crime writer Ian Rankin's bestselling novel 'Black and Blue'. This made way for another famous character to be born: Inspector John Rebus. But that is all history and fiction. Rebus is a character in a book. This is different. This is not a story, this is now and it's real.

Raymius turns the corner at Albion Street and stops dead. There's a fucking giant in the doorway of Janus standing like a sentry at Buckingham Palace.

Jesus! Maybe I shouldn't be thinking so much about Beanstalks and fucking fables.

The monster of a man is about the same height as a Coldstream Guard except he isn't wearing a black furry hat and is twice as wide. He rings the buzzer while eating something and is also speaking on the phone. He leans towards the intercom and then five stewards come outside, surround him and escort him upstairs. He's the only one who has to duck down entering the club so as not to smack his head off the concrete lintel.

This is all a bit too Tales of the Unexpected at ten minutes to seven in the fucking morning.

Raymius decides to wait for a minute or two. He lights up a cigarette. At the door of the club he listens for a bit before ringing the buzzer. JJ comes to the door.

"Back again, just can't keep away, eh?" Although JJ is attempting to be upbeat Raymius can tell he isn't nearly as relaxed as he had been last night.

"I've got a meeting with the Boss."

"Oh … The Boss, is it? I know, pal, he's expecting you and already knows you're here. I'll take you upstairs and you can have a coffee while you're waiting. He shouldn't be long. But hey, I'm sure you've got nothing better to do anyway, right?" JJ looks at Raymius the way you do when you expect a response.

"Eh, aye big man, that's bang on, just lead the way."

JJ takes him to the alcove next to the fire. Raymius has that morning-after feeling as he notices the mark on the table where a few hours earlier he had seen a demonstration of how to bond flesh and wood.

"I'll send one of the lads over to get you something from the kitchen. Have whatever you want, it's on the house." JJ smiles unconvincingly.

"Cheers, big man." Raymius returns the customary plastic smile and reaches for his cigarettes. He watches JJ talking to the lad behind the bar. The lad stops what he's doing and looks over at Raymius as if he wants to make sure he's got the right person. There is no one else around. Seems odd but then again, it is proving to be one of those mornings. He decides to text Clare while he's waiting. He turns his mobile on. No signal. *Fuck.* He switches it back off and puts it back in his pocket. The lad at the bar approaches with menus, cutlery and the whole entourage of condiments. He takes a chocolate mint.

"What can I get you, sir?"

Raymius feels like he's been asked what he wants for his last meal.

"Coffee, strong, black, brown sugar and twenty Marlboro Lights."

"Are you sure?"

Strange, Raymius thinks.

"Nothing to eat then?"

"Yeah, that's right mate, I've had breakfast, thanks, I'm sure."

"You OK if I put on some music?"

"Yeah no problem."

Raymius hears the high-pitched screech of feedback and then the sound system kicks in. To his delight, not too loud, but a bit of a weird choice for this early in the morning. A very familiar harpsichord intro but way too poppy for Mozart.

Quite eerie. Well, it is a nightclub.

Raymius listens intently to the first five lines but had it pegged after just one. He thinks: *Cool, comfortable and no such thing as a freebie!*

Raymius is pleased with himself for recognising and remembering the song and even the album - Destiny's Child's The Writing's on the Wall. He giggles to himself thinking about the difference between the cost of dating, marriage and Third World blow-jobs. He picks a magazine off the rack, gets to page three and looks up at the lad.

"You forget something?" Raymius asks.

The lad places the coffee on the table and hovers.

"Strong enough?"

He puts out his cigarette, drinks a mouthful and shudders at the bitter taste. He puts in an extra sugar.

"Wow, fully leaded eh?"

"Yes sir, fully leaded."

The lad walks off, totally underwhelmed. Raymius finishes off cup number one and is pouring the second, to see if it can taste any worse, when he hears Lloyd's familiar tone.

"Ah, Mr Punctuality!"

He looks up to see Lloyd being dwarfed by what only can be described as a fucking Honey Monster. He figures this guy could have his own ecosystem. He stands up as they walk towards him. He feels giddy, light-headed, like he's going to pass out or even faint. His eyes begin to blur, double followed by triple vision. He breathes deeply as everyone in sight starts to multiply and spin. He attempts to control his breath now and is just about managing his feelings of panic.

What the fuck's happening? Heart attack? Panic attack? Nausea? Think, think.

His eyes start to water, his mouth fills with acidic saliva, acid reflux.

He looks down and focuses on the mark. He can barely make out his reflection on the surface where last night he had watched Lloyd drive a car key through a terrified man's hand.

Focus, focus, focus on one point and fucking breathe, concentrate, think, think.

"Are we feeling OK, Ray? You've gone a funny colour, maybe you'd better sit back down…" The words filter into his brain like they're coming from the end of a long, dark tunnel.

"I'm sorry, gentlemen, but I think I might have to throw…"

As the coffee table rushes up to meet him, the last thing Raymius hears is the thud of his face slamming against its beautifully varnished surface.

service 1 *v* copulate with female of a male animal **2** *n* act of serving ball or shuttlecock **3** *n* fine wire or cord used to bind rope to prevent it from fraying **4** *n* delivery of a legal document such as a writ or summons **5** *n* work done for somebody else **6** *n* domestic servants' work **7** *n* the act of bringing food to someone or the way in which this is done **8** *n* maintenance of machinery **9** *n* a specific ritual that is performed to a prescribed form **10** *n* a religious ceremony **11** *n* government agency **12** *n* a set of dishes and cups **13** *n* meeting of public need **14** *n* one of a country's armed forces ...

Ribbon decided to change the venue for his meeting with Mac. Two phone calls last night and one this morning have created a completely different spin on what now needs to happen. Mac didn't get the change of venue till a short while ago. The first commandment: Always have the deck stacked in your favour. Ribbon likes texts; less dialogue. People tend to be more specific and one can usually get the info one requires without having to bother about rapport. And it's easier to lie.

He's changed the RV from the office to a more suitable venue. Cafe Uno, 'The only Italian you'll ever need to remember, No1 coffee-shop, No1 Royal Exchange Square'. Ribbon doesn't just like the jingle, the coffee is great too, but that doesn't matter because they won't be staying long. In the Merchant City it's easy to get lost in an ocean of tourists, students and the business community. Mac turns up a couple of minutes early. His boss is already there. Ribbon stands up, leaves a fiver on the table and walks towards Mac.

"What's all the cloak and dagger stuff for, Boss?"

Ribbon ushers him by the arm back outside. "Let's walk first and coffee later, Mac, there have been developments."

Mac knows his boss well enough to realise this isn't a request. They head across the road through the alleyway and up the steep cobbled streets of Ceremony Hill. Glasgow is essentially a collection of hills. Although the hum of the city is only a short distance away, within minutes they are off the trodden track thinking it could be Sunday afternoon. Certain streets are always practically deserted any time of the day if you know where to go. Ribbon is heading north to hit the river Kelvin and then the tow path that hugs the canal. Mac is unusually quiet but Ribbon can tell that there is a lot of noise going on inside his sergeant's head.

"Before I say my piece, Mac, you first. I guess it's best for me to let you get whatever it is that's bothering you off your chest. 'Cause what I'm about to tell you is going to change your career."

Mac's face goes red as he takes a gulp of air. "Boss, I know about the flat in Amsterdam, I've seen your Special Branch File and to top it all Sheena wants me to spy on you. I don't know what you're into, Boss, but the boys in their ivory towers are taking a keen interest."

Ribbon stops himself from laughing but can't hide his smile. "Wow, loyalty. Hmm, that's not exactly what I meant, Mac. There are a few things that you're not aware of that I need to give you a heads-up on. Maybe you'd better have a cigarette." Mac lights up. "Mac, there's stuff you know and stuff you don't know."

"Yeah, course, Boss." Mac gives Ribbon one of his confused looks.

"Bear with me, Mac. I've done this before, you haven't. There's stuff you know you don't know but more importantly there is always stuff you don't know you don't know. Roger so far?"

"Yeah, roger so far, Boss."

"No, I mean it, Mac, are you clear on this? 'Cause if you need me to spell it out, we've got as long as it takes today."

Mac thinks for a bit. "No, it's crystal, Boss, I get it. But I must admit I'm beginning to go out of my mind here and would really like to know what the fuck is going on."

"Patience, Mac, all will be revealed."

They reach the Kelvin; they are now on a wooded path that is deserted apart from the occasional squirrel and the odd jogger. It's like one of those scenes from Lord of the Rings when the fellowship embarks on their trek from the safety of the Shire to the foothills of Mordor. Ribbon stops and looks around. He offers Mac a mint. Mac declines and lights up another cigarette. Ribbon pops the Polo into his mouth.

"It's hard to believe that we are still in the middle of a city, eh Mac?"

"Aye Boss."

Ribbon smiles as he acknowledges the reality of why Glasgow means 'Dear Green Place'.

"Thanks for your candour, Mac, I appreciate that. Hear me out though and don't interrupt, I've given this speech many times now and it's best that you just listen and absorb. Sorry if this sounds a little bit by-the-book but it's best you keep any questions till the end. Like I said earlier, your life is about to change. It's one of those crossroads, one of those defining moments."

"Look, Boss, the reality is, whatever it is, I don't need to know…"

"Mac, you don't understand because you do need to know."

"Look boss, I appreciate this but if it's OK, I'd rather not know. I'll back you a zillion percent no question, but if I don't know then I don't have to lie."

303

"Yeah, Mac, unfortunately I guessed you might say that, but for fuck sake, shut up, and just listen. Jesus Christ."

Mac looks like a scolded child. "So are you going to ask me to take the red or the blue pill?" he asks nervously, almost sneering.

Ribbon's face is expressionless. "Yeah, Mac, something like that."

Mac swallows hard and wishes he hadn't tried to be flippant.

"You ready?"

"Aye Boss."

The path starts to snake upwards and they climb towards the canal. Ribbon checks to make sure it is only squirrels that are within earshot.

"In 1929 the NCIS was established. As you're probably aware this information is in the public domain. What is not and known by very few, is that at the same time SO1 was also commissioned from the highest executive branch of the government. For most people SO1 is essentially a myth and that's the way it will stay."

Mac can't hide his excitement.

"What do you think you know about the history of our secret police, Mac?"

"Fuck all Boss, like you say, it's a myth."

"Good, don't need to tell you to forget anything then. If you think about it logically, Mac, the advantages of having a police force that is secret do not require any explanation. In fact the emergence of a clearly recognisable uniformed police force is a much more recent necessity than that of covert operations. SO1 is officially endowed with authority superior to any other law enforcing agencies. We investigate, apprehend and some-times even judge our suspects in secrecy. We are known and accountable only to the executive branch of government that formed us. So there we are, Mac. What do you think of the show so far?"

"Well, at the risk of asking the obvious, Boss, what has all this to do with me?"

"A massive problem that our society faces is that the bad guys are a lot more sophisticated than the average person knows. We have moles in their garden and have done for many years but now it seems that we have strangers in our house, Mac, and we don't know how high up the rot goes."

"Like I say, Boss, what has all this to do with me?"

"Patience, Mac, patience." Ribbon pops another Polo and again offers Mac the top of the packet. Mac lights another cigarette.

"Our real world is in chaos, Mac. Balance versus chaos. Balance needs organisation. We can be sure of only one thing: Change. Nothing stays the same. The way we try to understand where we have come from is passed down through the ages by language. One of the most widely used is the English language, Mac. The Encarta Concise English Dictionary contains over twenty thousand more headwords than any other dictionary on earth and a simple headword like 'service' has more than fourteen different definitions. Thinking that our world remains organised without input from guardians like SO1 is a bit like thinking the Encarta Concise English Dictionary fell out of a tree."

"Sorry if I'm being thick, Boss, but at the risk of repeating myself, what the fuck has all this to do with me?"

"We need good people, Mac. We need the best people, the very best. I was recruited into SO1 in 1987 and last night I was given clearance to bring you under the covers. So Mac, how do you feel about being a guardian of the people, one of the good guys for Queen and country and all that?

"How long do I get to think about it?"

"Nice one, Mac."

"I don't know what to say, Boss."

"No need to say anything. Reality is, we have an up-against-the-clock situation. I got a phone call from our man at the Yard first thing this morning. One of our biggest bad guys is ringfenced in London and we're going for him today."

"Who is it, Boss? Do I know him?"

"The Professor that Buxton was educating you on, the guy who's responsible for all those missing persons you discovered when you were researching HOLMES. The guy with the nice handwriting."

"Christ. So are we headed for London?"

"No, Mac, we've got four moles hiding under the covers in Glasgow and we've just told them to come home. So I need you to help me do that. Look Mac, later, when we've got time, you'll go down to Hereford for six months and fast track your training, but right now I need someone I can trust."

They reach the canal. A few metres along the path there is the Canal Café, an old boat that has been converted into an eatery. To the right across the road is the start of civilisation, a few shops and workmen going about their day.

"Mac, I know this is a lot to take in but it's real, so deal with it, Sergeant. Look, I'm in serious need of calories and caffeine. I'll go inside and see if I can wake someone up on this barge to get us a brew."

Mac takes a seat at one of the tables outside, pulls over an ashtray and lights up another cigarette. They both force smiles and attempt to make light of the situation.

"I guess, Boss, they're not expecting a lot of business this early in the morning, this early in the year for that matter."

Ribbon shrugs and throws his arms out to the side in resignation.

"Hey, no one is going to get bent out of shape if we have a bit of breakfast before we win the war and save the day. What do you say to a bacon butty?"

Mac's face beams back in appreciation. "Tell you what, Boss, I'll have a bacon and egg doubler."

Ribbon makes his forefinger and thumb into the shape of a gun and points it at Mac. "Coming right up, Sergeant."

Mac waits for Ribbon to go inside and then has a look about to see who's around. He pulls out his mobile and starts to text.

'i have managed 2 get in big house. confirm 4 moles uground in Gla coming out 2day. If u r still in Lon leave now if you want 2 miss the party.'

He presses send. 'Message sent' flashes on the screen. He then follows the usual procedures before putting his phone back into his pocket and lighting up a cigarette. Mac looks up as he hears the café door creak open. Ribbon walks back outside with his mobile up to his ear. He sits back down next to Mac but doesn't say anything. He just looks at Mac and smiles.

"So, did you find anyone in there, Boss?"

"Yeah, Mac."

"Food's on the way then?"

"Yeah, Mac, it'll just be a few minutes."

There is a sinister silence before Ribbon asks the Who Wants to be a Millionaire question.

"So, Mac, who you texting at this hour?"

"Just the missus, Boss, you know how she is."

"Can I see?" Ribbon holds out his hand.

"Sure Boss," Mac obliges nervously.

On inspection as expected all Mac's outbox has been deleted.

"You know how it is Boss, training, SOPs, all that old-habits-die-hard stuff."

"Yeah, Mac, I know exactly how it is." He pops Mac's mobile into a plastic bag and away in his jacket pocket. Mac's eyes are darting everywhere but he's frozen on his seat like an animal lost in the middle of a dual carriageway.

"Breathe, Mac. And don't make any sudden movements. Look down at your solar plexus." Mac looks down. "There are another two dots the same colour, Mac, one on the front of your head and one to the right of your back as the marksman is looking at it. So long as he hits the mark it will go straight through your heart, missing any bones and, more importantly, me. Everyone is now expecting you to put out your cigarette in the ashtray and put your hands flat on the table. It's not good to deviate from any of those expectations, Mac. You know the drill."

Mac complies slowly and deliberately. "That's good, Mac." Ribbon pulls his own mobile phone out and shows Mac a copy of the text he'd just sent and then deleted. Mac's eyes widen. "You see, Mac, we have the technology now to capture texts so long as we are close enough and know when and where to throw the net. It's more difficult in the middle of a busy city with so much digital traffic but out here..." Ribbon looks around and admires the view from the canal across the open fields and up towards the Campsie Hills. "Well, like I say, Mac, we have the technology now and had you managed to do your training at Hereford you'd have found that out."

Ribbon stands up. "They'll be here for your debrief shortly. If I were you I'd enjoy the next few minutes while you can." He turns his back on Macmillan and begins to walk away. "I'm disappointed, Mac. I thought it would have been more difficult."

"Don't you want to know why, John?" Mac shouts, almost pleading.

Ribbon stops and turns only his head. "Jesus, Mac, I already know why, that's not complicated." He flares his nostrils. "You're a fucking cliché, Mac, a fucking cliché." As Ribbon walks across the road towards a council van he can hear the handcuffs being applied along with the usual babble of 'you-have-the-right-to-remain-silent' stuff – not that that has any real significance since this will never see the inside of any court. This decision has already been decided. The 'rights' are just one of those many pre-frames that's used to get a stranger in the house to comply. To make him think that he still has rights which of course he hasn't. He gave up those rights when he chose the other side of the fence. Ribbon reaches the van, opens its back door and sticks his head in. "Good work guys, what can you tell me I don't already know?"

"The message got picked up in Glasgow, Boss."

"Will the recipient be able to tell we intercepted it?"

"Unlikely, Boss, the delay was only seconds, the time it took to copy it could be caused by a tunnel or travelling through any black spot."

"Fair enough, lads, good job." He sighs. "Get me a secure line." Ribbon picks up the handset and punches in the number. A voice answers straight way.

"Go ahead, John."

"Hi Mike, go secure." There's a few seconds of silence.

"Go ahead, John, that's us in."

"Job's done Mike, that's the hamster in its cage. Well, one of them at least."

"John?"

There's a pause before Ribbon answers. "Yeah?"

"You heard from your guy yet?"

"Negative, Mike, he's missed breakfast and we've had no further comms yet but I'll let you know as soon as I do."

"Thanks, John, I'm going to be tied up in that meeting soon but I'll call you once I know what the PM's next move is. Roger that?"

"Roger that Mike, thanks, out."

Ribbon returns the black handset into its cradle. He throws his hand up to the boys in the back of their wagon and then closes the door. All around everything seems to be back to normal. Over the road the café door opens and a flustered face pops out and spots Ribbon.

"Are you wanting this bacon roll and coffee or what? It's going cold, y'know."

Ribbon shouts back: "Yeah, thanks love, I'll be right there."

catch *v* **6** stop with hands **7** begin to burn or ignite **8** to become infected with a disease **9** to surprise somebody who is in the act of doing something wrong or forbidden **10** to manage to meet somebody, especially one who is very busy **11** to strike someone a blow **12** to entangle **13** to reach or get alongside a person or vehicle moving ahead usually at speed **14** to arrive on time to board a bus, train or other form of public transport...

Vincent enjoyed killing them all. JJ had been the most trouble but then again ex-cops usually are. Being a professional killer is one thing, enjoying your work is a blessing. He has never worked with this bitch before and can't make his mind up whether he likes or hates her. Etta Yuille is not wearing any makeup apart from a subtle hint of lipstick. Her eyes look too small for her face and her long, perfectly manicured fingernails match her outfit. Vincent likes things in order. The Lab Rat is another matter. Vincent doesn't usually take an instant dislike to anyone. It leaves too much room for emotion. In Vincent's profession it's best to be impartial. He would gladly make an exception for this little geek in the white coat. But, unfortunately, the oddity comes free, bundled with the Bitch. Professional interrogators, that's how they market themselves. They have been referred to the Professor by Lloyd Oakley; how ironic. So, the Professor has asked Vincent to give them a try and although he can appreciate his employer's motives he is not convinced they are up to the task or worth the effort expended.

They've had their chances and so far Vincent is not impressed. So this is their last attempt. Vincent has made it absolutely crystal. Anybody can snuff a candidate. Getting the information first is the skill. This is definitely their last chance. They've already chalked up two stiffs with little or no relevant information. The Professor's terms of business are clear: If you are not an asset then you are a liability, no middle ground, no grey areas. Simple black and white, cut and dried. The Lab Rat has now toasted two people to death with his infernal fucking machine.

Vincent closes the vault, turns the key and locks the door. He likes the fact that he doesn't need to duck coming through it. In fact he likes the room, the bright white shiny tiles, the hi-tech fibre optics in each corner of the ceiling, he even likes the wire cages that protect the lights. He doesn't even mind that the room has recently begun to smell like a public toilet. The only real bit of ugliness apart from the little Lab Rat is his contraption, which is on a trolley hiding under a green piece of cloth. The trolley makes Vincent think of hospital. Vincent doesn't like hospitals.

Vincent looks over again at the Bitch. He is intrigued by her colour coordination. She could be right out of a comic book. Torture and execution are powerful aphrodisiacs; maybe later he'll rip off her little black outfit. Vincent imagines what she'd look like frightened, no, terrified, and begging for more.

They all look down towards Raymius as he starts to show signs of regaining consciousness. He opens one eye and surveys the trapdoor a few metres away from his face. He touches the large lump on his head and winces. The injury is the result of collapsing over a beautifully varnished table like a bag of marbles. Small potatoes compared to what is now on the menu.

"Have a seat, Mr Raymiuz Scott," she says. Raymius opens his other eye and attempts to get onto one knee. He stands up and sways like he's drunk. Raymius looks suitably fucked up, dazed and frightened, but confused enough to still have a sense of hope. Vincent knows that it's only human nature to hope. It is the interrogator's job to keep this fantasy alive but the reality is that Raymius has only two chances of getting out of this one – none and fucking none. Vincent stands up and pulls from inside his jacket one of his favourite toys, his 9mm Beretta. He points it at Raymius's right knee, a motivational gesture that probably isn't needed. He echoes Etta's instructions.

"Take a seat, Raymius."

Raymius looks to his right and sees two leather chairs. They'd been purchased from a local dentist. All the little extras such as the head, chin, arm, and ankle straps are customised additions courtesy of the Lab Rat. Raymius drags himself over and into the empty chair. He looks in the mirror attached to the armrest. His bright young eyes are bloodshot. Raymius appears to be trying hard not to be surprised about who is strapped into the other seat. Vincent takes a few moments to consider why this should be the case. The battered remains in the chair are simply that; remains. Vincent had enjoyed initiating the initial havoc that created most of the mess in the leather seat. Vincent had particularly enjoyed witnessing the ego disappear. And it was such a large ego to beat down. Vincent smiles to himself, looking at the puddle beneath the chair and recalling the last few moments, when its occupant had soiled himself. The Lab Rat and his fucking contraption had finished it off.

Vincent is still bewildered by the machine and has yet to see a positive demonstration with a successful result. Well, c'est la vie, this is definitely their last attempt. They need the information first before Raymius can be allowed to die.

Raymius sits in the free chair. He looks again at the mess in the other seat who is not sleeping, no breath. Vincent reaches over and places the barrel between Raymius's eyebrows and then pushes until his subject's skull falls back into the headrest. He grabs Raymius's right wrist and slams it into the groove on the armrest. The Bitch speaks.

"Vinzent, hang on a second." She turns to her left. She uses her finger and thumb to massage her earlobe with a slow pulling motion. She whispers to the Lab Rat and then turns back again to face Vincent. Her lips curl, her eyes close for the briefest of moments as her head shakes ever so slightly, her body language signalling a final no, like the way you would to an auctioneer. Let the games begin.

"Vinzent, letz see if Mr Scott will cooperate with our little inveztigation." She takes another puff of her cigarette. "I don't think we need the restraintz right now. If our guezt can clear up a few simple matterz for uz then we can let him go." All bullshit, but everybody looks pleased anyway. The Bitch leans over and whispers to the Lab Rat again. Raymius looks pleased by the announcement and smiles as the Beretta is lowered. Vincent's eyebrows crease and his nostrils flare. Vincent decides to let Raymius know that he still wants to anyway.

"Of course, Mr Scott, if you decide to be silly we may have to put a few holes into you first." The Lab Rat laughs like what Vincent has said is fucking hilarious. Maybe he's OK after all, as far as geeks go? He stops laughing as abruptly as he'd started. Vincent lets Raymius's wrist go and flop back to where it was before. Vincent produces Raymius's cigarette packet and holds it in his outstretched hand.

"Would you like one, Mr Scott?"

Raymius doesn't appear to want or need a cigarette right now but reaches for the packet anyway. His audience look on as his outstretched hand and arm tremble and then stops short of the packet. The audience make a terrible job of concealing their satisfied smiles.

"Go on, have a cigarette, Raymiuz," Etta says, more encouragingly this time.

"Not just now, thanks." Raymius withdraws his hand, coughs and continues with a shaky voice. "Maybe later if that's OK. I'm afraid if I have one now I might…"

It doesn't matter to his audience, who just continue to smile understandingly. Raymius guesses that it's Psychoburd's primary role to be soothing, to convince Raymius that Lloyd Oakley's square go with the meat shredder was a freak misunderstanding which they can all straighten out and soon that he'll be free to go. They are all still trying to deceive each other, even in this room of death.

"Are you prepared to help uz in our enquireeze, Mr Scott?"

"Do I have a choice?"

"We always have a choice, Mr Scott."

Raymius considers the situation. Every word now is a precious move in this game of chess. The 12th Commandment ticker-tapes through his mind. *Guard against your desire to believe them. It is natural to want to and natural to want to tell the truth. What they say means nothing. Giving them what they want won't help you, that's the thing you hold on to. That's the only idea that matters in this situation.*

She opens a folder. Her cigarette is clamped in the middle of her mouth with the smoke streaming into her eyes. She is smiling with her lips shut so the fag doesn't fall out but still smiling just the same. It makes Raymius remember photographs of the Barras. Old women gutting fish doon at the Saltmarket.

"What's your relationship with Emma Burgezz?" she asks.

"Who?" he replies. The audience move their heads closer together to whisper.

"Emma Burgezz," she says again, holding up a glossy photograph.

"I've never seen her before," Raymius replies.

She shakes the photo in the air like she's on a protest march. "You see? You see what happenz when ..." As she shrugs, the ash falls off her cigarette onto her lap. She brushes it off with her hand onto the white tiled floor. The photograph has been taken after Burgess was dead. The mark on her left temple could be mistaken for a bullet entry wound but he knows it isn't. It's the exact same mark as the one on Lloyd's temple.

She takes out another photograph and holds it aloft.

"How do you know Helen Carter?" she asks.

"I've never seen her before either." Raymius watches and waits once again while they exchange their secret whispers, knowing that Vincent is telling Psychoburd that he's lying.

"You want that cigarette now, I think," she says. Raymius shakes his head as she lights another one for herself. Her eyes roll up to left and then to the right, again she seems to meditate, for a while.

"Put on the strapz," she says.

"Wait," Raymius pleads.

"What iz it?" she says.

"Where am I?" he asks.

She fills her lungs and blows out a huge ring of smoke before she responds.

"We call thiz room the Deconzecration Chamber." She looks at the Lab Rat. The Lab Rat looks at Vincent and then gestures towards the console behind the chairs. Vincent looks back at Etta and nods.

"OK, Vinzent, start the tape," she says. Vincent once again pulls out the Beretta and moves towards the console. The Lab Rat gets up and starts moving towards the trolley. They both look at her once more.

"Do it," she says.

316

The Lab Rat can't help showing his excitement and anticipation. Vincent breathes a heavy sigh and shakes his head at Raymius. Etta maintains her poker face. Raymius's heart starts to pound. He looks down at his chest and can imagine it actually bursting out through his shirt. He closes his eyes, takes a deep breath and manages his state. She takes another lungful of smoke and then throws the butt on the white tiles.

"Damn it, do it now," she says again.

Raymius stands up. They all pause and look at him.

"Who-the-fuck's-in-charge here?"

After Vincent has started the recording he comes out from behind the console and walks towards Raymius, pointing the handgun at his head. "I'm in fucking charge," Vincent replies.

"What's on the trolley?" Raymius demands.

Vincent looks at the Lab Rat and nods. "Go ahead, show the man."

The Lab Rat looks like he's just been told what he's getting from Santa. He's almost skipping as he pulls off the green cover. Underneath is a machine with dials, lights and a rod with a rubber grip that tapers into a blunt steel point. The metal vibrator's calibration system has the usual accessories including car battery terminals with rubber caps. It doesn't look like your typical lie detector, except Raymius can imagine why maybe these people think it is. The Lab Rat speaks.

"It's quite simple, really, a modification of the device neurologists use to administer electric shocks to people who suffer from various mental disorders. Only here we have what I like to refer to as the GTI version that essentially has the capacity to administer a far more powerful jolt. The pain is in actual reality secondary. I have discovered from extensive research that most people don't even remember the pain. What makes this method so successful and the subject so eager to talk is actually an aversion to the whole process. This of course can simply be referred to as atavism. Some day I hope to write a paper." The Lab Rat, who sounds like he's come to the end of his television commercial, realises he might have banged on a wee bit too long. Vincent takes this pause as his cue to produce Raymius's mobile phone.

"You will give us the answers we want one way or the other, Mr Raymius Scott."

"Ask me what you want. I don't need that fucking machine. I've got nothing to hide, I'm a nobody for fuck sake." Raymius sits back down and everybody in the room seems to relax.

"Whom do you work for?"

"I don't work for anyone, I'm unemployed." Vincent holds the phone aloft.

"Who has a phone with no one in the address book?"

"I do."

"Who deletes all of his text messages?"

"I've not had any yet, I just got the phone."

"That's a cop's answer."

"It's the truth," Raymius pleads nervously.

"Who deletes all of his call history, dialled and received?"

"Like I said, I just got the phone," Raymius replies.

"That's lame and still something a cop would say."

Raymius manages to stop his Adam's apple from doing what it instinctively wants to do.

"When did you get your phone?"

"A couple of days ago."

"I suppose you're going to tell us that no one has your new number then."

"A few people have, but not many. I just haven't had time to save them in yet."

"Very convenient, Raymius. However that also just sounds like another cop's answer." Vincent produces another phone and holds it aloft. "For the last time, Raymius, what's your relationship with Emma Burgess?"

"I'm telling you, I've never heard of Emma Burgess."

They whisper again.

Vincent punches a few numbers on the other phone and seconds later Raymius's mobile starts to vibrate.

"Maybe you can explain, then, why Emma Burgess has your new number in her old phone?"

The game is over, checkmate. The Lab Rat holds up the steel rod. "This can be used to touch all of the extremities or to be inserted in any orifice. I applied the wand to her temple and administered a calculated, measured jolt. Carefully measured, I assure you, less than half power, not a bit more. She had a seizure and died before we could get all our answers. It may have been epilepsy. Did she have a history of epilepsy, Mr Scott?" The Lab Rat's high-pitched, squeaky voice gets higher and squeakier the more excited he gets and currently sounds like he's been sucking helium balloons all morning.

"Don't you fucking touch me with that."

"Have some dignity, do not weep, plead or pee your pants, like our poor big dead gangster. I applied the wand to Mr Oakley's temple and again only administered a calculated, measured jolt. Carefully measured, I assure you, less than a quarter power, not a bit more. He also had a seizure and died before we could get all our answers. Very unfortunate, extremely unusual, I assure you. Who would have thought such a fit-looking black man would have such a weak heart? We didn't know he had a heart condition. Did you know our Mr Oakley had a heart condition, Mr Scott?"

Raymius is now getting that this information is more for the benefit of the Honey Monster than it is for him. It is crystal that the Lab Rat is ecstatic at the prospect of having more data for his paper. Even under the present dilemma Raymius can't help thinking that the Lab Rat would have had more success if he had got the subjects to fill in a medical questionnaire beforehand. Under the circumstances he doesn't see the benefit in offering this suggestion.

Raymius considers the situation. Even if he manages to get that gun, shoot them all and then escape this room, there'll be guards everywhere and as soon as they hear the shots they'll come running. The smiling Lab Rat turns to his machine and flicks a switch. There is a hum, the kind that comes from an old-fashioned PC when it's re-booting. Three green lights come on. Raymius feels the panic; why not? The idea of being touched anywhere with this stainless steel fucking vibrator is panic-worthy. But there is another cold-blooded calculating part of Raymius that knows he will have to take at least one dose of electrified steel. The conscious mind and the unconscious mind, the two selves at war, duality.

"I mean it, don't you come anywhere near me with that fucking thing."

"Do it!" Etta screams.

Raymius feels paralysed as his world is welded in the moment. The pain is so sudden that dots appear before his eyes, dancing frantically. He takes Psychoburd's attempt at volume to another level and lets go of his own howl. Raymius grips the arm of the chair and is now unsure about whether he is acting or not. The line between panic and acting has vaporised. There is a crunching sound like when you tread on peanuts. The knuckles of his fists contract so fiercely that his fingernails stab into his palms. A dancing sickness races up his wrists, forearms, elbows, shoulders and one side of his neck. His gums and the fillings in his teeth feel like they are leaking with molten lead. If luminous is a feeling, he knows what it feels like. He bites his tongue and shoots sideways in the chair, his eyelashes and lids flapping like the shutters on the viewer of the old-fashioned 'what the butler saw'. Every muscle in his body feels like it's just been woken up and is now squawking like a hungry chick in an overcrowded nest.

He considers all the things he would do in order to stop a repeat of being touched with the Lab Rat's little lightsaber. There are no caveats that spring to mind; the list is infinite. He'll do anything. Even if it means telling them all they want to know. He will never experience that again. The atavism is complete. He will gladly swallow his own tongue and choke to death first. The Lab Rat approaches with his clipboard, pencil and high-pitched squeak.

"Tell me how it feels, now, while the experience is still fresh?"

"It feels like death," Raymius responds, truthfully.

The Lab Rat's voice increases another octave. "And that was only a tenth of the power." The Lab Rat's face is jubilant with pride. And he is the one. The one who has killed his friend Emma Burgess, standing beside his machine with his hands folded in front of him smiling and perhaps thinking about the paper he will write. The truth is no longer safe and there is no longer any sanctuary in a lie. Raymius takes in a deep breath and then pauses. They all become a little keener, eager to hear what Raymius has to say.

"Can I have that cigarette now?"

Two mouths smile triumphantly. Vincent looks at Etta and Etta nods. The Lab Rat looks a little disappointed. Vincent pulls out Raymius's packet. Raymius's hands are trembling now and this is also not an act. He puts the tab in his mouth and bends towards the flame. Its end catches fire and glows orange. He draws the smoke in deeply. He knows how to choke himself; he's been gathering saliva in the back of his throat. He breathes in the fluid with the smoke, deep into his lungs. This is enough to create an authentic scrapping cough like someone is grating the insides of his chest and amplifying the sound through a loudspeaker. He throws himself back in the chair and adds a gurgling growl. It sounds like a death moan. Shaking, jerking and drumming his feet till the finale, he stops the drum roll and his eyes continue, rolling all the way until his audience can see only the whites. Raymius has witnessed enough fits to know that pretty much anything goes. He's guessing that his captors are more concerned about the info they need rather than considering the authenticity of his induced fit. It doesn't look good to whoever the boss is, losing three sources of info due to negligence. All the time Raymius's panto is unfolding he holds on tightly to the cigarette, being careful to protect the business end.

"Shit, not again," Vincent screeches and shouts to the Lab Rat, "Don't let him fall out the chair in case he cracks his skull. You are fucking amateurs! How can we get the answers we want if you keep killing them?"

As the Lab Rat reaches for Raymius's waist he shouts back at Vincent.

"Don't let him choke on his tongue."

In an Eddie Murphy movie this would be great comedy, but Raymius isn't laughing and neither is Etta. In fact she isn't doing anything, she is frozen in the moment and her eyes once again are filing to a point. Raymius realises she knows. She doesn't know it yet, but she senses that something isn't quite right. She's not necessarily smarter than Vincent or the Lab Rat but she's instinctively more aware by a long way. And, she's not in the trees so she can see the woods; she knows. But it doesn't matter because the curtain is up and Raymius's play has begun.

Vincent holsters the Beretta and reaches for Raymius's mouth. Raymius pushes the orange end of the cigarette into one eye and expertly drives his middle finger into the other. Two hands shoot forward and pluck out the Beretta from its home. Vincent jumps backward and loses his balance. Raymius puts two rounds into his chest to help him on his way. On his back, Vincent flails like a dying insect, screaming a flood of profanity and pawing at his own face. But the cigarette breaks and continues to solder itself onto his eyeball. The burning smell reminds Raymius of Japanese teppanyaki as he smashes an elbow through the Lab Rat's nose. The white coat starts to turn red as it lies still on the floor. He gets a waft of Psychoburd's perfume, and as he turns she whips her leg up and round. Raymius manages to miss the first kick aimed at the side of his head, but not the second. She follows through and drives her high heel into Raymius's shoulder. Raymius feels the metal tip stab through his skin and scrape against his collarbone. He closes his eyes and controls his groan while his left hand holds her foot in place. He moves forward, taking more of her heel in his shoulder but also taking her off balance. While his forward motion takes her one way, his left hand twists her foot anti-clockwise and then upwards, taking it the other and successfully snapping her ankle. She falls to the ground screaming like a sack of cats hitting the bottom of a cliff. He double-taps two 9mm rounds into her forehead. The lights in her eyes are saying, *who the fuck are you? You are the one who is supposed to die.* And then the lights go out.

Vincent is up on one knee and turning to face Raymius. Raymius instinctively lets go of another round that tears through the middle of the Honey Monster's face and out the back of his head, taking with it a part of his brain and the last bit of fight.

The Lab Rat becomes conscious and makes for the door. He gets to it and is scrambling with the handle. Raymius can't understand why the red and white coat is still frantically attempting to do what cannot be done. It is obvious the vault is locked. Raymius lowers the Beretta and starts walking towards the Lab Rat, who has now developed stage fright and a puddle around the bottom of his left foot. When Raymius gets to the door he pushes the muzzle into the Lab Rat's mouth.

"Don't make me use this. Now, when I take this out of your face, turn round, slowly, and put your hands flat against the door. If I even think you're going to do anything stupid the game is over. You've probably guessed by now that this is not the first time I've fired a weapon. Understand?"

The Lab Rat nods, very slowly.

Raymius removes the Beretta from the Lab Rat's mouth and takes half a step backwards. The Lab Rat turns about and puts his hands flat against the door.

"Who are you?"

"I'm a police officer."

"What are you going to do?"

"I'm going to ask you some questions and if you give me the right answers I'll arrest you."

"And if I don't?"

Raymius moves the tip of the Beretta until it is in line with the Lab Rat's backside and then thrusts his arm forward…

"Do you have any idea what will happen if I shoot you now?"

The response is hardly even a whimper. "No."

"If I re-invent your arsehole, it'll take a long time for you to bleed to death. Unlike with your machine, I can assure you that you will never forget the pain. After about three minutes you will be begging for me to put a cap in your brain in order to release you from your agony. I don't need to write a paper on this, it's old stuff, and let me assure you that I've forgotten more about inflicting misery than you will ever comprehend. Your choice – at least you've got one, more of a choice than you gave to Emma, more of a choice than you were going to give me." Once again there are those lies. There is no honesty, not even in this room of death.

"What do you want me to do?" The Lab Rat manages to stutter out.

"I'm tired and I'm guessing you are too. Why don't we have a seat?"

The Lab Rat feels the prod of the Beretta into the rim of his anus and realises it's not a question. Raymius steers him to the front of the dentist's chair.

"Sit."

The Lab Rat turns, sits down and once again Raymius takes a half step backwards.

"What do you want me to do?" he asks again nervously.

"Fasten the leg restraints."

The Lab Rat bends forwards and complies like it's an unconscious act. Meanwhile Raymius studies the machine on the trolley. It's not nearly sophisticated enough for a geek like the Lab Rat. Three dials, one switch and two indicator lights. Raymius holds the rubber end of the steel vibrator up above the Lab Rat like he is about to knight him Sir Quivering Wreck. The Lab Rat wipes his swollen face. He resembles someone who's been doing push-ups in a sauna fully clothed.

"What are you going to do?" The Lab Rat repeats nervously.

"Nothing, I'm just curious, that's all. Relax, I'm a police officer. You tell me what I need to hear and we can all go home." The chess game continues, the pawn becomes queen, check. "So what's your name, lab guy?"

"Harold."

"You look hungry, Harold, when was the last time you ate?" Raymius watches the Lab Rat's nervous and confused response intently.

"Eh, no, I'm not hungry, not in the least."

Raymius puts on a surprised expression like he's humouring a child.

"Really, wow! I'm surprised, you look really hungry. Now, when was the last time you had a proper meal, Harold?" The Lab Rat's face distorts again, confused by the situation and the line of questioning. He squints and looks skyward, recalling the events prior to the current ordeal.

"Must have been yesterday since I've had a proper meal, but then again I don't eat much, especially when I'm, eh, working."

The Lab Rat's heart rate is returning to normal and his speech is becoming less of a screech. Once again Raymius looks intensely interested and concerned.

"And tell me, Harold, what is your most favourite dish? What is it that you most like to eat, when you're away from work and relaxing, on holiday perhaps?"

"Sorry?"

"Harold, humour me."

The Lab Rat's face once again distorts, still confused by the situation and the line of questioning. He squints once more and looks skyward again, recalling his happy food memories.

"I love a Sunday roast."

Raymius maintains his pleasant manner and smiles like he's going to take his order and announce that he'll be Harold's waiter tonight.

"What did you think the very first time you met Helen Carter, Harold?"

The Lab Rat's face distorts again as his heart rate starts racing once more. He thinks deeply about the question before answering.

"I've never actually met Helen Carter."

It's Raymius's turn to be confused by the response. He thinks for a while and then his face lights up.

"You little cunt, she's here, isn't she? Helen Carter is here somewhere, isn't she?"

"No she isn't, I've never met her, I'm telling you the truth," he replies, almost crying.

"Harold, when someone accesses their memory, their eyes search for the answer first. You must know that, don't you?" Harold's face is blank. "It's an involuntary response that is perfectly natural. Only highly trained individuals, talented actors and actresses can distort this natural process. Are you a talented actor, Harold?" Again, his face is blank. "Contrary to popular belief everyone to a certain extent is different. When you in particular access your memory, Harold, you look up and to the left. This is very common for a right-handed person. You are right-handed, Harold, aren't you?" The blank expression starts to show signs of panic. "When I asked you about Helen Carter you accessed the part of your brain that stores memory. If you had never met her, your eyes would have nowhere to look. You are not telling the truth, Harold, and we both know that, so let us not waste any more time."

He hands Harold the little steel vibrator. "Put it in your mouth."

"No."

Raymius cocks his head to one side and points the Beretta at Harold's groin.

"OK, OK, OK, I've met her, I've met her, but she isn't here, I promise, I'm telling you the truth."

Raymius stops and ponders for a second.

"OK, I believe you, but I'm running out of patience so here's what we're going to do. I've had a big day. But I'm not going to turn the machine on you, I promise, I'm not that sick. But I do need to know that you know what it feels like to be on the other side of your toy. Call it a lesson in remorse. Call it my way of rehabilitating someone who has lost his way. Call it what you like. Like you said, it's not the pain that makes you talk, it's the aversion to the pain. Now, I'm guessing you've witnessed the pain more than once?"

He nods. Raymius's eyebrows crease. "So we don't really have to go there, do we?" Harold shakes his head frantically in agreement.

"As a matter of interest, just how many times have you witnessed this machine work?"

The Lab Rat's face manages to look even more terrified and his red eyes now let go of big round tears that roll down his cheeks. His terror merges with remorse.

"Let's just stick to ballpark – more than a hundred or less than a hundred?"

"More."

Within Raymius, Vesuvius erupts. His face, however, is expressionless and his whole manner finds a new lease of calm.

"So like I said, Harold, think of your paper, think of your research. I want a few answers so let's play you-get-to-know-how-it-feels. And, so long as you don't bullshit me, you don't ever need to know what the pain really feels like. But you do get to experience the feel of the steel in your mouth and the tension of the aversion process. Like I've already said, think of your paper, think of it as invaluable research. What do you say, Harold? Deal or no deal?"

Harold looks as if he's been frozen to the seat.

"Look, Harold, I don't think there's anything you can tell me anyway so I'd just as soon shoot you in the balls." Raymius once again points the Beretta at his groin. "So what would you rather play with?" The Lab Rat puts his mouth over the steel rod. "Bite onto it with your teeth." Another whimper leaks out as Raymius reaches for the trolley.

"I just want you to experience…"

"Where are you going?" Harold protests.

Raymius stops and turns to face him. "I'm going to turn off your machine, but if you don't put the lollipop back in your mouth I might change my mind."

The Lab Rat puts the rod back in his mouth and bites down hard, the sweat once again starts running off his forehead.

"Put your head in the headrest and arms in the grooves of the armrest. Try to relax and enjoy the experience; think about your paper. I'm not going to do anything unless you get stupid. I told you, I'm a police officer, I'm going to call in soon and we'll take you down the station. It's not like all of this is down to you, you're small potatoes, just a hired hand. We're after Mr Big. Chill out, Harold."

Raymius goes over and puts his hand over the on/off switch. The Lab Rat's eyes start to dart from side to side. His nostrils are flaring and there's phlegm dribbling out the side of his mouth. Raymius smiles and with a relaxed voice says., "Hey Harold, if it's OK I'll get the formalities over with and read you your rights?"

The Lab Rat seems to relax a little again and nods frantically.

"I am arresting you as an accessory on the suspicion of murder." Raymius smiles. "You have the right to remain silent, anything you might say..." His hand changes direction to the power lever and he pushes it all the way home. He remembers the old tag line 'don't sell the sausage'. He looks with fascination and waits for the sizzle. As the red needles shoot past all the black and white numbers and get lost in the red wedges at the end of the little glass windows, Harold's teeth and lips weld themselves onto the stainless steel rod. The snapping sound is like when you accidentally stomp on a plastic CD cover. The Lab Rat's body vibrates inside his clothes like an alien is about to burst out. His cheeks turn a deep purple before they start to tear open and melt. Both eyes drop out to reveal orange and blue dislocated eye sockets. Flames shoot out of all remaining exits, making Harold's face resemble a pumpkin at Halloween that's been sponsored by Scottish Gas. As the steel vibrator falls free what appear to be bits of lips, tongue and teeth remain attached. He sounds like an old man having a wet dream. And then it all goes quiet. Raymius cocks his head to one side again with a certain degree of satisfaction.

There is a set of keys attached to the Honey Monster's belt. As he rips them from his middle he sees a bulge. After exploration he finds a couple of clips for the Beretta. The contents of both speed loaders are full. He's about to walk away but stops and remembers something else: his cigarettes. He nods his head. "Thanks, big guy." He knows he won't have enough rounds for the trouble he is about to encounter outside the vault door but at least he'll create enough chaos to make it all worth it and of course keep one in reserve, for himself. He is sure of two things: He won't give up and he won't be having another go of their fucking lie detector.

As he walks past the smouldering Lab Rat, he smiles. "... Anything you do say might be taken down and used against you in a court of law." He pauses and lights a cigarette. "So, Mr Harold Lab Rat, how would you describe that? While it's still fresh? In your mind!"

> **job** *n* **1** an activity such as a trade or profession that somebody does regularly for pay. **2** an assignment or an individual piece of work of a particular nature **3** something that is difficult to accomplish. **4** a crime or criminal act. 5 the book of the Bible that describes Job's afflictions and eventual reward **6.** in the Bible, a righteous man whose faith withstood severe testing by God...

The last key opens the door. No one is in the hallway. A mouse is nibbling at crumbs a few feet away, where the floor meets the wall. It looks up, startled, stares at Raymius for a nanosecond and scurries away out of a well-planned escape route. Raymius stops and listens for a while, his eyes surveying the emptiness. It feels like a bank holiday. Raymius does something he never thought he would ever do again; he takes a deep breath. His ears feel as if they are pinned to the back of his head. He goes back into the room and heads for the DJ's console. He proceeds to remove all the footage by saving everything on the hard drive to a USB memory stick that's protruding from the PC's tower. *I love the 21st Century,* Raymius thinks to himself. He gathers all the mobile phones and puts them in his pocket apart from his own, which he switches on and immediately texts John Ribbon.

"%"

A few miles away at the other side of Glasgow, Ribbon turns to the sergeant in charge of the Support Group he's with and hands him his mobile phone.

"Trace the signal, Sergeant."

"Roger that, sir."

Back a short way along the corridor from the chamber Raymius opens the door to a small room that a guard would normally occupy. It's empty. Raymius examines the chart on the wall and tries to make sense of what looks like an underground village. He's realising that Ribbon's hunch, as usual, is right. Raymius has found the lost village of Grahamston. If the book Ribbon gave him is right, he'll be in walking distance of Glasgow Central if he can only manage to find his way back up to street level.

All the monitors and electrics are off. He finds the master switch and powers up the system. He checks the screens marked CCTV and notices there are only two red lights on. He flicks the switch for the first and gets the Deconsecration Chamber. Raymius shudders as he sees the two leather chairs but feels comforted since everyone is still exactly where he left them. He flicks the switch for the other and smiles at the irony as he quickly checks the schematic on the wall for 13 on level C. He then locates the 'You-are-Here' point and the nearest elevator. He's at the lift within seconds, still expecting to run round a corner and into a firefight. But, apart from the hum coming from the elevator shaft, all is still deathly quiet. The lift clunks at his level and breaks back into the silence. The doors shudder open, he moves into the lift and figures out he's on level B. He presses the square aluminium button that reads 'C'. The lift starts to descend. Raymius feels as if he's travelling to the centre of the earth.

A few miles away, the sergeant in charge of the support group turns to DCI Ribbon and shakes his head. "Sorry, sir, we've just lost the signal and we've not had enough time to trace it."

Ribbon's head drops into both hands he tears at his own hair. "Shit."

The lift eventually stutters and slows to a halt. The steel doors open automatically. Again the whole place is deserted, like everyone has been laid off or gone on holiday. It's like a scene from the cargo bay in Alien Resurrection. Raymius realises that he has now found Glasgow's Catacombs. He holds back a gasp as he remembers the pictures he has seen of the Ossuary in Paris and looks around himself at almost exactly the same sight. Layer upon layer and layer of neatly stacked bones. *The forensic team are going to be employed down here for years,* he thinks. Again he's at his objective in seconds – room 13. He takes the security credit card attached to the Honey Monster's keys and swipes the electronic lock outside the door. It whirrs and opens. Panic is painted all over her face.

"Helen, I've come to take you home. Do you understand?"

No response. He holds out his hand. She throws her arms around him. Raymius cradles the back of her head as she buries her face into his chest.

"We need to go, Helen. Do you understand?"

No response. Raymius holds his fingers to his nose and sniffs.

"Peach…"

She looks into his eyes and nods.

"You're going to be OK, Helen, but we need to go, now!"

She starts nodding her head slowly while simultaneously shaking uncontrollably. He squeezes her hand firmly as she gazes at the stacks upon stacks of bones. The lift seems to take an eternity.

"Are you hungry? Breathe, Helen. We will be OK soon. It's almost over." The whole time Raymius knows that hell might break loose at any moment. He has no idea what's waiting for them on level A. He feels his phone vibrate but has no time to answer it. He takes the almost empty magazine out and replaces it with a full one. He presses the aluminium button.

The doors open and they are presented with what appears to be the cellar. He looks round at the beer kegs and notices an inscription on the brick wall.

Custodians: United Breweries PLC

They walk up the small, steep stairwell and open the door to be confronted with a pub peppered with no more than a dozen punters. He thinks about the line from Pulp Fiction as he fires a round into the ceiling and shouts: "Right you cunts, fuck off, this is a robbery." He points the Beretta at the big, fat, unshaven male behind the cash register, who echoes Raymius's instructions as the locals bimble out the bar in such a manner that Raymius thinks this must happen in here fairly regularly. Nobody seems remotely bothered about live rounds flying over their head and a few had actually taken the time to take their drinks with them. As the last punter leaves, shutting the door behind him, the barman barks back: "You have no idea who the fuck you're dealing with, skinny boy!"

Raymius fires another round into the glass mirror behind the sentries of optics. "The next one is for your brain. Call the police and tell them you are being robbed."

The big guy looks confused and seems as if he's about to offer another wisecrack. Raymius fires another round into the shards of mirror that remain hanging to the wall. "Now, I may have meant that or I may have just missed that big thick fucking skull you've still got. In case you haven't realised, I'm in a hurry."

The big guy has a reality check and starts frantically dialling 999. Apart from the dialogue the barman is having with emergency services and Helen's deafening silence, Raymius hears the words from the Jukebox. David Bowie singing Ground Control to Major Tom. Raymius thinks of an old saying of Ribbon's. *Life is always full of irony if you only take the time to look.*

"Police…"

"Armed robbery…"

"Now…"

"Naw! It's not a fuckin' hoax… Yeah, I know it's fucking serious, I'm the one that's got a gun in my face, hen… Grant Arms, Argyle Street… Jamie McKinney… Aye, right don't worry, I will." He puts the receiver back in its cradle. "Hope you know what you're doin', son."

A few miles away the support group sergeant informs Ribbon about the armed robbery and confirms it matches the location of the signal they've just traced. Ribbon responds: "Let's go and bring our guy home. Send all our available resources to Glasgow Central Station. If he can he'll head for the ramp, it's the closest RV point."

Back at the Grant Arms, Raymius is still issuing instructions. "Turn your podgy arse round and put your hands on top of your head, big guy." As the barman complies Raymius picks up an overcoat and woolly hat that's been left on a seat and hands them to Helen.

"Put these on. We're nearly home. You still OK?"

"What are you doin', Ray?" she manages.

"No time to explain, Helen, just trust me. We'll be safe soon, I promise."

She nods. As they slip out of the swing doors into Argyle Street, his mobile phone starts to vibrate. He safeties the Beretta and tucks it into his belt at the small of his back. He presses the picture of a little green telephone.

"I'm heading for the ramp, John."

"Good boy."

"You can tell Helen's uncle she's looking forward to seeing him."

"You OK?"

"Hell no, don't be long." Raymius hears the other end click. Ribbon is already en route.

"We'll be OK soon, the cavalry is on its way, Helen." As they walk under the bridge on the way to the escalators the public move out their way like they have the plague.

Ribbon gets an immediate update of Raymius's progress. "Alpha one, our man is on the move. He has someone with him, looks like a POW from an old Vietnam movie. It might be a woman."

Raymius picks up a polystyrene cup from Costa Coffee and sits down at the ramp, pulling Helen down beside him. She is still seriously in shock. She seems confused about the cup. He explains. "People are only curious about what's not normal. If you don't want to attract attention, sit in a busy place and get the right props for begging. Very soon you melt into the walls."

A loudspeaker from high above echoes out.

"The next train to depart platform one will be the 1700hrs express to London Euston." Raymius lights a cigarette and offers Helen a draw. Not a good idea to give her a whole cigarette, not yet anyway. A pound coin drops into the paper cup. Raymius looks up. Helen's head buries deeper into her newly acquired overcoat.

"Evening, Ray."

"Hi Arthur."

"As always you know there's plenty more where that came from if you and your new friend want to..." He stops. Raymius follows Arthur's eyes to Helen's leg; it's trembling over an increasing pool of pee. Raymius looks at Helen's face as her head starts to emerge from her coat. She's staring at Arthur and her entire body is now shivering. She looks at Raymius, her face radiating terror. His right hand moves to the small of his back. His fingers curl round the grip of the Beretta. Arthur forces a smile.

"Let me get you a little something for both of you." He steps back and begins to reach inside his jacket. "I'll just get my wallet..."

"POLICE! DO NOT MOVE!"

Everyone stops what they're doing to look round. "Step aside, sir." Arthur steps aside to reveal an entire armed support group unit with their weapons focused on both Raymius and Helen. Raymius raises his hands above his head and turns to Helen.

"Just do as they say, Helen. You'll be safe now." She turns to him.

"Oh Ray, what have you done?"

"I'm fine, Helen, just do as they say, we're both safe now." He watches Arthur disappear into the rush-hour traffic like a teardrop in rain. They are both escorted into the back of the support group's van. Ribbon is already there, waiting for them. He takes off their handcuffs, Helen's first. Raymius lights up another cigarette. The officer driving the van turns and looks through the wire mesh panel.

"You can't smoke in here!"

Raymius ignores him and offers one to Helen.

"I SAID NO..."

Ribbon holds his hand up to interrupt. "Let it go, constable."

"And who the fuck are you, sir?"

Ribbon knocks the window and gestures to the sergeant of the support group. He comes over and opens the driver's door. "Thank you, constable, I'll take it from here." He turns round and smiles at Ribbon, who is already smoking and is offering Helen and Raymius a light.

"Thought you'd given up, John?" asks Raymius.

"It's been a busy couple of days, fella." He turns to the sergeant. "Take us to the safe house."

"Sir."

Raymius lets go of a large intake of smoke and sighs. He looks at Ribbon with resignation. "When the uniforms turned up our Professor and I were talking on the ramp. I suspect he has just slipped out of Glasgow Central Station and through our fingers."

Ribbon gets on the radio. "Send a unit immediately to secure the CCTV footage for Glasgow Central Station... No, now, damn it! What bit about immediately don't you understand? Tell them to proceed with caution, the Professor is on the loose. He's probably armed and already started to clean the area."

In the control room at Glasgow Central Station, a security guard lies dead, his cracked skull still bleeding, his neck broken. The footage has already been erased and the copies removed. In a few minutes when the units arrive at the CCTV cameras overlooking the ramp, they'll find none of them are operational. They have all already been disabled.

Back in the van, Raymius takes another puff of his cigarette.

"I'm guessing it's too late. He knows, John, he's already gone. We've missed our chance."

"I know, Ray, you're probably right. He can disappear again, change his appearance. He can even change the shape and colour of his eyes. But he can't change what's behind them. He'll be back, he'll come up for air, stick his head up above the covers. And when he does, we'll be waiting."

Ribbon watches Ray take his mobile phone out of his pocket. "You still working, son?"

"I promised I'd text a friend."

THE END of book ONE...

EPILOGUE

Lie... (lies) 1. recline **2**. be placed on a flat surface **3**. be located somewhere **4**. be buried **5**. be in a specified position in a race **6**. be in a particular state **7**. Be in a particular direction **8**. be in store **9**. stay undisturbed **10**. unacceptable in law **11**. an animal's resting place **12**. position of a golf ball **13**. a false statement made with **14**. deliberate intent to deceive an intentional untruth a falsehood. **15**. something intended or serving to convey a false impression **16**. an inaccurate or false statement a falsehood **17. (Lying)** present participle of **lie**...

R aymius rubs the sleep from the corner of his eyes. He realises that he had nodded off and starts to replay today's headlines. Aaron's new uniform for school. Confirmation of his final marching orders. The Club Lounge. Priority boarding.

Raymius is happy with his place in life. A long time ago he had listened to the Universal Dinner Lady and only recently realised the truth. We create our own reality. He'd picked it himself. It's not the type of career you choose for cash. Fuck, he'd do it for free, most of the time. This time anyway for sure. He has no reason to feel depressed. Not being around Aaron and the heads-up from Ribbon is upsetting, but that is another story.

Aaron looked smart as a carrot in his new uniform. An odd expression he'd picked up from RSM Brandy Weatherburn. A man's man. A soldier's soldier. Aaron was standing straight as a pencil and beaming for the camera. *Good lad.* Raymius couldn't stop himself from laughing at his son's missing front tooth; the other one would be gone shortly too. He rubs his left ear on his shoulder and closes his eyes to increase the definition in his mind. He smiles and his chest fills with warmth. *What a handsome boy.* The lens blinked, followed by the flash, a buzzing vibration in his pocket, and an impatient shout.

"Let me see Dad, let me see?"

Raymius handed over the 'Olympus Trip' to Aaron as he pulled out his mobile. The text, even though it was expected, took away the joy in Raymius's face the same way the sun's light fades after the arrival of an unwanted cloud. He looked at Aaron's grandmother. Her face resembled the winter of discontent. She was already staring, waiting for him to state the obvious. He pressed the button with the picture of a little green telephone. Time to go, now. A voice answered immediately.

"Scot."

"Hullo Scot, go secure."

"Roger that. Secure."

"I've got the attachment. If there are any questions or problems I'll get back to you within the hour."

"Roger that."

"Out."

Raymius ended the secure connection. There were no questions, there were no problems. It was only a few hours ago but it felt like days. Another mission, another life, another plane. Raymius has swapped his **HS-USD: High Sensitivity - Ultra Slim Design** for a Creative Zen. A Digital Audio Player. He puts one of his new earphones into his left lug and pushes on. The Zen can still get radio but also has the ability to store about twenty of his favourite albums. No brainer.

Raymius breathes in the aroma of freshly ground beans from the coffee machine. *Now that is impressive. I'll be having some of that shortly.* After he presses play the noise from the hustle and bustle of his surroundings fades into the background and is replaced by what has recently become a new favourite. He closes his eyes and smiles as he remembers his last night in the Scotia Bar. That also feels like a lifetime ago. The Proclaimers' 1987 album, This is the story. Classic.

This is a story of our first teacher…

Raymius is now free of the usual suspects and suspects at some point he might miss the magical city of Glasgow, but fuck it. If you hang about in the sewers long enough you end up smelling of shite. No more Scotia Bar. No more squats, no more low-lifers. No more freezing cold wriggly tin hides at the top of Queen's Park. No more rats, sleepless nights and no more fucking rain. Ms Langan and her therapist had been appeased. All the usual suspects had been happy as fuck. For a while, anyway.

Shetland made her jumpers
And the Devil made her features

Clean white Egyptian cotton sheets are on his list of gubbings along with a chance to look and feel human again. No more binge boozing, no more mindbending lethargic hash heads. H had got five years for serious assault, having had his sentence reduced from attempted murder. Money no issue equals expensive lawyer equals five instead of ten. Gavin Brookfield had survived to get his jaw wired. That should keep a lot of people happy for a while in more ways than one. No more fucking cancer sticks either. The smoking ban is in full swing now and he doesn't miss it a bit. Last that he had heard Noonan had booked a trip for him and that bird with the road-sweeper headlights. Cuba. Raymius is also on his way to sunnier climes and still can't believe it. Beverly fucking Hills. Praise the Lord.

> *It's over and done with…*
> *It's over and done with*

Raymius has also swapped Deefor with a leather flight bag and Shanks's Pony for Virgin Atlantic's Upper Class. When he'd first reclined the seat as far back as it could go he was literally lying horizontally and thought to himself, *No, that's just too far.*

> *This is a story of watching a man dying*
> *The subject's unpopular*
> *But I don't feel like lying*
> *When I think of it now I acted like a sinner*
> *I just washed my hands*
> *Then I went for my dinner*
> *It's over and done with…*
> *It's over and done with*

He pulls out his little notebook. Some things never change. He's been working on his new legend. One important consideration had been what accent to adopt. All options considered, the conclusion was that the Scottish accent for this job would do just fine. He would of course have to re-calibrate the Glaswegian attitude. He has also swapped his red pen for a blue one.

To-do's Today
Aaron's new camera
Gardening World
Triple A batteries
Tony says take a holiday + consider CBT
Enjoy the flight

He thinks back to when Ribbon had floated the whole deal: "It's not just a job, Ray, it's a fucking Hollywood adventure. You play your cards right and you could end up doing shaving ads."

Ribbon couldn't resist making Lethal Weapon references since the very first one.

"Aye, fella, bollocks to Mel Gibson we should register you as a Lethal Weapon."

"You think about it. You think about it hard, but not too long. It's a two-way-fucking street. The suits need to know if you're still our man."

Ribbon had sworn more than once in one spiel and by all accounts he hardly ever swore at all. Raymius figured Ribbon was just as wound up as himself. The bastard was that the Professor had sent Ribbon another letter.

"Oldman knows about Aaron, fella. Sorry."

Raymius knows that Ribbon has given him information that by the rules he doesn't need to know. Raymius had said that it didn't change a thing, but it did. It changes everything. The Professor might be well informed about many things but he doesn't know Raymius the way Ribbon does.

"You'll have the house for a whole month to yourself. A pool and a fucking Jacuzzi. Beverly Hills Cop. The owner is in Europe on business, or at least that's the script. You've got more time if you need it. The owner can be delayed indefinitely but this is costing a fucking fortune so don't milk it indefinitely. You were right about the whole cook thing, you pick your own legend for this one. Let us know asap so that we can start to fill in the blanks if anyone starts snooping. It goes without saying the super-rich and famous are paranoid about who they let into their neighborhood, let alone their homes."

Ribbon still felt the need to say it just the same. It had been suggested to Raymius that he should hide under this cover as the cook. For a whole number of reasons, it didn't make fucking sense to be the cook. What spanner came up with that suggestion? It was Ribbon's job to address that training need.

The owner was some English tycoon who'd made his millions by retailing overpriced designer jeans. MI5 or 6 had some sensitive information which meant that our resident tycoon would be in complete cooperation. Intel had plenty of information that suggested Professor Oldman was back in business in Beverly Hills. It had his MO all over it. Most villains with sustainability have a process. The symptom of that process is the problem that nobody gets to see them that often and the ones that do don't get to hang about for too long. All Raymius had to do was confirm the professor was on the ground and then get out of Tinsel Town.

For the moment though, all Raymius has to do is chill out and enjoy the inflight entertainment.

A new feature of his Creative Zen is 'shuffle'. Raymius normally doesn't appreciate surprises but this is different. His attention is brought back into the moment by the irony of the intro starting on his playlist. Four beats to the bar. Four bars. C Major.

Dum dum dum dum
Dum dum dum dum
Dum dum dum dum
Dum dum dum dum

Easy-peasy, not complicated at all. Raymius thinks. *It's not like it's a sixteen-bit encryption, is it? Classic.*

When you go will you send back a letter from America?
Take a look up the rail track from Miami to Canada…

Raymius puts in the right earpiece and presses the little button to alert a flight attendant. He watches the button glow and is contemplating what the usual suspects will be up to at the Scotia when a tap on his shoulder interrupts his thoughts. He looks up and takes the right earpiece back out.

"Yes, sir, what can I get you?"

He looks for the inflight magazine or some sort of menu whilst trying not to look like he doesn't fly Upper Class all the time but at the same time his head is somewhere else.

Well broke off from my work the other day
Spent the evening thinking about all
the blood that flowed away
Across the ocean to the second chance
I wonder how it got on when it reached the promised land?'

Fuck, that was quick. I suppose oral sex is out of the question. Blow job lips. That's how Noonan would describe her. Aye, Noonan and that big orange bird. Amanda. I wonder what the Two Donnies and that wee cunt Dillon are up to c'est soir? Clare. Ah well. Too bad. That ship has sailed. C'est la vie.

Raymius returns to the moment realising that the stewardess is losing her patience and her plastic smile.

When you go will you send back a letter from America?
Take a look up the rail track from Miami to Canada…

Raymius takes out the left earpiece, presses pause and pops the Zen into his shirt pocket.

"Could I have a double espresso? Please."

"Sure thing, sir, anything else?"

"Some Champagne?"

The stewardess beams a perfect smile and her eyelashes flutter ever so slightly.

"That won't be a problem, sir. Will there be anything else?"

Raymius smiles back like he's Marlon Brando in the Godfather.

"I really need to go and take a leak first, will that be OK?"

"Not a problem, sir, I'll look out for you. Will that be all for now?"

Raymius smirks, pauses for effect and then says: "Aye, once I get back that'll be all for now. Caffeine and bubbles will be just fine. Thank you."

"You are most welcome."

As she walks along the aisle he adjusts his neck so that his eyes can follow her elegant gait down to the drinks. He enjoys her curves and her wiggle. He does the maths on how long it will take for her arse to devour the toffee it's chewing. He can also just make out the hint of a thong and would bet money it is that rich blood red colour to match her uniform. He contemplates how long it took for her to become a member of the Mile High Club. As she reaches her destination she has a word with her colleague before turning around and smiling back at Raymius. He returns the smile before realising that his head is inappropriately placed. He could imagine his wee mum saying; *"Sit up properly. Somebody might want to get past."*

Curiously the seat belt sign gets turned off almost immediately, followed by the usual bullshit from the Captain. Raymius can't remember any turbulence but then again, he did dose off for what was a while. He gets up from his seat to join the battle for the loo. It seems that he is not the only one who needs to get rid of what they consumed in the lounge before boarding. A wee posh or gay or both, Goth and a member of the blue rinse brigade beat him to it. He checks the time on the wee Goth's wrist watch and thinks; *Fucking hell, we must have been delayed. How long was I dosing for?*

The wee Goth looks at Raymius looking at his watch and reads his mind.

"I know. I didn't expect that long a delay. We had to wait for the usual stragglers to finally get on board. Some people, eh? Just as well the seat belt sign went off when it did. I was beginning to break into a sweat. Didn't think I was going to make it there."

The toilet door opens, the wee posh Goth curls the left-hand side of his lower lip, bites it, widens his eye sockets like his eyeballs are wanting to pop out his head and sort of dances off. He bids his departure apologetically.

"Sorry, excuse me, must dash, toodle-pip."

Raymius doesn't have a problem waiting it out but he is looking forward to enjoying the flight so the sooner he can sort his ablutions the sooner he can crack on with that. He is doing what he does and just taking it all in, who's with who, who's a frequent flyer, who's on business, who's on holiday but before he can sweep and record the whole cabin he gets interrupted with a nudge by the guy in the pink shirt and dark blue pinstriped trousers who's next in the queue behind himself. Pink shirt guy doesn't say anything. All that is needed is a gentle touch with his elbow and an exaggerated glance towards the vacant sign.

"Aye OK pal, got it."

Raymius closes the door slides the latch to occupado, lifts the lid and peers down inside the big white mint. The smell wafts up his nose nano-seconds before his eyes blur and then start to water. *Fuckin' Hell, now that's rich!* Raymius has always had an acute sense of smell. At times like this it is not a bene-fit, it is a hazard. On the side of the porcelain bowl about half way up is what appears to be a melted king-size chocolate bar. He's pretty sure it's not a Yorkie because it's the wrong shade of brown and has more of a Galaxy look to it, *definitely not Bourneville.*

Since there are no indications of nuts he's also ruling out Snickers. *Now there's another good point*, he thinks, pondering to himself. *Is it actually porcelain? It could be plastic that just looks like porcelain.* In an attempt to always gravitate towards the positive he smiles to himself, acknowledging that at least the beer and whisky are still having their effects and soon the caffeine and bubbles will be kicking in. He notices several yellow foreign bodies amidst the melted fudge and contemplates the market-ability of chocolate confectionary that hosts sweetcorn. *Dirty bastard.*

As he pees he starts the cleaning process like he was peeling muck from a wall with a fireman's hose. Raymius is not the type who would care if the next person in line thought it was him. Couldn't give a fuck what other people think, but you don't walk out and leave that kind of mess, even if it is somebody else's. In any case, from a professional point of view it wasn't exactly congruent with any strategy of maintaining anonymity.

"Can you remember anything about him?"

"Aye, he was the one who left that shite in the toilet! Dirty bastard."

Raymius has always been fascinated about how you can put people into definitive categories. Those who want to do the right thing but usually find some excuse not to; those who want to be seen to do the right thing; and those who just get it done.

After what felt like a four-pinter peters out, small remnants of chocolate-covered sweet corn still stick doggedly to the side of the pan. His hands, protected by an adequate supply of paper tissue, reach in, dip the water and rub the remains loose. He flushes and waits. When the aqua engineering has concluded, he inspects. He smiles, satisfied, and although nothing has penetrated the tissue this is one occasion when one ensures to thoroughly wash one's hands. He grins. *Job done.*

As he walks back to his seat he spots the senior citizen avoiding eye contact and cringes. *Ah well, fair enough, better out than in. SO1, Serve to Lead. Dirty auld bastard.*

The stewardess gives him one of those knowing smiles and he imagines that she's saying: *Better, eh?* In his mind, he retorts: *Too fucking right.*

The caffeine and bubbles arrives shortly after he does. No plastic smile this time. He looks at her name.

"Svetlana?"

"Yes."

"Russian?"

"Georgian."

"Excuse me, I am sorry. Izvinite, ya proshu proshcheniya."

"Ty govorish' po-russki? You speak Russian?"

"Yes, a little. Da, nemnogo."

"Otlichno, otlichno. Very good, very good."

They both giggle at each other in mutual appreciation. Raymius blinks first.

"My pronunciation is not great."

Your pronunciation is fine, sir, but you should work a little on your accent. To speak Russian correctly you must sound Russian."

Raymius snorts out loud then adjusts his tone down an octave and tries to sound more like Stellan Skarsgard playing Captain Viktor Tupolev in The Hunt for Red October.

"Of course, Svetlana. Spasibo bol'shoye."

"Fantastic! Otlichno, otlichno." I must be a good teacher.

"You have no hint of an accent, Svetlana, where did you learn English?"

"I moved to England when I was little. I went to school and university there."

"Cambridge?"

"Yes, well done again. Otlichno."

Svetlana begins to look like she has realised she is enjoying herself too much. She reaches over and plucks out a menu for food and a brochure for inflight entertainment. She hands them both to Raymius.

"Can I bring you a headset?"

"Not just now thank you, Svetlana. I've got a bit of reading to do."

jo3m

"It's a long flight, sir. You know how to reach me if you need anything." She looks at the flight attendant's button. "You know, a lot of people who are busy choose to fly Upper Class with us so that they can get their work done and forget the most important point."

"Really, what's that?"

"To enjoy the flight."

"Got it."

He picks up his essential reading but doesn't zone into the pages for a while because he is imagining Svetlana walking up the aisle chewing that toffee. His left eyebrow creases as his right creeps up his forehead. He shakes his head slightly and his nostrils flare before he sighs and then eventually smiles.

He necks the double espresso followed by a bubbles chaser. He flicks through the magazine, looks at the pages with the Post-its to remind himself why and thinks: *Gardening for Dummies.* He then looks at the contents and notices the poem of the month. *For fuck sake.* Inspired and adapted from a Glass Half Full by Felix Dennis.

Never go back. *I know this guy, he was big around the time of the Beatles, made his money with that old Bruce Lee magazine Kung Fu monthly. Now he's a fucking poet. Classic.*

Memories

A Blast from the Past

I ventured back to the haunts of my youth

The same bar stools were being warmed

By the same fat arses

Dead men

With that same old stare

No one was waiting for me there

I thought about the glorious past

The battles I've fought

How life goes so fast
The bridges I burned
The people I've bought
The present
My future, I've earned
Why would you want to go back?
Leave the well-beaten track
Open the cupboard that's bare
Holding your breath
In Anticipation
Then realization
No one is waiting
Nothing is left for you there
Inspired and adapted from a Glass Half Full

By Homer Spires

Homer Spires, now there is a name I don't recognise. Raymius pops the left ear piece back in. He knows that there is much waiting for him back home. Maybe it's time to consider a career change. While he was researching his new assignment, he couldn't help thinking that money gives you more than freedom; it gives you currency, power. But as the cliché goes, absolute power corrupts absolutely. Money doesn't change you, it just makes you more of who you are.

The beautiful people of Hollywood had made a bit of a mess and were perhaps only attempting to clean their own laundry. Tinsel Town may be a law unto itself but unwittingly if they have accepted Professor Oldman into their inner circle they have just embraced an individual who has a penchant for being judge and jury. The Professor is another man who has made a career out of getting things done.

Raymius puts in the right earpiece and presses the pause button to re-enter the world of the Creative Zen. It starts where it had left off.

...I've looked at the ocean tried hard to imagine
The way you felt the day you sailed from
Wester Ross to Nova Scotia
We should have held you, we should have told you
But you know our sense of timing we always wait too long

When you go will you send back a letter from America?
Take a look up the rail track from Miami to Canada

Lochaber no more, Sutherland no more
Lewis no more, Skye no more
Lochaber no more, Sutherland no more
Lewis no more, Skye no more...

Raymius presses pause once again. He takes out his left earpiece first. It was a feeling. A sixth sense, perhaps, but a smell that doesn't make sense. Perhaps he's not got rid of the effects of all that hash he'd consumed. *Paranoia can't last this long, can it? Flash backs in smell? Regression? Too much caffeine? The Champagne? All of it together in one wonderful nostalgic cocktail?*

"Your mind does play tricks on you from time to time. You have been in deep cover for a very long time, Raymius. How can you possibly know what effect all of this is having on your mental health? For goodness' sake, man, you really need to take at least a year off. Take a holiday. You cannot do a proper diagnosis until it's finished, done, over. The best you can hope for right now is that something in there doesn't snap."

That's what Tony had said.

It's only a scent, for fuck sake, they sell it in shops. It is possible that someone else bought some.

But I've never smelled that before, anywhere else.

Aye, but that was Glasgow.

Then a voice in his ear.

"Looking for business, sir?"

Raymius looks up, more astonished than surprised.

"Clare?"

"Well, actually it's Stephanie. I got your text, thanks, appreciate that."

"I like the uniform."

"Yes, I thought you might. John thought this would be best."

"What, the uniform?"

"Cute."

"It was all a bit last minute, wasn't sure I would make it. It's complicated."

"OK, let's stick with simple. Ribbon?"

"Yes, that's right, detective."

"Are we in protocol?" Raymius closes his eyes for a moment, cursing himself, and thinks: *What a prick! Did I really just say that?*

She puts her finger to her lips.

"Protocol? What are you talking about?" She leans over and whispers: "Don't be so fucking silly, are you pissed?"

"Where's the Glasgow accent?"

"Glasgow."

"Very convincing. Where did you..."

She doesn't let him finish. "RSAMD. Look, we have plenty of time to reminisce later but for now, at least I am still working."

Raymius thinks, *WTF* and then starts to take in the additional information.

"Figures. Stephanie, I never did ask you what your perfume was called. It's very distinctive."

"Thank you, sir, it's called Amber."

"Amber?"

"Hard translucent fossilised resin."

"Yes, I know what amber is, Stephanie, and since I also know what it smells like, it would be great if you could fill in the blanks."

She surveys the cabin before smiling and answering.

353

"Later."

"Irony?"

"What?"

"Amber."

"How's that?"

"A cautionary signal between red for stop and green for go."

"Cute. I wore it especially for you." She pauses and surveys the cabin again. "In case you didn't recognise me."

"Blonde, I like it. It suits you."

"Naturally."

Raymius splutters.

"Really?"

"Yes. Really!"

"So where can I buy some of this Amber?"

"You can't."

"Why not?

"I make it myself. Look how long are we going to do this for… Raymius?"

"It's a long flight, Stephanie, do you have a parachute and a boat?

"What?"

"Well if you don't then you and I are not going anywhere anytime soon."

"In case you have missed the obvious, I have things to attend to."

"Really? I thought perhaps John had organized a Kiss-o-gram."

"Very cute."

"OK, so this passenger is needing a little more attention, indulge me. So, you make your own perfume, Stephanie. Chemistry degree?"

"Pharmacy."

"Of course. I didn't see you earlier."

"I was last on… with a few late passengers."

"Of course. Like I said, nice uniform." He looks at the name tag again. "Stephanie, really?"

"What do you think?"

Raymius finishes his Champagne. "Fair enough." He hands her the empty glass. "Can I have another?"

"No problem, sir, I'll get Svetlana to sort that out for you straight away. I hear you speak Russian?" She takes the glass from him.

"Da."

She leans over a little and whispers again.

"Svetlana likes you. I think you might be in if you play your cards right. However, I've got 48 hours in LA before I head for Moscow. It's your call."

"Moscow?"

"Moscow."

She leans over and picks up the empty espresso cup. "I'll take this away too. Would you like another?" She leans closer, her lips almost touching his ear. "John Ribbon thought that this would be best. He told me to tell you that if you didn't understand… He said…" She has another survey of the cabin. Raymius is sitting back now with arms folded. She leans forward again to within a millimetre of his ear. "…At this moment in time and under these circumstances you don't need to. I know when you get a chance to think about it you'll work it out eventually."

"He said that?"

"Word for word."

"Figures. OK, Stephanie, if I don't get a chance to chat to you again before we land I guess I'll see you in LA. You know where I'm staying, of course?"

"Of course."

Raymius just looks and as he puts back in the left earpiece and presses play he asks:

"Anything else?"

"I'll send over Svetlana, sir. Enjoy your flight."

> *Lochaber no more, Sutherland no more*
> *Lewis no more, Skye no more..."*

> *When you go will you send back a letter from America?*
> *Take a look up the rail track from Miami to Canada*

> *I wonder my blood will you ever return*
> *To help us kick the life back to a dying mutual friend?*
> *Do we not love her? I think we all claim we love her*
> *Do we have to roam the world to prove how much it hurts?*

Minutes later Svetlana appears with an even bigger smile. He presses pause.

"Dobryy vecher Svetlana."

"Dobryy vecher, you called?"

"I think I am ready to order some food and watch some of the inflight entertainment."

"Great, glad to hear it. Have you finished with your reading?"

"Nope."

"Oh really, what's changed?"

"I think it's time to just enjoy the flight."

"What would you like to eat?"

"Surprise me."

"Excuse me?"

"Would you mind terribly choosing for me Svetlana? Some dinner and wine, you choose. I am sure whatever it is it will be fantastic."

"OK, fair enough, sir. No pressure." She smiles and then giggles. "Can I also suggest that you perhaps watch a movie?"

"If I said that I prefer the theatre would you recommend the cinema of the Ukraine?"

"Excuse me?"

"I'm sorry private joke. Yes, I'd love to."

"Excellent, I'll bring you over a headset."

"So long as it doesn't self-destruct."

"Excuse me?"

"No, excuse me, sorry, private joke – bubbles are working."

"Do you still want another double espresso and another Champagne?"

"No thanks, Svetlana, I'll just wait for food and wine."

"Shouldn't be more than ten or fifteen minutes."

"Perfect, no rush."

He wonders what he might have done if she had recommended the cinema of the Caribbean. *Aruba, perhaps?* Svetlana walks off to finish chewing that toffee and Raymius presses play.

When you go will you send back a letter from America?
Take a look up the rail track from Miami to Canada

> *Bathgate no more, Linwood no more*
> *Methil no more, Irvine no more*
> *Bathgate no more, Linwood no more*
> *Methil no more, Irvine no more*

> *Bathgate no more, Linwood no more*
> *Methil no more, Irvine no more*
> *Bathgate no more, Linwood no more*
> *Methil no more, Lochaber*

Raymius starts looking at the movie options. Classics. Hunt for Red October? *Naw.*

Lethal Weapon? *Naw.* Mission Impossible? *Definitely naw.* He starts to remind himself of the favourites on his Zen. He can pretend he's watching something and at least he knows it won't self-destruct. He finds what he's looking for. It is right at the top. He presses play. *Classic!*

'*My heart was broken, my heart was broken*
Sorrow... Sorrow... Sorrow... Sorrow...
My heart was broken, my heart was broken
Sorrow... Sorrow... Sorrow... Sorrow...'

He presses pause. It just didn't feel right. I love that song, but not right now. He flicks through his playlist. That's much better. FGTH. Perfect. No, not perfect. Epic. He presses play. The sound of air raid sirens is haunting. He puts in the right earpiece and closes both eyes. Annihilation Mix. Frankie Goes to Hollywood. Two tribes go to war.

About The Author by Sue Ashcroft

Hailing from the West coast of Scotland, my life-long friend Joseph Martin Morrison-Meade and I both grew up in the small seaside town of Gourock. His life has been a bit of a 'Do'.

The sports-mad teenager gave up his electrical apprentice-ship much to his step-father's disappointment. Joe became an officer in the British army, graduated from university and subsequently went on to have a corporate career all of which took him from the USA to Shanghai and then Moscow. In 2010 after two years living the London dream he became ill and had time at home in Scotland to reflect on what he really wanted from life. An artistic and a spiritual calling was tempered with a social conscience. Drawing from personal experience he founded a not-for-profit organisation offering personal, social and emotional development to under privi-leged school-leavers.

This debut novel 'Hiding Under the Covers' was awarded 2nd place in the Constable Trophy at the Scottish Association of Writers annual conference in 2007 and then gathered dust in a drawer. Over the last two years with help from Kim, Sinclair and Andy it has been rewritten and edited to make way for book 2 in the series; Stories from Silver Clouds. Joe lives at the Glasgow Harbour with his wife Kirsty.

Contact: jo3m@outlook.com

Sunshine On Leith

My heart was broken, my heart was broken
Sorrow Sorrow Sorrow Sorrow

My heart was broken, my heart was broken
You saw it, you claimed it
You touched it, you saved it

My tears are drying, my tears are drying
Thank you Thank you Thank you Thank you
My tears are drying, my tears are drying
Your beauty and kindness
Made tears clear my blindness

While I'm worth my room on this earth
I will be with you
While the Chief, puts Sunshine On Leith
I'll thank him for his work
And your birth and my birth

Words and Music by CRAIG MORRIS REID and CHARLES STOBO
REID ZOO MUSIC LTD. (PRS)
All rights administered by WARNER/CHAPPELL MUSIC LTD
www.proclaimers.co.uk

The Joyful Kilmarnock Blues

I'm not going to talk about doubts and confusion
On a night when I can see with my eyes shut

I'd never been to Ayrshire
I hitched down one Saturday
Sixty miles to Kilmarnock
To see Hibernian play
The day was bright and sunny
But the game I won't relay
And there was no Kilmarnock Bunnet
To make me want to stay

But I'm not going to talk about it
On a night when I can see with my eyes shut

When I started walking at Wishaw
My eyes obscured my vision
After five miles on my way
I began to learn to listen…..

I walked through the country
I walked through the town
I held my head up
And I didn't look down…..

The question doesn't matter
The answer's always "aye"
The best view of all
Is where the land meets the sky…..

Words and Music by CRAIG MORRIS REID and CHARLES STOBO
REID ZOO MUSIC LTD. (PRS)
All rights administered by WARNER/CHAPPELL MUSIC LTD
www.proclaimers.co.uk

Over and Done With

This is a story of our first teacher
Shetland made her jumpers
And the Devil made her features
Threw up her bands when my mum said our names
Embroidered all her stories with slanderous claims

It's over and done with

This is a story of losing my virginity
I held my breath and the bed held a trinity
People I'm making no claims to a mystery
Sometimes I feel like my sex life's all history

I'm not saying these events didn't
Touch our lives in any way
But, ah, they didn't make the impression
That some people say

This is a story of watching a man dying
The subject's unpopular but I don't feel like lying
When I think of it now, I acted like a sinner
I just washed my hands then I went for my
dinner

Yeah
It's over and done with

Words and Music by CRAIG MORRIS REID and CHARLES STOBO
REID ZOO MUSIC LTD. (PRS)
All rights administered by WARNER/CHAPPELL MUSIC LTD
www.proclaimers.co.uk

Letter From America

When you go will you send back
A letter from America?
Take a look up the rail track
From Miami to Canada

Broke off from my work the other day
I spent the evening thinking about
All the blood that flowed away
Across the ocean to the second chance
I wonder how it got on when it reached the promised land?

I've looked at the ocean
Tried hard to imagine
The way you felt the day you sailed
From Wester Ross to Nova Scotia
We should have held you
We should have told you
But you know our sense of timing
We always wait too long

Lochaber no more
Sutherland no more
Lewis no more
Skye no more

I wonder my blood
Will you ever return?
To help us kick the life back
To a dying mutual friend
Do we not love her?
I think we all claim we love her
Do we have to roam the world?
To prove how much it hurts?

Bathgate no more
Linwood no more
Methil no more
Irvine no more

Words and Music by CRAIG MORRIS REID and CHARLES STOBO
REID ZOO MUSIC LTD. (PRS)
All rights administered by WARNER/CHAPPELL MUSIC LTD
www.proclaimers.co.uk

Lightning Source UK Ltd.
Milton Keynes UK
UKHW020738161118
332438UK00005B/206/P